ANN VICKERS

By
SINCLAIR LEWIS

Introduction to the Bison Book Edition
by Nan Bauer Maglin

University of Nebraska Press
Lincoln and London

Copyright 1932, 1933 by Sinclair Lewis
Introduction to the Bison Book Edition copyright © 1994 by the
University of Nebraska Press

First Bison Book printing: 1994
Most recent printing indicated by the last digit below:
10   9   8   7   6   5   4   3   2   1

Library of Congress Cataloging-in-Publication Data
Lewis, Sinclair, 1885–1951.
Ann Vickers / by Sinclair Lewis; introduction to the Bison Book edition by Nan
Bauer Maglin.
p.   cm.
Includes bibliographical references.
ISBN 0-8032-7947-7 (pbk.)
1. Women social workers—United States—Fiction.   2. Women socialists—
United States—Fiction.   3. Feminists—United States—Fiction.   I. Title.
PS3523.E94A67   1994
813'.52—dc20
93-46687   CIP

Reprinted by arrangement with Howard Gould, executor of the Estate of
Michael Lewis, c/o McIntosh & Otis, Inc.

∞

ANN VICKERS

OTHER NOVELS BY SINCLAIR LEWIS
AVAILABLE IN BISON BOOK EDITIONS:

Free Air
The Job

To
DOROTHY THOMPSON
whose knowledge and whose help
made it possible for me
to write about Ann

INTRODUCTION

By Nan Bauer Maglin

I am going to do something that is important and that, so far as I can remember, has scarcely been touched upon in all fiction, and has never
been adequately done except in the case of Mr. Shakespeare's Portia.
In doing it I am thinking of Genia Schwarzwald—of Frances
Perkins—of Susan B. Anthony—of Alice Paul—of such lovelier and
more feminine, yet equally individual women as Sarah Bernhardt—of
Jane Addams with all her faults—of Nancy Astor—of Catherine the
Great—and if you don't mind being put in with such a gallery, a good
deal of yourself.[1]

After winning the 1930 Nobel Prize in literature (shocking the lit-
erati who thought of him as a "scribbler" and angering Theodore
Dreiser), Sinclair Lewis wanted to prove himself. And so, on November 21, 1931, putting aside the research he had done for a
novel about labor, Lewis, in this letter to his wife, Dorothy
Thompson, declared his intention to write a novel about the life of
a Great Woman.[2]

First serialized in *Redbook* from August 1932 to January 1933
and then published by Doubleday on January 25, 1933, *Ann
Vickers* became a best seller, pulling Doubleday out of the red and

inspiring "the hope that it might be breaking a cycle of four years' failure in the publishing business"[3] despite the Great Depression. *Redbook* heralded the book in superlatives, calling it a masterpiece: "One of the novels which probably will be held representative of the best of our time as long as literary records of America are preserved." Everyone wanted to cash in on the success of *Ann Vickers:* the "March of Time" made a dramatization of it for the newsreels, RCA-Victor wanted to make a recording of it; *The Saturday Evening Post,* which had not run a book advertisement for years, promoted *Ann Vickers.*

Reviews and reactions were varied.[4] A man from Michigan who read the November installment in *Redbook* was outraged, declaring in a letter, "I have yet to read anything so rotten, as stinking and filthy as that story." Certainly, the novel is daring for the time. It follows Ann Vickers from age ten in 1899, growing up in Waubanakee, Illinois, to her forties in the New York radical intellectual/artistic scene. Ann moves through college, into the suffrage movement, settlement-house work, charity work, and then, prison reform. Her personal odyssey includes an abortion, close friendships with women, an affair with a married man that produces a baby. Although *Redbook* captioned each selection somewhat sensationally—A novel of a woman's *emotional* turmoil; *Ann Vickers:* An eager girl tries to remake the world; *Ann Vickers:* Who kept her head but gave her heart away—in fact, much of the really radical content of the novel had been, according to Martin Bucco, excised by *Redbook.* "The editors deleted nearly a thousand paragraphs and thousands of phrases and single words, most dealing with politics, religion, and education." Furthermore, they removed all references to violence, cruelty, squalor, and prison conditions. They certainly eliminated all allusions to pornography, seduction, sexual intercourse, abortion, and childbirth. To Bucco, "the serial heroine is Wordsworthian, [while] the book heroine is Marxian."[5] Nonetheless, even with all the deletions, the reader quoted above was shocked!

When the book appeared, some reviews were negative because of content, politics, political slant or style. The reviewer in *Commonweal* called it "shallow, and amoral." Another Roman Catholic periodical, *America,* regarded the book as obscene. Ellen Glasgow, writing to Allen Tate, asked if he had read *Ann Vickers,* "a whole mob of a book." She was unhappy with what she labeled "the literary oligarchy of the Middle West." Many reviewers of repute found fault with the novel. Criticizing Lewis from the left, Malcolm Cowley in the *New Republic* felt the novel to be fragmentary and a failure because of Lewis's mixed feelings: Ann "is a feminist and Lewis is really hostile toward feminism. Ann is a reformer and Lewis has learned to distrust reformers." In the *American Mercury* Lewis's friend H. L. Mencken allowed for "a few bright spots" but thought *Ann Vickers* "might have been written by Fannie Hurst." Some friends of Dorothy Thompson from her suffrage days were not amused by Lewis's representation of the feminist movement.

But *Ann Vickers* had plenty of admirers. The *New York Times Book Review* called it one of Lewis's best: "unlike some Lewis novels, this is not a tract, but a moving fictional biography." *Booklist* gave thumbs up: "intellectually inclined and bold." A woman writing for the *Saturday Review* praised it as "one of the fairest, most alive, best books I have read." The *New Yorker* liked the "remarkable woman" Lewis had created. Several journalists commended the novel as a social document on prison reform. To the *New York Herald Tribune Books* reviewer the novel was "beautiful and terrible and . . . true."

Those people who knew Sinclair (Red) Lewis and Dorothy Thompson understood that *Ann Vickers* was based to some extent on Dorothy's life. The dedication is to Dorothy, "whose knowledge and whose help made it possible for me to write about Ann." Whereas Mencken does not find much of Dorothy in the book, Mark Schorer in his biography of Sinclair Lewis sees the novel as "drawing on the background of his wife's life, partly on that of his own—prewar Christian Socialism, feminism and settlement-house work, charity organization, liberal and radical thought, prison reform, sexual emancipation, the Depression, careers for women, equal rights."[6] In fact, what makes the point of view of the novel confusing or contradictory and cynical relates to the trouble in their own marriage (especially Lewis's unease about Thompson's independence and success as a foreign correspondent/journalist) and to Lewis's own ambiguous and increasingly hostile feelings about left/liberal politics. As Schorer noted in his introduction to the 1962 Dell edition of *Ann Vickers:* Lewis was trying to depict sympathetically what he resented in real life: the liberal and radical movements. Although it is interesting to pick out the parts that clearly evoke Red or Dorothy, the book's great value is in how it mirrors a generation of women who came of age during a period when America was undergoing great transformations. Ann Vickers follows a path taken by a group of first-generation (mainly native-born, white, middle-class and Protestant) college women between 1890 and 1930 that led to professional commitment to social change and the questioning of traditional gender arrangements.

The novel opens with Ann at age ten already a budding socialist and feminist. Oscar Klebs, a German cobbler, teaches her about socialism while her own experiences point to an elementary kind of feminism. "Except in the arts of baseball and spitting, she knew herself as good a man" as her male playmates. Understanding that it is a man's world and feeling that she can never compete in terms of traditional femininity, she makes up her mind that she really only has one choice: "The boys, the ones I want, they'll never like me. And golly, I do like them! But I just got to be satisfied with being a boy myself."

Ten might be a rather precocious age to be making such a momentous decision, but the feminist Inez Haynes Irwin, one of seventeen women (women much like Ann Vickers/Dorothy Thompson) writing in the 1926–27 *Nation* series "These Modern Women," recalls a parallel development in her own life:

> Like all young things I yearned for romance and adventure. It was not, however, a girl's kind of romance and adventure that I wanted, but a man's. I wanted to run away to sea, to take tramping trips across the country, to go on voyages of discovery and exploration, to try my hand at a dozen different trades and occupations. I wanted to be a sailor, a soldier. I wanted to go to prize fights; to frequent barrooms; even barber shop and smoking room seemed to offer a brisk, salty taste of life. I could not have been more than fourteen when I realized that the monotony and soullessness of the lives of the women I knew absolutely appalled me.[7]

Ann's critical attitude toward gender roles continues through college. While at Point Royal College for Women, she organizes a socialist club and does other things no "proper lady" would do. After graduation, from 1912 to 1916, she becomes a full-time activist for the suffrage movement. At twenty-three, Ann and four other women are sent as a team of organizers to Clateburn, Ohio, which is a major organizing center for the national suffrage movement. Actually, between 1906 and 1913, when the National American Woman's Suffrage Association had no formal headquarters, the small city of Warren, Ohio—for which Clateburn appears to be the analogue—was considered the informal headquarters.[8] Working out of the Buffalo headquarters in 1914, Dorothy Thompson stumped for suffrage in the small towns of western New York.

Organizing in a small midwestern town and the surrounding region was not easy. Housewives, especially, tended to be hostile, making such deprecatory remarks as "If you had to *work* like me, you wouldn't have no time to think about the vote, no more'n I do." Nevertheless the suffragists succeed, despite the harassment of police and male hecklers, in holding several large meetings. But Ann eventually becomes fed up with their struggle. She tires not only of the tedium of addressing envelopes

> but of the whole theological vocabulary of suffrage: "economic independence of women," "equal rights," "equal pay for equal work," "matriarchy." Like such senile words as "idealism," "virtue," "patriotism," they had ceased to mean anything. And she was tired too of the perpetual stories about women's wrongs. There were plenty of wrongs, Heaven knew: young widows with three children working twelve hours a day for just enough to starve slowly on; intelligent women ridiculed and made small by boisterous husbands. But the women who came to tea at the Fanning mansion merely to say that their husbands did not appreciate their finer natures, to them Ann had listened long enough.

Rightly portraying the class politics of the suffrage movement, Lewis draws the activists mostly in such a mocking way (reminiscent of the tone Henry James takes in *The Bostonians*) that the reader may not be sure of his support for the movement. Interestingly, Dorothy Thompson had planned to write her own history of the women's movement from 1910 to 1920, but found herself "so fundamentally out of sympathy with it" that she did not pursue it.[9] *Ann Vickers* is in some sense that book.

The novel tentatively presents the possibility of women living and working together as an alternative to marriage. Ann and four of her comrades (including Maggie O'Mara, waitress and labor organizer, created by Lewis to show that the movement did appeal to working-class women) call themselves "The Ball and Chain Squad" after a two-week stint in jail because of a struggle at a suffrage meeting; Ann remains close to at least two of them over time. She also begins a supportive friendship with Dr. Malvina Wormser, who remains her mentor throughout the novel. Lewis, however, goes out of his way to portray intimacies between women in a hostile way. Eula Towers' "involuted sex" repels Ann (Eula becomes a doctrinaire Communist) and the destructive relationship between Dr. Isabel Herringdon and Eleanor Crevecoeur leads to Eleanor's suicide. One wonders what Dorothy Thompson's reaction to this was. She had many close women friends and some of them were romantic relationships. She and Barbara De Porte, whom she called "her beloved," went to Europe together in 1920, and she and Christa Winsloe (author of *Mädchen in Uniform*), in a relationship begun just before *Ann Vickers* was published, were nearly inseparable over the next few years. On December 28, 1932, she wrote in her diary: "So it has happened to me again, after all these years. It has only, really, happened to me once before with G. [Gertrude Tone]. (Then I was twenty, and G. was 37. . . . Sometimes I think I loved her better than anyone, and there's a queer tenderness between us still.) . . . To love a woman is somehow ridiculous. Any way it doesn't suit me, I *am* heterosexual. [Dorothy wrote this last sentence in German.]"[10]

Sociologically, Ann Vickers represents the career woman, successor to the 1890s "new woman." Between 1890 and 1920 the number of professional women increased over 226 percent. From 1910 to 1920 the number of women in professions such as chemistry, architecture, and law doubled. By 1920 women were 5 percent of the nation's doctors, 1.4 percent of the lawyers and judges, and 30 percent of the college presidents, professors, and instructors. In both law and medicine, as in business, academia, and even in social work, where 62 percent were women, women were far less likely than men to advance to high positions.[11] After her involvement in the suffrage movement, Ann goes from settlement-house work to dispenser of money for a female philanthropist to officership of the Organized Charities Institute to educational directorship of Green Valley Refuge for Women to superintendency of a "modern prison" in Manhattan in 1925. She writes a book on prison reform, receives an honorary doctorate, and speaks to groups around the country. She is labeled a "Great Woman."

During the 1920s, Ann becomes more moderate, gradually replacing her earlier radical views with liberal ones. Lewis is portraying the effects of an era that saw the receding of the prewar radical wave. There was no mass women's movement. The only significant women's struggle was the Woman's Party for the Equal Rights Amendment in the early part of the decade. The period was dominated by the growth of conservatism and the hysteria of the Red Scare. Moving away from his straightforward, realistic style, writing four pages (421–25) in an associative, poetic form, Sinclair Lewis satirizes Ann, her husband Russell Spaulding, and their left-wing intellectual crowd by listing the TALK he could apparently no longer abide: "radical talk, progressive talk, liberal talk, forward-looking talk, earnest talk, inspirational talk," which takes in everything from Stalin, Gastonia, homosexuality, race equality, and the Theatre Guild to Freud, Sam Gompers, Communist agitators out on bail, Columbia instructors, and members of the Lucy Stone League. It was fashionable to note that Thompson abandoned her liberalism and her feminism when she became prominent; Peter Kurth claims that is not so; rather she became as we would say today a "difference" feminist. She loved to write and talk politics abroad; her first passion was writing against Hitler. At frequent gatherings, Lewis would drink, often sulking in the corner, while Thompson would hold forth.

The novel also traces the unfolding of Ann's personal and emotional life. She sleeps with a Jewish soldier, gets pregnant, and has an abortion. During her marriage to Russell Spaulding, she has an affair with Judge Barney Dolphin, a married man who is indicted in a bribery scandal. She deliberately becomes pregnant by him, raising the child while he is in jail. Lewis's ability to write convincingly and in detail in both the abortion and pregnancy/labor scenes is worth noting, reminding us that he was a good writer. The negative portrayal of Ann's husband is especially interesting. Russell found it as hard to live with a "Great Woman" as did Lewis. In that November letter to Dorothy, Lewis explained that Ann's "great tragedy . . . is that she has never found any man big enough not to be scared of her." In the novel, Ann, who had left Spaulding during Barney Dolphin's trial, does find a man who is not scared of her. After two years Barney is pardoned and they plan a life together in the West. At novel's end, Ann is pictured as free and complete. She is:

> the Captive Woman, the Free Woman, the Great Woman, the Feminist Woman, the Passionate Woman, the Cosmopolitan Woman, the Village Woman—the Woman.

While this success story of the work world that "feminize(s) Horatio Alger pluck-and-luck heroes"[12] may seem contrived, Lewis apparently believed in the ending. In the June 1929 *Pictorial Review,* he answered in the affirmative to the question "Is America a Paradise for Women?"[13] Of the three female-centered novels Lewis wrote exploring the choices and pressures that women felt personally and socially during the first third of the twentieth century (*The Job,* 1917; *Main Street,* 1920; *Ann Vickers,* 1933), only *Main Street* ends badly for the protagonist, a mother/housewife who "experiments" with government work and suffragism. Central to the focus of each novel is the dilemma: work or marriage. The resolution of that dilemma is, in each case, crucial to the character's self-realization. Marriage, children, and satisfying work are attained in *The Job* and *Ann Vickers* but not in *Main Street.* In *Ann Vickers* neither is social commitment put aside—although who knows what will happen in the next installment of her life with Barney in the West.

Mass media women's magazines played heavily on the themes of marriage and work, varying their tune according to the needs of society and the job market. During the period of Una Golden's work history (1906–1915 in *The Job*), the message conveyed was that it was all right for women to work but their ultimate goal in life should still be marriage and the family. Once World War I was over, the virtues of work were no longer sung. The traditional woman in the home is called the "Newest New Woman" in the April 1921 issue of the *Ladies Home Journal*. Readers are warned that a woman who puts her career before her home is "a distinct danger to the state." Lewis smartly realized that the revolution in women's lives during the first three decades of the twentieth century was not only the stuff for interesting stories but important politically. *Ann Vickers*, like *The Job* and *Main Street*, is a historical document that preserves for us the struggles of women to solve some of the same problems existing in different forms today.

Dorothy Thompson's own evaluation of Sinclair Lewis's writing upon his death in 1951 gives the best reason to reprint *Ann Vickers* and suggests why this novel can speak to women, young and old, looking to determine their own narratives in a nontraditional way. Lewis, Thompson wrote, lives on not in the lofty heights of high culture but rather

in public libraries from Maine to California, in worn copies in the bookshelves of women from small towns who, as in their girlhood, imagined themselves as Carol Kennicotts. . . . he is an ineradicable part of American cultural history in the twenties and thirties, and no one seeking to recapture and record the habits, frames of mind, social movements, speech, aspirations, admirations, radicalisms, reactions, crusades, and Gargantuan absurdities of the America *demos* during those twenty years will be able to do without him.[14]

NOTES

1. Quoted in Peter Kurth, *American Cassandra: The Life of Dorothy Thompson* (Boston: Little, Brown and Company, 1990), 172. All the women named are probably known by readers today except for Dr. Eugenia Schwarzwald, one of the first women in Europe to earn a Ph.D., and a mentor to Dorothy.

2. At first Lewis called the heroine Ruth Vickery; *Ann Vickers* suggests H. G. Wells's *Ann Veronica*.

3. Vicent Sheean, *Dorothy and Red* (Boston: Houghton Mifflin Company, 1963), 234.

4. All reviews and reactions come from Kurth, *American Cassandra;* Robert E. Fleming, *Sinclair Lewis: A Reference Guide* (Boston: G. K. Hall and Co., 1980); Mark Schorer, *Sinclair Lewis: An American Life* (New York: Dell Publishing Co., Inc., 1961).

5. Martin Bucco, "The Serialized Novels of Sinclair Lewis," in *Sinclair Lewis, Modern Critical Views,* ed. by Harold Bloom (New York: Chelsea House, 1987), 64–66.

6. Schorer, *Sinclair Lewis,* p. 581.

7. Inez Haynes Irwin, "These Modern Women: The Making of a Militant," *Nation,* CXXIII (Dec. 1, 1926), 554–55. All the essays have been reprinted in *These Modern Women: Autobiographical Essays from the Twenties,* ed. by Elaine Showalter. (New York: The Feminist Press, 1989).

8. For the suffrage movement, see Ellen Carol Dubois, *Feminism and Suffrage: The Emergence of an Independent Women's Movement in America, 1848–1869,* (Ithaca, N.Y.: Cornell University Press, 1978); Aileen S. Kraditor, ed. *Up from the Pedestal: Selected Writings in the History of American Feminism* (Chicago: Quadrangle, 1968); and Eleanor Flexner, *Century of Struggle: The Woman's Rights Movement in the United States,* (Harvard University Press, 1959).

9. Kurth, *American Cassandra,* 139.

10. Kurth, 178. See Blanche Wiesen Cook, "Female Support Networks and Political Activism: Lillian Wald, Crystal Eastman, Emma Goldman," in *A Heritage of Her Own: Toward a New Social History,*

ed. by Nancy F. Cott and Elizabeth H. Pleck (New York: Simon and Schuster, 1979).

11. Mary P. Ryan, *Womanhood in America: From Colonial Times to the Present* (New York: Franklin Watts, 1979), 140–44. See also Alice Kessler-Harris, *Out to Work: A History of Wage-Earning Women in the United States* (Oxford University Press, 1982), esp. 224–36.

12. Laura Hapke, *Tales of the Working Girl: Wage-Earning Women in American Literature, 1890–1925.* (New York: Twayne Publishers, 1992), 124.

13. Dorothy Thompson answered no to the question in that same issue. Here you see Thompson arguing for female values and Lewis arguing that women have the opportunity for equality and even have control in some areas.

14. "The Boy and Man from Sauk Centre," *Atlantic Monthly,* reprinted in the appendix to *Dorothy and Red.* Of course, to get a full picture of women in the first two decades one should read a range of writers, including Fannie Hurst, Zora Neale Hurston, and Anzia Yezierska, to name a few.

ANN VICKERS

1

SLOW yellow river flowing, willows that gesture in tepid August airs, and four children playing at greatness, as, doubtless, great men themselves must play. Four children, sharp-voiced and innocent and eager, and blessedly unaware that compromise and weariness will come at forty-five.

The three boys, Ben, Dick, and Winthrop, having through all the past spring suffered from history lessons, sought to turn them to decent use by playing Queen Isabella and Columbus. There was dissension as to which of them should be Isabella. While they debated, there came into that willow grove, that little leaf-littered place holy to boyhood, a singing girl.

"Jiminy, there's Ann Vickers. She'll be Iserbella," said Winthrop.

"Ah, no, gee, she'll hog the whole thing," said Ben. "But I guess she can play Iserbella better than anybody."

"Ah, she can not! She's no good at baseball."

"No, she ain't much good at baseball, but she threw a snowball at Reverend Tengbom."

"Yes, that's so, she threw that snowball."

The girl stopped before them, arms akimbo—a chunk of a girl, with sturdy shoulders and thin legs. Her one beauty, aside from the fresh clarity of her skin, was her eyes, dark, surprisingly large, and eager.

"Come on and play Iserbella 'n' Columbus," demanded Winthrop.

"I can't," said Ann Vickers. "I'm playing Pedippus."

"What the dickens is Pedippus?"

"He was an ole hermit. Maybe it was Pelippus. Anyway, he was an ole hermit. He was a great prince and then he left the royal palace because he saw it was wicked, and he gave up all the joys of the flesh and he went and lived in the desert on—oh, on oatmeal and peanut butter and so on and so forth, in the desert, and prayed all the time."

"That's a rotten game. Oatmeal!"

"But the wild beasts of the desert, they were all around him, catamounts and everything, and he tamed them and they used to come hear him preach. I'm going to go preach to them now! And enormous big bears!"

"Aw, come on play Iserbella first," said Winthrop. "I'll let you take my revolver while you're Iserbella—but I get it back—I get the revolver while I'm Columbus!"

He handed it over, and she inspected it judiciously. She had never had the famous weapon in her hand, though it was notorious through all of childland that Winthrop owned so remarkable a possession. It was a real revolver, a .22, and complete in all its parts, though it is true that the barrel was so full of rust that a toothpick could not have been inserted at the muzzle. Ann waved it, fascinated and a little nervous. To hold it made her feel heroic and active; it is to be feared that she lost immediately the chaste austerity of Pedippus.

"All right," she said.

"You're Iserbella and I'm Columbus," said Winthrop, "and Ben is King Ferdinand, and Dick is a jealous courtesan. You see all the guys in the court are crabbing me, and you tell 'em to lay off and——"

Ann darted to a broken willow bough. She held it drooping over her head with her left hand—always her right clutched the enchanted revolver—and mincing back to them she demanded, "Kneel down, my lieges. No, you Ferdinand, I guess you got to stand up, if you're my concert—no, I guess maybe you better kneel, too, just to make sure. Now prithee, Columbus, what can I do for you today?"

The kneeling Winthrop screamed, "Your Majesty, I want to go discover America. . . . Now you start crabbing, Dick."

"Ah, gee, I don't know what to say. . . . Don't listen to him, Queen, he's a crazy galoot. There ain't any America. All his ships will slide off the edge of the earth."

"Who's running this, courtesan? I am! Certainly he can have three ships, if I have to give him half of my kingdom. What thinkest thou, concert?—you Ben, I mean you?"

"Who? Me? Oh, it's all right with me, Queen."

"Then get thee to the ships."

Moored to the river bank was an old sand barge. The

four children raced to it, Ann flourishing the revolver. She led them all, fastest and most excited. At the barge, she cried, "Now, I'm going to be Columbus!"

"You are *not*," protested Winthrop. "I'm Columbus! You can't be Iserbella *and* Columbus! And you're only a girl. You gimme that revolver!"

"I am, too, Columbus! I'm the best Columbus. So now! Why, you can't even tell me the names of Columbus's ships!"

"I can too!"

"Well, what were they?"

"Well, I can't just—— Neither can you, smarty!"

"Oh, I can't, can't I!" crowed Ann. "They were the *Pinto* and the *Santa Lucheea* and—and the *Armada!*"

"Gee, that's right. I guess she better be Columbus," marveled the dethroned King Ferdinand, and the great navigator led her faithful crew aboard the *Santa Lucia*, nor was the leap across that three feet of muddy water any delicate and maidenly exhibition.

Columbus took her station in the bow—as much as a double-ender scow possesses a bow—and, shading her eyes, looking over the thirty feet of creek, she cried, "A great, terrible storm is coming, my men! Closehaul the mainsail! Reef all the other sails! My cats, how it thunders and lightens! Step lively, my brave men, and your commander will lend an hand!"

Between them they got down all the sails before the hurricane struck the gallant vessel. The hurricane (perhaps assisted by the crew, standing on one side of the barge and jumping up and down) threatened to capsize the unfortunate caravel, but the crew cheered nobly. They were encouraged, no doubt, by the example of their commander, who stood with her right leg boldly thrust forward, one hand on her breast and the other holding out the revolver, while she observed, loudly, "Bang, bang, bang!"

But the storm continued, viciously.

"Let's sing a chantey to show we have stout hearts!' commanded Columbus, and she led them in her favorite ballad:

> "*Jingle bells, jingle bells,*
> *Jingle all the way.*
> *Oh! What fun it is to ride,*
> *In a one-horse open sleigh!*"

The storm gave up.

They were approaching Watling's Island now. Peering across the turbulent water, often broken by the leap of a pickerel, Ann perceived savage bands roaming the shore.

"See, yonder, among the palms and pagodas! Pesky redskins!" warned Columbus. "We must prepare to sell our lives dearly!"

"That's right," agreed her crew, gaping at the dread row of mullen weeds across the creek.

"What d'you kids think you're doing?"

The voice was perfectly strange.

They turned to see, standing on the bank, a new boy. Ann stared with lively admiration, for this was a hero out of a story book. Toward such mates as Ben and Winthrop, she had no awe; except in the arts of baseball and spitting, she knew herself as good a man as they. But the strange boy, perhaps two years older than herself, was a god, a warrior, a leader, a menace, a splendor: curly-headed, broad-shouldered, slim-waisted, smiling cynically, his nose thin and contemptuous.

"What d'you kids think you're doing?"

"We're playing Columbus. Want to play?" The crew were surprised at Ann's meekness.

"Nah! *Playing!*" The stranger leaped aboard—a clean leap where the others had panted and plumped. "Let's see that gun." He took the revolver from Columbus, casually, and worshipingly she yielded it. He snapped it open and looked into the barrel. "It's no blame good. I'll throw it overboard."

"Oh, please don't!" It was Ann who wailed, before Winthrop, the owner, could make warlike noises.

"All right, kid. Keep it. Who are you? What's your name? My name is Adolph Klebs. My dad and I just come to town. He's a shoemaker. He's a Socialist. We're going to settle here, if they don't run us out. They run us out of Lebanon. Haa! I wasn't scared of 'em! 'You touch me and I'll kick you in the eye,' that's what I told the policeman. He was scared to touch me. Well, come on, if we're going to play Columbus. I'll be Columbus. Gimme that gun again. Now you kids get busy and line the side of the boat. There's a whole slew of redskins coming off in canoes."

And it was Adolph-Columbus who now observed, "Bang, bang, bang!" as he introduced European culture to primitive Americans by shooting them down, and of all his followers none was more loyal, or noisy, than Ann Vickers.

She had never before encountered a male whom she felt

to be her superior, and in surrender she had more joy than in her blithe and cocky supremacy of old.

In this town of Waubanakee, Illinois, a little south of the center of the state, Ann Vickers's father was Superintendent of Schools, known always as "Professor." His position made him one of the local gentry, along with three doctors, two bank presidents, three lawyers (one of them justice of the peace), the proprietor of the Boston Store, and the Episcopal, Congregational, and Presbyterian ministers.

Physically, Waubanakee does not much enter Ann's story. Like most Americans who go from Main Street to Fifth Avenue or Michigan Avenue or Market Street, and unlike most Britons and Continentals from the provinces, after childhood she kept no touch with her native soil; never returned to it after the death of her parents; had no longing to acquire a manor there, as a climax to careers and grandeurs, or, like an Anglo-Indian pro-consul, to be buried in the village cemetery.

Her mother died when she was but ten, her father a year before Ann went to college. She had no brothers or sisters. When she was middle-aged, Waubanakee was a memory, a little humorous, a little touching—a picture she had seen in youth, unreal, romantic, and lost.

Yet that small town and its ways, and all her father's principles of living, entered into everything she was to do in life. Sobriety, honest work, paying his debts, loyalty to his mate and to his friends, disdain of unearned rewards —he once refused a tiny legacy from an uncle whom he had despised—and a pride that would let him neither cringe nor bully, these were her father's code, and in a New York where spongers and sycophants and gayly lying people, pretty little people, little playing people, were not unknown even among social workers and scientists, that code haunted her, and she was not sorry or Freudian about it ... and, though she laughed at herself, if she had not paid all her bills by the fourth of the month, she was uneasy.

She once heard Carl Van Doren say in a lecture that before he had left his native village of Hope, Illinois, he had met, in essence, everyone whom he was ever to meet. Ann agreed. The Swedish carpenter at Waubanakee, who talked of Swedenborg, differed only in accent from the Russian grand duke whom thirty years after she was to meet in New York and hear amiably flounder through a froth of metaphysics.

Yes, so deep was Waubanakee in her heart that all her life Ann caught herself naïvely classifying acquaintances as Good People and Bad People, as implicitly as had her Sunday-school teacher in the Waubanakee Presbyterian Church. Here was a Charming Chap, witty, smiling, belonging to the best circles of New York, and never repaying the money he "borrowed," never keeping his dinner engagements. Well! To the little Ann Vickers of Waubanakee, who was never quite extinguished in that Great Reformer, Dr. Ann Vickers (Hon. LL.D.), this man was Bad —he was Bad just as the village drunk of Waubanakee was Bad to her father, the Professor.

It was a prejudice she could never much regret.

She came far enough along in American tradition to be as little ashamed of an American provincial origin as a British Prime Minister is of his Scottish village birth, or a French Premier of Provence. Till her day and moment, it had been fashionable among most Americans with a keen awareness and some experience of the world either to sigh that pride in Arkansas is insular and chauvinistic or, with a reverse humility, to boast of its rustic perfections. But Ann had the extraordinary luck (along with some 120,000,000 other Americans) to live in the magnificent though appalling moment when the United States began awkwardly to see itself not as an illegitimate child of Europe but as the master of its own proud house.

There are but frayed cords binding such ambitious, out-stepping American girls as Ann, not only to their native villages, but even to their families, unless they are of recent Jewish or German or Italian origin. If they thus lose the richness and security of European family solidarity, equally they are free from the spiritual and social incest of such nagging relationships.

But in Manhattan, Ann was some day to be mildly glad that through her father and Waubanakee she was related to the bourgeois colony which, up to 1917, was the only America.

2

WAUBANAKEE did not vastly care for the newly come cobbler, Oscar Klebs, father of the dashing Adolph. In Ann's childhood, the prairie towns, from Zanesville to Dodge City, still had no notion that they were part of the Great World. They felt isolated—they were isolated.

Oh, it was all right to be German (only they said "Dutch") like Oscar Klebs.

"There's some darn' good Dutchmen, by golly—just as good as you and me. Take the priest of the German Catholic Church. Course a lot of his congregation are dumm Dutch farmers, but he's a real guy, he certainly is, and they say he's studied in Rome, Italy, and a lot of these places. But believe me, he hasn't got any more use for these darn Europeans than I have. But now this Dutch shoemaker, this fellow Klebs, they say he's a Socialist, and I want to tell you, we haven't got any room in this country for a bunch of soreheads that want to throw a lot of bombs and upset everything. No sir, we haven't!"

But it chanced that the only other cobbler in town was a drunken Yankee who could never be trusted to half-sole shoes in time for the I. O. O. F. dance on Saturday evening, and, regretfully, irritably, the reigning burghers of Wau-banakee took their work to a man who was so anarchistic as to insist, even right at the bar of the Lewis & Clarke Tavern, that the Stokeses and Vanderbilts had no right to their fortunes.

They were cross with him.

Mr. Evans, president of the Lincoln and Douglas Bank, said testily, "Now I'll tell you, Klebs. This is a land of opportunity, and we don't like these run-down and I might say degenerate Europeans telling us where we get off. In this country, a man that can do his work gets recognition, including financial, and if I may say so, sir, without being rude, you can't hardly say it's our fault if you haven't made good!"

"By golly, sir, that's right!" said the hired man for Lucas Bradley.

Professor Vickers was dimly astonished when Ann brought her everyday shoes to him and complained, "Papa, these need half-soling." Customarily, Ann was unconscious of worn soles, missing buttons, or uncombed hair.

"Well, my little girl is beginning to look after her things! That's fine! Yes, you take 'em around tomorrow. Have you done your Sunday school lesson?" he said, with the benign idiocy and inconsequentiality characteristic of parents.

This was on Sunday, the day after the miraculous appearance of Adolph Klebs, the king-Columbus. On Monday morning, at eight, Ann took the shoes to Oscar Klebs, in his new shop which had formerly been the Chic Jewelry Store (the first word to rhyme with Quick). On the shelf above his bench, there was already a row of shoes with that curiously human look that empty shoes maintain— the knobbly work-shoes of the farm-hand, with weariness in every thick and dusty crease, the dancing slippers of the slightly dubious village milliner, red and brave in the uppers but sleazy and worn below. Of these, Ann saw nothing. She stared at Oscar Klebs as she had stared at his son Adolph. He was quite the most beautiful old man she had ever seen—white-bearded, high and fine of forehead, with delicate pale blue veins in a delicate linen skin.

"Good-morning, young lady," said Oscar. "And what can I do for you?"

"Please, I would like to get these shoes half-soled. They're my everyday shoes. I got on my Sunday shoes!"

"And why do you wear a different pair for Sundays?"

"Because it is the Sabbath."

"And isn't every day the Sabbath for people that work?"

"Yes, I guess it is. . . . Where's Adolph?"

"Did you ever stop to think, young lady, that the entire capitalist system is wrong? That you and I should work all day, but Evans, the banker, who just takes in our money and lends it back to us again, should be rich? I do not even know your name, young lady, but you have luffly eyes—I t'ink intelligent. T'ink of it! A new world! From each so much as he can give, to each so much as he needs. The Socialist state! From Marx. Do you like that, young lady? *Hein?* A state in which all of us work for each other?"

It was perhaps the first time in the life of Ann Vickers that a grown-up had talked to her as an equal; it was perhaps the first time in her life that she had been invited to consider any social problem more complicated than the question as to whether girls really ought to throw dead cats over fences. It was perhaps the beginning of her intellectual life.

The little girl—she was so small, so innocent, so ignorant!—sat with her chin tight in her hand, in the terrible travail of her first abstract thinking.

"Yes," she said, and "Yes." Then, thought like lightning in her brain, "That is what we must have! Not some rich and some poor. All right! But, Mr. Klebs, what do we *do?* What shall I start doing now?"

Oscar Klebs smiled. He was not a smiling man—he suffered, as always the saints have suffered, because Man has not become God. But now he almost grinned, and betrayed himself, chuckling:

"*Do?* Do, my young lady? Oh, I suppose you'll just go on talking, like me!"

"No," she said pitifully. "I don't want to just talk! I want Winthrop Zeiss to have as nice a house as Mr. Evans. Golly! He's lots nicer, Winthrop is. I want to—— Gee, Mr. Klebs, I'd like to do things in life!"

The old man stared at her, silently. "You will, my dear, God bless your soul!" said he—the atheist. And Ann forgot to ask again about the glorious Adolph.

But she did see Adolph, and often.

Oscar Klebs's shop became her haunt, more thrilling even than the depot, where every afternoon at five all detachable children gathered to watch the Flyer go through to Chicago. Oscar told her of a world that hitherto had been colored but flat, a two-dimensional mystery in the geography; of working in 1871 in a lumber camp in Russia—where some day there would be a revolution, he said—of the Tyrol (he combined with atheism an angry belief that in the stables of the Tyrol the cows do talk aloud at Christmas midnight)—of carp that come up and ask you for crumbs in the pool at Fontainebleau—of the walls of Cartagena, which are ten feet thick and filled with gold hidden there by pirates—of the steamers on which he had sailed as mess-boy, and what scouse is like in the fo'c'sle—of the lone leper who sits forever on the beach in Barbados, looking out to sea and praying—of what sort of shoes the Empress Eugénie wore—of prime ministers and tavarishes and yogis and Iceland fishermen and numismatists and *Erzherzogen* and all manner of men unknown to Waubanakee, Illinois, till the Socialism to which Oscar converted her was not very clearly to be distinguished from the romance of Kipling.

And while he talked to the ruddy girl, on her stool, her eyes exalted, Oscar Klebs kept up a tat-tat-tat, tat-tat-tat, like a little drum.

And Adolph came in.

He never sat down. It was hard to think of that steel spring of a boy ever sitting. He belonged not to the sedentary and loquacious generation of his father, but to a restless new age of machinery, of flashing cam-shafts, polished steel, pistons ramming gayly into a hell of exploding gas. dynamos humming too deep for words. Had he been a boy in 1931 instead of 1901, he would have responded to all

his father's ponderous propositions with "Oh, yeah?"
But in 1901 his "Yuh, sure!" was equally impertinent,
sharp, and antagonistic to fuzzy philosophizing. Tall,
mocking, swift, leaning against doors and walls as though
he were about to leap, his hands ever in his pockets, he was
to Ann Vickers the one perfect hero she had ever known.

Now the theory was that Ann was being respectably
educated by her father and mother, by the Waubanakee
public schools, and the Sunday school of the First (and
only) Waubanakee Presbyterian Church, with the select
and frilly children of Banker Evans for social guidance.
Actually it was from the cobbler and his son, and from her
father's vices of paying debts and being loyal, that she
learned most of what she was ever to know, and all this
was dual and contradictory, so that she was herself to be
dual and contradictory throughout her life. From old
Oscar she learned that all of life was to foresee Utopia;
from Adolph she learned that to be hard, self-contained,
and ready was all of life.

Sitting by the Waubanakee River (which was no river,
but a creek) she once or twice tried to tell Adolph what she
regarded as her ideas:

That Oscar was right, and we must, preferably immediately, have a Socialist state in which, like monks, we labor
one for another.

That it wasn't a bit nice to drink beer, or to appear in
certain curious revelations, behind barns, of the differences
between little boys and little girls.

That algebra was pretty slick, once you got onto it.

That the *Idylls of the King* by Mr. Lord Tennyson
was awful exciting.

That if Jesus died for us—as, of course, He did—it was simply horrid of us to sleep late on Sunday, and not take our baths in time to get to Sunday school.

Adolph smiled always while she was earnestly talking. He smiled while his father was talking. All his life he was to smile while people were talking. But it cut Ann and made her a little timid. She did mean, so intently, the "ideas" which she babbled forth—on a sand barge, by a slow river flowing in the shadow of willows that slowly waved in the tepid August airs.

If his supercilious smile was really from a higher wisdom, fitted to the steel of the machine age, or if it was only a splendidly total lack of intellect, neither Ann nor any one else will ever know. Some day he was to be the manager of a fairly good garage in Los Angeles, and Oscar to sleep irritably in the Catholic Cemetery of Waubanakee, Illinois.

Even without old Oscar, Ann would never have been completely a conformist. In Sunday school in the Girls' Intermediate Class (teacher, Mrs. Fred Graves, wife of the owner of the lumber yard) she first exploded as a feminist.

The lesson was of the destruction of Sodom, with the livelier portions of the tale omitted. Mrs. Graves was droning, drowsy as a bumblebee, "But Lot's wife looked back at the awful city instead of despising it, and so she was turned into a pillar of salt, which is a very important lesson for us all, it shows us the penalty of disobedience, and also how we hadn't ought to even look at or hanker for wicked things and folks. That's just as bad as if we actually had something to do with them or indulged——"

"Please, Mrs. Graves!" Ann's voice, a little shrill. "Why shouldn't Mrs. Lot look back at her own home-town? She had all her neighbors there, and maybe she'd had some lovely times with them. She just wanted to say good-bye to Sodom!"

"Now, Annie, when you get wiser than the Bible——! Lot's wife was disobedient; she wanted to question and argue, like some little girls I know! See, it says in Verse 17: 'Look not behind thee.' That was a divine command."

"But couldn't the Lord change her back into a lady again, after He'd been so cranky with her?"

Mrs. Graves was becoming holy. Her eyes glittered, her eyeglasses quivered on their hook on her righteous brown-silk bosom. The other girls crouched with the beginnings of fear—and giggling. Ann felt the peril, but she simply had to understand these problems over which she had fretted in "getting" the Sunday school lesson.

"Couldn't the Lord have given her another chance, Mrs. Graves? I would, if I was Him!"

"I have never in my life heard such sacrilegious——"

"No, but—Lot was awful mean! He never sorrowed and carried on about Mrs. Lot a bit! He just went off and left her there, a lonely pillar of salt. Why didn't he speak to the Lord about it? In those days folks were always talking to the Lord; it says so, right in the Bible. Why didn't he tell the Lord to not be so mean and go losing His temper like that?"

"Ann Emily Vickers, I shall speak to your father about this! I have never heard such talk! You can march yourself right out of this class and out of this Sunday school, right now, and later I'll talk to your father!"

Stunned, anarchistic with this early discovery of Injustice yet too amazed to start a riot, Ann crawled down the church aisle, through an innumerable horde of children giggling and sharpening their fingers at her shame, into a world where no birds sang; a Sabbath world of terrible and reproving piety. Her indignation was stirring, though, and when she reached home, to find her father just dressed for church, shoe-shined, bathed, and wearing the Prince Albert, she burst out with the uncensored story of her martyrdom.

He laughed. "Well, it doesn't sound very serious to me, Annie. Don't worry about what Sister Graves will say."

"But it's very important about how that nasty man Lot acted! I got to do something!"

He was opening the front door, still laughing.

She fled through the kitchen, past the hired girl, astonished in her cooking of the regulation fricasseed chicken, through the back yard, to the path up Sycamore Hill. She scolded to herself, "Yes, it's men like Lot and the Lord and my Dad—laughing!—that make all the trouble for us women!" She did not look around; she kept her sturdy back toward the village till she had dog-trotted halfway up the hillock.

She swung about, held out her hands to the roofs of Waubanakee, and cried, "Farewell, farewell! Sodom, I adore thee! All right, God!" And she raised expectant eyes to Heaven.

3

FROM eleven to fifteen Ann cuddled to her a romantic
affection for Adolph Klebs. It is not to be supposed that
she made herself more than normally and wholesomely
ridiculous by mooning over him, or that she had nothing
else to do. She was busy—like a puppy. There were adventures every day, then: skating, sliding, fishing, swimming, trapping a rabbit—just once, and releasing it afterward with screams of pity; nursing dogs and cats and
ducklings, often to their great distress and inconvenience;
discovering Vergil and Lord Macaulay and Hamlet and
the vast new art of motion pictures and the automobile.
Hearing a lovely elocutionist gentleman with black wavy
hair recite Kipling at the entertainment of the Order of the
Eastern Star. Baking and sweeping and ironing—she
loved ironing; it made things so crisp and smooth. Doing
all the housework in the not infrequent hiatuses between
hired girls. Always, caring for her other-worldly father,
who seemed far more of an orphan, more bewildered and
disorganized than herself: laying out his handkerchief,

putting his muffler on him, hustling him out for a Sunday afternoon walk. She came to look on the race of males so protectively that it was questionable whether she would ever love one whom she could not bully and nurse.

But daily she saw Adolph and his mighty ways.

They were in the same class in school, and though all his scholarship consisted in smiling condescendingly when he didn't know the answer, he seemed superior. He could swim better, fight better, skate better, and pitch better than any boy in the gang. He was not afraid of the town policeman, even on Hallowe'en, when the gang perilously stole certain outhouses and arranged them as a miniature street in the school yard, with signs from the Main Street stores upon them, to the delight of the ribald next morning. And he could dance better—but other girls besides Ann had learned this, and sometimes at a party of the young set, she ached for his "Mave honor thdance thyou?" all through a barren evening.

Perhaps the grandest party Ann had yet seen was given by Mrs. Marston T. Evans, wife of the president of the Lincoln & Douglas Bank, president of the Midstate Plow & Wagon Works—the Lorenzo de' Medici, the J. P. Morgan, the Baron Rothschild of Waubanakee—for their daughter Mildred, on her fifteenth birthday, which happened to be two months after the fifteenth birthday of Ann Vickers.

Ann had always admired, had envied a little, the Evans mansion. It was white, with a green turret, very tall; it had both a parlor and a library. The parlor had a parquet floor, dark and much polished, with a genuine tigerskin rug, and on the wall two genuine hand-painted paintings, very ancient, perhaps seventy-five years old, said to be worth hundreds of dollars apiece. In the library there were rows of books in gilt and leather bindings, behind locked glass doors.

All that Saturday in May, while the hired girl helped prepare her party dress, Ann wondered whether Adolph Klebs would be at the party. She had not dared to ask him, and rumors differed. Adolph did not answer personal questions; he had a witty way of retorting, always, "Who stole the fish-pole?"

It was hard to think of a socialistic cobbler's son invited by Mr. and Mrs. Marston T. Evans. But Mildred was believed to be "crazy about him."

"I'll die if he isn't there—and my dress so pretty!" agonized Ann, seemingly so sturdy and independent over the ironing-board.

Her new party dress was not a new party dress. Last summer it had been a new white organdy with a red sash, noble for summer evenings. Now she had with her own hands (which for a week looked like those of a Solomon Islander) dyed it pale blue, and all day the cook and she had been sewing on little white cuffs and collar, and ironing the frock till it flared out fresh as new.

She had a lace shawl of her mother's for her head, and her father had voluntarily bought for her cobalt-blue dancing slippers. (Sometimes, years after, she wondered whether her father, the Professor, so sober over his school records and Carlyle and *Educational Review*, had really been so incurably adult a parent as she had thought him. She missed him, when he was dead and she would never hear again the chuckle that once had infuriated her.)

The party was to be late—some of the gang said they were expected to stay till eleven, and they were summoned for eight o'clock, not seven or seven-thirty, like an ordinary bourgeois party in Waubanakee.

There was no moon as she scampered to the party, a little late after her dressmaking. But there was an afterglow warmer and more tender than moonlight, which, for all its celebrity, is a somewhat chill and mocking illumination, made of the breath of dying lovers. The thick sycamores along Nancy Hanks Street showed sculptured blocks of leafage against the afterglow, and the bark-stripped gashes on their trunks were mysterious blanks in the dusk. The air was full of village murmur, of distant laughter and clopping horses and the barking of a farmyard dog—a shadow of noise. And Ann was happy.

She was excited, a little startled, as she came round the corner and saw afar the exceeding glory of the party. There were lighted Japanese lanterns on the Evans lawn, and not just a string or two, as at a church festival, but lanterns hung from the box-elders along the front picket fence, lanterns in every spruce and rosebush scattered on the lawn, lanterns entirely across the immense front porch! It was Paris! And, nearer, Ann saw that on the lawn—right outside, outdoors, in the evening!—was a Refreshment Table heaped with every known delicacy in the world: several kinds of cake, innumerable pitchers of lemonade and other delicate drinks, with three visible freezers of ice cream, while a girl help—not the regular Evans hired girl but an extra one, for the evening—was already serving ice cream from these freezers to young ladies and gentlemen palpitatingly holding out saucers.

Refreshments right from the beginning of the party, maybe all through it, and not just at the end!

But, fretted the conscientious spirit that was always nagging at the adventurous in Ann, wouldn't maybe some of them get sick to their stomachs, with so much rich food all evening?

Sudden and brilliant as a skyrocket the music flashed, and she saw that there was dancing—on the porch, outside, outdoors!—and to no mere phonograph, but a full, complete orchestra: piano (moved right out on the porch!), fiddle, and clarinet; and the clarinet was played by no less a one than Mr. Bimby of the Eureka Dry Goods Store, leader of the Waubanakee Band!

It was too much. Ann fled. She—the diver, the walker on ridgepoles—had social panic; she dashed into darkness and stood biting the end of her forefinger. (She was later to feel just so when, after blandly presiding over a large meeting of wealthy, high-minded, and complacently dull ladies, importantly gathered for impossible reforms, she was suddenly escorted into a screaming night club in New York.)

With no more exhilaration but with aching dutifulness she marched back to the Evans mansion and through the gate. It got worse. She felt herself dressed in old calico. The other girls were so dainty: Mildred Evans in lace over pink satin; Mabel McGonegal (the doctor's eldest) in ruby velvet with a rhinestone necklace; Faith Durham in airy Japanese silk—so dainty, so feminine, so winsome, so light; herself so ordinary and stodgy!

(She did not note that most of the twenty other girls displayed even more familiar and less exotic frocks than her own. At any party Mildred and Mabel and Faith managed to preen and giggle and arch themselves into the foreground. They were not very good at Latin or cooking, but they were born to be brilliant, to marry Lithuanian counts, to be movie stars, or to live gloriously on alimony and cocktails.)

Like a sturdy old farm dog amazed by a high-stepping greyhound, Ann stared at them as they revolved to the heavenly strains. But Mrs. Evans sailed up to her so graciously, she so benevolently cackled, "Why, Annie dear, we've missed you—we did hope you wouldn't fail us—you must come and have a nice fruit lemonade before you dance!" that Ann was restored. And what a lemonade that was! The great soda fountain had not yet in its morning splendor dawned on the Western World; at the drug store you took vanilla ice cream soda or you took vanilla ice cream. The fruit lemonade which Mrs. Evans introduced to Ann (without explaining just what a non-fruit lemonade might be) was seething with cracked ice, sliced pineapple, sliced orange, and two red cherries! Ann sipped as in paradise, until she realized that Mrs. Evans had left her.

Alone! She wanted to sneak away.

She saw then that, shadowed by a spruce, sitting on a camp stool and also drinking a fruit lemonade, was Adolph Klebs.

"Hello, Annie. Come on over and sit down," he called, and he was actually wheedling.

It was a tribute Adolph was not likely to have again in this life that Ann set her lemonade down on the refreshment table not only unfinished but with one of the cherries

unsecured. Beside Adolph was another canvas stool, and
Ann squatted on it, her chin on her hands.

"Why aren't you dancing?" she said.

"Oh, the hell with 'em! They're too tony for me. I'm
the crazy old shoemaker's kid! Why aren't you? Your old
man is rich, like them!"

She did not stoop to the false modesty of denying this;
it was true, of course—her father made twenty-eight hundred a year. But: "Oh, you're crazy! They're all crazy
about you! Why, Dolph, you're the best dancer in town!
The girls are all crazy to dance with you!"

"Hell with 'em! Lookit, Ann, you and me are the only
square kids here. Those girls, they're just a bunch of flirts.
They can't go hunting and swim and everything like what
you can, and they ain't half as smart in school, and—and
you never lie, and they're all a bunch of liars and so on.
But you're a dandy kid, Annie. You're my girl!"

"Am I? Am I honest your girl?"

"You bet your sweet life you are!"

"Oh, Dolph, that's dandy! I'd like to be your girl!"

She held his hand. He awkwardly kissed her cheek.
That was all of their caressing. Long kisses and greater
intimacies did exist, in this evening of the Age of Innocence,
but "necking" was not yet a public and accepted sport.

"Let's go and dance. We'll show 'em!" she said stoutly.

As they crossed the lawn into more brilliant light, she
realized that her Man was as magnificently clad as Morgan
Evans—a real blue serge suit, an enormously high collar,
an elegant green bow tie with figures of tiny white clover
leaves and, fashionably matching it, a green silk handkerchief drooping out of his breast pocket.

Though it was curious that he, the shoemaker's son, had
no pumps, like some of the aristocrats, but only his high
thick black shoes.

A square dance was just finished; a two-step starting as
Ann and Adolph defiantly mounted to the porch. Oh, that
foaming, moonlight music, to which the entranced ro-
mantics sang:

> *"Oh, this is the day they give babies away*
> *With a half—a pound—o' teeeeea!"*

In Adolph's arms she was not earnest. Her strength
flowed into his and she was borne effortless round and
round. She was a soap-bubble, a butterfly, an evening
swallow. She forgot her rivals with their elegancies; she
hadn't even to dodge them in dancing. Adolph led her,
with magic sureness. Though they danced morally, eight
inches apart, his dear, strong, nervous hand was against
her back, electric as a battery.

Then the music ceased, she tumbled from Heaven, she
stood bewildered, while Mrs. Evans shrieked in her clear,
strong, Christian voice, "Now, children, let's play 'Skip
to Malloo'!"

Ann and her Beau were separated. His shyness before
the grandeurs of this new Fête of Versailles seemed to
have waned. No one bounced more blithely in the game,
sang louder. Adolph was older than the others, but he was
adaptable. Last night he had been surreptitiously drinking
beer with worldly men of twenty; tonight he dominated
the children. When they danced again, Ann looked for

Adolph, her glance toward him like outreaching arms, but he danced first with Faith, then with Mabel McGonegal, courtly daughter of the doctor (she could play the banjo and recite French Canuck dialect poems), and at last with Mildred Evans herself.

Mrs. Evans, looking on, clucked to her lord, "You see, the Klebs boy is quite a gentleman."

"Yes. After all, this is a democracy. After all, I was born on a farm myself," marveled Mr. Marston T. Evans.

But Ann Vickers watched that swaying waltz of Adolph and Mildred with the eyes again of a hurt old farm dog.

She was "sitting out." She had danced a two-step with her faithful comrade-at-arms, Winthrop, but after the quicksilver of Adolph, it was agony. She had seemed to be dragging Winthrop like a cart. They bumped into every one. And though Winthrop's hearty and irritating humming followed the music, his honest feet protested against all frivolity and walked right on through the nonsense.

They played Post Office.

When the Postmaster, stationed at the door of the darkened library, with Adolph within as the fortunate receiver of kisses, inspected the girls to see which he should choose, they looked more than commonly self-conscious. Adolph was at once an outcast and king of the party; he was a Robin Hood fluttering the provincial court.

"Uh—uh—Ann!" called the Postmaster.

Giggles.

"She's crazy about um!" Mabel whispered to Mildred.

Ann did not hear, which was well for Mabel. Ann's vengeance was in a modest way terrible as the Lord's.

She did not hear. On wings she sailed into the darkened room. It had ceased to be an elegant library and became a cave of wonder and exaltation. She knocked against things that surely had not been there. She was lost and joyous. She held out her hands to—what? Of bodily ardors she had in her innocence no idea. It was the essence of love she wanted, now, not its husk . . . however realistically she was some day to know that flesh is not the foe but the interpreter of love.

"Come on!" she heard Adolph grunt.

He dabbled at her; his kiss licked the corner of her jaw; he muttered, "Now it's your turn!" and her knight was hastily opening the door, and gone.

It was Ben who came in then. Since babyhood he had adored Ann, followed her, brought her apples, and never kissed her. Now that he was turning man, it would mean something to him to kiss her. So he giggled rather idiotically as he groped for her. "Gee, I'm scared!" he snickered. He found her in an armchair, and as he diffidently embraced her he cried, "Why, golly, Annie, you're crying!"

"Oh, oh, please don't kiss me, Ben!"

"But you're crying! Was Adolph mean to you?"

"Oh, no, no, it's just—I ran against a table in the dark."

Quietly they sat, Ben monotonously patting her shoulder, till she whispered, "I'm all right now. I better go out."

As she appeared in the door, there was a storm of laughter from the young people, in a circle facing the library door. "Oh, what you an' Ben been up to! Oh, I guess that was some kissing, Annie!"

And Adolph leered at her.

Only by the sternest and most conscious will did she

keep from marching out and going home. She had a definite desire to kill; kill all of them. She made herself sit down, saying nothing. She never did know which girl it was who now went into the library to submit herself to the tepid caresses of Ben.

But she was aware enough when Adolph was summoned to entertain Mabel McGonegal in the dark.

It had often been whispered in the gang that Mabel was a flirt, that she was "awful sweet on the boys." The party, all save Ann, watched the library door with embarrassed giggles, with all the stirrings of puberty, for five minutes.

"And he stayed with me for five seconds!" Ann raged to herself.

Mabel came out, tossing her slightly ruffled head. But she was, unlike Ann, worldly wise. Before they could mock her, she screamed, "And maybe I didn't get kissed right!"

In Ann's heart was cold death.

But when Adolph, in his turn, reappeared, swaggering, proud, she did not agonize as she had expected, but suddenly laughed, as she thought, "Why! He's just a tomcat! He walks like one!"

And in that instant her love for the hero was gone, so that she did not suffer when she heard Adolph mutter to Mabel McGonegal a canonical, "May see y' home?"

Herself she was "seen home" by Ben, stumbling foolishly beside her and prefacing all his observations by "Aw, gee," or "Lookit."

The afterglow was gone.

At Ann's gate, Ben complained, "Aw, gee, Ann, why haven't you got a fellow? You never did have a fellow. Gee, I wish you were my girl!"

Ben was profoundly astonished and embarrassed by being smacked with a hearty kiss, and more astonished that Ann followed it up with, "You're sweet, but I'll never be anybody's girl!" and dashed into the house.

4

"I HATE that Evans house! All shiny! I like it here!"
raged Ann, when she had left Ben and come into the brown
and comfortable dowdiness of the Vickers sitting room. . . .
Gritty Brussels carpet; Hoffmann pictures of Christ; old
college textbooks, and Walter Scott and Dickens and
Washington Irving and the "English Men of Letters"
series and *The Jungle* and *The Birds' Christmas Carol* and
Cruden's Concordance; a highly tufted sofa with an autograph sofa-cushion; and Father's slippers in a wall-case
worked with his initials.

"I like it here. It's safe!" said Ann, and trudged up to
bed.

She took off her splendor of organdy frock scornfully.
But she was too neat a soul to do anything so melodramatic
as to tear it, to hurl it regally on the floor. She hung it up
precisely, smoothing out the skirt, her fingers conscious
of the cool crispness.

She brushed her hair, she patted her pillow, but she
did not go to bed. She put on her little mackintosh (the
Vickers household did not, in 1906, run to dressing-gowns)

and sat in a straight chair, looking about the room solemnly, as though she had never seen it before.

It was of only hall-bedroom size, yet there was about
it a stripped cleanness which made it seem larger. Ann
hated what she called "clutter." Here were no masses of
fly-spotted dance-programs, with little pencils, hanging by
the mirror on the bureau; no snapshots of bathing parties
on the beach during that wonderful camping party; and
not a single Yale or University of Illinois banner!

One shelf of books—Hans Christian Andersen, *Water
Babies, Lays of Ancient Rome, David Copperfield* (stolen
from the set downstairs), Le Gallienne's *Quest of the Golden
Girl,* her mother's Bible, a book about bees, *Hamlet,* and
Kim, its pages worn black with reading. A bureau with
the comb and brush and buttonhook in exact parallels.
(Like many rackety and adventurous people, Ann was far
more precise in arranging her kit, wherever she was, than
the steady folk whose fear of living is matched by their
laziness in organizing their dens.)

A prim cot-bed with one betraying feminine sentimentality: a tiny lace-insertion pillow. The straight chair.
A reasonably bad carbon print of Watts's reasonably bad
view of Sir Galahad. A wide window, usually open. A rag
carpet. And peace.

It was Ann herself, this room. Since the death of her
mother, there had been no one to tell her what the room of
a well-bred young lady should be. She had made it. Yet
she looked at it now, and looked at herself, as alien and
strange and incredible.

She talked to herself.

Now it is true that Ann Vickers, at fifteen, was all that

she would ever be at forty, except for the trimmings. But it is also true that she could not talk to herself so acidly sharp as she would at forty. Her monologue was cloudy; it was inarticulate emotion. Yet could that emotion have been translated into words, there where she sat, huddled in her little mackintosh, her nails bitter against her palms, it would have run:

"I loved Dolph. Oh, dear Lord, I did love him. Maybe even not quite nice. When that funny thing happened to me, that Father told me not to worry about, I wanted him to kiss me. Oh, darling, I did love you. You were so wonderful—you had such a thin hard body, and you dived —dove?—so beautifully. But you weren't kind. I thought you meant it, what you said to me tonight under the spruce tree. I thought you meant it! That I wasn't just a husky girl that could do athletics but nobody could love her.

"I shan't ever have a real Beau. I guess I'm too vi'lent. Oh, I don't want to be! I know I plan all the games. I don't want to. I just can't keep my mouth shut, I guess. . . . And all the rest are so damn stupid! . . . Dear Lord, forgive me that I said 'damn,' but they *are* so damn stupid!

"Ben. He would love me. He is so kind.

"I don't want to be loved by any spaniels! I am me! I'm going to see the whole world—Springfield and Joliet and maybe Chicago!

"I guess if I ever love anybody that's as husky as I am, he'll always be scared of me——

"No, Dolph wasn't scared. He *despised* me!"

Suddenly—and there is no clear reason why she should have done so—she was reading the Twenty-fourth Psalm

from her mother's Bible, which was worn along the edges
of the black, limp-leather binding, and her voice now,
articulate and loud, rose as she chanted:

"Who shall ascend into the hill of the Lord? or who shall stand
in his holy place? He that hath clean hands and a pure heart; who
hath not lifted up his soul unto vanity, nor sworn deceitfully.

"He shall receive the blessing from the Lord, and righteousness from the God of his salvation. This is the generation of
them that seek thy face, O Jacob. Selah.

"Lift up your heads, O ye gates; and be ye lift up, ye everlasting doors; and the King of glory shall come in. Who is this
King of glory? The Lord, strong and mighty, the Lord mighty
in battle.

"Lift up your neads, O ye gates; even lift them up, ye everlasting doors; and the King of glory shall come in. Who is this
King of glory? The Lord of hosts, he is the King of glory. Selah."

Her father was knocking, with a worried, "Ann! Annie!
What is it? Are you sick?"

She hated men then, save the King of glory, for whom she
would sacrifice all the smirking Adolphs and complaisant
fathers of this world. She felt savage. But she said civilly:

"Oh, no. I'm sorry, Daddy. I was just reading—uh—
rehearsing something we thought we'd do. I'm terribly
sorry I woke you up. Good-night, dear."

"Did you have a nice party?"

Ann was always to lie like a gentleman, and she caroled:
"Oh, it was lovely. *Good-night!*"

"Yes, I'll have to give it up. The boys, the ones I want,
they'll never like me. And golly, I do like them! But I just
got to be satisfied with being a boy myself.

"And I don't want to.

"But I'll do something! 'Be ye lift up, ye everlasting doors!'

"He was so strong. And slim!

"Oh, *him!*

"I'll never be cheap again and want anybody.

"That picture doesn't hang straight, not quite.

"Girls like Mabel! That hang around the boys!

"I won't ever give 'em, I won't ever give the boys another chance to make fun of me for being square with them!

"'Be ye lift up!' I'm going to sleep."

Though often she saw him in the grocery to which he tranquilly retired from the arduous life of learning in the high school, though it was the period when her gang was definitely aligning itself into Girls and Fellows, Ann showed no more interest in Adolph Klebs.

"Jiminy, Ann Vickers is funny," observed Mildred Evans. "She's crazy! She says she don't want to get married. She wants to be a doctor or a lawyer or somethin', I dunno. She's crazy!"

Oh, Mildred, how wise you were, how wise you are! Today, married to Ben, have you not the best radio in town? Can you not hear Amos 'n' Andy, or the wisdom of Ramsay MacDonald relayed from London? Have you not a Buick, while Dr. Ann Vickers jerks along in a chipped Ford? Do you not play bridge, in the choicest company, while she plays pinochle with one silent man? Good Mildred, wise Mildred, you never tackled the world, which will always throw you.

Good-night, Mildred. You are ended.

That Christmas Eve, when Ann was seventeen, was a postcard Christmas Eve. As she scampered to the church for the Sunday school exercises, the kind lights of neighbors' houses shone on a snowy road where the sleigh tracks were like two lines of polished steel. The moon was high and frosty, and the iced branches of the spruce trees tinkled faintly, and everywhere in the good dry cold was a feeling of festivity.

Ann was absorbed and busy—too busy to have given such attention to clothes and elegance as she had in her days of vanity, at fifteen. She did wish she had something more fashionable than her plaid silk blouse, and she a little hated the thick union suit which her sensible father had bought for her but—oh, well, her days of frivolity were done.

She was teacher of the Girls' Intermediate Class of the First Presbyterian Church, which had once been taught by Mrs. Fred Graves, now asleep in Greenwood Cemetery, and from which a girl named Annie Vickers had been driven for flippancy about the necessity of disciplining women. The Girls' Intermediate Class was to present the cantata "Hark, the Herald Angels Sing" at the Sunday school exercises, and Ann was hurrying—hurrying —because it was so important that she should be there, that she should take charge of things, that her class should impress the audience.

The church was a very furnace of festivity as she came up to it. The windows were golden, the door was jollily framed in a wooden Gothic arch. On the church porch were all the small boys who, though perhaps neglectful of their Sabbath duties for fifty weeks out of the year, had been edifyingly attendant the past two weeks.

Inside, the church was a cave of green and crystal. Even the helpful mottoes painted on the side walls, "Blessed be the Name of the Lord," and "Are you saved?" were almost hidden by holly wreaths. But the splendor of it all was the Christmas tree on the platform. Ten good feet it rose, with candles and papier-mâché angels—for on Christmas Eve the Presbyterian Church permitted itself to be so Roman as to admit angels, along with the Christ Child. Candles against the deep green; candles and white angels and silver balls and plentiful snow made of rich cotton batting. And at the foot of the tree were the stockings, one for each of the Presbyterian children, even those who had been convincedly Calvinistic only for the last two weeks; stockings of starchy net, each containing an orange, a bag of hard candy, including peppermints printed in red with such apt mottoes as "Come on, baby!" three Brazil nuts (better known in Waubanakee as "niggertoes"), a pamphlet copy of the Gospel According to St. John, and a Gift—a tin trumpet or a whistle or a cotton monkey.

They had been purchased by the new pastor, young Reverend Donnelly, out of his salary of $1,800 a year— when he got it. He was not altogether wise, this young man. He frightened adolescents, including Ann Vickers, by the spectacle of an angry old God watching them and trying to catch them in nasty little habits. And his sermons were dull, suffocatingly dull. But he was so kind, so eager!

And it was Reverend Donnelly (not, locally, the Reverend
Mister) who dashed down the aisle now to greet Ann.

"Miss Vickers! I'm *so* glad you're early! We're going to
have a glorious Christmas Eve!"

"Oh I do hope so. Ismyclassready?" demanded the
energetic Ann.

The exercises went superbly: the prayer, the singing by
the choir and congregation of "Come All Ye Faithful,"
the comic song by Dr. Brevers, the dentist, the cantata,
with Ann leading, very brisk with her baton; and they
came to the real point of the exercises—distribution of the
Christmas stockings by Santa Claus, very handsome and
benevolent in a red coat and snowy whiskers. Privately,
Santa was Mr. Bimby, of the clarinet and the Eureka Dry
Goods Store.

Mr. Bimby speaking:

"Now, boys and girls, I've, ur, come a long way, all the
way from the ice and snow and, ur, the glaciers of the
North Pole, because I've heard that the boys and girls of
the Waubanakee Presbyterian Church was particularly
good and done what their parents and teachers told them
to, and so I've given up my dates with the Pope at Rome
and the King of England and all those folks to be with
you, myself, personally."

Ann Vickers, as a participant, had a seat in one of the
front pews. A little uneasily she watched a candle drooping
on a lower bough of the Christmas tree. She rebuked herself for her phobia, but she could scarce attend to Mr.
Bimby's humor as he rollicked on:

"Now I guess there's some of you that haven't been
quite as good as maybe you might of been, this past year.

And maybe some of you ain't gone to Sunday school as often as you might of. I know that in my class—I mean, I got a phone call from my friend Ted Bimby, the teacher of the Older Boys' Class here, and he says sometimes on a nice summer morning——"

The candle was drooping like a tired hand. Ann's fingers were tight.

"—some of the boys would rather go off fishing than hear the Word of the Lord, and all them lessons that you can learn from the example of Jacob and Abraham and all them old wise folks——"

The candle reached the cotton batting. Instantly the tree was aflame, a gusty and terrible flame. Reverend Donnelly and Santa Claus Bimby stood gaping. It was Ann Vickers who sprang onto the platform, pushing Bimby aside.

The children were screaming, in the utter reasonless terror of children, fighting toward the door.

Ann snatched up the grass rug which adorned the pulpit platform, threw it over the incandescent tree, and with her hands beat down the flames which the rug did not cover, while her whole scorched body hurt like toothache. She raged, she said, "Oh, dear!" in a tone which made it sound worse than "Oh, damn!"

Just as she dropped, she was conscious that the fire was quenched and that Dr. McGonegal was throwing his coonskin coat over the tree. She was hoping the coat would not be burned.

For two weeks Ann lay abed. She was, said Dr. McGonegal, to have no scars save a faint smirch or two on her wrists. And for that two weeks she was a heroine.

Reverend Donnelly called every day. Mr. Bimby brought her a valuable bead wreath. Her father read *David Harum* to her. The Waubanakee *Intelligencer* said that she was kin to Susan B. Anthony, Queen Elizabeth, and Joan of Arc.

But what excited her was the calling of Oscar Klebs— his Homeric brow, his white beard, his quiet desperation.

Rather fussily and somewhat incredulous at such a proletarian caller, Professor Vickers brought in the old man, with a falsely cheery, "Another visitor for you, dear."

The authority of being a heroine gave Ann a courage toward her amiable but still parental parent that she had rarely shown before. She dared to drive him out with an almost wifely inclination of her head toward the door, and she was alone with Oscar.

The old man sat by her bed, patting her hand.

"You were very fine, my little lady. And I am not so bigoted I t'ink it all happened because it was in a church. No, maybe not! But I come—— Little Ann, don't let it make you t'ink that you are a herowine! Life, it is not heroism. It is t'ought. Bless you, my little lady! Now I go!"

It was much the shortest visit she had. And for a week, freed from the duty of being brisk and important about unimportant affairs, she lay abed, thinking—the one week in all her life so far when she had had time to think.

Oscar Klebs seemed always to be sitting beside her, demanding that she think.

"Um—huh. I enjoyed it too much," she brooded. "Being a heroine! I put out that fire before I had time to realize it. Annie, that was nice of you, putting out that fire. Yes, it was, dear! Mr. Bimby was scared, and so was Reverend Donnelly. You weren't! And what of that? You just move quicker than most folks. And yet you couldn't make Adolph love you!

"Oh, dear God, make me solid! Don't let me ever be too tickled by applause!

"'Who shall ascend into the hill of the Lord? or who shall stand in his holy place? He that hath clean hands and a pure heart.'

"But by golly I did put out that fire, while all those *men* stood goggling!"

5

Point royal college for women is a pleasant place of Georgian brick buildings, of lawns and oaks and elms, on the slope of a hill above the Housatonic River, in Connecticut.

Ann Vickers's father had left her, at his death—he died very quietly and decently, for he was that sort of man —a thousand dollars, all his estate. For the rest of her tuition she waited on table at Dawley Hall, the college dining-room, and corrected papers in sociology.

She was a Junior, now, in the autumn of 1910.

Ann Vickers, aged nineteen, was "appallingly wholesome-looking." That was her own phrase for it. She was rather tall, large-boned, threatened by fat unless, as she always did, she fought it. Her hair was brown and only by savage attention did she keep it from being mutinous. Her best feature was her eyes, surprisingly dark for her pale skin, and they were eyes that were never blank; they flashed quickly into gayety or anger. Though she was threatened with plumpness about her hips, she had beautiful slim legs, and long hands, very strong. And she, who thought of herself as a quiet person, a field mouse among these splendorous shining girls from Fifth Avenue and Farmington and Brookline, was actually never still, never meek, even to the daughter of a Pittsburgh steel millionaire. She was always being indignant or joyful or deep in sorrow or depressed—in what Lindsay Atwell was later to call her "small mood." When a play came to Point Royal, and the other girls said "That was a nice show" or "I didn't think that was so swell," Ann walked for hours—well, minutes—after it, hating the villain, glorying with the heroine, sometimes loving the hero.

She was, without particularly wanting to be, Important. She was on the basketball team, she was secretary of the cautious Socialist Club, she was vice president of the Y. W. C. A. and, next year, as a Senior, likely to be its president.

For two years she had roomed alone. But this year she was sharing a handsome apartment (it had running water) with Eula Towers, the pale and lovely Eula, given to low lights and delicate colors, to a pale and lovely leaf-green art—a *fin de siècle* exquisite held over ten years too long. Eula was doing most of the drawings for the Class Annual: portraits of young ladies with swan necks and a certain lack of mammary glands, pre-Raphaelite young ladies, very artistic and pretty dull.

Ann had always admired Eula, and never known her. To Ann, who could bandage a leg bruised at basketball, or fret over the statistics in a sociology paper, or with false jollity reconcile the dreadful controversy in the Y. W. as to whether they should have a joint camp-meeting with Bethel College Y. W., it was overawing that Eula should be able to draw portraits of the faculty, that she should wear five bracelets at once, that she should sometimes wear a turban, and that for the Point Royal *Literary Argus* she should have written the moving poem:

> *Night—and the night is dark and full of fear—*
> *Night—and I walk my lonely ways alone—*
> *Oh you are far, and dear—you are too dear—*
> *Under the deadened Moon.*

And Eula was rich. Her father was a significant whole-sale drug dealer in Buffalo. While Ann insisted on paying her half of the rent, she did let Eula furnish and decorate their two rooms, and what a furnishing, what a decoration that was! Eula was all for fainting pastels and a general escape from the bright exactitudes of the wholesale drug business. They had a study and a bedroom. The study, which she called "the studio," Eula furnished in black and lavender; gold and lavender Japanese fabrics against the cream-colored plaster walls provided by the unesthetic college authorities; black carpet; a couch, covered with black silk, so wide and luxurious that it was impossible to sit on it without getting a backache; chairs of black-painted wood with lavender upholstery; and pictures and pictures and pictures. . . . Aubrey Beardsley, Bakst, Van Gogh, a precious signed photograph of Richard Mansfield, and what appeared to be several thousand Japanese prints, not necessarily from Japan.

This groundwork once laid, Eula attended to dimming the light and excluding the air. The three gas-mantel lights, one on each desk and one from the ceiling, she cloaked with triple lavender silk shades. The two good windows, looking on oaks and grassland and far hills, she corrected with curtains of lavender silk and drapes of black velvet.

And on a little table she had a gilded cast-iron Buddha.

Ann was agitated but silent. She fretted that she "didn't know much about all this art."

The beauty and wonder complete, Eula glowed to Ann, "Isn't it lovely! The rooms at Point Royal, oh, they're so hard and bold, most of 'em. So dreadfully masculine and vulgar and bromidic! We'll have a real salon, where we can talk and loaf and invite our souls. And dreeeeeam! Now here's what I plan for the bedroom. Let's keep the black motif, but have old rose for the subsidiary theme. Black velvet drapes again, but——"

"Now look here!" Ann's reverence for high and delicate things was gone in a demand for light and fresh air, two of the greatest gods in her small, hard Pantheon, along with courage, loyalty, and the curiosity of an Einstein about what makes the world go. "This room is certainly swell, dear. It certainly looks pretty. Yes, I guess it certainly is pretty. But I'm not going to have any heavy curtains or any swell lamp-shades in the bedroom. I got to have air. And if you don't mind, I'm going to move my desk in there and study by the window, with just a green glass shade on the lamp. You keep this room. And then in the bedroom we'll have a coupla cots and a coupla bureaus and a grass rug, and that's enough."

Eula smote her breast at this Philistinism. (It was in 1910: they still used the word "Philistine.") She wailed, like a silver trumpet in a funeral march, "Ann! Oh, my darling! I did it only because I thought you liked—you liked—— Oh, if you had only *said!*"

"Sure, it's swell to have the sitting-room like this. But gotta have one room to work in. You see how it is!"

"Oh, of course. My *darling!* Whatever you want!" Eula advanced on Ann like a snake: she clasped Ann to her, kissing her neck. "I just want to do what you want! Anything that my talent can add to your greatness——"

"Oh, stop it! Quit it!" The curious thing is that Ann was more alarmed than angered by this soapy attack. It seemed unholy. With no visible gallantry, she fled. "Got to hustle to the gym," she grumbled, breaking away, seizing her tam-o'-shanter.

"I don't understand it. I don't like it when girls hug you like that. Gee, I just felt somehow kind of scared. Not nice, like Adolph!" she marveled, on her way to the library.

But after a happy hour with Danby's *Principles of Taxation and Its Relationship to Tariffs*, she sighed, "Oh, it's just one of those idiotic schoolgirl crushes. Just because she kisses you, you get up on your ear. You think you're so sacred! . . . But we're not going to have any Babylonian—Carthaginian, is it? whatever it is—decorations in the bedroom!"

They didn't.

Eula, though she squeaked plaintively against windows open on cold nights, declared in company that she was enchanted by "the fine Spartan simplicity of our sleeping-quarters."

Six girls were in Eula's "salon," this third day of their Junior year. The room was not yet completely furnished, but the wide black couch and a few hundred Japanese prints were in place. The six sat about a chafing dish in which Welsh rabbit was evilly bubbling. It was rather like six young gentlemen of Harvard or Yale or Princeton in a dormitory room about a precious bottle of gin in 1932, except that the Welsh rabbit was more poisonous.

They talked—they trilled—they gabbled—they quivered with the discovery of life. The first two years of college, they had been schoolgirls. Now they looked out to the Great World and to the time when they would be Graduates and command thrones and powers and principalities, splendid jobs in the best high schools, or lordly husbands (preferably professional men); when they would travel in France, or perform earnest good-doing upon the poor and uneducated.

"There's so many girls in the class that just want to get married. *I* don't want to get married. To wash a lot of brats and listen to a husband at breakfast! I want a career," said Tess Morrissey.

It was 1910. They talked then, ardent girls, as though marriage and a "career" were necessarily at war.

"Oh, I don't! I don't think it's quite nice to talk about family life like that!" said Amy Jones. "After all, isn't civilization founded on the hearthstone? And how could a really nice woman influence the world more than by giving an example to her husband and sons?"

"Oh, rats, you're so old-*fash*ioned!" protested Edna Derby. "Why do you suppose we *go* to college? Women have always been the slaves of men. Now it's women's hour! We ought to demand all the freedom and—and travel and fame and so on and so forth that men have. And our own spending money! Oh, I'm going to have a career,

too! I'm going to be an actress. Like le belle Sarah. Think!
The lights! The applause! The scent of—of make-up and
all sorts of Interesting People coming into your dressing-
room and congratulating you! The magic world! Oh, I
must have it. . . . Or I might take up landscape gardening,
I hear that pays slick."

"I suppose," Ann snarled, "that if you went on the
stage you'd do some plays as well as get applauded!"

"Oh, of course. I'd like to help elevate the stage. It's
so lowbrow now. Shakespeare."

"Well, I don't care," said Mary Vance. "I think Amy
is right. It's all very well to have a career, and I want to
keep up my piano and banjo, but I do want to have a
home. That's why you get a swell education—so you can
marry a really dandy fellow, with brains and all, and
understand and help him, and the two of you face the
world just like—like that French king, you remember,
and his wife."

"I'm not afraid of the world. I'm going to be a painter.
Study. Paris! Oh, dear Paris, gray old town beside the
Seine. And canvases that will hang in the salons forever!"
opined Eula.

"Yes, and I want to write," mooned Tess.

"Write *what*?" Ann snapped.

"Oh, you know. *Write!* You know—poems and essays
and novels and criticisms and all like that. I think I'll
start out reading manuscripts for a publishing house.
Or I might take a position on a New York newspaper.
I've got the cutest idea for an essay right now—about how
books are our best friends and never turn you down no
matter if you do hit bad luck. But what are you crabbing

about? You don't mean to say you're going to fall for this husband and hearthside stuff, after getting educated? Aren't you going to have a career, Ann?"

"You bet your life I am! But where I differ from you dilettantes—you Marys—I always did think Martha got a raw deal that time!—but where I differ is, I expect to work! I want all the cheers and money I can get, but I expect to work for them. Besides! I want to do something that will have some effect on the human race. Maybe if I could paint like Velasquez and make your eyes bung out, or play Lady Macbeth so people would fall off their seats, I'd be crazy to do it, but to paint footling little snow-scenes——"

"Why, Aaann!" from Eula.

"—or play Charles Klein, that's all goulash! I want to be something that affects people—I don't know what yet—I'm too ignorant. Maybe a missionary? Or is that just a way of getting to China? Maybe a lady doc? Maybe work in a settlement house? I don't know. But I want to get my hands on the world."

"Oh, yes," that future literary genius, Tess, said virtuously, "of course I want to help people, too. Elevate them."

"Oh, I don't mean pass around the coal and blankets and teach the South Sea Islanders to wear pants. I mean ——" If Ann was struggling harder than the others to say, to discover for herself, what she meant, it was because in some elementary way she did have something to mean. "It's like what you get in this new novel by H. G. Wells, this *Tono-Bungay*. I'd like to contribute, oh, one-millionth of a degree to helping make this race of fat-heads and grouches something more like the angels."

"Why, Ann Vickers!" said the refined Amy Jones. "Do you think it's nice to call the human race, that the Bible says were created in God's image, a bunch of fatheads?"

"Well, John the Baptist called his hometown folks a generation of vipers. But I don't think we're as good as that—we haven't got as much speed or smoothness as a nice viper. We need more poison, not less. We're all so—so —so darn soft! So scared of life!"

Into the room slammed Francine Merriweather, and the discussion of the purposes of life, which had become exciting, curled up and died instantly as Francine shrieked, in the manner of Greek tragedy:

"Listen, sistern! What do you think! The Sigma Digamma gang are going to run Snippy Mueller for class president, and Gertie for chairman of the Lit.! We got to do something!"

"Do something!" cried Ann. There was singularly little of the savior of mankind in her now; she was all briskness and fury. "Girls! Let's put up Mag Dougherty for president! Let's get busy! And if you don't mind, I think I'll just pinch me off the vice-presidency for myself! And we'll nominate Mitzi Brewer for secretary."

"Why, you said just yesterday she was nothing but a tart!" wailed Edna Derby.

"Oh," vaguely, "I didn't mean it that way. Besides, if we ring her in, prob'ly we'll get the whole vote of the Music Association. They're a bunch of simps, but their votes are just as good as anybody else's."

"Why, Ann Vickers, you sound like nothing but a politician. I don't believe you mean a word you said—all about making mankind like H. G. Wells and all that."

Ann was authentically astonished. "Me? A politician? Why, politicians are horrid! I wasn't thinking about any politics. I was just thinking about how to get the best class ticket—I mean, the best that we can put over!"

As sharply as practical affairs had cut into their solution of the problems of life, so sharply did a yet more interesting topic cut into politics when the newly come Francine thrilled, "Oh, girls, have any of you met the new European History prof, Dr. Hargis? I saw him in his office."

"What's he like?" the maidens cooed in chorus.

"Listen! He's swell! Be still, my fluttering heart! What the Regents have let in on this nunnery! He's one of these good-looking red-headed men."

"*Are* there any good-looking red-headed men? Women, yes, but men!" sniffed Eula.

"Wait'll you see this Greek god! The kind of red that's almost golden. And curly! And lovely gray eyes, and all tanned, like he'd been swimming all summer, and swell shoulders and a grin—oh, how you young Portias are going to fall for him!"

"How old is he?" in a chorus.

"Not over thirty, and they say he's a Chicago Ph. D., and Germany and everything. I bet he dances like a whiz. Do I take European History? All in favor signify by raising the right hand! The ayes have it!"

But Ann vowed privately, "Then I *won't* take European History. . . . Still, there is that one hole in my curriculum yet. . . . But I'm not going to have any Greek gods in

mine. Men are troglodytes—whatever that is! . . . What
was it Father used to say: 'Men is veasels and vimmen is
vipers and children is vorms'? No, men are just animals.
. . . But still, I couldn't stand much of Eula here. . . . But
I'm never going to fall for any male again, as long as I live.
. . . But I do suppose I might consult this Hargis person
about the course."

6

GLENN HARGIS, M. A., PH. D., Assistant Professor of History in Point Royal College, was in his office in the basement of Susan B. Anthony Hall; a small office: pink plaster walls, that carbon print of the Parthenon which is so familiar that it must be contemporaneous with the Parthenon itself, a flat desk, very meager, a World Almanac, a Point Royal catalogue, and a large class record, the latest New Haven *Journal-Courier*, Dr. Hargis himself, and that was all, till Ann Vickers strode in and this dungeon, accustomed to dismal discussions of cuts, marks, flunks, themes, and required reading, suddenly came alive.

Dr. Hargis, at his desk, stared up at her rain-shining cheeks and excited eyes. She stared down at him. He was, Ann noted, certainly not the "Greek god" that the hungry Francine found him, but he was a square, healthy, personable young man, with a broad forehead and cheerful eyes. He was smoking a pipe. Ann observed this with unexplained approval. Most of the male teachers at Point Royal were gray and worried and timid, and given to morality and peanut butter.

He stood up. His voicè was unexpectedly thin, almost feminine, as he piped, "Yes? What can I do for you?"

As they sat down, he puffed his pipe grandly, she thought. Herself she leaned forward in the torture-seat in which, the year before, so many students had tried to explain to the professor of mathematics why young females sometimes prefer dancing to a mastery of differential calculus.

"I have a nine-thirty free," she hurried, "and I can choose between Harmony, Shakespeare, and Gen European History to 1400."

"Why not Harmony or Shakespeare? Fine fellow, Shakespeare. Taught about cakes and ale—a subject much neglected in this chaste atmosphere, I should judge. Or Harmony? My Gen to 1400 class is pretty full."

"Oh, I couldn't do anything with Harmony. I'm afraid I haven't got much artistic temperament. I used to play the organ in church, but that's as far as I ever got with music. And Shakespeare—my father and I used to read him aloud, and I hate this picking him to pieces that they call 'studying' him."

"Very pretty, but then you ought to hate picking European History to pieces, too."

"No, because I don't know anything about it."

"Tell me, Miss Uh—tell me precisely why would you like to study Gen European, aside from its convenience in occurring at nine-thirty?"

"I want to know it. I honestly do! I want to know! I hope some day to—— A girl accused me of being a politician, yesterday, and I denied it, and then I got to thinking: perhaps I'd been lying to myself. Perhaps I will be a

politician, if women ever get the vote. Why not? There has
to be some kind of government, even if it's not perfect,
and I guess there can't be one without politicians."

"Politicians, my dear young lady, are merely the
middlemen of economics, and you know what we all think
of middlemen. They take the Economic Truth and peddle
small quantities of it to the customers, at an inordinate
profit."

"Well, aren't—aren't teachers, even college professors,
middlemen of knowledge?"

He grinned. "Yes, maybe. And writers are middlemen
of beauty—they adulterate it judiciously and put it up in
small packages, with bright patent labels and imitation
silk ribbon, and sell it under a snappy trade name. Perhaps.
And lawyers are the middlemen of justice. Well, maybe
we'll let you be a politician. But what has that to do with
Gen European and the hour of nine-thirty?—a chilly and
dreadful hour in these Northern latitudes!"

"Well, if I did get to be a politician, I'd like to be the
kind that knows something beyond getting a new post-
office building for Passawumpaic Creek. Now that there
won't be any more great wars, I can see America being
in close touch with Europe, and I'd like to work for that.
But anyway, I want to know!"

"You are accepted for my class." He rose; he beamed.
"And it may interest you to hear that you are the first
young lady in this cultured establishment that I have
accepted gladly. Because you 'want to know.' Your
confrères—or cosœurs, if you prefer—seem to have as
cheerful an antipathy to scholarship as the young gentlemen I have known in the University of Chicago and my

aboriginal Ottawatamie College. Doubtless, though, I shall find myself wrong."

"You won't," said Ann, glumly. "Women are industrious, but they rarely know what they're industrious about. They're ants. You'll find lots of girls that will work hard. They can recite everything in the book. But you won't find many that know why they're studying it, or that'll read anything about it you don't tell them to."

"But you, I take it, will!"

"Why," with a surprised candor, untouched by his irony, "you know I will!"

As she walked to the Student Volunteers' meeting, Ann gloated, "He's swell! He's the only prof here that it's fun to talk to!"

The Student Volunteers are an intercollegiate body whose members are so specifically pledged, so passionately eager, to become missionaries that, out of the forty-two Volunteers enrolled this year in Point Royal, five did later actually become missionaries. The Volunteers at their meetings sang hymns and prayed and heard papers on the rapid spread of Christianity in Beluchistan, Nigeria, or Mexico—which last, from the standpoint of Point Royal, was not Christian at all.

Today they had a real missionary, just returned from Burma. She did not talk of gilt domes and tinkling temple bells nor in the least of sitting with delicate native wenches when the mist was on the rice fields and the sun was dropping low. She talked of child mothers, of fever, and of scabby babies playing in the filth. Now Ann Vickers was less interested in mosaic temples than in feeding starved babies; nor was she cynical when the missionary sighed,

"Oh, if you will only come help bring them the tidings of Jesus, so that the heathen may, like our own beloved Christian country, be utterly free from the spectacle of beggars and starving babies!" Ann nodded agreeably—but she had heard nothing. She had been thinking of red-headed Glenn Hargis.

Was he really witty, or just (her words, in 1910) "sort of flip and brash?"

How was it that she liked pipe-smell better than the glossy, warm scent that hung about Eula?

And, dejectedly, why was she so absent of mind, when they were receiving a missionary message right from the Field?

And, was Dr. Hargis married?

He was not.

Within twenty-four hours every girl on the campus knew that.

It was against Point Royal custom to have on the faculty a bachelor, especially a good-looking bachelor. But it appeared that Dr. Hargis was a cousin of the late president of Point Royal, the sainted Dr. Merribel Peaselee, and therefore guaranteed to be sound.

"Well, maybe," said Mitzi Brewer, the Junior Class Problem, "but he looks like pie for breakfast to me!"

"Don't be disgusting!" said Ann. "He has a very fine mind. He doesn't think about anything except the lessons that history can teach us about how to reorganize human society. He has a real ideal of scholarship."

"Well, Annie, he can't teach me anything about how to reorganize society. Kick out the dean, run a free bus to

the Yale Campus, and a dance every evening. And how
would you like that? You're pretty doggone pure, Ann.
It hurts, when I look at you. But wait'll you feel your
oats, lamb! When I'm home knitting socks for my sixth
sprig, you'll be busting out, and yeaow!"

"You make me sick!" said Ann, with a feebleness which
astonished her.

Though in her personal habits Ann was as respectable
as the dean, Dr. Agatha Snow, though she was almost
tediously wholesome and normal, with her basketball and
course in domestic science, yet privately she had been
restless about the conservatism of all thought (if any) at
Point Royal. The shadow of old Oscar Klebs still hovered
gray behind her. She was irritated that not a dozen of the
girls considered the workers as anything but inferiors;
that they assumed that New Washington, Ohio, was
necessarily superior to Vienna, Venice, and Stockholm
combined. Though she regarded herself as a solid Christian, even a future missionary, she was distressed that it
should be regarded as ill-bred to criticize the Bible as one
criticized Shakespeare. It was not that Point Royal, in
1910, was as "fundamentalist" as a frontier camp-
meeting of 1810. The girls did not accept the Bible unquestioning because they were passionately uplifted by it,
but precisely because they were not enough interested in
the Bible, in Religion, either to fight for them or to doubt.
They hadn't enough faith to be either zealots or atheists.
Ann knew that there were greater women's colleges—
Vassar, Wellesley, Smith—in which some small proportion
of the girls did actually regard scholarship as equal in rank

with tennis. But Point Royal, like a host of Midwestern denominational colleges, exhibited perfectly that American superiority to time and space whereby in one single Man of Affairs may be found simultaneously the religion of 1600, the marital notions of 1700, the economics of 1800, and the mechanical skill of 2500.

This irritation, and her memory of Oscar Klebs, had driven Ann to form the Point Royal Socialist Club. It was rather mild, and very small. The average attendance was six, and they sat on the floor in one of the girls' rooms and said excitedly that it wasn't fair that certain men should have millions while others starved, and that they would all read Karl Marx just as soon as they could get around to it. Once Tess Morrissey, a stern young woman, said they ought to study birth-control, and they gasped and talked with nervous lowered voices. "Yes, women should be allowed to govern their own destinies," Ann whispered. But when Tess, from her work in biology, murmured of actual methods of control, they looked uncomfortable and began to discuss the beauties of woman suffrage, which was to end all crime and graft.

No one in the Socialist Club saw anything inconsistent in Ann's belonging to it and to the Student Volunteers. It was the era of a fantasy known as Christian Socialism. It was the era of windy optimism, of a pre-war "idealism" which was satisfied with faith in place of statistics, of a certainty on one hand that Capitalism was divinely appointed to last forever, and on the other that Capitalism would be soon and bloodlessly replaced by an international Utopian commonwealth rather like the home-life of Louisa M. Alcott. It was from this era that everyone who in 1930 was from thirty-five to fifty-five years old imbibed those buoyant, Shavian, liberal, faintly clownish notions which he was to see regarded by his sons and daughters as on a par with Baptist ethics and the cosmogony of Moses.

Ann Vickers, with the most aspiring mind of her class, as a college Junior in 1910, was nevertheless nearer mentally to William Wordsworth and the pastoral iconoclasms of 1832 than to the burning spirits who as Juniors in 1929 and 1930 and 1931 and 1932 were to be so clearheaded that they would be bored by the ghostly warriors who in the 1930's went on blowing defiant conch-shells over the body of a dead Victorianism quite as much as by the original Victorian proprieties; and who would despise more than either of these the sour degeneracy of the decade just before them, when the wrecked Odysseuses of the Great War had from 1919 to 1929 unceasingly piped, "Let us eat, drink, and be nasty, for the world has gone to hell, and after us there will never again be youth and springtime and hope."

So unprophetic of this new crusade was Ann and all her generation that though in 1932 she was to be but forty-one years old, yet her story must perforce be almost as much of an historical romance, a chronicle of musty beliefs and customs, as though she had lived in Florence of the Medicis. So is it with all of us who are old enough to remember the Great War as an actuality. In the forty or fifty years that we have lived by the lying calendar, we have gone through five centuries of hectic change, and like Ann we behold ourselves as contemporaries at once with Leonardo da Vinci and the dreadful beard of General Grant and the latest vulgarian of the radio and the latest twenty-two-

year-old physicist who flies his own aëroplane and blandly
votes the Communist ticket and, without either clerical
sanction or the chatter about "sexual freedom" of the
slightly older radicals, goes casually to living with his girl,
and who familiarly tames and spins and splits the atom
which, when we were his age, seemed as mysterious and
intangible as the Holy Ghost.

Outside these pious socialistic retreats, Ann heard no
more of revolution than if she had been a bridge-player.
She hoped that she would hear something of its gospel from
the lively Dr. Glenn Hargis, and she did, during his first
lecture.

It was in Classroom C2, in Susan B. Anthony Hall, a
room of hard shiny chairs with tablet-arms like a Thompson's Lunch, of blackboards, a low dais for the instructor,
and a dismal portrait of Harriet Beecher Stowe. It had that
traditional and sanctified dreariness characteristic of all
classrooms, marriage-license bureaus, hospitals, doctors'
waiting-rooms, and Southern Methodist Churches. In this
cavern, designed to make learning uncomfortable and
virtuous, the forty girls were an old-fashioned garden, and
Glenn Hargis, glistening on the dais, a red-headed gardener.

He grumbled for a few minutes about the cooking and
laundry of scholarship—office appointments, themes, required reading—then smiled on them and launched out:

"Young ladies, if I am granted the skill, I wish in this
class not so much to add anything to your knowledge as to
try to subtract prejudices. Despite the living evidence
of uncovered Pompeii today, we tend all of us to feel that
people who lived before 1400 A. D., certainly people who

lived before 500 A. D., were somehow as different from us as men from monkeys. It is the most difficult feat of scholarship *cum* imagination to understand that the citizens of Pompeii, when it was sealed by ashes in 79, had elections and electioneering and political posters, graft and reformism and the pork barrel, exactly like ourselves: that ladies went shopping and bought sausages and wine, that haughty and probably faulty plumbers fussed over the water pipes.

"A characteristic misconception of ancient history as being fundamentally different from our own is heard frequently in the idiotic discussion 'Why did Rome fall?' An ecclesiast will tell you that Rome fell because they drank wine and had races on the Sabbath and permitted dancing girls."

Ann nodded. She had heard the Reverend Mr. Donnelly and half a dozen other Reverends explain just this, in Waubanakee.

"The vegetarian will prove that Rome fell because the degenerate late Romans departed from their pristine diet of herbs and fruit, and gorged on meat. The professional patriot will explain the fall by the Roman degeneracy in military training and armaments. And in the early days of America, when bathing was just coming in, there were sages who explained that Rome fell solely because the Roman dandies took to daily hot bathing.

"But none of these retrospective prophets ever consider the fact that actually Rome never did fall!

"Rome did not fall! Rome *changed!* It was invaded by barbarians—the ancestors of the present English, and rather like them in rude health and possessiveness. It was invaded by plagues. In the Middle Ages it was an insignificant town, plainly inferior to Venice and Naples in that they had seaports, while Ostia Mare, the San Pedro of Rome, had silted up. But Rome did not fall. It has gone on, always, through changing fortunes, and is today along with New York, London, Berlin, Paris, Vienna, Peking, Tokio, Rio, and Buenos Aires one of the—let me see: how many does that make?—one of the nine, or is it ten, ruling cities of the world, with a population nearly equal to the entire Roman Empire of the classic day!

"It is such a point of view that I want you to seek, that I want myself to preserve, throughout this entire course; to keep the scientific attitude, and to inquire, whenever wiseacres explain, in classroom or pulpit or by the cracker-barrel, just why Rome fell, why the Dark Ages were dark, why the people endured the tyranny of feudalism, and why the Protestant Reformation was divinely appointed—to inquire whether Rome really did fall, whether the Dark Ages were so very much darker than South Chicago in 1910, whether a feudal serf was necessarily more miserable than a freeborn Pittsburgh miner in this blessed year of star-spangled civilization, and whether there may not be quite decent and sensitive persons who get as much solace from the high mass, even today, as from a sermon by Gypsy Jones."

In that pre-Mencken day, Dr. Hargis was preaching heresy so damnable that Ann broke her quick breathing of delight with a gasp of fear. She glanced about. Some of the girls looked shocked, some of them looked bored . . . and most of them were obediently making examination-passing notes in their neat little books with their neat little fountain pens, precisely as they would have if Dr. Hargis had said that the leghorn hat was invented at Sienna in A. D. 12 by a lame maiden aunt of Augustus Cæsar. She was relieved, and turned again toward Glenn Hargis as she had turned toward no masculine magnet since Adolph Klebs.

7

IT SHOULD have warned her.

When, after this first class, she impulsively went up and murmured, "Oh, Dr. Hargis, I've never enjoyed a lecture so much in my life, and I hope they won't think you're too radical, here," he giggled, "Me radical? Why, my dear young lady, I'm the soul of conservatism—a good Republican, and a vestryman in the Episcopal Church, and I really *like* the pictures of Millais and Leighton!"

"But that—about the Pennsylvania miners and the serfs?"

"Oh," airily, "that was just by way of illustration!"

And confusedly she gave place to fellow students who desired to ask Dr. Hargis whether Gibbon and Buckle were Required Outside Reading or just Optional.

Trudging home, Ann thought, with a maternal anger, "It's a shame for him to be so flip about his gifts, when he has so much. But maybe he's much more radical than he knows. Just caught this silly Ph. D. hand-wavy manner. I suppose it's part of the trade—the way Mr. Klebs used to look at a shoe sole, look wise. Scientific attitude. I wonder if I'll ever learn it. I will! Or am I just sentimental? . . .

He's sweet. His eyebrows almost come together. He has such thick red hair on the backs of his hands."

They met, as people inexplicably do meet when they are interested in each other; they met after class, at conferences in his office, at Y. W. C. A. teas, at the chaste orgies of cocoa and exotic Huntley & Palmer biscuits held by the Dean on Thursday evenings, at the debating society, of which he had been appointed director. The Ann who had despised that synthetic and self-conscious argument called "debating" suddenly found it a powerful training for politics. Scores of girls had shown a delicate interest in Dr. Hargis. But, so far as Ann could make it out, the domestic Amy Joneses of the college bored him because they were less interested in the Carlovingian kings than in cake-dough and the inexpensive decoration of small houses; the Mitzi Brewers because their come-hither eyes menaced the job of an earnest young assistant professor. Aching for him and his blindness, Ann watched him circle round one girl after another, and when he seemed to settle —but oh, in the purest, most friendly way, you understand —upon herself, she felt that she ought to be supercilious to him, and she wasn't.

They were friends.

They talked by the hour in the lounge-hall of the Y. W. building. He dropped his superior airiness, which she analyzed as a protection against the greedy students who would expect him to know everything and who would snigger at catching him out in an error.

And they walked—but on the campus, strictly.

It was the rule at Point Royal that males, either faculty

members or visiting cousins, might stroll with the girls on the campus, in fair view of the titters and yearning eyes of the other vicariously excited young ladies, but they might not go walking or picnicking elsewhere. For all the brave discussions at Point Royal, for all their biology and physiology, their pretended impersonality about the mistresses of kings and the economic causes of prostitution, for all their assumption that they were both normal and, as they had it, "up to date," ready for matrimony and child-bearing, or business on half-equality with men, these girls were in a convent, herded by nuns, male and female. In the co-educational state universities, the girls might be jolly and casual enough with young men, and, daily seeing them fumbling in library and laboratory, not take them too seriously. But in this cloister even the girls who had been wholesomely brought up with noisy brothers were so overwhelmed in the faint-scented mist of femininity that they became as abnormal as the hysterical wrens in a boarding-school.

They were obsessed by the thought and desire of men, and most of them took it out in pretending to despise men —when there were no men about. But when there were —— The plainest masculine teacher, the Reverend Henry Sogles, M. A., Professor of Latin and Greek, had after each class a twittering of girl students about him, listening with reverence to such interesting remarks as that Sophocles was a better writer, also more moral, than David Graham Phillips. And they scurried to find his worn, high, dusty overshoes. A minx who had stepped out of a French print found them under a desk and handed them to him, breathing quickly.

But it was when a student had a personable young male visitor that the girls went boarding-school mad. As the unfortunate came up the Main Campus Walk, scores of pretty heads hung out of windows. As he came into the dormitory, timidly, hat in hand, he was aware of a squeaking and peering and scampering up the stairs as though from thousands of active mice. As he sat awkwardly in the drawing-room and tried to be gallant to his current only love, it was strange how many young ladies had to edge into that room to find a book. And afterward they discussed every detail of the errant god, from his doubtful yellow shoes to his splendidly high collar.

They heard of girls from the greater women's colleges going quite naturally to dances at Yale or Harvard. And they themselves, home on vacation, danced at the country clubs which, all over newly rich America, were suddenly turning cow pastures into rich tourney fields. Yet once back in Point Royal, this essence, this ritual, this scent of femininity swept over them again, made them dizzy and unreal, as one who walks in fog. They fell into an orgy of daintiness—lace and ribbons, imitation French underclothes, little silver penknives inadequate for the constant chore of pencil-sharpening, teacups fragile as they could afford. For one another they dabbled perfume and exclaimed of its softness—yet not for one another but for imaginary heroes.

In each class a few girls revolted against this daintiness by arrogantly displaying thick flannels and serving tea in stoneware mugs, and a few, still fewer, put on a conspicuous, smartly tailored masculinity and were timidly yearned upon by the overloaded girlhood about them.

This cloying hypnotism of involuted sex Ann Vickers had resented; had fought it with basketball and hearty, if perhaps heartless, praying at the Y. W., and with the dry sexlessness of economics. Yet it caressed her always with treacherous sweetness, and this year she cursed (in respectable Presbyterian curse-words) to find herself more stroked and bewhispered than ever, by Eula Towers, her roommate.

The first month, Eula alarmed her. The second month, Eula bored her. The third month, Eula infuriated her. And each month of Eula made Glenn Hargis's hairy maleness seem more desirable.

She could not quite dismiss Eula. That chiffon-misted esthete, despite her generous exhibition of fake, did know a great many things which were closed to the brisk, efficient mind of Ann Vickers. She taught Ann to be excited over Keats and Shelley, Beethoven and Rodin, though Ann never could abide Eula's real idols, Swinburne and Edgar Saltus and Oscar Wilde. With a shrill whinnying of laughter, she ridiculed Ann out of her placid liking for Elbert Hubbard. Mr. Hubbard had a "very fine message," Ann insisted, until Eula demanded just what Mr. Hubbard's "message" might be. And in a piquant hour Eula closed up forever one of Ann's favorite booklets. It was such a nice little book, Ann sighed, and Reverend Donnelly had sent it to her one Christmas. It was an anthology of extracts from the most poetic sermons of American pontiffs, starting with Henry Ward Beecher, and it was called *Heaven-Kissing Hearts.*

"Oh, my God!" shrieked Eula, in an hysteria of delight, clutching her ankles, throwing wide her arms, yelping with a joyous vulgarity rare in her esthetic life. "*Heaven-Kissing Hearts!* Why not Seagoing Livers? Or Pansy-Faced Heroism?"

Ann, to be honest, never did exactly know what was the matter with her nice little book, which she had loved so much that she had often planned to read beyond the twenty-first page. But she gave it up and hid it in her trunk, and one day admitted that she did prefer, now, Eula's favorite:

> *The owl, for all his feathers, was a-cold;*
> *The hare limped trembling through the frozen grass,*
> *And silent was the flock in woolly fold.*

But when she showed herself grateful to Eula, when she stirred out of the fortress of briskness which she had erected against that insinuating young woman, then Eula flung herself on her, kissed her, and breathed, with a tenderness sickening to the outdoor Ann, "Oh, my darling, I'm so glad to see you smile! You have been distant and aloof, as though something were troubling you. Oh, I have wanted so much to sympathize, to help you! Oh, yes, let me kiss your hand! It's my reverence for you!"

"Hey! Quit! Are you trying to get a hammer lock on me, Strangler? You oughta go out for wrestling, not sketching!" snarled Ann, with a voice unrecognizable to herself— a voice hateful not with hatred but with pious fear.

And Eula wanted to crawl into bed with her on cold mornings and smoke the nastiest scented cigarettes, murmuring, "Oh, let's not go to class today! Classes—muck! Let's just lie here and dream about what we'll do when

we're free from this prison. Think—you and I will have
a villa in Capri, and dream all day long above the purple
sea, under the violet-crowned hills! Dearest, would you
like a cup of coffee? Lie still, lie still! I'll skip out and make
you one on the alcohol stove!"

"You will not! I got an eight-thirty test!" lied Ann,
emerging and dressing with a speed which would have astonished her father.

There were only four or five Eulas in all of Point Royal,
but they were enough to make Glenn Hargis, and walks
with him on the moth-eaten grass of the campus, an adventure brave and cleansing.

By no especial arrangement, they fell into the habit of
meeting on the oak-scattered promontory where a Civil
War cannon and the statue of Elizabeth Cady Stanton
looked on the brown Housatonic, wrinkled with gold in
the sunlight of Indian summer, and across the river to an
upland farm with red barns rising from poplar groves.
He talked, there, exuberantly, of German universities, of
cafés on Unter den Linden and the Kurfürstendamm, of
the simple law student who proved, really, to be a Herr
Graf and who had taken him for a holiday to the old family
Schloss in Thüringen, and of the rare, exalted week (paid
for by months of doing without breakfast or new shoes)
which he had spent in Egypt, where he had seen the exca-
vation of a king's tomb and, viewing those fresh natural
colors of paintings buried four thousand years, had recognized all history as a living thing, so that he was not bound
to the year 1910 and to this meager Connecticut campus,
but walked and talked also, this moment, in Thebes in

2000 B. C., and perhaps in some Asiatic or South American New Thebes of 3000 A. D. "It did something to my life, as an astronomer's life is richer when he looks through his tube and adds the moon and Mars to his own pasture!" cried Hargis, in one of the few moments when he dared to be unbarricaded, simple, sentimental.

She liked his intellect—no, his knowledge. She guessed that he was vain, finicky as an old maid, not large enough to be awkwardly sincere; and because he was the one resonant male in this nunnery, and because he had evidently chosen her from all the sisters, she was pitiful and cared not at all for his childishness.

But she could not go on being meek and reverent with him—the bright young student with the sage master. She did not deceive herself about him, as she had with Adolph Klebs, which was discerning, for Adolph Klebs was far more of a piece, far more consistently selfish and contemptuous, than Glenn Hargis, Ph. D. She was soon answering him with a placid "Uh-huh" instead of a breathless "Oh, yessss!"

He resented it. "You don't take me seriously!" he said plaintively.

"Well, do you?"

"I most certainly do! Well, perhaps I don't. But *you* ought to. I don't pretend to have any better mind than you, Ann, but I happen to know more."

"So does everybody. I'm the executive type, I guess. I'll always have people working for me that know more than I do, only I'll run 'em. I don't think it's any especial virtue to be a walking encyclopedia when you can buy the nice sitting kind, second-hand, for fifty dollars!"

"I'm not an encyclopedia! My purpose in class is to inspire the students to think for themselves."

"Well, I'm thinking for myself—about you, Dr. Hargis, so you ought to like that."

"You are the most offensive young woman!"

"Honestly, I don't mean to be! I guess I am. I don't mean to be. But somehow, all men, including my father—especially he—have always seemed to me like small boys. They want to be noticed. 'Mother, notice me! I'm playing soldiers!' And that Boston preacher they had in chapel last Sunday: 'Young ladies, notice me! I'm so noble, and you're just poor little lambs that I've got to lead.' If he'd heard some of the giggles at the back of the chapel!"

"And," irritably from Hargis, "I suppose you charming maidens giggle at me in class, at the back."

"No, we don't. We get awfully thrilled. You make Richard Cœur de Lion as real as President Taft."

"Well, I ought to. He was a lot realer. Did you know, by the way, that Richard was a fair poet and a first-rate literary critic? He said . . ."

Dr. Hargis was off, agreeable as ever when he forgot himself, and Ann was off, listening, agreeable as ever when she forgot him as a man and listened to him as a book talking.

When, palpably, Dr. Hargis was unable to impress this effective young woman by bullying, or by being a sad, lonely little boy, he adopted tactics against which she was helpless. He became quippish; he made fun of the store of naïveté that she still had—that she was always to have. And she, who thought swiftly enough when there were jobs to be done, was slow and confused when it came to defending her own illusions.

He made fun of her for fretting over anyone so obviously flabby as Eula, for worrying over the status of the current basketball team, for caring whether or no the new class secretary, Mitzi Brewer (her own evil creation), was playing the cat and fiddle with the records, for her simple beaming pride in receiving high marks in the dry realm of mathematics, for her zealous belief that it would ever matter a hang whether women got the vote, for her Waubanakee conviction that a glass of whisky was a through-express ticket to hell.

Then his fumbling fingers touched her religion, and she really winced and in anguish betrayed herself to his mastery.

It started innocently, a mere bout of intellectual gymnastics, and it ended in her wretchedly doing the most dramatic thing of her life so far—in tearing out of her heart, for the doubtful sake of honesty, something dear to her as love.

They had hung over the cannon on Stanton Point, and beat their chilly fingers against their legs, in the colorless November air; but in their intoxication of talk they had been unconscious of cold.

"We had the nicest meeting of the Y. W., last evening. Harvest Festival. It wasn't like an ordinary meeting. Everybody seemed so sort of happy," said Ann.

"Well, well, my dear Ann, and what did we do at our Happy Harvest Festival?"

"Oh, you needn't sneer! It was nice. We sang, of course, and we prayed—but *really* prayed, not mechanical. Everybody seemed to get excited and wanted to join in.

Honestly, do you know, even Mitzi Brewer was there,
and when the leader called on her——"

"I suppose you were the leader?"

"Yes, I was, if you want to know! There! And when I
called on Mitzi, why, she actually got up and made the
nicest prayer."

"And what invocation did our kittenish friend Miss
Mitzi offer up to the Divine Throne?"

"Oh, you know. Just prayer. About how she didn't
always do what she ought to, but she hoped to be guided."

"Hm, our Mitzi must have been up to some special
deviltry lately. Seems to me I've heard something about
her and that handsome young garage man at the Falls.
Very suitable. So you had a chaste Harvest Festival, and
probably sang, 'Bringing in the Sheaves.' Splendid! Of
course, being Christians and very modern, you wouldn't
do anything so primitive and ignorant as to have a festival
of the early Romans. Do you remember that June festival
in 'Marius the Epicurean'? Ceres and Dea Dia carried
in sacramental chests by white-clad boys—the altars with
wool garlands and flowers that were later thrown into the
sacrificial fire, and the smell of the bean fields, and the
priests in old, stiff, ancestral robes. And Marius had the
duty of laying honeycomb and violets on the urn of his
father. Violets and honey! Oh, those hill pagans weren't
a bit up to date! They didn't listen to Mitzi praying off
her last flirtation, and they didn't drone 'Work for the
night is coming, when man works no more'—which I have
always considered the worst *non sequitur* in literature."

"Oh, probably the Romans sang something just as bad!
I don't believe Mr. Pater knew all the stuff they sang!

Anyway, we were happy. There was a real—oh, sort of a quiet, twilight happiness there—real religion."

"You're so exquisitely, so touchingly childish about your religion, my dear child! You're perfectly convinced that all the miracles happened. You take the tale of the loaves and fishes feeding the multitudes as though it were documented historical fact, instead of a charming myth. You actually believe in the Bible as history, not as poetry."

"But, good heavens, don't you? Why, you're a vestry-man!"

"Of course I do. It's the *mores*. I shave, too, but I don't regard it as sacred; if it were the fashion for amiable young professors to wear a beard, as it was not long ago, I'd wear one. Oh, yes, I've been a vestryman, but you'll notice that I don't often attend. Now don't say 'hypocrite!' I know clearly what I do and what I think. You haven't dared to. You've never applied the test of reality to these vague emotions of yours that you call 'religion,' the tests that you'd apply to a medieval historical record. After all, Ann, you're typical of all women; you're realistic enough about things that don't touch your emotions; you weigh the butter and count the change, so the poor wretched serving-maid can't cheat you out of one cent. But you refuse to ask yourself what you really do believe, and whether your belief came by honest thinking or was just inherited from the family. And some day you'll have the same—probably worthy but certainly irrational—the same faith in your husband and your sons! Just a commonplace woman, after all, my dear Lady Scholar!"

"I think you're beastly!"

"I *know* I am! I don't for a moment, though, want to

rob you of the consolation of your superstition. I just want you to understand yourself—that's the chief purpose of college, isn't it?—and so long as you're a sweet, serene, wholesome *Hausfrau*, don't try to be a razor-edged intellectual also!"

"I am not wholesome! I won't have you—— You're— you're——"

"'Beastly,' I think it is?"

"Well, you are. You are so!"

She was querulous all the way back to her dormitory, while he trod lightly, a school-teacher smile of satisfaction on his face at having quelled her. He said good-night with cheerful affection.

Neither affectionate nor cheerful was Ann during the week before they talked again.

Worst of all, she raged, it was true that she had never evaluated her creed. She had weeded out some details; after a good deal of emotional suffering, she had, in Freshman year, decided she did not believe in the Virgin Birth or in Eternal Damnation. But she had never faced herself and demanded whether she believed in a Future Life, the concrete existence and omnipotence of God, or the divinity of Christ.

She did face herself now, with considerable worry. Eula took this week of agony in Gethsemane to propose that they get up a public poetry-reading, and she was throbbingly shocked when Ann turned on her with "Don't bother me—go to hell!"

Ann hung over her Bible. The miracles did seem improbable to her, now that she saw them with unsoothed,

irritated, unfamiliar eyes. What was all this about Jesus's
driving devils out of a possessed man, and into a herd of
two thousand grazing swine, so that they went mad, fled
into the sea, and were drowned? Not very probable, she
worried, and a strange way to treat innocent swine and
their ruined owner!

And in Luke IV she came with new eyes upon the tale
of the devil's taking Jesus up on a mountain, showing
Him all the kingdoms of the world, and offering them to
Him if He would worship.

Ann gasped: "Why! It's a symbol, obviously! A dramatic fable, but only a fable!"

With astonishment she perceived that all her life she
had taken it as a chronicle of exact fact; she fancied that
she had taught it as fact, in the Waubanakee Sunday
school. Viewing her own mind as impersonally as though
she had just met herself, she discovered that she had never
thought about the Bible and the church-creed of her childhood, but swallowed it undigested. Even the vague agnos-
ticism of old Oscar Klebs had been only phrases, which she
had adopted without applying them to her actual creed.

"And all the miracles—they're like that—beautiful
myths—real only as Santa Claus is real to a four-year-old
enchanted by Christmas!" she marveled.

She felt like one who has for years unknowingly been
deceived by a husband, while everyone else has known and
giggled. She tried to recover her serene faith by reading
the Nineteenth Psalm:

The heavens declare the glory of God; and the firmament
showeth forth his handiwork. Day unto day uttereth speech, and
night unto night showeth knowledge. There is no speech nor

language where their voice is not heard. Their line is gone out through all the earth, and their words to the end of the world. In them hath he set a tabernacle for the sun, which is as a bridegroom coming out of his chamber, and rejoiceth as a strong man to run a race.

The law of the Lord is perfect, converting the soul; the testimony of the Lord is sure, making wise the simple; the statutes of the Lord are right, rejoicing the heart; the commandment of the Lord is pure, enlightening the eyes. . . . More to be desired are they than gold, yea, than much fine gold; sweeter also than honey and the honeycomb.

For the first time it seemed to her great poetry; she rolled it out magniloquently, thankful that Eula was not at home to snicker. But for the first time, also, it seemed to her to have nothing to do with daily life. It was all words, however lovely the words, like "Kubla Khan." And she again heard Glenn Hargis's fluty mocking: "You take it as though it were documented historical fact, instead of a charming myth."

With a sturdy ferocity she marched out to meet Dr. Hargis on Stanton Point.

As they walked the path on the edge of the cliff, looking on the valley gray with frosted grasses, he jeered, "Have you thought anything more about your interesting medieval religion?"

"I have!"

"And have you decided about the seven loaves and a few small fishes? Splendid way to solve the economic——"

"Oh, hush! I've decided. Tomorrow evening—in another couple months I'd probably be elected president of the Y. W. C. A., but at the meeting tomorrow evening, I'm

going to resign and tell 'em why. I no longer believe, and if
I don't, I can't lie about it."

"You mean you're going to stand up before all that
massed spectacled purity and say you don't believe in
Christianity, any more than you do in Buddhism?"

"Of course!"

"But, uh—what business is it of theirs? It's your
private problem. Not a matter of lying, at all; simply that
there's no law that compels you to tell every ragtag and
bobtail what you think."

"Maybe not, except that I've led meetings, I've prayed,
I've confessed my faith—on false grounds, it seems. Oh,
I'm not going to try to deconvert them. No! Let them keep
their faith, if they like it. But I owe it to myself to tell
them where I stand now."

"But look here, Ann!" Dr. Hargis's mockery was gone,
and his joy in having shown himself superior to the young
female. His eyes were helpless and babyish; his thin voice
was a squeak: "I don't know that I care to be mixed up
in this, and have my private opinions dragged out for the
inspection of a bunch of jabbering provincials. Not that
I'm in the least afraid, you understand! But if they knew,
especially the president, that I'd influenced you, it might
seriously interfere with my mission of teaching history
intelligently!"

"Oh, you needn't be afraid. I won't expose you!"

"Don't be an idiot! I? Afraid? Of these hick teachers?
Nonsense! I just don't care to give them a chance to in-
fringe on my privacy."

"I told you. I won't expose you. Dafternoon!"

She was off, a loping lioness.

The next evening, addressing the meeting of the Y. W. C. A., she said gravely and briefly, with no nervous wrigglings or exultations of self-inflicted heroism, that she was unable to accept the Bible or any Christian creed as anything more than a brave, bright fable, like the cycle of King Arthur. She announced that she was resigning as vice-president—and suddenly, with the jolly helpfulness of all politicians, that she *did* hope they would elect Amy Jones in her place!

She did not mention Dr. Hargis, either then or afterward in her room when all her friends save Eula wailed, "What *has* come over you? You must be mad! If you do think that way, why do you give all the fanatics such a chance at you?" (Eula made hay by weeping that her dear, darling, belovedest Ann could believe whatever she wanted; she would follow Ann through hell fire or even exegesis.)

It was, in rather a dull month at Point Royal, a sensation. The president, who was pious though she was the sister of a popular Episcopal bishop, summoned Ann to struggle with her, and read Newman to her—the early, correct Newman, before he was deceived. At a special meeting of Y. W. directors, a frightened, anæmic girl named Sarah prayed loudly for Ann, to her annoyance. It was curious, but now, in a week, it seemed to Ann as though her struggle had been over and forgot for years.

Only to Dr. Hargis could she talk about it; certainly not to Eula, with her wreathing damp thin arms.

Though she a little despised Hargis's panic, she felt that they shared together the danger of exile and—oh, he was a male, and she needed the security that, or so she had heard, only males could give a weak woman.

8

It was December; too cold now for them to meet beside the cannon. Nor did either of them want to encounter the rebuking faces of praiseworthy young ladies at the Y. W. C. A., though at the Y. W. was the only spacious and comfortable lounge in the college—not the Social Hall, with its Morris chairs, mass photographs of former classes, spectacled and dolorous, and tables covered with missionary magazines, but rather the Y. W. cafeteria and the small flowery tin tables where, any afternoon, were to be seen such erotic tableaux as the lady professor of geology giving tea and cinnamon buns to the pastor of the First Universalist Church, and the head of the physical culture department, a bouncing young lady don who was rumored to have been seen smoking cigarettes at Mouquin's, in New York, giggling in a corner, over Coca Cola and Nabisco Wafers, with a giddy clothing-merchant from the town of Point Royal.

Such comparatively aseptic café life Ann and Hargis would have enjoyed, but they could not stand chatter; they were absorbed in each other; and they met in the

waiting-room of Ann's dormitory, a below-stairs closet
with a large rusty radiator and eight stiff armchairs.

"I can't stand this hole!" snapped Hargis. "Let's sneak
off into the country, Saturday afternoon."

"Against the rules, Glenn." If she had overlooked his
cowardice, if again they were intimates, mind sliding into
mind with no more self-defensive quibbling, yet she no
longer accepted him as a superior officer; she called him
"Glenn," and refused to salute him.

"Oh, hang the old rules!" he whimpered.

"Certainly. I just don't want to be expelled. Too much
bother."

"You needn't be—rather, we needn't be. Look, lamb.
Last Saturday I tramped up Mt. Abora, and I found an
old woodman's shack—log cabin—door gone. Be a splendid
place to make a fire and have picnic lunch—wooden table
left—wonderful view down the valley. I'll get all the stuff
for the lunch—girls'd be snooping around and asking
questions if you did. Come on! Let's get away from this
cursed convent and be human beings. Damn it, I believe
I'll go into the advertising business. I'm sick of being a
little tin teacher: can't say what you think. I've got a
friend, a classmate, who's got one of the very most important advertising positions in Chicago! He wants me
to join him! Oh, let's get out. You needn't be afraid of me
in the wilds, Annie!"

"I'm not! Mt. Abora?"

"Yes. Tramp up the Letticeville road, and meet me by
the old brick church, twelve o'clock, noon, next Saturday.
Will you? Will you?"

Log shack, camp fire in open air, view down the valley

from a mountain throne, escape from the stares of close-pressed girls—it was enticing, and she hesitated only seconds before she nodded. "All right. Twelve. G'night."

Afraid of him! Heavens! And yet the tease, the playboy, he did have glistening eyes and meaty hands.

She had not seen him before in English tweeds, grass-colored, with plus fours. Anyway, they were practically English, for they came from Marshall Field's, in Chicago, along with the crinkly orange tie of raw silk, very worldly and artistic. And he told her, thrilling, that his knapsack was a real German rucksack which (far horizons in a little canvas!) he had carried in the Schwartzwald.

He carried it lightly. He seemed sturdier than ever in the folds of tweed, and he stepped lightly and sang. For all his splendor and Europeanism, as they tramped he did not discourse highly, but took her into his own rank by snickering intimately—as though they were both Juniors or both faculty members—about such scandals as the lady president's moral union suits, betrayed by the lumpiness beneath her thick cotton stockings; the fond, loose-jawed, yearning glances which Professor the Reverend Mr. Sogles cast upon the bouncing physical culture instructor, and him with a poor bed-ridden invalid wife, who was so patient; and the rumor that the wife of Professor Jaswitch (French and Spanish) wrote all his lectures and corrected all his papers for him.

"She's an awfully smart woman. But they say she drinks cocktails!" said Ann. She was ashamed of herself for it, but she was enjoying this gossip—as, of course, she should have.

"Cocktails? And what, my brave young Ann, may be the matter with cocktails? I wish I had some with us, for our lunch."

"Why—why—they destroy the brain-tissue! That's scientifically proven! You can find it in every physiology!"

"I congratulate you on having read every physiology. In Russian and Spanish, also?"

"Oh, you know what I *mean!*"

"Certainly! But do you? Matter of fact, a cocktail might be good for you. Might elevate you above your bloodless earnestness about things that don't matter; might make you almost human and jolly! Wouldn't you like to live, for once—love, or war? Wouldn't you?"

His insistence was like a finger poked into her ribs. She was uncomfortable.

But otherwise he was neither airily professorial nor shroudingly amorous.

It was a scene out of a Western motion picture, or a novel about the rude, survirile hill-billy who kidnaps the frail city maid and makes her like it. The cabin was of rough logs, clay-chinked, authentic. Inside, were a puncheon floor, empty bunks, a rusty box-stove, and an unplaned table in the center, so that sitting at it you looked through the doorway, over a stony pasture, quiet with four inches of snow, and down the valley where the spruces were massed in dark clusters. She had gone a hundred years back from the Point Royal campus, and seemed to herself in a frontier life vigorous as the cold, sweet mountain air.

And Hargis, did he not combine the virtues of the romantic pioneer and those of the Cultured Traveler?

"Come on now!" he bullied. "Here's a good pile of kindling and small wood—gathered 'em when I was up here the other day, and if I must, I'll admit I gathered 'em with the treacherous hope that Ann would share 'em with me! Come on, shake a leg! Be useful and start a fire— here's matches—while I unpack."

But it was the Cultured part of him that from his ruck-sack produced, along with the sandwiches and hard-boiled eggs and coffee pot, a slim brown bottle.

"Why, it's wine!" she marveled.

"It certainly is! Rudesheimer. Genuine!"

"I don't think—I don't remember ever seeing a bottle of wine before. Just in pictures."

"Do you mean to tell me you've never tasted wine?"

"No, never. I've had a few glasses of beer, German pic-nics, back home, but I never cared much for it. But— wine!"

"Does it afflict that chronic moral sense of yours?"

"No. I'd love to taste some. Of course, it's against the rules. But then," agreeably, "so is being up here with you at all, Glenn."

"Exactly, my dear!"

She was truthful; she had never tasted wine. Her alco-holic adventures, besides the beer, had been an annual teaspoonful of hot whisky for a cold. So was it with half the college girls, even with the more serious and unpopular brands of college men, in 1910. The pendulum was to swing with American feverishness—in fact, in America, generally, a pendulum is not a pendulum; it is a piston. By 1915, the excellent wines of California were triumphing; Americans were everywhere beginning to drink them; yet in 1920 the girls were again like Ann—they knew nothing of wine, though they had this slight difference, they knew all about gin, and about raw alcohol colored with burnt sugar, called "whisky." But by 1930 Prohibition had, despite all, proven itself a blessing, for it had taught American women to drink wine with their men, as European women had always done; taught not merely gin-experimenting schoolgirls, but the worthiest matrons, the testiest women college professors, the most devout uplifters, such as Superintendent Ann Vickers, LL. D.

With the wine, fussily wrapped—he screamed at her womanishly, "Oh, do be *careful* of those!"—he had brought two thin glasses on stems.

After a sandwich she tasted her wine. It seemed a little flat to her, flavored like mild vinegar. She was disappointed. Was this the nectar, the liquefied jewels, that launched young women on luxurious sin? She longed for a strawberry malted milk.

"Another glass, Annie?"

"Thanks, no. I guess you have to get used to the taste, to appreciate it."

"Oh, come on! When I've brought it all this way? Of course you have to get used to it. Well, never mind. All the more for me, my dear!"

She was grateful to him for not insisting. And now the cool wine had turned to a glow in her stomach. She poured herself half a glass, while Hargis had the unexpected good sense not to comment. She felt warm and happy; the white strong valley was enchanting in its stillness; and Hargis was talking softly of vine-covered booths beside the Rhine.

They sat on the bench by the table, facing the open door. Lunch done, without comment he gave her a cigarette. For perhaps the dozenth time, she tried smoking, and for the dozenth time did not like it, though she found it part of all this magic: frail wine, far hills, secret cabin, Rhenish vineyards in the sun and, after so much feminine flutter and cooing on the campus, a Man.

She was not startled; she was comfortably pleased when he put his arm round her and drew her cheek down to his shoulder. She snuggled there, warm against the tweed. But she was annoyed when he lifted her cheek to kiss her, when he touched her breast.

Not much experienced, she had yet known enough dances, enough sleigh rides, not to be utterly naïve. "Oh, Lord, do all men follow this same careful-careless technique? All the same? And expect you to be surprised and conquered? Just as all cats chase mice the same way, and each thinks it's the first bright cat to discover a mouse? Now the idiot will drop his arm and paw at my thigh."

He did.

She sat up, furious that in betraying himself as just another Model T out of the mass-production, he betrayed her also as nothing but a mechanism, to be adjusted like a carburetor, to be bought like a gallon of gas. She threw off his arm, as his hand smoothed her thigh. "Oh, stop it!"

"Why, Ann! Why, my Ann! Are you going to spoil it by —— You go and spoil it all by thinking beastly thoughts, when we were so happy, together, away from the campus——"

"'Beastly!'" She was more furious. "I don't mind your

trying to seduce me. (Only you can't!) But you're old enough to not do the injured small boy!"

"I wasn't trying to seduce you!"

"Weren't you?"

"You make me sick, all you nuns, with your books and your little committees and your innocent little songs! Emotionally ten years old! Green-sick! And you'll keep yourselves from life till you're safely decanted and marry insurance men and live in bungalows with plate-glass in the front doors! When you might *live*—have all the world—purple Greece and golden Italy and misty England——"

"I don't see just what being seduced has to do with visiting purple Greece and misty England. New way of paying for Cook's Tours, I should think!"

"Everything! It has everything to do with it! Women who aren't afraid, who have rich, exciting emotional experiences, they don't get stuck in suburbs; they see the world—no, not just see it, like a tourist, but know it, live in it where they choose, mistresses of their own fates. You jeer, you try to be funny, when I bring you the wisdom and grace of Europe, along, of course, with what the European hasn't got, what the American man has, the loyalty and dependability and kindness and—— You idiot!"

To her considerable astonishment, she was seized and kissed soundly, so that she choked. She stopped despising him, and stopped being rational and lofty, and her lips seemed alive. "Oh, please!" she begged.

"Don't you *want* to be a real woman, not just an educated phonograph? Don't you want to feel, to have your whole body burn, to know glory, and not just timidity in a pinafore?"

"I do but—I'm not ready——"

"Shocked like a Sunday school brat!"

"I'm not shocked at all! Good heavens, this is the modern age! It's not 1890! I've studied biology. But one doesn't do these things lightly. I'd have a lover, if I wanted him enough, that particular him!"

"You wouldn't! You're too afraid!" He kissed her again, coarsely, fiercely. She was blinded a moment, for a moment thrilled, as though she were a barren estuary through which the returning tide was gushing. Then she was cold and empty as he overdid it. He was too realistic to be real.

"Stop it, I said!" she demanded. He loosed her but he stared hopefully, the ambitious little boy, sure that he really was going to the circus, and he urged, "You have no passion!"

"Oh, yes I have! Since we seem to be rather frank, I'll tell you that I did feel the beginnings of a thrill, just now, till you decided to try the rôle of cave-man. Wude and wuff! Oh, Dr. Hargis!"

"No passion. Printer's ink for blood. You're a biological monstrosity, you and all the girls here. Too *superior*, you think, to meet a man on his own honest grounds! Biological monstrosity, that's what the so-called well-bred American woman is! Not one atom of healthy, splendid passion!"

"Could it possibly occur to you that I might have plenty of passion for some men but not for you? Possibly you aren't the heroic and tempting male you think you are.

Once, I wanted to fall for a shoemaker's son who worked in a grocery. He *was* a male. But you—fingering at seductions, turning your history into little smart-aleck attitudes! I'd rather be seduced by the Anthony Hall janitor!"

He threw his coffee pot into the rucksack, swung the sack brusquely round his shoulders, and tramped off, down the wood-road, not turning back.

She wanted to call to him. She didn't want to be seduced —not now at least—but he was her intensest friend—at his worst he was warmer and more solid than any girl——

She piped up a feeble "Glenn!" but too late. He was out of sight.

Then she was touched by the small boy who had been so proud of his little lunch, his European knapsack, his copper coffee pot, his wine that he could not afford.

"Maybe he was right. Maybe I just talked myself into virtue," said the moral young woman who had defied the vile seducer.

Then all effort to find out what she really thought was lost in a gray loneliness as the valley below her turned gray and chill and lonely.

9

She had never been very conscious of her body. It was an acquaintance often encountered, rather than an intimate. She had known it glowingly tired after basketball or tramping; she had known it softly relaxing in sleep under a comforter on a winter night, or rejoicing in hot corn-bread and cool milk, or upsetting her self-respect by being sick. Yet mostly it had served her, without much demand. Now it was all demand, inescapable.

The caress of Hargis had awakened her body to its rights, its possibilities of joy. Ann lay sleepless—after more than common irritation at the good-night of Eula, sticky as honey, slippery as cold cream—and her loins ached, her breasts ached, and in dismay she found tantalizing images of Glenn Hargis charging like traffic through her brain: his gray eyes that taunted her placidity; his hands, not puffy, but with the skin stretched taut over hard knuckles; his chest, not feminine and pneumatic, but solid as an oak barrel; his skin, not soft like talcum powder, but faintly rough, like the good bark of a beech tree. She lay in her iron cot, her arms behind her head, her hands under the pillow, staring, longing for him to come to her.

It was a fairy story that, wordlessly, she told herself over and over: Eula would somehow, some miraculous how, be gone, and she would awaken to see Glenn striding in, not meeching, not apologetic, not insincerely trying to show himself a dominating cave-man; he would come to her bed, sit on its edge, and murmur, "No matter what, we need each other—both so lonely, so longing."

The clever Dr. Hargis could have captured her any time in the month after the picnic on Mt. Abora. He showed no signs of knowing it.

She never went to his office now, never talked with him after class nor once walked with him. In class, he badgered her with unbelievably small-boyish resentment, so that everybody talked of it, gleefully. He mocked her eagerness in answering questions. "Will you please give more attention, young ladies: Miss Vickers is about to share her excitement with us. I don't know that inspired intuition is the soundest method of establishing historical fact, but I may be mistaken." He rode her for the split infinitives in her themes—she grimly saw to it that there was nothing else he could pick on and, contemptuously, continued to give him the split infinitives, even when she had awakened to their heinousness.

She was, till passion died clean out of her and she again slept healthily as a cat, incredulous of his pettiness in revenge. The only thing more surprising than to find a person spectacularly false to his being is to find someone always running true to it, with not one natural human slip. She had thought him weak but original; she found that, in his obstinate spite, his refusal to be for a moment gallant, he was strong as a venomous wronged woman.

Once she was openly angry at him. He had been sniffing that medieval serfs were better off than the "free" workmen of today; and now she perceived, as she had not during the first lecture, that he was not really indignant about the insecurity and wretchedness of the workers but, rather, contemptuous of them as natural morons, fitted only for subjection to slavery.

"Do you mean, Dr. Hargis," she protested, while the class stared moon-faced and happy at this row between the reputed sweethearts, "that we have made no progress toward a reasonable state at all? That the struggle of the workers and the liberators has just been a farce—Wolfe Tone, Cromwell, Washington, Debs, Marx?"

"Why, certainly, we have progressed, my dear Miss Vickers, *provided* you consider President Taft an improvement on Queen Elizabeth, Howard Chandler Christy an improvement on Leonardo da Vinci, and William Jennings Bryan a more edifying philosopher than Machiavelli! *De gustibus!* I should never venture to argue about opinions. I have only facts on my humble shelves, you see!"

College professors, some of them, used to talk like that; nasty little gang slogans like "*de gustibus.*" Perhaps a few of the breed still exist.

Before spring, Ann was solaced by forgetting him, outside class hours. Through her Senior year, having no class with him, she never saw him save at faculty teas, and her passion turned into bustling activities of a vaguely social aspect.

Since she was out of her religious whirligigs, Y. W. C. A., Student Volunteers, class prayer-meetings, decorating the chapel, her brisk extrovert soul, her very Theodore Roose-

velt of a soul, demanded other crusades, and she blithely
went into them with all the illusions, the priest-worship,
the love of familiar ceremonial, the belief that she could
mother and change the world, that she had shown in
religion.

She pounced on the Socialist Society, which was rather
sickly, and, canvassing for members, doubled its size.
They triumphantly presented a portrait of Eugene V.
Debs to the college library, and the president of the college,
a sly, tricky, cynical old lady, ruined their defiance by
ordering the portrait accepted and hung in a back corridor
of the library, where no one ever went. (After Ann's
graduation, the frame was used for the portrait of the
Reverend Mary Wilkerbee, missionary to the Flathead
Indians.)

Ann also galloped into the Debating Association, and in
Senior year took the course in Public Speaking.

Her religious apostasy and rumors of her intimacy with
Dr. Hargis had queered her with all the high-minded young
ladies not members of the Socialist Club. Indeed, though
she had been a certainty as class president for their last
and most sentimental months together, she was not even
nominated. She was not greatly welcomed in the Debating
Society, and she felt a little frightened; she who had been
a leader of the class was frightened as the little girl who
had gaped at the Japanese lanterns at the birthday party
of Mildred Evans.

But in the try-outs for the Debating Team, in her Senior
year, Ann shone. She had always been an earnest speaker,
convinced that she had something important to say; she
had always been credulous enough to enjoy and be height-

ened by direct applause. A few lessons in Public Speaking taught her to stand straighter and more still and added to her natural urgency a professional trick of imbecile gestures which—for no perceptible reason, unless that the gestures were inherited from sound, seasoned witchcraft— seemed to carbonate audiences till they fizzed like soda water. This new staginess, backed by her genuine sense, made her a riotous debater, and she was chosen leader of the team that went on a great adventure, far to the north, to debate with the celebrated and undefeated team of the Southern New Hampshire Christian College for Women the topic: "Resolved: That the Church is More Important than the School." Ann, who didn't believe anything of the kind, led the affirmative. A pirate voyage! Going off with two splendid other girls, unchaperoned! A cheering crowd of twelve to see them off, with flowers and a two-pound box of Park & Tilford candy, and a copy of *Life!* Strange men in the train staring at them invitingly, till they all giggled in communal delight! The sweet seriousness of planning their strategy for the debate! New towns, cold upland air, the excitement of arriving, and an even larger, more cheering crowd of sixteen wonderful S. N. H. C. C. W. girls welcoming them! Two luxurious rooms for them in a sorority house, and a private bath! And an enormous audience of two hundred, but so generous and friendly!

After the other debaters had prettily spoken their pieces in favor of church or school, like nice girls in a class in elocution ("the question, don't you think, my dear friends, is whether the Little Brown Church in the Wildwood, the Little Brown Church in the Vale, for all its dearness to our hearts and mem'ries, is any more sacred than the vision of the devoted schoolma'am in the Little Red Schoolhouse by the Road Where the World Goes By ")— after all these pansies and dewy rosebuds of thought, Ann tore loose, forgot nice ladyness and, quite convincing herself for five minutes, savagely trumpeted the glories of the church—inspirer of the crusades, architect of the most glorious buildings ever seen, prophet which taught the schools the moral basis without which their little lessons would mean nothing, founder of our perfect democratic government, arouser of the heathen bowing down to wood and stone. "The school, yes, it is our older sister, kind-hearted and loyal, but the church, it is our mother, who gave us birth and life and all we have! Forgive me, oh, forgive me if I offend the decorum that many think proper in a debate—forgive me if I speak too hotly—but who can be calm and decorous when folks analyze, when they criticize, when they mock at one's own, only mother?"

The applause was like a cloudburst, the unbeatable S. N. H. C. C. W. was beaten, and Ann was guest of honor at the sorority house, with a licentious spread of coffee and lettuce-and-tomato sandwiches and deviled eggs. The name of the last, coming after a religious debate, inspired many an innocent joke. And next week Ann's picture was on the first page of the *Weekly Point Royalist*, and she was invited to address the Woman Suffrage Association of Torrington and the Young Women's Society of the First Disciples' Church of Amenia.

But her spirited defense of the Little Brown Church in the Wildwood got her into complications. The officers of the Y. W. C. A. pounced on her, like six kittens on a tennis

ball, and demanded why, if she was so filially devoted to
the church, didn't she come back to the Y. W.? When she
refused, a little feebly, Miss Beulah Stoleweather, faculty
adviser to the Y. W., bubbled, "After all, Ann, you really
are with us. You see, my dear, I know you better than you
do yourself! At heart, you're a complete Christian—so
much more than you know! Haven't I heard you say 'God
bless you!' at parting? You'll see! You'll be with us again!"

So Ann was restored to respectability. But she was not
satisfied. Her nights of longing shamelessly for arms about
her had awakened something that could not now be content with committees and buttery words from lady faculty
advisers. She was furious that she had not been elected
class president . . . "not, of course, that she wanted to be
anything so bothersome and committee-ridden as president. But it was the principle of the thing. Well, she'd
show 'em! She'd go out of college something far more
popular, grand, and memorable than any idiotic little
class president!"

In a fury of popularity, in a maelstrom of politics without policy, she raged through Senior year, regaining whatever she had lost by apostasy and the rumor of having
been jilted by Dr. Hargis. Her room—her single room, not
scented this year by the presence of any Eula Towers,
thank God!—became the gathering-place of all the debaters, economists, future settlement-house workers and
other intellectuals of Point Royal, and over hot lemonade
they settled Suffrage, World Peace, and the Problem of
Wages.

She called on girls whom she disliked. She was blandly
affable on the campus to girls whose names she did not

remember. Especially she plotted in and for the Debating Association. She awed the whole college by the stupefying project of wangling a debate with Vassar, which had regarded Point Royal as on a level with agricultural schools, Catholic academies, and institutes for instruction in embalming. (Two years later, it happened, but Ann was gone then.)

Heaven knows what effect, good or evil, this Senior year of dictatorship had on Ann's later ventures into more masculine politics. It is not pretended that the good little Ann of Waubanakee was not somewhat soiled, yet the rather helter-skelter and embarrassed young woman did gain new power, and might have gone on booming into cynicism and grandeur but for her hour with the grotesque Pearl McKaig.

Pearl was the high-ranking scholar of the class after Ann's. She was a thin, undersized, priggish, knubbly-browed child, humorless, eager, and precocious, two years or three younger than the average of her class. She took scholarships as a drunkard takes free whiskies; and her classmates laughed at her, and petted her, and hated her for her naïve frankness.

She had tried out for the debating team and failed—one of her few failures, since she had never tackled athletics. Her speeches in try-outs were as statistical as a thermometer and as dry as flour. But she hung about, opening her pale eyes in worship as Ann flashed and stormed and juggled with words; she joined the Socialist Club, and agreed in stammering ecstasy when Ann bubbled that we all belong, of course, to the gentlewomanly and highly educated caste, and it is our duty to help the Less-Fortunate

Workers. And when Ann, busily passing her on the campus, waved with amiable recognition, Pearl flushed
happily.

Yet it was Pearl McKaig who came to Ann's room, just
when Ann should have been leaving for a Vernal Vespers
Meeting of the Campus Tree Planting Society, to Say a
Few Words, and plumped down in the Morris chair, stared
unspeaking till Ann wanted to scream, fumbled at her
insignificant chin, and burst out:

"Ann, you're—you speak lots more easily than you did
two years ago, when I first heard you in Y. W."

"Yes?"

"Lots more eloquentiy. You know better how to catch
the crowd."

"Oh, that's just——"

"And you're interested in lots more things. You aren't
just a small-town girl any more. I still am, I guess."

"Well, of course——"

"You could be an awfully big woman—nation-wide."

"Oh, nonsense, my dear!"

"Then why, Ann—why have you sold yourself? Why
do you want to be popular with every kind of fool on the
campus?"

"Well, really——"

"You've got to listen! Because I love you! And because
I'm the only one that dares tell you—maybe the only one
that knows! When you resigned from the Y. W. I was
there. I admired you, oh, terribly. I got out then, too—
only I didn't say anything to anybody. Just quit going.
And I guess nobody much noticed, with *me!* You were
wonderful. And now you hang around with the Y. W.

leaders and kid them and pat their backs and make 'em think that maybe, inside you, you're kind of sorry you ever got out, only you got to stand by what you said. And you're getting pompous. Yes, you are! Like that Reverend Dr. Stepmoe that comes here and calls everybody 'sister' and mentally pats your back—prob'ly he does physically too, with the girls that got softer backs than I have! You're pompous! And affable! All things to all men, and still more to all women! Suave! Managing! Executive! Snappy! Clever! So jolly, when inside you're sore as a crab! Bright and quick! And false! Oh, Ann, don't sell out! And don't think you're so important—you're too important to wall in your heart by thinking that. And now you'll never speak to me again. . . . That's how much I love you, though!"

Pearl fled from the room, wailing.

Ann Vickers did not go to the Vernal Vespers nor say the few well-chosen words. She sat into the darkness, cramped in her soul as her shoulders were cramped with sitting.

"It's all true," she said blindly. "Now I need my re-'ligion again, to pray for humility. Probably I'll never get it; probably I never had it. But after that—only I could *kill* that brat, with her boiled-egg forehead and her smirking righteousness, for making me doubt myself!—but anyway, after that, maybe I'll be a little less obviously offensive. Humility! 'Blessed are the poor in spirit for——'

"No, I'm hanged if they are! Blessed are the rich in spirit for they shall not *need* the Kingdom of Heaven! Blessed are the fearless in heart, for God shall see them!"

But she was strangely quiet till graduation and after;

she refused an offer as assistant in economics during the Bryn Mawr summer school, and went to work in a steamy Fall River cotton mill, where she learned how much less the gentlewomanly caste knew than French Canuck mill-hands about love, birth, weariness, hunger, job-hunting, and the reason for labor unions and the way of concealing bricks for window-smashing during strikes.

And thus she did learn humility—enough of that dangerous element to enable her to get through a world that equally praises and despises it.

10

For ten years after her graduation, in 1912, Ann had a wild medley of jobs. For a year she studied nursing at the Presbyterian Hospital, in New York, as a basis for social work, which was to lead to politics on the inevitable day when women should have the vote. Her friends told her that she ought to be in a graduate school, or a school for social workers, to read books and hear lectures about the downtrodden; but she preferred to learn with eyes and hands and nose, decidedly with nose, something of the agonized bodies of the people with whom she would have to deal.

With the campaign for woman suffrage booming, she became an organizer, in the New York Headquarters, whence she was sent to a certain city in Ohio—call it Clateburn, for disguise. She was the best of the young women of that piratical crew, and they were pirates. Years before the organization of the aggressive National Woman's Party, with its cheerful rioting and its pestering of senators in their sacred offices, there were in several American cities groups of young devils who made miserable the lives of the congressmen that for years had enjoyed the sunniest seats on the fence, from which they purred that women were the saviors and life-givers of the race, the conservers of culture and good breeding, the inspirers of all that was noble in the male, but that their delicate bloom (though proof against washtubs, diapers, and minding the chickens) would be rubbed off in the awful sordidness of polling-booths; that certainly women ought to have the vote *some time*, but not quite yet. This "some time" was apparently of exactly the same date as the "some time" when Britain would find hoary India, and America find the Philippines, capable of self-government, when employers would clap their heels in joy at giving non-union employees wages equal to union members, when married couples, universally, would cease quarreling, when prostitution and love of hard liquor would disappear, when college professors would have a knowledge of life equal to that of the average truck-driver, when farmers would know the rudiments of agriculture, when atheists would rationalize all the pious into happy materialism, when dogs would be born house-broken, and cats would play tenderly with mice.

Suffrage Headquarters in Clateburn were in an 1880 residence known as the Old Fanning Mansion. It was a large and hideous pile, covered with brown plaster crossed with white lines not so much to imitate stone as to symbolize it. The surly portico had Ionic pillars of wood covered with brown paint over which sand had been scattered, so that they resembled brown sandpaper and greatly vexed the finger-tips of Western Union boys waiting with messages at the door—suffragists always, in idle moments, send agitated telegrams to one another. The roof was flat, with a pressed zinc cornice.

The Fanning Mansion resembled an aged hospital, except that it was less sympathetic.

Inside, the high-ceiled, flatly echoing, immense parlors were crammed with desks and tables which were piled with dreary suffrage tracts and envelopes to be addressed. On the third floor were slant-roofed bedrooms, once belonging to the Fanning servants, occupied now by four of the suffrage workers, including Ann.

The Empress and Lady High Executioner of the Clateburn Headquarters, whether because of the large contributions with which she had bought importance, or because of her heavy-handed energy, was Mrs. Ethelinda St. Vincent, a large, determined lady with purple hats and a bosom like a sack of wheat. Eleanor Crevecoeur, of Headquarters, said that Mrs. St. Vincent had been Miss Ethel Peterson, daughter of a plumbing corporation, till she had married Mr. St. Vincent who, though he manufactured binding-twine, was an aristocrat, which meant that he had gone East to college, that his family had been in Clateburn for two and a half generations, and that the twine factory had been founded not by himself but by his father.

Mrs. St. Vincent was given to dropping into Headquarters after the theater—she called it "after the theater," though the ribald Eleanor said that it meant "after the movies"—and if she found the young workers idle and chattering, at 11 P. M., she blared, "Do you ladies feel that suffrage is merely a job, like working in an office, and that you must watch the clock?"

But she never was assaulted, for the suffragists had read Luke VI:37: "Give and ye shall be forgiven."

Mrs. St. Vincent had entertained, in her Georgian house

on St. Botolph Avenue, the more prominent suffrage speakers, including an Englishwoman with a genuine title, who had been shipped to Clateburn, and this intellectual atmosphere had won her her election to the Phoenix Musical Club of Clateburn.

But the real executive and boss of Headquarters was the paid secretary, Miss Mamie Bogardus, known to all the workers and to much of Clateburn outside as "The Battle-axe," and to the Ohio press as "The Carrie Nation of Suffrage."

Miss Bogardus was to the eye and ear the comic journal picture of a suffrage war-horse: a tall, scraggly spinster with ferocious eyes and a loud, shrill, ragged voice. (What has become of them, the haggard Amazons, the "shrieking sisters," of before-the-war?) She was impudently aggressive or completely fearless, depending on your interpretation. If she thought the aldermen were grafting, no decent awe of their magisterial dignity restrained her; she went to their meetings and rebuked them, very audibly, with figures. If she saw a man mistreating a child, a horse, or a fiddle, she up and told him so. She was presumably a virgin, at fifty; she neither smoked nor drank; and she said often and publicly that all males (of seven and up-wards) were clumsy as dogs, dirty as monkeys, tyrannical as grizzlies, and dull as guinea pigs. She wore the most astonishing garments in Ohio. With a mannish suit and flat mannish shoes, she combined canary-yellow blouses with scarlet buttons—such buttons as were not missing—turbans of golden Chinese fabrics, always raveled and awry, and at least a dozen necklaces of cheap glass beads or wooden disks. Her infrequent frocks for afternoon or evening were of crêpe de Chine, in violent crimson or fainting lavender, always mussy, the skirts hiked up above her toes and dragging behind and askew over the hips. Everyone asked where she managed to find such dresses, since no sane dressmaker would make them and the Battle-axe herself was clumsy as a ditch-digger when she took a needle between her large, liver-spotted fingers.

She ran the junior suffrage workers ragged. She scolded them worse than did the voluptuous Mrs. Ethelinda St. Vincent, and she was at Headquarters more often for the scolding. She scratched them out of bed at seven, and yammered when they staggered off to sleep at midnight. She sniffed at the infrequent young men who came calling, and asked them in a voice like ammonia whether they smoked. She complained if her girls dressed decently, because that was wasting money that should go to the Cause, and she complained worse if they were not exquisitely neat, because that "might give the wrong impression." Almost anything they did or didn't do might, according to the Battleaxe, "give the wrong impression."

When Ann Vickers arrived in Clateburn, she was so horrified by this embattled fury that she almost gave up the job.

And within a fortnight she had found that Miss Mamie Bogardus, the Battleaxe, was the bravest, the most honest, the kindliest, and the most wistful woman alive. If she was aggressive, it was because she was convinced that most men and women let themselves be misgoverned through cowardice or sloth; if she was slovenly, it was because all her acute thought was going to her work. Though she drove her lieutenants, she was the first to defend them, as Ann discovered when she heard the Battleaxe privately snarling, even at the rich and succulent Mrs. St. Vincent, "You quit picking on my girls; I'll do all the picking necessary!" And when one of them was really sick, it was the Battleaxe who kept her in bed and brought up a bowl of beef tea—not particularly well seasoned.

The public, the press, even some of the suffrage sympathizers, and all men lively and full of moist wisdom in front of bars, said that Miss Bogardus was a suffragist because she had never caught a man; that she wanted something, but it wasn't the vote.

It was true, Ann guessed, only to the extent that the Battleaxe had never found, and resented the fact that she had never been able to find, a man big enough to understand her loyalty, her piercing honesty, and a passion too tempestuous to wrap itself in little pink prettiness. Ann was presently certain that Miss Bogardus, if she were married and the mother of ten lusty sons, would be equally the fighter, would equally hunger and thirst after righteousness.

Ann remembered her American history (a topic not popular in the Clateburn press, save as it dealt with baseball batting-averages, George Washington, and the development of the automobile self-starter) and saw in Miss Bogardus the pioneer grandmother with a baby on one arm and a rifle for the Indians on the other.

Besides Miss Bogardus and Ann, there were two other paid agitators, Eleanor Crevecoeur and Patricia Bramble. Both of them were to Ann romantic and endearing comrades-at-arms. To describe Pat Bramble, in any record, no matter how realistic, the word "dainty" would have to be fetched forth from the boarding-house of shabby and pensioned words. Dainty. Out of a Victorian novel. Kin to Little Nell and Miss Nickleby and Harry Maylie's Rose, with the difference that she had the vocabulary of a fo'c'sle hand, the cynicism of a fashionable priest, the joy of an Irish trooper, at least during suffrage riots, in fighting policemen, and the honesty of Mamie Bogardus. But she was small and willowy enough to please even the lickerish eyes of Dickens; she was golden of hair and her cheeks were petals; and in private she smoked only rose-petal-tipped cigarettes, where Eleanor flaunted a small pipe.

Eleanor Crevecoeur was the mystery of the Fanning Mansion. Ann Vickers was complex only as environment clashed with her simple desires for frankness, efficiency, kindness, and sexual freedom; Miss Bogardus was as obvious as any other woman of the frontier; Pat Bramble had a sound foundation of commonness under her airy daintiness; but Eleanor Crevecoeur was always a divided personality, and divided not merely into two recognizable factions, but into three or four or a dozen.

She was twenty-eight, now, to Ann's twenty-three and Pat's nineteen. She was tall and rapier-thin; thin legs, thin tapping feet, thin veined hands at the end of arms so frail that it seemed the wind would snap them, with a brown eager face and a nose too large and hooked. But she was not at all ugly; there were in her too much fire and will; men drifted to her and laughed with her where first they had smiled at her.

The chief mystery about her was her origin. She could

ape Pat Bramble's blasphemy and wholesome commonness, but it never seemed altogether natural. In Clateburn
suffrage circles it was whispered that Eleanor was from a
noble French family; that there had been a Marquis de
Crevecoeur who had married a wild, blown-haired wench
who was the daughter of an Indian princess (whatever an
Indian "princess" may be) and an English general.

Neither Ann nor Pat ever had the truth. Of Eleanor's
childhood they knew only that she came from Canada and
had for some time gone to a convent school. They suspected that the legend of her nobility grew from the fact
that, in a city like Clateburn, composed of Smiths and
Browns and Robinsons, of Müllers and Schwartzes and
Hauptschnagels, of Joneses and Lewises and Thompsons,
and of Cohens and Levys and Ginsbergs, the name Crevecoeur sounded aristocratic. Ann looked it up in the dictionary, and announced to Pat, impressively, that it really
meant "heartbreak" and was guaranteed to be romantic.
But Pat looked it up in a larger dictionary and bawdily
announced to Ann that *crèvecœur* also meant "a French
variety of the domestic fowl, heavily crested and bearded,
and having a comb formed like two horns—see Fowl."

One other girl, though she did not live in the Fanning
Mansion, was with them nearly every evening: Maggie
O'Mara, organizer for the Waitresses' and Lady Dishwashers' Union, and herself of late a waitress and lady
dish-washer. She was ruddy and bright-eyed; she had arms
like a washerwoman; she was a whooping and successful
soap-box speaker; and she was, she pointed out, all the
vulgar things that Pat and Eleanor pretended to be.

And these four, Ann, Pat, Eleanor, and Maggie O'Mara,

made up the group which, for causes presently to be stated, came to be known throughout Ohio suffrage as the "Ball and Chain Squad."

Their private life—not that they had much private life, aside from six or seven hours of sleep in cold lone beds, with a theater perhaps once a week and a dance sanitarily flavored with liberal conversation once a month—was never free from the itching topic of Woman and women; Woman's rights and Woman's duties and Woman's superiority to man both in constructive mentality—whatever that might mean—and in physical endurance of weariness and pain.

They cooked and dined in the old kitchen of the Fanning Mansion, a stone-floored cavern looking out on a yard decorated with chickweed, sunflowers, and archaic heaps of ashes and tin-cans. They were supposed to take turns cooking, but usually it was Ann, assisted by Maggie O'Mara, who came as guest and remained as amateur hostess, who got the dinner; and always it was she, or Maggie and she, who wiped the sink and the linoleum strips on the stone floor, and washed out the dish towels.

Ann whistled then. She liked using her hands, as she had in nursing-school, and as a child, when she had cared for her casual father. And, as half-trained nurse, it was she who understood bedmaking, and night after night she remade the aristocratic but tumbled couch of Eleanor Crevecoeur, whose idea of domesticity was to shake the sheets and blankets, yank the top coverings straight, pat them once, and call it a job.

In these moments of housework only was Ann an individual at the Fanning Mansion. Otherwise she was a Worker in the Movement, a private in a jammed barracks, a conjunction in a particularly long and complicated sentence.

The others, even Maggie O'Mara, did not seem to mind being mere units in the collective mass; they did not seem to have, even, an ambition to be chief and most titled unit. But the Ann who made speeches when she was told to, addressed envelopes when she was commanded, ridiculed males when it sounded proper, was still the Ann Vickers of Waubanakee, free woman of the woods and river, lone bandit who had wanted to socialize crime in childhood, provided she remained dictator.

The Ball and Chain Squad got away from Woman only when, in whispered confidences at midnight, sitting cross-legged on beds or on the floor, with the Battleaxe asleep in the hall across the way, they talked about Man.

Even then, in 1914 and 1915, with the World War begun, though some anonymous genius had already invented Sex, it had not come into popular use and quantity production. Maggie and Eleanor might refer frankly to communal sleeping, Pat might use the sacred words as expletives, Ann might be free from the reticences of Waubanakee, yet none of them felt they could discuss Lesbianism, incest, or any of the other drawing-room topics of fifteen years later. But it is not recorded that their private emotions were different from those of 1930. It came out in anxious queries and uneasy desires for confession.

Pat, to whom flocked all of the rare males who were tabby enough, or venturesome enough, to invade the Fanning Mansion socially, was as cold sexually as any other rosebud, Ann guessed. Maggie O'Mara only laughed. "You're all babies, with yer fine educations. What do I think of loving up the boys? Well, I'll just say I'm no virgin!"

"Well, I am," said Pat, "and I think it's a lot less trouble!"

Eleanor cried, "You both make me tired! Sex! You neither of you know a damned thing about it. To you it's guzzling corned-beef and cabbage. If you want to know, and I don't suppose you do, I'm a nymphomaniac. If I let myself—only I've got a will like a steel trap; you can laugh if you want to, but it's true!—if I let myself go, I'd be diving into men's beds all the time. Like a crazy woman. I'm not a virgin either, my proud Maggie! Twice I've tried it, and I had to quit—I just ceased to exist, *then*—my whole body was like flame, with skyrockets shooting off at the center. I never will again, unless I meet a giant, and wenches like us, that try to untie our brains, just don't meet giants. But if I go to the movies with any male between the ages of eight and eighty and see a film about catching herrings or making glass, and the back of his hand brushes mine once—why, when I get back here, I snap 'good-night' so he thinks I'm cold as a frozen axe, and run upstairs, and all night I pace the floor. We suffragists that hate men! Sure! And I bet that when the Battleaxe was young, she was bad as I am! Oh, nice young ladies don't feel passionately, like men. No indeed! We mustn't experiment; we must fold our gentle hands and wait till some male mouse comes up and flicks his whiskers at us. Hell! Well, Ann, what's your confession? Vulgar like Mag, or inhuman like Pat, or crazy like me?"

"I—don't—know! Honestly, I don't!" stammered Ann.

Since Glenn Hargis, she had longed to escape any mania that would obscure her clear and cheerful eyes. So when men came calling at the Fanning Mansion, to sip chilly tea and eat bakery cakes, or in the evening to help address envelopes and confer about raising funds—worthy males, unexplained business-man husbands dragged in by feminist wives, liberal clergymen, usually unmarried, very young or very old faculty-members from Clateburn University, and back-patting politicians gambling on these probable future feminine votes—it was Pat and Maggie and college girls come in as part-time helpers who talked with them, occasionally danced with them to the phonograph, down aisles between desks and tables, while Ann and Eleanor vanished away, or sat in corners.

"Some day, some man that I want to kiss, like Adolph, is going to want to kiss me, like Glenn Hargis, and then I'm going to forget all the statistics on the underpayment of woman workers, and kiss him back so hard the world will go up in smoke. Or am I just an icicle, like Pat?" fretted Ann.

They worked; they worked like sailors in a gale, like students before a final examination. It was a life of perpetual midnights. They smiled when bedraggled housewives said, "If you girls were married, like me, and had to cook and wash and take care of the kids, if you had to *work*, like me, you wouldn't have no time to think about the vote, no more'n I do!"

They were sent out to address meetings—women's clubs, men's church clubs, the W. C. T. U., the D. A. R., and incessant suffrage rallies in narrow halls where you got sniffly colds from lack of ventilation. Alone, or commanding flying squadrons of amateur workers, frequently smart flappers who darted and giggled and did not greatly increase the dignity of the Cause, they went canvassing for funds and political support, among handsome houses and poor tenements, in Chinese laundries and grain elevators and the offices of millionaire brokers, where occasionally some weak-chinned underling wriggled playfully at them and cooed, "Come on and give us a kiss and then you won't want a vote!"

And sometimes they found an illiterate husband (quaint word!) who admitted that he was all for the women having the vote, but entirely against "suffrage," which he had identified as meaning teas at the Fanning Mansion, which would interrupt his wife's labors for him. And once a housewife (yet quainter!) chased Ann with a broom when Ann asked to talk with the husband. "You get out of here! I know you an' your kind! You ain't going to get the mister away from me, with your sneaking and prying and—and—— A bunch of chippies, that's what you are! Beat it!"

Among the four girls and Miss Bogardus, it was Ann who was usually chosen to scrabble the publicity material which they were always sending to the newspapers: notes about the rare success of the meeting at Odd Fellows' Hall, about the sympathy of Senator Juggins, about the coming to Clateburn of the celebrated Reverend Dr. Ira Weatherbee who had "accepted an invitation" (given at the muzzle of a shotgun) to address the ladies of the Sycamore Avenue Christian Church.

Eleanor Crevecoeur wrote more lucid and fetching prose than Ann but, probably for that reason, she could not scrawl publicity with the liveliness and false jollity suitable to the art. It may be that Ann's debating had given her the proper glibness. Certainly she became a brisk and popular propagandist; and later, she was able to advance any cause by writing Sunday newspaper articles full of statistics selected with pious discrimination. She wrote with passion about the evils of the world, but she was never able to see why one adjective was juicier than another; and she was wistful and a little hurt, years afterward in New York, when newspaper friends hinted that she was a dear sweet woman but her journalism was atrocious.

Ann, Pat, and Eleanor were each of them sent out, alone, from Clateburn to help local Mothers in Zion organize suffrage associations; out to small, suspicious, masculine towns, where woman's entire place was still in the home, which meant in the kitchen and the nursery. They were received by acid matrons who croaked, "Well! I'm kind o' surprised Headquarters couldn't find nobody but a young gal like you to send us, when we've worked so hard and all!" Supported only by three or four of these old warhorses—which support, since they were usually known as the local cranks, pests, and Mamie Bogarduses, was worse than nothing—they hired a grocer's delivery wagon or a shaky automobile and spoke on street corners, while the slowly gathering audience catcalled and whistled and made sounds of kissing; and at night they slept in funereal black walnut beds in the unaired "spare-rooms" of the local Cassandras. For breakfast had fat bacon and chicory. And in the evening, when they came back to the Fanning Mansion, on the local train, often in the acrid smoking-car, came back discouraged and clean beat, the Battleaxe yammered at them, "What are you sitting around for? We're 'way behind on addressing envelopes!"

Envelopes, then, till another midnight, with another God-forsaken journey to the hinterland in view for next morning. If Ann had had time, in those days, to read Kipling, she would probably have rended the book for its assumption that it was only the male (and only the British male, at that) who could make punitive expeditions to the native tribesmen and with serenity face the hairy, horrid throng. Pat Bramble and she made such punitive expeditions twice a week, and did not return to any mess and whisky-soda or C-spring barouche at Simla, either.

Envelopes!

Envelopes to address!

Envelopes, with "N. A. W. S. A., 232 McKinley Ave., Clateburn, Ohio," neatly printed in the upper left-hand corner in a watery blue. Envelopes. In piles. On tables, along with city directories, telephone books, blue books, and mimeographed sucker-lists, for addresses. Envelopes containing mimeographed appeals for funds, appeals to "Write your congressman and senator," appeals to "Vote in the primaries only for candidates who understand that Women Are People"; envelopes with little four-leaved tracts reminiscent of Waubanakee—except that it was the vote and not the Blood of the Lamb that was to save and make perfect the entire world—and envelopes with thick little cards in which you could, if you longed to, insert a

quarter, moisten the red wafer, and return to Suffrage
Headquarters.

Ann believed—Ann and Pat and Eleanor and Maggie
all believed—that the vote was necessary, both that
women might enter public affairs, and that they might be
freed from the humiliation of being classed (*vide* any of
Ann's hundreds of speeches of that period) with children,
idiots, and criminals. But she did get tired of envelopes.
She went insane over the thought of envelopes. For years
after she had done with suffrage-organizing, she was to be
plagued by the recollection of piles of yellow envelopes,
printed in blue with "N. A. W. S. A., 232 McKinley Ave.,
Clateburn, Ohio," and below it the oval union label, and
the symbol F16. Envelopes that piled up mountainously in
her dream till they toppled and smothered her. Faith,
hope, envelopes, these three; and the greatest of these was
envelopes.

11

No task of Ann, Pat, and Eleanor was considered weightier than forming a guard of honor for the feminist celebrities who were referred to, after midnight at the Fanning Mansion, as "the Visiting Firemen."

Some of the Visiting Firemen were pretty terrible. And some were charming—"inspiring" they called it.

A year after Ann had begun organizing, there came to Clateburn for a suffrage-rally in haughty Symphony Hall the renowned Dr. Malvina Wormser of New York. She was chief surgeon of the Agnes Caughren Memorial Hospital for Women, in Manhattan; president of the Better Obstetrical League; an officer in all known birth-control organizations; author of "Emancipation and Sex"; and D. Sc. of Yale and Vassar.

The Ball and Chain Squad were nervous about Dr. Wormser's coming. They expected a raw-boned, horse-faced woman, as much sterner than Mamie Bogardus as she was more famous.

Dr. Wormser was to be the guest of Mrs. Dudley Cowx, the one really smart woman in the Clateburn organization. Mrs. Cowx (a Dodsworth by birth) had gone to school in

Montreux, Folkestone, and Versailles as a girl; she had a summer villa at Bar Harbor; and her sister had married a German baron. At suffrage rallies she wore tweeds, rather severe except for the fresh ruffles at her throat; and she snubbed the flamboyant Mrs. Ethelinda St. Vincent whenever they met. She did not snub the Ball and Chain Squad; she nodded to them and thereafter ignored them.

That Mrs. Cowx should be entertaining Dr. Wormser in her Norman château on Pierce Heights made the good doctor the more intimidating.

At ten on the morning of Dr. Wormser's show in Clateburn, while all the organizers and volunteers were answering the telephone and addressing envelopes—envelopes!—into the Fanning Mansion came a small, plump, dowdy woman with white hair, cheeks round and powder-pale, bright eyes, and soft little pads of hands. To Ann, near the door, she said—and her deep voice was astounding in such a wren of a woman, "Is Miss Bogardus in? I'm Malvina Wormser. I believe I'm to stay with a Mrs. Cowx, whoever she is, but I trotted straight here from the train. You look pale, my dear. I might prescribe a tonic, but I honestly think a little rouge would do just as well—grand psychological effect."

For all her belligerent frankness, Miss Bogardus had trained herself and her serfs to be cautious in talking with the press. The reporters, or at least their editors, longed for something scandalous from the Fanning Mansion: some hint that it was a free-love colony or, nearly as good, a frenzied zoo of man-haters, anarchists, atheists, spiritualists, or anything else eccentric and discreditable. The

Battleaxe explained to her young ladies that they might attack the water and gas departments, the city orphanages, President Wilson, or even the Allies in the Great War now dragging on, but they must do so only as Christian gentlewomen and solid taxpayers. They must be convinced, no matter what they thought privily, and they must convince others, that the vote would not lead to "moral laxity" (another folk-phrase of the era) but would immediately end prostitution, gambling, and the drinking of beer.

In horror, then, after admiringly greeting Dr. Malvina Wormser, Miss Bogardus heard the little doctor cheerily booming the most poisonous opinions at the delighted reporters who had run her to earth at the Fanning Mansion:

"Do I believe in free love? What do you mean by that, young lady? How can love be anything but free? If you mean: Do I believe that any authentic passion—not just a momentary itch in the moonlight—is superior to any childish ceremony performed by some preacher, why of course. Don't you?

"Do I think women are brighter than men! Tut! What a question! Not brighter—just less mean. But don't try to get me to riding men. I'm a forlorn old maid, but I adore 'em, the darlings—the poor silly fish! What do you suppose men doctors would ever do without their women nurses and secretaries? I know! I was a nurse myself, before I became a doc. And now my chief satisfaction in life," Dr. Wormser chuckled fatly, "is that I don't have to stand up when a surgeon enters the room! You see? Silly customs like that—just what a man *would* institute—poor lambs, we have to take care of 'em and their little egos! That's why we need the vote, for *their* sake!

"Do I think a woman'll ever be President? How do I know? But let me point out that women rulers—Queen Elizabeth, that lovely rakehell Catherine of Russia, the last Chinese Empress, Maria Theresa of Austria, Queen Anne, and Victoria—were better rulers than any equal number of kings. *Or* presidents!

"You boys and girls might as well know that I don't believe in hedging and pussy-footing. This is going to be a long struggle. Not just getting the vote. That's a matter of a couple of years. Then we got to go on. Birth-control. Separate apartments for married couples, if they happen to like them. What women need is not merely a vote but something more up here." She touched her forehead. "Don't need just exterior opportunity, but something interior, with which to grab the opportunity, when we get it, and use it. Freedom's no good to a pussy-cat, only to a tigress! And women have got to stick together. Men always have had the sense to—drat 'em. Sex loyalty. We ought to lie for one another and sneak off and have a good drink together, like the men.

"I believe that there is no field that men control now that women can't enter, completely. Medicine, law, politics, physics, aviation, exploring, engineering, soldiering, prize-fighting, writing sweet little rondels—only I hope women'll be too sensible for either the prize-fighting or the rondels, which are both forms of male escapism, and singularly alike if you look at 'em!

"Only I don't expect women to imitate or try to displace men in any of these fields. I'm not one of the gals who believes that the sole difference between males and females is in conception. Women have special qualities which the human race has failed to use for civilization. I know a woman can be as good an architect as any man—but she may be a different sort of architect. I bring something to medicine that no man can, no matter how good he is. And if you think women can't go to war, remember what the Teuton tribes, marching with their women along, did to the beautiful, virile, professional men soldiers of Rome! But the pig-headed masculine world forgot that lesson for fifteen hundred years and never discovered it till Florence Nightingale happened in and bullied the masculine British War Office into some of the common sense that any normal girl would have at seven!

"No, I don't want to rival men. But I don't want to be kept by the tradition of feminine subjection from the privilege of working eighteen hours a day. I'm not much of a democrat. Believe inferiors ought to be subjected. If they *are* inferiors! But if a girl secretary is smarter than her male boss, let him be *her* secretary. Listen! In 1945, maybe you'll have to go to England (where they invented this Inferior Women myth, so men could have their clubs) to find anybody so benighted that he'll even know what you're talking about when you speak of considering candidates for a job as male and female, or on any other basis except their ability!

"I speak of 1945 because I have a hunch that after we get the vote, we'll be less ardent feminists. We'll find that work is hard. That jobs are insecure. That we must go much deeper than woman suffrage—maybe to Socialism; anyway, to something that fundamentally represents both men and women, not just women alone. And a lot of suffragists that pretend to hate men will find the dear brutes are nice to have around the house. We'll slump. But then we'll come back—not as shadows of men, or as noisily professional females, but, for the first time since Queen Elizabeth, as human beings! There! You ought to be able to get sufficient out of what I've said to make trouble enough for me to satisfy even a suffrage speaker! Goodday."

The reporters gone and Dr. Wormser departed to Mrs. Cowx's for lunch, after having posed for the press photographers, the Battleaxe wailed, "This is going to be terrible! They'll make the home editions of the afternoon papers with the whole story, and it'll be dreadful! There'll be a big enough audience tonight! No fear of that! But how nasty they'll be! Ready for trouble! You girls—I'd meant to have you on the platform, but you'll have to mix with the crowd and see if you can stop any row, if it starts. Oh, dear, when we've been so careful! Free love!"

Ann had never before seen Mamie Bogardus tremble. They were all respectful to her, and tender, that afternoon. They themselves trembled when they had dashed out for the four o'clock editions of the afternoon papers and read the front-page blasts.

This is, in part, what the newspapers made Dr. Wormser say:

Love is nothing but a temporary itch caused by moonlight, but even so, it is more important than lasting marriage, because marriages are performed by ministers, who are all childish. Free love, that is, taking any sweetheart any time you choose, is not only permissible but necessary for any free woman.

Men are much meaner than women. Men doctors boss
their nurses around and treat them simply terribly.

The next president of the United States will be a woman,
and she will be lots better than any man. Marie Louise of
Russia was the greatest king who ever lived.

As soon (two of the papers printed in bold face, and one
in red, a paragraph more or less as follows): *as soon as we
get the vote, then we're going on and advocate birth-control,
Socialism, and atheism. All married couples will live in
separate apartments. And women will imitate men and sneak
off and get drunk together. Women must lie about one another's whereabouts, to fool the men.*

Women will make better soldiers, prize-fighters, engineers, and poets than men, and men are fit only to be the
secretaries and servants of women. I know that talking
frankly like this will get me into trouble, but all suffrage
speakers love publicity, and I guess I'll get plenty on
this.

Till time to leave for the Symphony Hall meeting, the
girls went mouching about the Fanning Mansion in a
misery too deep for talk. Even Maggie O'Mara, when she
came in from the Waitresses' Union office to join them, was
depressed to silence. They put on, not frocks suitable to a
public feast of reason and politeness, but jackets and sailor
suits.

And with all her anxiety, Ann was furious, because she
had painfully saved up enough to buy a blue taffeta evening frock so inspired, she felt, as to impress an audience
even of Mrs. Dudley Cowxes. She *did*, she raged, want to
be something for once besides the frowsy, grubby organizer

who snooped into tenements and addressed envelopes and spoke on the corner of Main Street.

"I like pretty things! Suppose I were to meet some grand man there tonight, wearing this old gym skirt. Damn!"

The Ball and Chain Squad and Miss Bogardus went solemnly to Symphony Hall in a trolley-car (not once a year could any of them afford a taxi) and they felt that every man on the long seat across the car was glowering at them as immoral and dangerous women. Before they slipped by the stage-entrance into the security of the "artists' rest-room," they diffidently sneaked through the crowd in front of Symphony Hall. That noon, only half the tickets had been sold. Now a blue and gilt attendant was bawling, "Standing-room only—all seats sold— standing-room only!" And there were three thousand seats in the hall.

Despite the attendant's warning, hundreds were penned against the triple doors, trying to get through. The panting, ruffled crowd was snarling: ". . . ought to ride 'em out on a rail—bunch of floosies—all crazy, that's what they are—wouldn't have a woman doc for a sick cat—free love, I'd like to show 'em some free love, with a club—bunch of crazy anarchists . . ."

The crowd did not rise to the dehumanized horror of mob rage. There were among them too many sympathizers with suffrage, too many who did not believe that Dr. Wormser had been accurately quoted; and the interesting thing is that these defenders were either prosperous "leading citizens," or rugged and shabbily clean workmen; none of them worthy citizens in between wages and directorates.

The portico of Symphony Hall, with its tall marble pillars like highly polished bread pudding, its serene though slightly imbecile bust of Mozart in a niche, and its associations with evening clothes and chypre and the Annual Ball of the St. Wenceslaus Society, did not encourage violence. No, Ann guessed, the mob would not talk of lynchings, but they might keep Dr. Wormser from being heard, and it suddenly seemed to her that Dr. Wormser was the most important and sensible person she had ever known.

Back of the stage, they found Dr. Wormser looking serene, though her hand trembled. The slim Mrs. Dudley Cowx, in severe black crêpe with only a string of corals, was with her, and Mrs. Cowx seemed less afraid than any of them. "Those cursed newspapers!" she snapped. "Will some of you explain to me why every single reporter and editor on a paper can be a liberal, or perhaps a Red, and the paper itself as conservative as the measles? Don't worry, Dr. Wormser. I have my Dudley and two large and quite beautifully stupid brothers out there. They'll have stopped at the club for a drink, and by this time they'll be equal to handling at least three hundred bullies."

But Mrs. Cowx's suave chatter did not loosen the tension. It was a dreary apartment, this "artists' rest-room," with plaster walls against which cigarettes had been crushed out, clusters of shaky kitchen chairs, and dismal piles of slatted folding chairs and music stands. The Battleaxe sat by a table, her fingers drumming the most irritating tattoo upon it; Dr. Wormser strode, or rather rolled, up and down, her lips moving as she rehearsed. The clock moved so slowly on to eight-thirty, hour of the speech, that it seemed to have stopped.

From in front they heard laughter, derisive whistles, a hash of excited voices, then stamping feet.

"Eight twenty-seven—oh, let's get started, Doctor, and get it over," groaned Miss Bogardus. "Listen, you four girls. The minute the Doctor starts talking, you all skip to the back of the house, and if anything starts, see what you can do."

She stalked out, ahead of an apparently meek little Dr. Wormser, and as they appeared on the stage they were met by a hurricane of ironic clapping, pounding feet, and a blare of "Hurray for the Battleaxe! Hurray for the lady doc! Votes for the skirts!"

The Ball and Chain Squad hurried through the pass door, up a side aisle, to the back of the house, which was jammed with people standing, in time to hear Miss Bogardus's introduction as chairman. If she had been nervous behind the scenes, this old war-horse, this professional who had played her Lady Macbeth to much worse houses, did not seem nervous now. She beamed on the audience as though she were Editha with the Burglar, as though she loved them all and had no doubt that they loved her—and the Vote.

"I'm afraid that in the unavoidable haste of getting out the newspapers, our friends the reporters considerably exaggerated the radicalism of the speaker for this evening," began Miss Bogardus, before a stilled hall; then flatly, without ornamentation, she introduced Dr. Wormser as probably the greatest physician since Benjamin Rush.

For their home-town scourge, Miss Bogardus, the gang

had something of the same jeering fondness that they might have had for a celebrated local drunkard who always broke hotel windows and assaulted policemen in his heightened moments, or for a politician caught with a daughter of joy, or a notoriously mendacious fisherman, or any other romantic but strictly native eccentric. But when the alien infidel, Dr. Wormser, began, the crowd exploded.

In the thick-woven bawling, Ann could hear no individual voice save one, coarse, powerful, drunken, which belched, "Gwan back t' N' York!"

Dr. Wormser was so small and pleasant and comfortable-looking, she stood so bravely, holding out her pudgy little hands in appeal, that the crowd quieted, and she was able to speak.

"Ladies—and gentlemen—and also anti-suffragists!" (Laughter and whistling.) "I agree with you! If I knew myself only through reading the papers this evening, I would thoroughly disapprove of myself!" (Laughter.) "I would tell Malvina Wormser to get out of this lovely city and go back to the sinfulness of New York!"

Light clapping—through which tore the raucous voice Ann had heard before: "Gwan back then! Skiddoo! We don't want you!"

Ann had elbowed through to the back row of seats, and she saw that the heckler was halfway down the center aisle. He had risen, turned about for applause. He was a bulky, red man, swaying, grinning fatuously. Encouraged by this Agamemnon, the lesser breed of youth without the law began again to whistle, to stamp.

There were half a dozen uniformed policemen gaping

foolishly beside Ann. She seized the sleeve of one; she demanded, "You've got to throw that man out! He'll start a riot."

"Aw, he ain't doing nothing, lady. He'll shut up."

The red man started singing.

Ann lost her temper completely, instantly, and beautifully. She scrouged her way through the mass, she darted down the aisle, like a retrieving spaniel; and Maggie O'Mara followed her like a bull-terrier, Eleanor Crevecoeur like a coursing greyhound. But Pat Bramble was not in sight.

The policemen followed them like a parade of ice wagons.

Ann caught the red one's collar. Her voice was not loud, but it was venomous: "You get out of here, you drunk!" He shook her loose, and Maggie slapped him. It was a grand stinging slap; the slap of a waitress trained in midnight lunch-rooms. While the whole audience rose, shrieked, peered, and Dr. Wormser was forgotten, the red one reached for Maggie, but suddenly, somehow, Eleanor was in front of her, too cold, blade-thin, and calm for even a sot to attack.

(But where was Pat? She was a coward, a deserter!)

"Here, you! Take him out!" Ann demanded of the foremost policeman.

But other males growled, "He's got a right to talk—you and your tough molls—oughta be ashamed yourselves—call yourselves ladies?—let a bunch of hellions like you have the vote?"

The policeman said, rather hastily, "You git back to your seat, lady! You're making all the fuss, not this guy! You beat it, and we'll take care of the rumpus." And retired, in broad blue-bottomed dignity, while the red one bawled over Eleanor's thin shoulder, "Yeh! Come on, boys, let's spank the whole lot of 'em, and then start in on the lady doc! Come on!"

A cyclone. Sudden. An express-train bursting through house-walls into the parlor. A herd of crazed steers, down the center aisle. Pat Bramble was leading a cheerful gang of young men in University of Clateburn sweaters. "Take him out!" cried Pat, pointing to the red one. He vanished under sweaters; his reversed heels and ankles were seen kicking above the crowd at the back of the hall. "And take that one—and that one!" demanded Ann.

Two men, then half a dozen, were hauled over the protesting heads of auditors and lugged out like limp ragbags. Now the policemen became gallant and active, and, supported thus by the U. of C. sweaters, began to drag out anyone who so much as squeaked—including a venerable and feminist U. of C. male professor, who was rumored to have voted twice for every known pro-suffrage candidate since he had been eighteen.

The policemen and the sweaters paraded the aisle. All was quiet, and Dr. Wormser charged on again, for a blissful hour, and ended to reasonable applause.

But the Ball and Chain Squad did not hear her address. They were back of the stage, exhausted. Eleanor was weeping. Maggie was glaring, furious that the beautiful fight was over.

"Where the heck did you get all those young giants?" she asked Pat.

"What a chance I took! I'd noticed 'em, front row of the balcony. I knew *from his* pictures one of 'em was Tad

Perquist, football captain. I skipped up to him and I said,
'Oh, Mr. Perquist, I'm a friend of your sister. You've got
to come and help.' I took a chance on his having a sister.
He came, with all those earnest young scholars, and what a
lovely bit of research they did!"

But Ann, sitting apart, was brooding, "It's disgusting!
Our real work, committees, canvassing, envelopes—those
envelopes!—we never get credit for them. And now we go
melodramatic, like college boys, and probably the newspapers will all say we're fine brave wenches, because we're
just as dumm as men and try to settle things by violence,
like men. . . . But I wish I'd slapped him once, just once,
like Mag!"

As they left the hall, guarding Dr. Wormser, a frail,
delicate little old lady pounced on Ann and Eleanor and
sizzled, "Young women, I have been a suffragist for forty
years. My dear late husband and I have contributed a
great deal of money, a great deal of money, for what we
considered the Cause. But after tonight I am entirely opposed to woman suffrage. You and your fellow ruffians
were not at all ladylike, not one bit!"

Eleanor whooped, "Not ladylike? Oh, Lord, the next
movement I take up is going to be the Needlewomen's
Guild!"

But Ann did not laugh. She was depressed. The evening's
melodrama had shaken her out of the hypnotizing routine
of the Fanning Mansion. She brooded, "I've stopped being
an individual. I'm a cog, whether it's riots or addressing
envelopes. One more year—got to give them another year
—and I'm going to quit and find out what Ann Vickers is

now, and whether she's become anything besides 'one of those young women at Suffrage Headquarters.'

"And then I suppose I'll get into some other confounded uplift movement and be another cog in another wheel.

"Is all this reform mania like that?

"Anyway, I won't get into another riot. Just exhibitionism, that's what it is! Finished!"

12

THE next of the Visiting Firemen was neither so distinguished nor so amiable as Dr. Malvina Wormser. She was a Miss Emily Allen Aukett, one of those prominent women about the reasons for whose prominence everyone was vague. She was referred to in suffrage magazines as an "author, lecturer, and reformer," but what she had written, what she had lectured about, and for what reforms she had battled, nobody at the Fanning Mansion was quite certain, when National Headquarters sent her out from New York to inspire and quicken the local laborers.

They were directed to see that Miss Aukett was handsomely housed and fed, and they were warned that she would require a hot supper before retiring, also taxicabs for viewing the battlefield and for taking the air.

"Huh! Hot supper! Taxis! Our idea here of a hot supper is a nice long glass of hot water!" grumbled Miss Bogardus to Ann. "You and Eleanor will have to steer her and baby her. I'm not guaranteed to be safe from biting, as you've probably observed!"

Miss Emily Allen Aukett wore more bracelets than Eula Towers of Point Royal, and she was full of lavish toothy smiles. She was thirty-five by candlelight and forty-five by the sun. She cooed, but she criticized. She hinted that the room they gave her at the Fanning Mansion was rather dreadful, and the Fanning Mansion food a little worse. She suggested they hire a "nice negro mammy" to do their cooking—they who often could not afford pie.

"It's so refreshing to be out here in your simple, vigorous Middle West, after New England and London and Paris," she gushed to Miss Bogardus, who had been born in Maine.

Miss Bogardus would not have minded if Miss Aukett had wrung her audiences in her two speeches—a rally in Schützenverein Hall, on the North Side, and an address to the Old Elm Station Ladies' Literary Society. But Miss Aukett was too refined to do any wringing, and not sufficiently refined to do anything else. She said a few chaste things about the Wrongs of Women, but she hadn't thought up any new ones, and all of Clateburn, even Mamie Bogardus, was a little sick of the regulation Wrongs. What she did blithely and toothily lecture about was her acquaintanceship with the great of the world: the time she had crossed the ocean with General Wood and the cute thing she had said to him when they were docking; the observations on the nobility of motherhood that Elbert Hubbard had confided to her.

And at night, twitchily exhausted after her orgies of eloquence, she was rather curt about the hot supper, consisting of cocoa and warmed-over tea-biscuits and honey, of which Ann had robbed her own perpetually hungry self.

"Honest, Miss Bogardus, I don't want to kick, but that Aukett woman is a pest," Ann complained later that night,

while Miss Bogardus was trying to finish on time her editorial for the *Ohio Suffrage Banner*, due three days ago.

"I know it, my chick. I used to think that any girl that
believed in suffrage had been saved, but I guess we back-
slide like the men. What shall we do with her?"

"You know we four have to go down and try to organize
in Tafford, and it's the toughest proposition in the state.
Why not send the Aukett with us?"

"I will. Now skip to bed, child, and get—— Or no.
It isn't midnight, Ann. I know you're tired, but that nasty
Bandolph woman laid down on us tonight and didn't get
her pile of envelopes all addressed. These awful volunteer
workers! Don't you want to finish them, dearie? And Miss
Aukett—I'll tell her she'll love Tafford!"

Tafford was a small industrial city, but an old one, with
three-generation industries, watches and rifles and type-
writers, demanding well-paid, cautious, skilled craftsmen
rather than newly come roustabouts, Polish and Hunky
and Italian, and it lacked the Socialism to be expected in
factory towns. It was, like Hartford, Conn., or any American city named Springfield, so conservative that it resembled an English cathedral town, minus the cathedral.
Tafford snubbed suffrage; particularly did the mayor, Mr.
Snowfield, whose high-nosed and jet-encrusted wife was a
vice president of the Ohio Anti-Suffrage Association. But
there was in Tafford one old stalwart, a Mrs. Manders,
widow, a sister Battleaxe to Mamie Bogardus, who went
on fighting for the vote, went on asking Clateburn Headquarters for speakers, and could not be choked off, because
her father had been an Ohio Methodist Bishop and a divi-

sion superintendent on the Underground Railroad before the Civil War.

To the mercies of Tafford, the Hon. Mr. Snowfield, and Mrs. Manders, the Battleaxe sent Emily Allen Aukett, but as guard she mercifully sent Ann, Pat, Eleanor, and Maggie O'Mara. Mrs. Manders had engaged the Grand Opera House and placarded Tafford with announcements that the citizenry would hear, in Miss Emily Allen Aukett, "one of the greatest thinkers and authors in the world." Mrs. Manders met them at the 5:18 from Clateburn, and looked sharply over the five, trying to find which one was the great thinker and author. She sniffed when, on the platform, Emily danced forward with outstretched hand and teeth, and gurgled, "I am Miss Aukett—these are my lieutenants—such dear girls—so lovely to be in this bustling Mid-Western city, with its vigor and simplicity, after Paris and London and New York."

"Don't know if it's so lovely," piped Mrs. Manders. "Tried to get you by wire on the train. Owner of Grand Opera House broke our contract. Guess the antis got to him. Scared him. Tried to get another hall. Couldn't. They've got us sewed up."

"Can't we hold a street meeting, or vacant lot, Mrs. Manders? (I'm Ann Vickers, from Headquarters.) We're used to it, and I'm sure Miss Aukett wouldn't mind."

"But I'm afraid I do mind!" wailed Miss Aukett, with diminished though still pestilential sweetness. "I feel that in a street meeting you can't put so much reasoning into your message. And such unimportant people!"

Mrs. Manders (and she looked as motherly and dove-gray and pious as any other deacon's widow) rasped,

"Guess the unimportant folks will get all the message to-night! I know a nice vacant lot; a little muddy but no bricks for the children to throw. We'll take a chance on going to the calaboose. Too late now to get a permit from the mayor for a street meeting. Not that you need one legally—vacant lot, private property. That won't stop the police in this town!"

Ann, Eleanor, and Pat looked casual as mercenaries. Maggie chuckled. Miss Aukett choked. Then Miss Aukett smiled. But all the gold and benevolence had gone out of Miss Aukett's smile, and she sounded as though she had bitten something gritty: "I'll do what I can, of course. I always do. But I'm afraid these young women will have to do the rough-and-tumble speechifying. They're used to it!"

Mrs. Manders was a hustler. She had immediately caused to be hung on a shop across from the entrance of the Grand Opera House a hand-scrawled poster:

TAFFORD IS AFRAID OF THE WOMEN!
Won't Let Us Speak as
Announced at
GRAND OPERA HOUSE TONIGHT
COME TO OPEN AIR MEETING
BLAIR & STAFFORD STS. 8 P. M.
Hear the Sensational Truth
TONIGHT—WEDN.

At the corner of the lot she had stationed a small boy with a drum and a lame Spanish War veteran with a bugle. They were proud of their art and willing to demonstrate it. When the crusaders came up in Mrs. Manders's asthmatic Pope-Hartford car at five minutes to eight, the lot was full. The audience were not unsympathetic, like the respectables at Symphony Hall in Clateburn; most of them were the dispossessed, the unemployed, the boiler-tenders, the janitors, the roustabouts, the scrubwomen, and they admired the pluck of the lady bandits; they cheered jovially as Mrs. Manders and the girls coaxed the automobile into the center of the crowd, unpacked leaflets, and set up a gasoline flare. But under that murky and nervous flame, the crowd looked wild: unshaven jowls, corded throats above collarless shirts, hats smeared with coal dust or lime, bold eyes of women dishwashers.

Miss Emily Allen Aukett gasped to Eleanor, the only female in the gang who seemed to have traces of recognizable gentility, "Oh, they're a dreadful mob! Do persuade Mrs. Manders that it's dangerous! We must get out of here!"

"Yeay! Go it, girls. Give 'em hell! Hurray for the vote!" roared the crowd, as Mrs. Manders climbed on the rear seat of the car and held up her two hands.

"They'll mob us!" sobbed Miss Aukett.

Mrs. Manders had spoken to the audience as to neighbors; Ann had begun her familiar—too familiar!—exordium about women's looking not for privilege but for a chance to work, when a police car came shrieking up the street in imperative agony. A dozen officers, clubs waving, headed by a lieutenant, were seen buffeting through the crowd.

"Thank God!" whimpered Emily Allen Aukett; and the ladylike Eleanor Crevecoeur turned on her with, "You chump! How much will you take to go back to New York?"

It is improbable that, in her terror, Miss Aukett heard.

She slipped out of the car door; she cuddled as near as she could to the big police lieutenant when he pushed through to the side of the car; she poured out on him the bland, bright balm of her smile. He did not notice. He was demanding of Ann, who was looking down at him from her station on the seat of the car, looking down at his malignant mouth in the torchlight, "Hey, you, lady! Where's your permit to speak?"

"We don't need one. Don't need one at all," Mrs. Manders said primly. "You'll please to go on about your business, officer. This is not a street meeting. Private lot. Don't need——"

"The hell you don't need a permit! Lookit how the crowd's stretching out into the public highway! That makes it a street meeting. Now, you shut your traps and get out of here or I'll run the whole bunch of you in!"

The primness of the bishop's daughter vanished, and Mrs. Manders yelled back, "Run us in! Go on! We want to be run in!" (Miss Emily Allen Aukett was seen by a coldly grinning Eleanor to slip behind the lieutenant and off into the crowd.) "That's the only thing that'll impress the muttonheads like you, that make up this town!"

"That'll be enough out of you, Mrs. Manders! I know all about you. Ought to be ashamed of yourself, old gal like you, preacher's daughter, associating with these chippies from out of town! Bunch of Reds and anarchists! If you wasn't related to the best families, I'd pinch you—yes, and if I got any of your lip, maybe I'd have an accident with my night stick! Your swell relatives won't stand your acting-up much longer, you take it from me; I've got the low-down. Now you—— Boys! Clear the crowd! Pilwaski!

Get in here and drive this car to this old gal's home—
you get in, too, Monahan, and see that none of these hell-
cats get loose!"

As Pilwaski drove their car off, Ann saw the admonishment of a mob by the officials whom that same mob had
hired to guard the peace. She wanted to leap out, to kill
the policemen, to battle and kill until they killed her, but
she was held in by Officer Monahan, and from the elevation of the car saw something she never could forget;
something that made her fundamentally a revolutionist
even in the days when she was to be a cautious public
official. The big lieutenant at their head, eight policemen
waded into the crowd. Eight against five hundred! It
would sound heroic, as told in the newspapers. It wasn't.
She discovered something that later made it impossible
for her to accept the emotional pacifism fashionable everywhere (save in Russia and Japan) from 1920 to 1930: that
an unarmed mass is helpless against an armed trained
squadron; that neither age, sex, arguments, nor sweet
reasonableness is proof against guns and clubs.

The policemen started into the crowd, simply and sys-
tematically banging every head in sight—old men, women,
boys of eight, along with mature workmen. When anyone
protested, he was hit twice, and kicked in the sides as he
writhed in the mud. When they had slashed halfway
through the audience, and everyone was fleeing, stumbling,
pushing at the man in front, the eight policemen collared
the first eight auditors at hand, kicked them into the patrol
wagon that had followed the police car, and drove clanging
away.

As Mrs. Manders's car, Pilwaski driving, edged after

the patrol wagon, Ann looked back to see men with blood dribbling in divided streams from cut foreheads down into their blinded eyes, or lying face up in the mud, or staggering with fluttering hands, sobbing. She ceased that moment to be merely a feminist and became a humanist, in the only orthodox sense of that harassed word.

Miss Emily Allen Aukett had, by taxicab, reached the residence of Mrs. Manders before them. She was crying prettily beside a pot of geraniums.

Mrs. Manders ignored Emily. When they were in the parlor, safe from the ears of Officers Pilwaski and Monahan, she declared, "We'll go to the mayor tomorrow morning and tell him we want a street-speaking permit. We won't get it. But maybe some day the citizens will see who owns the streets, along with the gas and water! What say, Miss Vickers—you girls?"

"Grand!" said the Ball and Chain Squad.

"Oh, no!" wailed Emily Allen Aukett. "I told you beforehand what would happen tonight! It's all so undignified!"

Then spoke the daughter of the bishop: "Yes, and so is giving birth to a baby, my dear woman! You needn't worry. Your train leaves at 11:16 tonight. I'll drive you down. Now, you others, we'll leave here at nine in the morning . . ."

Before she went to bed, Mrs. Manders telephoned to the death-watch at the evening papers that there might be something interesting on the steps of City Hall tomorrow; telephoned to the mayor at his house to expect them at nine-thirty. For the first time the girls heard the Methodist

Boadicea chuckle: "Why, your honor, I'm surprised at such language, though I do remember you were a shocking, nasty little boy when you used to steal Father's apples and . . ."

Mrs. Manders beamed. "He'll be sure to have the police there."

"And you won't have me there, thank Heaven," sniffed Miss Emily Allen Aukett.

Five years later Ann was to meet Miss Aukett in New York, to have tea at her apartment in Tenth Street, and to discover that, secure and at home, Miss Aukett was gracious, amusing, clear-headed, and, worst of all, that she really did know the celebrities she had pretended to know. Ann sighed, "Oh, no one ever understands anybody, except the people you met just last evening!" That Miss Bogardus, the snapping-turtle, should be the kindest of women; that Eleanor Crevecoeur could and did shock Mag O'Mara; that Glenn Hargis, the virile, should be weaker than Eula Towers and more timid than the Reverend Professor Henry Sogles, M. A.; that the bumptious and cowardly Emily Aukett should be courageously disdainful of popularity; that she herself, Ann Vickers, should give her life, her most ardent ambition, to uplift and reform and general pediatrics for adults, yet all the time wonder whether any of it was worth while—where did it leave her in the study of mankind?

They came meekly enough up the steps of City Hall, between the massy columns which were revered in Tafford as solid marble, but which, owing to some unfortunate accident in the civic labors of Mayor Snowfield's party, were actually shells filled with broken stone. Six reporters, seven photographers, and nineteen policemen were awaiting them on the steps.

"Yuh can't go in there, lady," said the police captain to Mrs. Manders.

"I am a citizen of Tafford, and I demand my right——"

"You go on down in the street and demand your rights there!" said the captain. A policeman seized each of the women, not painfully, but with considerable rudeness.

Mrs. Manders, Eleanor, Ann, even Maggie stood quietly enough, and Ann was thinking, "We can be back in Clateburn by three this afternoon. I think I'll take a vacation and clean up my room——"

But Pat Bramble, the small and dainty Pat, snatched herself loose from her policeman, lowered her head, and rammed him agonizingly in the gendarmish belly. He howled, he slapped her, he grappled her wrist and twisted it till she screamed. Mechanically, not thinking much about it, the other three girls fell to their duty, struggling with the policemen, trying to slap them, while Ann remembered the rebuking old lady at Symphony Hall, and casually reflected, in the calm space inside her brown hatless head, that was so furiously yanking itself away from the policeman's pressing shoulder, "Not at all ladylike, not at all ladylike . . . I hope the photographers get this; ought to be swell publicity for the Cause. . . . Not at all ladylike, not at all ladylike."

And with that she bit her policeman.

To be arrested, anywhere, for any reason, had always seemed to Ann as permanently disgraceful as being caught in adultery. Anyone who had ever been arrested was a *criminal*, essentially different from human beings; doing appalling things for no comprehensible reason, belonging to a bewitched world of courts and prisons and torture-chambers and agonies of inhuman guilt. A criminal was as sorcerous as a ghost; a judge or a jailer as awesome and unordinary as a Catholic priest; and the precincts of a court, a prison, anything connected with an arrest, was made not of brick or stone or wood, but of leprous and unterrestrial material that obscured sun and air and secure sleep.

Yet as they drove off in the Black Maria, with its two long seats covered with quite ordinary black oilcloth, a massive policeman standing on the steps at the back and shutting off the light, she did not seem to herself to be in any bewitched and terrifying place, but only in a rather bumpy and uncomfortable Ford truck with the curtains drawn. She did not feel like a criminal. She wondered if many prisoners did not feel not like criminals, but merely like human beings who had been arrested by rather dull policemen.

They were held for half an hour in a bull-pen at the municipal courthouse, along with three prostitutes, a negress shoplifter, and a very drunken lady. Ann had no horror of them. She did not believe that she, a Respectable Young College Woman, had been put upon by being confined with these drabs, but the opposite, that they were not so different from herself, and that possibly they were no more to blame for being arrested than herself and the bishop's daughter.

And now Ann, Pat, Eleanor, and Maggie became what

they were hereafter to be called: "The Ball and Chain Squad."

They were arraigned before a magistrate, neither sadistic nor humorous: a commonplace plump man with a commonplace tan mustache, to whom sentencing offenders was as unemotional a routine as eating pork and beans.

Standing before the magistrate's high and greasy pine desk, the five were charged (to Ann's wonder and Eleanor's snicker) with breach of the peace, use of abusive and profane language, resisting officers in the discharge of their duty, and causing a crowd to collect. The five officers, each of whom was as large as any three of the defendants, gave testimony that "these here women" had threatened to assault the mayor, that when they had been told that the mayor would be unable to see them, they had set upon the officers, struck them, bitten them, and caused them serious distress.

The magistrate looked down on Mrs. Manders, then at her police guardian. Ann thought that he winked at the policeman as he demanded, "But this elderly lady—she didn't join these young women in their shocking behavior!"

"No, yonor. She tried to prevent 'em. They're strangers from out of town—claim they come from Clateburn. They claim to be anarchists or suffragettes, or something like that, and it looked to me like they was trying to mislead the old dame."

"They were not! If they're guilty, I'm twice as guilty!" wailed Mrs. Manders.

"Mrs. Manders discharged. The others, two weeks in county jail. Next case!"

"I demand to go with these girls! This is a disgrace——"

"Officer! Take the old lady out. Next case, I said."

As the Ball and Chain Squad were led through the right rear door, Ann looked back to see Mrs. Manders, kicking and slapping, lugged out to freedom by three grinning giants in blue.

13

LIKE the worthy magistrate who had sentenced them, their jail was neither fiendish nor amusing. It was just drab, dirty, and perfectly senseless.

They heard enough, from their fellow criminals, of other county jails and state prisons, for women as well as for men, that were dens of secret and irresponsible cruelty; of solitary confinement in dark, damp, lice-crawling cells till the victims went insane, of strait-jackets and whipping, of stout women keepers, vicious as any man warder, who enjoyed stripping prisoners, lashing them, nagging them to frenzy and, in punishment for the frenzy, playing the icy fire-hose on them. Incredulous that such things could happen, in the United States, they heard a prisoner describe a Georgia county jail in which not one of the women prisoners had any clothing beyond a thin skirt, not even shoes, and in which the man jailer—there was no matron—walked among the bare women whenever he chose, and the gallant town loafers wandered in to look at these wretches on the toilet—and no one cared, and the

Good Citizens, when they were told, did not believe it.
But in this particular jail at Tafford, it was not cruelty,
but the waste and stupidity, the good-natured ignorance
of the sheriff and the constant, sneaking, sickening, amorous approaches of the deputy sheriffs that exasperated
the Ball and Chain Squad. They were confined to the
women's wing of the county jail: a lofty room, ill-lighted,
dreary and, now that December was coming on, clammily
cold. Round the room were two tiers of cells for sleeping,
kept unlocked save in the rather common cases of hysterical or violent inmates. On the bunks in the cells were
mattresses covered with damp gunny-sacking. In the
center of the vast room were some dozens of rickety
straight chairs, a few greasy tables, a rusty stove—and the
prisoners.

When the four girls were sentenced, the floor was
muddy, the chairs sticky to the touch, the cracks in the
walls alive with lice. They began reforming at once. Possibly had they remained a year, their fresh and innocent
vigor would not have lasted, but for their fortnight, they
were as optimistically busy as a Mormon missionary. As
the matron "didn't guess it was necessary" for them to
clean up, they bought mops, brushes, soap, insecticide,
with their own money, and, bawdily but cheerfully assisted by two of the prostitutes, they got rid of the grease
and some of the garbage-like smell. They started classes in
English, in economics; and one of the other prisoners, a
born Parisian, in for stealing furs from checking-rooms,
gave them lessons in French, though they never afterward
dared to use most of the words she taught them.

They had plenty of books, for they had not been in jail

twenty-four hours before Miss Bogardus had swept down from Clateburn, and after giving a spirited interview to the papers, called on the Ball and Chain Squad, kissed them all around, cried, said that there was a considerable argument as to whether judges or policemen were the worst jackasses, and left with them all the books that in her haste she had been able to pick up around the Fanning Mansion or buy at the Clateburn Station news-counter. They included the Gospel According to St. John, the second volume of *Les Miserables*, *The New England Cook Book*, *The Jewel of Jandaphur*, by E. Phillips Oppenheim, *Gulliver's Travels, Arranged for Children*, *The History of the Mammoth Cave*, an aseptic novel called *Helen o' High Tor*, and Weininger's *Sex and Character*, of which Miss Bogardus had remembered nothing except that it had something to do with women.

Mrs. Manders came, daily, and brought the newspapers, *Life* and *Judge*, cold chicken and large, meaty, perdurable plum puddings, which were more interesting than Weininger to four healthy young women starving on a menu consisting entirely of gluey porridge, sour bread, oleomargarine, dematerialized coffee and tea, lukewarm boiled potatoes, stew crusted with grease, molasses, and orange marmalade made of carrots.

Washing the tin dishes in which these luxuries were served was the only occupation the other prisoners had, save for incessant conversation. All day, sometimes half the night, the women talked—petty thieves, prostitutes, women who had maltreated their children or slashed their lovers, drunks, dope-fiends. They told smutty stories and sang "Frankie and Johnnie"; they boasted of their lovers and sobbed about the cruelty of their husbands and the stinginess of the customers for whom they had scrubbed floors or washed clothes. Seventeen of them, aside from the suffragists; all talking, hating the world and a little bewildered by it.

Seventeen of them, out of whom, by count, fourteen seemed to Ann no more "criminal" than herself. Poverty, unemployment, early underfeeding and, on the part of the prostitutes, plain feebleness of mind and puerile love of silk and bright lights, had sent them here. Fourteen slovenly women who presently seemed to her as good friends and understandable as Pat or Eleanor or Maggie— and some of them less calculating than Pat, less ribald than Eleanor, less belligerent than Maggie.

As day by day they became more knowable and more human, more like girls in Waubanakee or Point Royal, so did the jail itself seem less extraordinary and strange with dread. It was not a "prison," smacking of mysterious terror; it was, like the Black Maria, just a *place*, a place where she happened now to be, as she might have been in a railway station, bored with waiting and thinking about the inefficiency of the world. For it was not the cruelty of the whole system of laws and courts and prisons which she resented now so much as its futility. "Let's assume that the court is right and that I am a criminal," she fretted. "All right. What does the state accomplish by shutting me up here for two weeks? The theory is that I am a violent rowdy who injures the little policemen and threatens the mayor. What is there about sitting idle for a fortnight among professional prostitutes that is going to make me so gentle, that is going to teach me so much self-restraint, that when I come out the policemen and mayor will be safe?"

She saw that war was stupid, that conducting business for the profit of a few owners was insane, that thrones and crowns and titles and degrees were as childish as playing with tin soldiers, but that in the entire range of human imbecility, there was nothing quite so senseless as imprisonment as a cure for crime . . . and that the worse the crimes became, the more serious it was that there should be only so barbaric an effort to cure.

And that perception, mingled with the remembered sour smells and slimy tables and acrid food, with the picture of women prisoners puzzled and hopeless and stupefied, and the guards' sly amorousness, was to send her one day into prison reform, and to keep her in it even when she longed to escape from the naggings and exhibitionism of reform to the security of a man, a house, children, land, and the serene commonplace.

Land and children and a hearth and her man!

She had never so closely yearned for them as in this idleness. Skittering about in Waubanakee, bustling in Point Royal, tub-thumping in Clateburn, she had been too busy to consider adequately what this individual Ann Vickers was, and what she wanted.

Perhaps, she sighed (looking at one of the cockroaches, which bred faster than they could slap them to death)—perhaps she was one of the Marthas who could never be so showily wasteful as to anoint the world with the spikenard of sexual exaltation, who would always be serving the dinner for Lazarus and Jesus, who would be for and of the mass, and never an "individual." But it was an individual

enough Ann who thought about men in the sordid and
perverted feminism of the jail, among women staled and
bound by sex.

Men! They had existed at the Fanning Mansion scarcely
more than at Point Royal. To the Fanning Mansion had
come only hog-tied husbands, literary bank-clerks, and
Socialists who called you "comrade" and immediately
chucked you under the chin in an alleged spirit of fra-
ternity. But the girls had been too driven for any vast
yearning. They had time now, and Ann daydreamed and
dreamed by night of a lover and mate who should have the
irony of Adolph Klebs, the ruddy freshness of Glenn
Hargis. He came to her down the rough grass of a hillside
pasture, and they raced through uplands, light as the
shadows of the clouds. . . . She met him in a worn doorway,
in a city worn and old and thunderous, on an afternoon of
fog and watery street-lights; there was something illicit
and exciting about it; they slipped away together—she
shivered happily as she took his arm—and had tea in their
secret place. . . . Together they walked through the alleys
of Venice and came back to an apartment in a *palazzo*,
with lofty ceiling riotous with little loves, and a vast blue
and golden bed at the distant end of a room floored with
scarlet tiles and lit by a crystal chandelier. . . . And by
magic, they were in a Connecticut cottage with a vegetable garden smaller than the chandelier, but more exciting.

Everything from every romantic novel, every motion
picture she had seen, came to her now and appeared more
real, in her detached brooding, than the cockroaches on
the rusty bars of her cell, the screaming prostitute five feet

away, the piles of envelopes awaiting her back in Clateburn.

The Ball and Chain Squad were released in a storm of roses, confetti, and a brass band playing "Tipperary." The four, with Mrs. Manders, Miss Bogardus, and the Reverend Chauncey Simsbury of St. Gondolph's P. E. Church, addressed two thousand Tafford people, who clapped lustily and went out to vote against municipal suffrage for women.

At Clateburn, at the station, were all the press photographers in town, sixteen commercial photographers, and seventy-two amateurs, with a battalion of reporters, and another brass band. At Symphony Hall they addressed three thousand, and the only man who tried to heckle them was thrown out by two enthusiastic business-men of the kind who went to the barber's every fortnight.

They had had no time for any dinner beyond chocolate almond bars between train-arrival and the Symphony Hall rally. When they escaped from the hundreds of lady stalwarts who came up to shake their hands after the rally, and reached the fortress of the Fanning Mansion, they found that the flustered Miss Bogardus had forgotten to prepare supper. They supped on cold canned corned-beef and moldy biscuits.

But their cots in the Fanning Mansion attic seemed like couches in a Mohammedan paradise.

Her brooding in jail had encouraged Ann to escape from the righteous bondage of the suffrage movement. The very virtuousness and self-sacrifice of Miss Bogardus, which made her expect equal virtue and sacrifice from others, was a worse tyranny than dungeons. In this world no one ought to be more than decently virtuous; it is too hard on the neighbors. Ann was more afraid of the Battleaxe than of any squad of policemen. But she was tired—not only of envelopes, which Miss Bogardus had them addressing again within twenty-four hours after leaving jail, but of the whole theological vocabulary of suffrage: "economic independence of women," "equal rights," "equal pay for equal work," "matriarchy." Like such senile words as "idealism," "virtue," "patriotism," they had ceased to mean anything. And she was tired too of the perpetual stories about women's wrongs. There were plenty of wrongs, Heaven knew: young widows with three children working twelve hours a day for just enough to starve slowly on; intelligent women ridiculed and made small by boisterous husbands. But the women who came to tea at the Fanning Mansion merely to say that their husbands did not appreciate their finer natures, to them Ann had listened long enough. She began to sympathize with the husbands.

Yet it took her four months of bullying her fear, of whispered conferences with Pat and Eleanor, to escape from Clateburn and the envelopes. Probably, in her perfectly normal cowardice, she would not have eloped from the Fanning Mansion till the suffrage amendment had been passed if Pat and Eleanor had not confessed that they too planned to invade New York and be human and sinful and free of envelope-addressing. They would see Ann there—why didn't she pioneer for them?—they would *try* to back her up when Miss Bogardus indicted her treachery.

In 1916 Ann found a job with a committee "investigating conditions" in the textile and garment industries in New York, with an insult instead of a salary but with board and room at the Corlears Hook Settlement House guaranteed, in return for teaching classes of foreigners.

A little dazed, free, and not quite sure what to do with freedom, her good little Mid-Western-cum-Connecticut conscience writhing over the Battleaxe's crisp, "If you don't feel happy here, we won't try to keep you," Ann rode miserably through coaxing April to the towers of New York.

When from the elevated platform she saw the spire of the Woolworth Building, then looked down on a throng of Chinamen, Italians, Hungarians, Yankees, of billionaire bankers, and sailors just in from Java, and intellectual Jewish lawyers, and whistling structural steel workers, her spirit soared with the tower, quickened with the quick-flowing blood of a great seaport, and she cried, "Now I'll *do* things. . . . I wonder what?"

14

Wᴴᴇɴ America entered the war, in 1917, Ann Vickers
had risen from ordinary resident of the Corlears Hook
Settlement, in lower New York, to assistant head-resident,
in direct charge of the classes in elementary English, com-
position, modern drama, economics, physiology, and cooking, for the poor of the neighborhood, of the clubs for
mothers, girls, and militant small boys, of the dramatic
association, and of the lectures delivered gratis by earnest
advocates of single tax, trout-fishing, exploring Tibet,
pacifism, sea-shell collecting, the eating of bran, and the
geography of Charlemagne's empire.

She had been rushed from the social solitude of the
Fanning Mansion into a typical, inescapable New York
maelstrom of acquaintanceships, with the telephone always ringing. Pat Bramble, after teaching for a term in
Denver—she had apparently been discharged for inefficiency—had come to New York and was some sort of
glorified stenographer for an advertising agency; Eleanor
Crevecoeur had come as assistant editor on a trade-paper
devoted to household furnishing, for which she wrote

lyrics about lavatories, panegyrics about wall-board, and martial melodies on the convenience of folding luggage-stands in guest-rooms.

In New York Pat Bramble was as cool, sweet, and frostily virginal among the rugged copywriters, and the salesmen whose socks, ties, and handkerchiefs matched, as she had been among the male spinsters whom she had met at the Fanning Mansion. But Eleanor observed, "Like you girls, I kid myself that I came here to make a career, but what I really came for was to catch me a good husky male," and quite successfully, without marriage-license, she went to living with a large, athletic young graduate of the University of Oklahoma, one Mr. Ewbank, secretary of a taxicab company, whose only social gifts were imitating a Chinese laundryman, playing bridge, and keeping restfully silent when his betters, the women, discussed taxation and immortality.

As soon as she had arrived in New York, Ann had diffidently called on Dr. Malvina Wormser, the embattled suffrage speaker whom she had guarded at Symphony Hall in Clateburn. The plump and cheerful little doctor embraced her, gave her a prescription for a cold, and immediately annexed her to the human zoo of which, like all women doctors, she was proprietor. Dr. Wormser's flat, a high-ceiled upper floor of an old-fashioned mansion on Fifth Avenue, in the Thirties, was filled with German medical books, Chinese pottery, dust, violins which Dr. Wormser believed to be Strads, oak cupboards from Sussex, piles of unread magazines advocating the causes of vegetarianism, Macedonia, Chinese orphans, and colonic irrigation, with cigarette butts, inscribed volumes of agonized poetry, obstetrical customers, begging letters, and people. Here, Ann met architects, wounded French officers, wounded German spies who were always supposed to be Swiss bankers, male and female bacteriologists, Episcopal rectors who had been unfrocked for orthodoxy —i. e., for taking the Bible seriously, secretaries of publishers, and women chemists, of which last category one half were spectacled and harsh, and the other half golden and frivolous and regularly kissed behind Japanese screens at Dr. Wormser's impromptu dances.

"You'll like my bunch," Dr. Wormser said to Ann; "and it will train you for the day when you become the first American woman ambassador. You'll see that all the earnest scholars that come here think I'm light-minded and frivolous, and all the hell-raisers think I'm depressingly serious, and so between them, I never get any of them for patients, and I have to make my living out of free clinics and free advice to rich women who ought to be spanked. I have some nice Benedictine here. Come tomorrow evening. There's either an aviator or a conchologist coming, I forget which."

But Ann's most constant intimacies were necessarily with her neighbors, her fellow residents of the Corlears Hook Settlement, and out of the twenty of them, seven were males: Columbia graduate students, a young liberal lawyer who despised the law and worshipped Clarence Darrow, a middle-aged librarian, the inevitable liberal clergyman who argued humorously, and a certain rich young ruler who was eager to do anything for the downtrodden except to sell all that he had and distribute unto the poor. He lived among the poor, but he retained his room and his evening clothes at the house of his father, who owned four acres of New York tenement real estate.

Ann had breakfast and dinner with them, at a long table with the atmosphere and the routine fodder of a boarding-house in a college town. The rooms of the men residents were close enough to hers, along the third-floor corridor of the settlement house, for chatty visits in dressing-gowns and pajamas. She liked their quality and their rough smell; it was more adventurous to go to the theater with these men than with Eleanor. But, she sighed, they were all seven so—so liberal! They were judicious and full of lively conversation, but they had in them neither fire nor earth.

The Corlears Hook Settlement House entered the war along with President Wilson. Like the great Socialist thinker, Mr. Upton Sinclair, all the settlement workers except Ann proclaimed that while they were pacifists, opposed to all other wars, *this* crusade was to overthrow the Prussian military clique, after which there would forever be universal peace. Ann, remembering old Oscar Klebs of Waubanakee, and her professor of German in Point Royal, could not believe that the Germans were of an especially belligerent breed, but her friends screamed her down. (This is ancient history, now, forgotten particularly by the people who made it and who address peace societies three times a week and go back to Berlin and explain to their German friends that they, personally, were always against the war.)

The settlement made bandages, sent out its workers to collect for the Y. M. C. A., and entertained the new sol-

diers passing through New York. It was the headquarters
for "social workers" from other cities, who did their
bayonet practise with peculiar purity of purpose. In June,
1917, the settlement had a large dance for the guest
officers, and the Italian and Jewish children of the neighborhood, accustomed to settlement-workers with floppy
poetic ties, now had the privilege of seeing uniforms.

For the dance the large hall used for lectures and concerts had been cleared. Entwined American, British, and
French flags concealed the portraits of Jesus and Karl
Marx. On the stage, settlement workers were serving
coffee, lemonade, and ice cream. There was no liquor,
though the guests did one by one disappear to the room
of the rich young ruler, who was also in uniform.

Ann's slight prejudice against the war had not kept her
from dancing, on this June evening, with the windows open
to cheerful Ghetto sounds, street cries, tinkling barrows of
peddlers, children dancing to the hurdy-gurdies. The orchestra jazzed marching-songs into one-steps, and she
circled with young, eager men glorified by adventure,
rejoicing to be out of the dust and hypocritical virtuousness of their "social work."

"Gal! Better come over and drive a truck! We'll have
a swell time Over There! I'll buy you a bottle of fizz in
Gay Paree!" the best of her partners bawled cheerily at
her.

He was agate-faced, smooth as agate. He was a Ph. D.
in philosophy.

She liked to dance, though she did gird at herself, "Now
for Heaven's sake, Annie, don't bounce as if you were
playing basketball!" But the gayer and more wanton

the warriors became, the more cramped with creeping depression was she. They were her brothers, these young men, even if they were a little sentimental and excitable, like all males. That this solid chest against which she agreeably leaned in dancing should in a few months be a heap of ragged muck, crawling with maggots—oh, God, no cause was worth it, and certainly not the cause of shooting the cousins of Adolph Klebs!

She slipped away to the stage and took the place of a flashing Jewish girl of the neighborhood—a good Socialist except when she saw the tailored uniform of an officer— at the splintery pine planks which made up the refreshment counter. She sat in a slatted folding chair at the end of the counter, melancholy.

A man in captain's uniform ambled across the stage, dropped sighing into a folding chair beside her. He looked like a Welsh evangelist; thin, sallow, not tall, with unsteady hands and imploring dark eyes. He seemed to be two or three years older than Ann—she was twenty-six now.

"Tired, Captain?" she said.

"No—yes—I suppose so."

"Some ice cream?"

"Heavens, no! I've just had too many highballs up in Room 17—that millionaire duffer's place. Six, I guess. Highballs, I mean. And the hell of it is, I don't feel them."

"Really?"

"Yes, *really*. And I wish I did."

"Why?"

"So I'd forget, of course. Eh? Forget where we're going. I'm a neurotic—like most social workers, the other portion being dumm—but same time, I wonder how many of the other heroes down there are as scared as I am. Yes, scared, that's what I said! When I'm going to sleep—if you can call it sleep, now!—I picture a big Heinie jumping down on me in the trench, with a bayonet, straight at my belly. Hell! Forgive me for being a cry-baby! I don't usually talk this way. Tonight it's just that some fool girl I was dancing with said, 'Captain, bayonet a couple of Fritzes for me, will you!' and I just went to pieces! Ought to be ashamed——"

"Oh, I can understand! Why shouldn't you feel neurotic, if it's natural to you? I'm not a lady patrioteer! Can't you transfer—you're infantry?—to some other branch where you won't—you know, with your nerves all on the surface; s'pose perhaps mine would be, too—not face bayonets?"

"No. I can't. Just because I *am* a damned neurote! I'm just the sort that *would* go into the trenches, and over the top. I'll either get shot for cowardice—and bawling in battle!—or I'll get the Congressional Medal. No; got to carry on. Owe it to myself!"

"I do think that's awfully brave—even if it's perhaps foolish. By the way, my name is Ann Vickers—I'm a resident here."

"My name is Resnick—Lafayette Resnick—Lafe, to pretty girls like you. What was your college?"

"Point Royal. . . . I am not pretty! Nice eyes—that lets me out."

"Nice? Lovely! And swell ankles. And thank Yahveh, no magazine-cover prettiness. I should have said handsome rather——"

"What was your college, Captain?"

"B. A., University of Minnesota. M. A., Chicago. Been

working toward my Ph. D. in sociology. Don't suppose I'll ever get it now—not even in time for my obituary— 'body found horribly mangled; his Phi Beta Kappa key had been driven by the bayonet six inches into his guts.'"

"*Stop it, will you!*"

"Oh, you're right. Do forgive me, Ann. Honestly, I'm not like this often. Guess the highballs did get to me, more than I thought. *Timor in vino!*"

"And after your M. A.?"

"The usual. Saving the world, especially the unfit— people like myself, but without my Pop's suspender-and-nightshirt-selling money. Taught for a year in high school in Winnetka. Wrote criticism of the movies in Milwaukee —say, I met Victor Berger; you know, he's the St. Paul of the Socialist party; Debs is the St. John, and old Karl the Messiah. Got fired for saying what I thought—bad habit of neurotics; see how it almost got me in Dutch with you, tonight. Since then, probation officer in Chicago. And now, a hero!"

"Stop it!"

"Try to! And what about you, darling?"

"Oh—the usual also. Suffrage organizing. Investigating. A little nurse's training."

"Nursing? Then you better join us and come on over. See you in Paris."

"That's the second invitation I've had tonight."

"But I mean it, terribly. The other galoot just thought you were a sweet girl. I think you're—oh, if you had charge of me, I might give up the delicate delights of being neurotic and be normal. You might even marry me before we sail. Though God knows what you'd get out of it! But it happens I've never had a gal that was man enough to boss and mother me and sweet enough to cuddle. You are! The invitation *aux noces* is quite serious, by the way, Ann."

"To the—— Oh, yes. Well, it's seriously received and placed on file."

"'We'll let you know in case any vacancy turns up.' Oh, I know! I'm afraid you're *not* very serious about it. Or maybe you have a nice helpful highbrow husband in the background?"

"No, Captain; if you really care to know, this is the first proposal of marriage I've ever received. And I've always thought I had some talent for mothering—I suppose most females think so—but I warn you, I'm not quite so stolid and dependable as I seem. I have nerves, too, under the fat."

"Not fat!"

"Tendency, anyway. If I didn't exercise. Yes, I have plenty of nerves concealed. I once bit a policeman!"

"I adore you! Let's get out of this—this damn military-plus-Yiddish atmosphere. Little too *kosher*——"

"But aren't you——?"

"Of course I am, idiot! Grandfather a rabbi (or so my Dad claims; but I think he ran a butcher shop on the side.) Can't we—— You live here? Got a nice sitting-room or something where we can get away from hearing 'em try to harmonize 'Smile, Smile, Smile' in here with 'Ole Clo'' out on the street?"

"No, just a single room, very single, under the matronly eyes of the head-resident."

"Is she venomous?"

"Well, I'd say she was efficient."

"Then let's go to—I know a restaurant—fact there's one across from my hotel, where a bold soldier in uniform can get a drink as if he were as grown-up as a civilian. Staying at the Hotel Edmond, on Irving Place—little one, you probably don't know it; most respectable, highbrow place; they give you copies of the *Nation* and the *New Republic* instead of a Gideon Bible. Let's go up there and have a drink. . . . Do you mind a drink?"

"No, not *one*. But I can't get away. I ought to be down on the floor right now. I'm more or less in charge of this dance."

"Dine with me tomorrow night?"

"Yes."

"Meet me at the Edmond at seven?"

"Yes."

She was sure enough of his "intentions," as they were politely called. She was not at all sure of hers. She was not unwilling to "mother him." (Detestable vicarage phrase, she thought!) But she was not sure that, at twenty-six, edging toward spinsterhood, she did not want considerably more. Certainly she was not afraid of him. She realized that he incredibly had meant his proposal of marriage— for the moment. Could she consider it? His skin was goose-fleshed with twitching nerve ends. He would be cruel from timidity and cold from the heat of Levantine passion; he would lie to her and pinch the folds of her soul. But he would be clever; he would know suave surfaces; he would show her a world colored like the geography book—not just brown common earth, but scarlet and yellow and blue and garish green. He would torment her, but he would, surely, never be smug and heavy and jocular, like all the men she had known, all except Adolph and Glenn Hargis.

Well. She would be wise. Not soppily romantic, like the slum girls who were always "getting into trouble" and galloping in to her for help. She would walk with Lafayette Resnick as she would with Pat Bramble.

"No. *Lafe*. Not Lafayette. Anyway, it's better than Irving or Milton or Sidney!"

She was at the Hotel Edmond at a quarter after seven. She had had to walk up to Twenty-sixth Street and back in order to be late enough for pride.

She had thought of wearing her new gray suit—she was smarter in a suit than anything else—but however Lafe might talk of appreciating reason in women, he would like them unreasonably feminine, and she had put on a semi-evening frock of soft lavender in which, she rather hoped, she was fragile as Pat. "Anyway, I do have a good mouth and a pretty nice skin," she grumbled, while she was dressing, five minutes after having scolded a Jewish stenographer for putting so much of her salary into rayon stockings and so little into green vegetables.

She wondered how Lafe would look. Strange thing—she remembered nothing about him except his eyes, like those of a wild deer caught in a trap.

The modest lobby of the Hotel Edmond, lined with panels of red burlap divided by pilasters of mock-marble, was filled with respectable middle-aged ladies with literate but worried faces and some inattention to their hair. They all looked as though they had come from New England retreats to New York to see editors about their contributions, to see married daughters about their new babies, or to see newly enlisted sons about their chances of a commission, and as though, in all cases, they had been disappointed. They sat in imitation mahogany armchairs, waiting. It was a place of waiting, and the air was a little stale.

Through this tension of mild bovine worry Captain Resnick dashed, and he *was* like a brown wild deer, as she had remembered. He was quick and brown and slender, and the welcoming light of his eyes, the two thin hands that caught hers, dissolved all her doubtfulness, made her certain that they had known each other long and loyally.

"Come up to my apartment. We'll have a drink and skip right out."

"All right."

It was a drab enough little suite, a pocket in space, with comfort-grudging brown velvet chairs, and chromos of female children with doting animals: spaniels, cats, and pigeons unhygienically feeding at their mistresses' lips. Lafe had added a silk kakemono of chrysanthemums and a tooled crushed levant edition of Goethe, which made the suite possibly a little more dismal. It was Lafe himself and his gaiety, unrestrained as his depression last evening, which really lighted up the place.

"Let's see something of this town together, shall we?" he demanded, as he poured a cocktail. "I have a week's leave, then I have to report at Camp Lefferts, in Pennsylvania. Do you know New York much?"

"No. *Kaffeeklatsch* and Blinzes and *gehackter Leber*. Zionism and the Bonnaz, Singer Embroiderers, Tuckers,

Stitchers, and Pleaters' Union. The Corlears Hook Dramatic Association in a Yiddish version of *Ghosts*. Concerts at Carnegie Hall. The Metropolitan Museum and Grant's Tomb. And a red-ink joint where you get half a bottle of red with dinner for seventy-five cents. That's all. I suppose there is more to New York!"

"There is! Quaint old-fashioned Amerikanski places where there are no Yids or Hunkies, but foreigners from New England, who still eat corned-beef hash and clam chowder and beans and brown bread. Let's go find 'em!"

"I'm terribly tied up at the Settlement, you know. I'm assistant head-resident."

"Really? Salaams! But I'm the United States Army. I'm saving you from invasion by the Germans. Think! I have only a week before—— And it'll take all of that to make up for my having been such a chump with you last evening, neuroting all over the place! You see, I had an unfortunate boyhood. My father and mother and——"

Ann sat on the lumpy day-bed in the parlor of the suite; Lafe sat at her feet, pointing his story by waving his empty cocktail glass.

"—and cousins and aunts and uncles, they all—and you know how hard this is on an imaginative kid—understood me perfectly! I was nervous and jumpy. All right, they didn't mind! Jews are too intelligent to believe there is any virtue in pain or any heroism that doesn't pay! Then I was fanciful and poetic. All right, they encouraged me—they enjoyed selling forty-nine-cent overalls (with Kantluze buttons) to buy me books and send me to a prep school. I wanted to be an explorer, a chemist, a

New York stock-broker, a composer, an anarchist, a Christian missionary. Fine, go ahead!

"I met some prejudice in college—not much—and I was just as much prejudiced against the Goys' dumm Anglo-Saxon lack of taste, so that was all fair. I've never had to fight. That's why getting into this war, once the first thrill of adventure was over, has scared me so much. What use will I be in the trenches? High explosive shells blowing up!"

He clung to her hand; she impulsively leaned over to stroke his hair, not soft like her own, but confusingly male; thick, harsh, sleek, and black as a horse's mane. He seemed to her—just then—so gay, so needle-fine, so honest about his fear, while the other recruits pretended to bland blond heroism. As he kissed the side of her hand, as she wonderingly touched the taut muscle below the hinge of his jaw, she was outraged by the picture of him hanging, a dried leathery stiff, on the insane zigzag of barbed wire.

Never letting go of her hand, yet holding it lightly with his warm dry palm, he darted off into stories of his boyhood, always with a humorous deprecation of his own eccentricity, of his oriental crimson amid the October brown of Bavarian Catholics and the icy blue of Minnesota Swedes and Norwegians and Vermonters. How he had learned the Greek alphabet out of a dictionary and impressed the entire boys' realm by chanting, "Alpha tau omega tau zeta omicron!" How passionately he had admired the Methodist Church and its mystic, incomprehensible hymns like "Rock of ancient, cleffer me."

He sprang up to cry, "Let's have dinner here, brought up. You won't mind? It'll be heaven for me, after these months when I've never been alone—jammed in barracks, on trains, being so hearty and communal!"

"No, I don't mind!"

She expected him to be more pretentious than Dr. Glenn Hargis when he exhibited his bottle of Rudesheimer at their mountain picnic. But quite casually Lafe Resnick ordered dinner from the room-waiter, brought out Burgundy from a bureau drawer, went on talking, and made her talk. She found herself giving him Waubanakee and Point Royal, Mamie Bogardus and jail. She found herself puzzling aloud as to what it was all about; whether she would not have "done as much good" if she had become a secretary to a banker; but insisting that, good or not, she was not going to be submerged in business or marriage.

Suddenly it was a quarter to eleven, by her wrist watch, and she was in a warm bath of Burgundy, with a diminutive cognac or two. Lafe was crouched with his head on the couch, his cheek against her knee. Half uneasily and half regretfully, she murmured, "So late! I must fly!"

He raised his head slowly, as in a daze looked at his watch. "Is it late? Quarter to eleven. Is that late? Must you go?"

"Yes! Really!"

"I'm so sorry—you darling! I wish you were staying. You let me talk about myself! But you'll dine with me again tomorrow evening—you must; only a week, remember!—and I won't even mention the gallant Captain Resnick! You'll come?"

"Y-es, if I can change a date. Phone me in the morning."

"Good-night, angelic!"

He kissed her at the door, and as she stood in the corridor, she was dizzy and astonished with the fire of that kiss, in which all her individuality had been burnt away, so that for a second she had not been a separate person, but one flesh with him, fused in an electric flare.

Her eyes were sightless on the subway as she swayed with the cars, swayed with remembrance of him.

She was confused when, awakening at three in the morning, she could not recall how Lafe looked nor how he had spoken. Even then she did not suspect that she had never once seen him and never heard him; that from the first second to the last she had read into his boastful whining all the wise gallantry for which she had been longing in man, and into his glittering eyes a cleansing passion which was not his at all but only the projection of her own desire.

She did not know.

15

THAT second evening when she arrived at the Hotel
Edmond (absurd name for lovers!) she was glad that Lafe
sent down word that she was to come straight up. She
could not have endured greeting him among the peering,
waiting ladies in the lobby. And she could not have endured it if he had been suave and glib when she knocked
at the door of his room. If he had chattered, she would
have been impertinent to him; if he had straightway urged
a drink on her, she would—she could not have avoided it
—have rasped out some jeer about his "plying his girls
with liquor."

But he said nothing at all. He looked pale, beseeching.
With no word, trembling a little, he embraced her, kissed
her, led her by the hand to the bumpy day-bed, and sat
silent beside her, his arm trustfully about her. After her
night and day of agitation, she rested in the feeling of his
presence; and his kiss, her kiss in answer, seemed part of
an eternal relation. When they sank to the couch together,
he was not fumbling and technical and ludicrous like

173

Glenn Hargis. He lay beside her quietly, his hand under her cheek, and very quietly he talked of things they might some day do together. . . . Study in London, with a flat in Bloomsbury and walks through High Wycombe. . . . Do an investigation of Mid-Western agriculture and its future; not just graphs, but something really human, that would stand as a classic, like Bryce.

It was he who discovered that it was already nine. Without the fussiness of asking whether she wanted to go out, he ordered dinner. And when the waiter had taken out the last tray, she curled in his arms as naturally as though they had been intimates these many months. So natural, so sweet, so unrestless, she thought in drowsiness, as his nervous finger traced the outline of her lips, her throat.

For ten days then—he had his leave extended by some necromancy which he never explained—they were together at odd hours every day and most of every night. If the settlement house staff stared a little at the tardinesses of the immaculately punctual Miss Vickers, they said nothing, for she was abrupt with jocular male liberal humanitarians who liked to gossip.

It was only the more exciting, after having met with a feeling of perilous secrecy at a kosher restaurant for lunch, to meet again for dinner only six hours later, at the Hotel Edmond or at an Italian café or in the cosmopolitan but polite Bohemianism of the Brevoort. In those six hours they had thought up so many things to say that only by virtuous restraint had they kept from telephoning; significant, exciting things, such as that she was curiously like Ethel Barrymore, that he really must read *Ethan Frome*, that why couldn't he with entire self-respect transfer to the morale corps, that it was nonsense for her to plan going to a gymnasium for regular exercise—her ankles would always remain slim and he didn't think so much of these skinny flappers, anyway, that Beethoven's greatness didn't prevent one appreciating Mozart, that tanks must be more terrifying than machine-gun fire, that the I. W. W. were more logical than the American Federation of Labor, that Mrs. Buzon Waverley, of the Cleveland Federated Charities, was a terrible politician and soft-soaper, that Lafe's green and purple pajamas were hideous and very funny, that they longed to go to the Green Mountains . . . that there was really no topic worth their earnestness, as they leaned over tablecloths speckled with cigarette ashes, save their own curious selves.

She met him in a worn old doorway, in a city worn and old and thunderous, on an afternoon of fog and watery street-lights; there was something illicit and exciting about their meeting; they slipped away together and had tea in a secret place.

It was on Cedar Street, where he had mysterious business with a stock-broker, in a quarter of New York where on slate-colored afternoons the tortuous streets retained a memory of London.

He stopped at the squeak of a beggar woman with a basket of pretzels and dropped a quarter into her hand.

"That's a fine thing for a professional charity worker to do! Encouraging parasite beggars!" she said.

"I know it! I wanted to give somebody something use-

lessly—like pouring out sacrificial wine before the altar—
to tell the Gods how happy I am to have found you!"

She came in early one afternoon, when she would not
be able to see him till nine in the evening, and brought him
red roses. He stared; there was a tear in his eye. "I've
never had any girl bring me flowers! I've never heard of a
woman bringing a man flowers!" he cried.

They wanted to arrange the parlor of his suite to make
it more nearly homelike. They had almost belligerent conferences as to whether the day-bed ought to remain along
the wall, beside the radiator. Puffing and straining, grunting, "Swing y'r end round!" they lifted it and tried it in
a corner, beside the door.

Hopeless!

The parlor was *sui generis*, like a Ford car, and nothing
they could do would change it. But she did buy for him
on Mulberry Street a majolica coffee set, and they had
coffee from it, while he exulted, "Think! This is just the
first of the funny homes we'll have together, all over the
world!"

She had read once somewhere in H. G. Wells, "The
jolly little coarsenesses of life," and had sniffed at the
phrase with the primness of Point Royal and Waubanakee.
She understood it now. She laughed at Lafe's socks—those
absurd lumps attached to threadbare but once voluptu-
ously purple garters. She laughed at the small-boyish
absurdity of an "athletic" undershirt, with its little
bobbed tails. She laughed at his combination of an old-
maidishness equal to her own in arranging his comb,

brushes, nail-scissors, and shoehorn in absolute parallels on the bureau with a masculine heedlessness in scattering cigarette ashes on the floor.

Lafe was much given to handsome accessories. Ann was obligingly impressed by his gold cigarette case, his gold-and-platinum watch chain, his ruby solitaire ring, his imported English military brushes, his leather-and-crystal flask, his thin damascened pocket knife from Sweden. But what touched her was his very unhandsome old slippers— red morocco, peeled, the backs crushed flat on the heels. "Oh, you poor darling! I'll be domestic and send you some new slippers for Christmas," she cried, absurdly pressing the slippers to her breast. . . . And stopped, writhing. Where would he be next Christmas? In no place where men wore slippers!

She had thought, she had even said, to Eula Towers and to Pat Bramble, that there must be something sickeningly vulgar about a man's shaving. If *she* ever married, all those sordidnesses would be shut away, in bathrooms! Yet now she smiled to see him smearing lather on his black bristles, comically leaning his head on one side and pulling the skin taut with the fingers of his left hand while he scraped, all the time arguing with her about Vachel Lindsay. Good hard male bristles—luxurious cream of shaving soap—man's humorless enthusiasms!

And she learned certain bawdy words and flinched over them, while he laughed at her.

It was he who spoke of marriage.

"Let's bounce out and do it right now!" he cried.

"Shall we be married by an alderman, like sensible people, or by a rabbi or by a Presbyterian preacher or—— It would be fun to make a grand show of it and be hitched by a High Church Episcopalian padre with his nice little dress on——"

"Episcopal!"

"Eh?"

"Episcopalian is the noun—it's an Episcopal church, and so on."

"All right, my love! You can't expect a small-town Jew boy to understand all the fine points of this cat's-cradle game that you call religion! But I mean, let's get married at St. Something's, with all the agony. I *guess* the Episcopalians would marry us. We haven't either of us been divorced—not yet! And we've committed only a reasonable amount of adultery. And think of the sensation. We'll invite everybody we know. It'd be a circus to see all those good conscientious agnostics in a swell Episcopalian church!"

"Darling! Be serious."

"I am!"

"Are you sure you want to marry me?"

"Am I!"

"How do you know?"

"I adore you!"

"How do you know?"

"Oh, Lord, that's unanswerable. I just do! But it seems to me—— Do you want to marry me, Ann?"

"I'm not sure. It would keep me from being bored."

"Then let's up and at it, with a heart for any fate!"

"No, please think seriously. You're going to France, and

over there you'll meet grand American girls driving am-
bulances, and pretty French ones. You'll be furious, then,
if you're tied to me. You'll say, 'I never really knew her.
I was just crazy with war-hysteria.' Then you'll hate me."

"Never! I know what I want!"

"But you have liked girls, uh, fairly intimately, before,
haven't you?"

"Oh—yes—no, not really. Anyway, I mean I never
would again, not if I were sure of you! And besides—you
know I might not come back."

"Oh!"

"But I might not, you know. Got to face it. And something might happen to you. We don't seem to have taken
any precautions and—oh, I think I'm radical enough about
this sanctity of marriage rot, but it would be kind of hard
lines on a kid if he had to explain to his friends in school—
I mean it would be kind of tough on him to have to explain
he didn't have any Dad, any name. Yes. We'd better."

"Oh, that couldn't possibly happen. Things like that
don't happen to a social worker. No, really; don't laugh.
They just don't, somehow. Besides, I could do something."

"Not so easy."

"Don't be silly. It must be. I guess it's funny; I talk so
authoritatively to the girls at Corlears House about sex,
but I don't really know much about the technique of not
having babies. But I can find out. Besides, as I say, there
isn't a chance . . . middle of the month, this way; oh, don't
make me so beastly and unromantic! I just mean—— No.
I won't marry you now. I will like a shot when you come
back——"

"If I come back!"

"Well, all right then! *If* you come back, and still want
to. Darling! It's time for me to hustle."

He did not again speak of marriage. She was glad. It
showed how completely, without chatter, they understood
each other.

Like all lovers, though it was beguiling to meet in secret,
she had to show off the beloved to her friends. She took
him to Dr. Malvina Wormser's where, under the doctor's
soothing touch, Lafe purred and became rather funny
about the top sergeants who worshiped "disCIPline."
But Dr. Wormser was beyond earth, like Gene Debs and
Cardinal Newman and El Greco, like stars and comets and
the depth of midnight blue; she was not comprehensible,
like trees and ice-storms and dust, like Pat and Eleanor
and Adolph Klebs and Pearl McKaig; and it is knowable,
earthy friends whom a lover would impress with the
wisdom of her love, as it is not to celestial heroes but to
familiar rivals that the strong man would show his power,
the famous man his renown.

Ann telephoned to Pat Bramble and Eleanor Crevecoeur for a party. It was to be held at the flat on Thirteenth
Street where Eleanor was living in pastoral sin with her
inarticulate male mistress, George Ewbank of the Glide-
well Taxicab Company. The flat was the top floor of a
loft building, with a warehouse of a living-room, plastered
with the violently colored originals for magazine covers
which Eleanor had stolen from the fashion journal to
whose staff she had climbed from the furniture trade-paper
on which she had begun her New York career. There were
also dusty strips of batik, couches, insufficient chairs, and

the large, wide, stammering, restful presence of George Ewbank. Behind the living-room (inevitably known as "studio") were a bedroom, a bath, and an elementary kitchen.

And there was Pat Bramble, fragile and shining as ever and still china-smooth, save for a line or two beside her eyes; Eleanor Crevecoeur, so radiant that she seemed to the glance, if not to the tape-measure, less edgy; and Lafe Resnick; and Ann, almost slender in a tight and hopelessly extravagant coral evening frock. It was, then, a metropolitan, sophisticated, socially conscious group, typical of New York and a goal for Main Street and Zenith, and it was only to be expected that the conversation would be brilliant.

"This is my friend Captain Resnick—Miss Crevecoeur, Miss Bramble, Mr. Ewbank—our host—Captain Resnick."

"How do you do," said Eleanor.

"Well, I see you've gotten into the army. I guess I'll have to be getting in," said George.

"You will not! With all those French hussies over there? Fat chance!" said Eleanor.

"Well, I don't know. Fellow has to sort of do his duty. Don't you think so, Resnick? That's the way I feel about it, anyway. Do his duty. Guess I'll have to be getting into the army. Not drafted yet, but I guess I'll have to get in," said George Ewbank.

"Yes, I guess we all have to do our bit," said Lafe.

"Yes, you can't duck it. I'm an ardent pacifist, but I'm convinced it's up to all of us—way things are, I mean, with what Germany stands for and all—to do our bit, *now*, I mean," said Pat Bramble.

"You're all idiots. But I suppose I do understand what you mean. But I'm agin it," said Ann.

"Now, Ann dear, this is no time, things being what they are, to be flip about the war. It's a big beastly job that we've got to do," said Eleanor.

"Yes, that's the way I look at it. Got to do our bit. I mean—I'm a dues-paying, card-carrying party Socialist, but I guess with the situation what it *is*, we all got to carry on and finish up the job," said Lafe.

Ann was delighted that Lafe fitted in so well with these old friends, that presently he sat beside Pat, held her hand and flirted gayly—but not meaning it, of course!—and that they seemed to like him. She began to make him do his tricks. "Tell us the story about the obstetrician and the professor of agriculture," she begged, and "Listen! Captain Resnick insists Russia will go Communist this year. Tell 'em about it, Lafe."

When she went out with Eleanor to serve dinner (the best cold turkey and salad and pickles from the delicatessen on Sixth Avenue), Eleanor gurgled, "My dear, he's lovely. But he's a nervous devil, isn't he! But he's awfully keen. And sweet. Are you very chummy with him?"

"Fairly so. Yes."

"Thinking of—— Where the dickens is that cranberry sauce? Damn that cat, it's been at the turkey! Are you and he thinking of marriage?"

"Oh, no. Not really. I'm like you. I think this marriage bond is just a superstition. I wouldn't want to bind him even if he wanted it." And privately, "Let him try and get away!"

At one o'clock, Lafe was calling them all by their first

names, he had kissed Pat and Eleanor—Eleanor gasped and wilted and grew blank of eye—and he had sat at the piano for an hour, playing Gilbert and Sullivan.

As he put Ann on the subway, Lafe yawned, "They're a nice bunch, darlink. Even George, even if he is a little dumm. It'll be great to have 'em come stay with us some day. When we have a cottage on Cape Cod. Gee, think of it—early morning and fog over the beach and the ocean and you and me—rush out for a dip before breakfast!"

"Yes!"

They came to the end of their ten days, and next morning he would take train for Camp Lefferts, in the Pennsylvania hills. They had all night, at the Edmond. She had told the head-resident at the settlement that she was going out to Connecticut for the night.

She awoke at dawn. Lafe's arm was about her, his cheek against her shoulder, and he breathed placidly. She slipped softly from bed and smiled down on him—the unbuttoned jacket of his screaming saffron pajamas, the olive tinting of his chest, his arm that, once she had crept from its encircling, lay with the pajama-sleeve drawn above the soft dark inside of his elbow. His relaxed hand, palm up, was curved, and never free from a slight twitching. But, she thought proudly, he seemed so much less drawn and anxious than when she had met him. How strange his slimness, the young oriental prince in that absurd bed of rumpled cotton sheets! Probably the bedstead was of imitation brass, if there was such a thing as imitation brass!

She crept to the window, looked out on the street, which was crowded with still emptiness. Summer, summer dawn, and her lover there, dreaming of her embrace. The pavement below her smelled fresh from early sprinkling. A milk-wagon horse clopped amiably down the street.

Gramercy Park, to her right, had not, in 1917, yet been overwhelmed with apartment houses; Madison Square Garden, to the left, not become a cemented haunt of civic righteousness; there was neither American Legion flagpole nor communistic rallies, only ragged, contented trees under which, on worn benches, slept the tramps. Trees! A lover, she thought, should have trees about her to symbolize her love, its sturdiness and endurance at the trunk, its delicate pattern of fantastic twigs for fulfilment. Across the street from her was a lone elm, sunk in cement. It was drooping and many boughs were withered, yet its green was gallant, and since it was alone, with no vulgar forest to mock it, it was to Ann a Forest of Arden, bright glades, dim copses, song and feasting. The sun was coming up, joyous on a drab gray house across the street. Summer and sunlight and a tree and her lover sleeping! She smiled round at him, smiled out on the street, and halted, the smile dried and her eyes fading. She had heard the distant marching of men, *clump*, clump, *clump*, clump, *clump*, clump, and suddenly it was not summertime or lovers' time but only war.

That *he* should have to face the black horror—he, the quick and overstrung! She remembered, with sad anger at herself, that she had been irritated sometimes by his neurotic jumpiness. He was afraid of dogs, the best-natured fawners, sure that they would bite him. He was doubtful about cats—said they had malicious eyes—and afraid of crossing through street traffic, of the murky thundering subway, of taxicabs on a skiddy wet day.

Absurd! Why couldn't he try to be a little stolid, like an Adolph? But that such an over-tempered blade should be ground between boulders . . .

(And she loved him so! She hadn't known she could love with such flooding surrender.)

It was the abomination of desolation. Again she saw him —*there:* They had trotted out in an attack. Bitter gas, searing the tissue of their lungs, swept over them—over Lafe—blinding him to the horrors of moldy corpses, riven stumps, smashed motor trucks. The gas was a threshing scorpion in his lungs. (She felt it, whimpered with it.) He stumbled, slid down a shell-crater, fell over a rotting body. It was too steep; he could not crawl out; could not escape this body of death. He wailed, unheard. Then, overhead, an aëroplane with the German crosses on its wings crept snail-like through the upper air, dropping bombs in a trail that came nearer, nearer——

"Oh, I can't! I won't let him!" she screamed.

She turned aghast toward the bed. She had awakened him.

"What's the matter? What was that noise?" he said nervously.

"Oh, oh, nothing. Just somebody—newsboy, I guess— down on the street!" (How swiftly Love taught to lie!)

"Eeeeeuh! Golly I'm sleepy! Come on, sweet, crawl back in. Oh, God! I forgot. It's today I go to camp. To the gallows! My last night in the death house! Any day, then, they may ship us to France!"

She was as angry as she could make herself—but not for herself, only to brace him. "It's scarcely complimentary to call a night with me a night in the death house!"

"Oh, I didn't mean—— You know——"

"And besides! You've got to stop writhing, making yourself scared and miserable! Simply lack of decent inhibitions. You look here, my boy! If you don't stop your exhibitionism, I'll come to camp and I'll march you out on the parade ground by the ear, before your colonel and all, and tell them I've come to take you back, and I'll set you at gardening in the suburbs, and you'll hate that worse than being a hero!"

She succeeded in getting a thin smile from him, and promptly she herself broke. She clung to him, sobbing, and now first it was that he forgot himself in comforting her. Her head on his breast, he soothed her. "We'll sleep a little while yet, beloved. Don't have to get up and pack till seven. Must be early. Sleep, and forget what a yammering brat I am."

And she might have slept, but looking through the curtained double door into the parlor of the suite, she saw the majolica coffee set she had bought for him in Italiantown. "We'll use it this morning, and then not again, maybe never again," she agonized to herself, and kissed him desperately, so that he altogether awakened and was too conscious of her nearness to sleep again.

She crossed the ferry with him and saw him off at the Baltimore & Ohio station—not a swift express, not a vociferous troop-train, but a vulgar local, with half a dozen detached soldiers taking it.

She met a girl she knew, Tessie Katz, young, vibrant, hook-nosed, handsome, a fur worker who sat about the Corlears Hook Settlement and often brought her troubles (mostly amorous) to Ann. Tessie was also seeing off her hero, a round-faced young man like a bartender, with corkscrew curls and a foolish mustache. Tessie hung on his shoulders and wailed, till she noticed Ann. She had always seemed to regard Ann as one of the vestal virgins, and her dramatic sorrows did not keep her from watching Ann and Lafe with thrilling wonder.

It was embarrassing. But Ann forgot it, for Lafe was clinging as desperately as a child. "You'll write me every day, Ann? Twice a day! You'll give me your blessings? Listen! I won't whine. Honestly, I don't, among the men. They think I'm a blinkin' little man of granite. It's just your darling sympathy that makes me let loose. Off, now! At it! And back with a Cross of the Legion of Honor— back to you!"

"All abooooooard!"

"God keep you, dear!" Ann fled, not looking around, not daring to betray her smeary eyes.

But as she rested, leaning against a pillar, Tessie Katz caught up with her.

"*Hel*-lo, Miss Vickers! I didn't know you had a fellow, too! Gee, he's a swell-looking guy! The real kolinsky! And a captain! My!"

"Why, how do you do, Miss Katz! Were you seeing someone off, too?"

"Yeh, my boy friend. He's just a privut, but lissen, that bozo is full of pep. He'll be a sergeant or captain-general or something before this man's war is over. Say, he isn't the fellow I was telling you about last month. *That* poor fish! He was just a big bum. But Morris, he's a peach. He's going to marry me, just soon's he gets back."

Ann Vickers did not feel that her own love, her own grief, was burlesqued by Miss Tessie Katz's tragedy. Tessie was her friend, her sister. The two young women clung arm in arm, and murmuring together climbed painfully to the top deck of the ferry-boat.

Only for a minute was Ann the superior uplifter again. "Tessie, I think—you know how they all gossip around a settlement house—I think I'd just as soon you didn't say anything about my seeing Captain—seeing the Captain off."

"Sure, you bet your life, Miss Vickers. None of their business. What they don't know won't hurt 'em none. And—— Oh, my God, how I am going to miss that bum, Morris, and maybe him getting shot to pieces!"

They held hands and wept, shamelessly, under the summer sun.

16

Ann fancied that her ten days of truancy had made the Corlears Hook House staff, especially the plump and polite head-resident, suspicious, and she flew at her work. It was not her conscience alone that quickened her. She felt keener, gayer, more whole and fulfilled than ever in her life, and more capable of driving herself, of driving others. Her patchwork of little neighborhood tasks seemed to take on some purpose and point, though exactly what the point was she did not know.

She persuaded a Broadway manager to help the Corlears Dramatic Association produce a neighborhood revue, and it had a success not yet known in any activity of the settlement. They repeated it four times, and orthodox parents who had been doubtful about permitting their young to go to Corlears House now regarded it as next in importance to *Schule*.

The credit went to the Broadway manager, who had spent one hour on the scheme, to Ann Vickers, who had spent perhaps ten hours, to the head-resident, who had spent none at all, and not to the native authors, nor to the cast, who had worked from 8 P. M. till three in the morning every night for a month. This taught Ann the art of being an executive; of not wasting her time on little speeches, and giving little advices to the unfortunate, and addressing envelopes—envelopes!—but of getting an improbable idea and smiling on the underlings who sweat blood to carry it out.

She got great glory with the head-resident and began now to be regarded, therefore to regard herself, as a driver, a leader, a person whose opinion on anything—taxation, alcohol, immortality, the best hotel at Atlantic City, or the morality of short skirts—was valuable, and to whom any large and vague job could be entrusted.

But she was not quite lost in the slough of politics and success and impressiveness. She laughed a little that her new vitality should be due to such relations with Captain Resnick as could scarcely be confessed in the liberal but strictly chaste confines of a settlement house.

And she was living all the while not in her success but in letters from Lafe.

For three weeks he wrote every day; he wrote of his colonel's comic breeches, which stuck out behind like a bustle, and of his adoration for Ann; he wrote that he was reading Napoleon's campaigns, and that when he went to sleep he could see nothing behind his closed lids save the curve from her shoulder to her breast; that he had hiked with his men twenty miles, and that he had imagined, every step, that he was tramping with her through the Salzkammergut.

Her own letters to him were a little longer. But then, of course, he was busy, as menfolk must always be.

When he had packed, on their last morning at the Hotel Edmond, he had said, "Look! I'll have the porter send you down this Japanese kakemono and this complete Goethe and the coffee set you gave me. Can't use 'em much in a dugout! You keep 'em for me. Will they remind you of me a little when I'm so far away, my darling?"

They had actually come, and when Ann opened the box she found hidden among them Lafe's disreputable old red slippers, the very lines of his feet in the welter of wrinkles. She sobbed over them. They were dearer infinitely than the bleak handsomeness of the morocco-bound Goethe. She hid them among her lingerie, and daily she took them out.

One afternoon she invited Tessie Katz to have coffee with her out of the majolica cups, and the two girls, the volatile city Jewess and the small-town Mid-Western Nordic, forgot all differences as they contested for chances to talk about Morris and Captain Resnick.

After three weeks, Lafe wrote only every other day—then twice a week—then once a week.

He had insisted, in New York, that she must spend a week-end in Pennsylvania as soon as he could find a comfortable inn near Camp Lefferts. He seemed never to find the comfortable inn.

For ten days she had no letter, and when one came it was all about discovering an amiable Jewish family in Scranton, not far from the camp. He had had a day and night's leave and spent it with the new friends. The Birnbaums. The father, lawyer and bank-director; clever, scholarly,

sometimes funny, imitating Pennsylvania Dutch. The
cooing mother, who fed him goose. The daughters, Leah
Birnbaum, twenty-two, and little Doris, nineteen.

Such darlings, clever, etc., swell—Leah is simply a wiz at
chemistry, and golly that does get so much farther down into
the sources of human life than all our darn old sociology, etc.,
doesn't it—you would just love them!

"I would not!" remarked Ann and, after she had read
the letter over again, "Oh, she does, does she! Leah! With
her damn smelly test tubes!" Five minutes afterward,
when she was ironing out handkerchiefs, she stopped
aghast. "A day and a night! He could have come up to
New York. I'm going down and see—— No, my beloved,
I can't come to you till you say you want me!"

He had been gone for ten weeks, and for another ten
days she had had no letter. She made bountiful excuses; of
course he was insanely busy; training, marches, musketry.
But—— She had had only two letters in eighteen days.
No excuse deleted the fact.

Ten weeks? Ten years!

Only by violently calling on her conscience and will did
she keep up her new energy. "What's the matter? You
look a little frazzled," said one fellow worker and another.

In mid-afternoon, she was racing through the main-floor
corridor of the settlement house, between a committee on
the prevention of cruelty to abandoned cats and the circle
for making bandages for the Red Cross, when Tessie Katz
stopped her. She had not seen Tessie in three weeks. She

was alarmed. Tessie's lips and fingers were twitching like palsy.

"Why, Tessie! Not at work today? You're lucky. What is it, my dear? You look worried."

"Oh, my Gawd, Miss Vickers, I am worried! Worried ain't no word for it. Look, Miss Vickers, I got to talk to you, I just got to!"

"Couldn't you wait till this evening?"

"I can't wait! Honest, I'll go bugs if I don't find out! Can't I see you a minute? Now!"

"Come in my office. Or shall we go up to my room?"

"Oh, I'm scared to death somebody will butt in. Can't we go somewhere where nobody will horn in? Please, Miss Vickers, please!"

"Well—let's try Clubroom D. Nobody there, this hour."

Clubroom D had piles of folding chairs and collapsed card-tables, a couple of highly fretted emerald-green easy-chairs presented by an enthusiastic Grand Street dealer, a cupboard of dishes, and a gas-stove in a curtained alcove. The room was barren as a country railway station, yet warm with the memory of a thousand Kaffeeklatsches, a thousand interchanged confidences of Jewish and Italian matrons about their American grandchildren.

Tessie did not wait for the revered Miss Vickers to sit down; she slopped into an armchair, pressed her fingertips into her eyes, and sobbed.

"Stop it! Unless you want people to come in. Now, what is it? Don't be afraid of me, Tessie. Nothing'll shock me. Especially not in wartime. I know how it is," said Ann briskly.

"Gee, oh, gee, Miss Vickers, I guess maybe you guess

—— Oh, Gawd, and I was so careful! I'm going to have a kid. That dirty Morris! I'll claw his eyes out! He ain't written to me, not one word, for a month."

"Are you sure?"

"It's over two months now. And my boss will fire me— he's awful' strict—he's a swell boss—he never tries to make none of us girls. But it's my Dad I'm scared of. Oh, Gawd, Miss Vickers, honest, he'll kill me!"

"Want to marry Morris?"

"That *Mamzer!* Oh, I wouldn't mind. But I guess he's got a new girl and he'll tell me—oh, gee, you don't know how violent that guy gets—he'll tell me to go jump in the lake! If I only had a fellow like yours! But it's my Pop. We're orthodox, and Morris, he ain't hardly better than a Goy. Honest, if I was to marry him, Pop would come after us both with a shotgun. And if I was to have a kid without marrying, he'd come after me with a coupla guns!"

She was trying to be humorous. Her voice cackled with the effort. She even smiled sweatily. But Ann could not smile back. Tessie's brittle, anæmic youth was gone already, in ten weeks. Her hair was stringy and dribbled out in greasy locks under the brim of her cheap, smart pink hat, and in her cheap, smart near-silk stockings were long runs through which peeped black hairs. She looked forty, and ill, and abandoned.

Ann flitted across to sit on the arm of Tessie's chair, to smooth her shoulders, and there was more tenderness than usual in the cool, professional voice by which a social worker protects herself from the agony of too much sympathy:

"It's hell, Tess. I understand. What can I do?"

"I got to get rid of it, somehow. I've tried exercising and running up and down stairs till . . . I fainted, this afternoon, just after I run up five flights to our fur loft. I guess I got to have a doctor do something. A girl told me about one, but he's a stinker. You got to find the name of a good one for me!"

Instantly, in ten seconds, Ann skimmed through the whole subject of abortion and came out convinced. . . . Life demanded that normal women bear children, without the slightest consideration of the laws passed by preachers, or by small-town lawyers in legislatures. But these laws still remained. And society punished by a lifetime imprisonment in the cells of contempt any girl who was false to them and still true to the life within her that was the only law she knew. Then it was as righteous for a girl thus threatened to flee from her neighbors' spitefulness as it was for a revolutionist to flee from the state's secret police.

"Yes," said Ann. "I'll find someone. Got any money?"

"Not a red. And I dassn't borrow."

"I have a little. I don't need it. Come see me tonight—no, tomorrow evening."

"Oh, Gawd, you been nice! I wish I was like you, Miss Vickers. See you tomorrow evening. Be good!"

Already hysterically gay as she had been hysterically frightened, Tessie skipped out by the basement entrance of the settlement house, stopping to repair her streaked make-up.

Ann Vickers tramped slowly up to the clattering slate floor of the main corridor. Her knees felt watery, and her back was raked by claws of pain. Each dragging step sounded flat and dull on the carpetless stairs as the drum of a funeral cortège. She did not go to the Red Cross Circle. She trudged ever more wearily, often stopping with one hand on the balustrade, one on her back, to the second floor, to the third, and down the unending hallway to her room.

She opened the door, closed and locked it. She stood bowed as in contrite prayer, her arms drooping lifelessly beside her.

"'Wish I was like you, Miss Vickers!'" she groaned, in bitter caricature of Tessie Katz; then, "I've got to face it. Ten weeks. There's no doubt. But—*me*—Ann Vickers! And I can't even write to Lafe that I'm going to have a baby, unless he shows some sign that he wants me. I don't know what to do!

"And my 'social work'—oh, that's all ended, of course."

17

Just as it is felony to help a condemned murderer cheat the state of its beloved blood-letting by passing poison to him, so that he may die decently and alone, with no sadistic parade of priests and guards and reporters, so is it a crime to assist a woman condemned to the tittering gossip that can be worse than death by helping her avoid having what is quaintly known as an "illegitimate baby" —as though one should speak of an "illegitimate mountain" or an "illegitimate hurricane." A physician who keeps a rich woman abed and nervous is a great and good man; a physician who saves a girl from disgrace is an intruder who, having stolen from society the pleasure of viciousness, is rightly sent to prison. It is, then, difficult for respectable people to find an abortionist; it is only the notoriously sinful who are rewarded for their earnest cultivation of vice by being able to find ways out of its penalties.

Had Ann been a pickpocket or a professional gambler, she would have had no difficulty in unearthing an abortionist on whom she could depend to care for Tessie Katz. Being an industrious servant of humanity (at something like a quarter the salary of a good insurance saleswoman

and a tenth that of a pleasantly bawdy actress), it was as
hard for her to get information about abortionists as
about unclaimed diamond mines. She whispered to fellow
settlement workers, she hinted to Dr. Malvina Wormser,
and it was not till she remembered that Eleanor Crevecoeur was happily living in sin that she found the address
of the savior. (Eleanor had six addresses of what were
called "specialists," guaranteed to be careful, cheap, and
discreet, all neatly noted down, with telephone numbers,
in her little black book.)

It was a youngish Italian doctor on East Broadway who
was most recommended. Ann called on him and found him
brisk, chuckling, cinematographically professional with
his quirked mustache and tiny beard.

"I, uh—I want to speak to you very privately," hesitated Ann, feeling rustic, not at all like the crisp social
worker. In the curtained fastnesses of the consulting-room
(where no one overheard them save the doctor's nurse, his
secretary, and a fellow savior, comfortably awaiting him
behind the curtains) Ann ventured, "Doctor, I'm a resident at a settlement house. There's a poor girl there, just
a working girl, on low wages, who—well, she got into
trouble. The man won't marry her, and her parents would
turn her out. It would be a great mercy to help her. Of
course she has no money, but I'd—I don't get a high
salary, but I'd see you were paid, and right away, if you'd
make it reasonable."

The doctor yelped with laughter. (He was a kindly
person, who was supporting three relatives in America
and five in Italy. He played the clarinet and was a cham-
pion swimmer.) He stood over Ann's chair, caressed her

shoulder, and insinuated, "Now, now, little girl! You don't have to be shy with the doctor. That's our business! Wartime—I know how it is. Maybe I'll go over to the Piave myself—and Lord knows how many angry girls I'll leave behind! Sure—wartime—perfectly normal, darling— and you look like a grand sweetheart! When did you have your last period?"

"When—— I tell you, it's *not* myself! How could you! Ridiculous! I tell you, it's a Jewish girl who's one of my charges."

"And you're going to pay for her, on a reformer's salary? Hmmmm. Well, you'll have to—even docs have to live, you know—I'll have to ask you to pay for her in advance."

"Very well. How much?"

"Why—why—— Well, fifty dollars is the very least I can do it for, and that's pure charity."

"Very well. When shall I bring her? (I'll have the money with me.) And how much would it cost you to keep her here or some safe place for three or four days afterward, so there won't be so much danger?"

"Ten dollars a day. Got a fine room upstairs. That includes a nurse, part-time, and I'll keep a close eye on her, just like she was my own sister. Sure, I'll do her a fine job. You'll be satisfied—why, sure, I betcha you'll be sending me all the girls from the settlement. You're a fine educated young lady—I could tell, the minute you come in—I was just joking about thinking it was you and not the Yid."

Ann staggered as she walked to the subway. Curious how faint she felt sometimes, these days.

When she had gone to the doctor, she had had a notion
of engaging his services not for Tessie alone but for herself.
Impossible! Impossible!

It was no physical fear. She was certain that the little
scoundrel of a doctor would be skillful, but even if it had
been dangerous, she would have had no physical fear.
She did not worry about dying now. It would be so lucid a
solution of her disgrace if she died. But it would be intolerable to her dignity as a social worker, as a physician
to fretted souls and aching purses, to submit herself to
that jocular little quack.

She had been assuming these past days that of course
she would imitate Tessie. Perhaps that way out was closed.

Suicide?

But she could only say the word to herself. "Suicide."
It was only a word, fantastic, meaningless, like "abra-
cadabra"; it was not an act that she could imagine the
busy Ann Vickers humorlessly performing. To fuss about
solemnly stuffing silly wads of paper into door-cracks and
turning on the gas! To put on her best nightgown and
carefully shoot herself in the forehead! Nonsense.

"Either I haven't got enough imagination or too much
I dunno!"

Have her baby, then! Be disgraced! All right! Change
her name and take the baby and get an honest job washing
dishes!

"Yes, it sounds so easy," she jeered at herself. "But how
would you like washing dishes, for keeps! And you might
not even be good at it!"

Oh, dear Lord! What escape for a woman who had been
such a fool as to forget her dignity and egotism and grant

her whole self to another human being; who had been so
naïve as to believe the sages meant it when they preached
that love was a greater way of life than hard insensibility or
giggling coyness; who took seriously the myth that *Tristan
and Isolde* and *Romeo and Juliet*, and the Song of Solomon,
as duly read in all Protestant pulpits, were loftier than
the saws of Polonius? What way out for a woman who had
apparently been created by the Lord God Almighty in
accordance with His regular biological principles, and not
by a Y. W. C. A. secretary?

Tessie's operation was (unlike some of them, Ann had to
admit) safe and competent. In a week she was back at
work, a little silent, her rouge standing out more than
formerly on her drained cheeks, but rescued from her
sentence of social death.

They became friends, Ann and the fur worker. Tessie
had learned many unholy and fascinating things from the
Italian doctor and his lively nurse. Ann discovered from
her (not looking at Tessie, as she listened, but bending
over the majolica coffee set) that abortion was impossibly
dangerous after the fifth month.

And she was three months into peril now.

She had not had a letter from Lafe Resnick for a fortnight, and then only a meretriciously jolly anecdote about
a drunken colonel, and a hint of further intimacies with
the Birnbaums . . . what a shrewd old advocate the father
was, what lovely girls Leah and Doris.

There was no hint as to when he might be ordered to
France, as to when he might be coming through New York.

"I must see him! I'll go to the camp! Perhaps he's

wondering why I don't come—thinks I don't want to,"
she fumed, for the hundredth time and, for the hundredth
time, "Oh, he's not such a shy bud. He's not so inarticulate. He'd let me know."

But with all her agonizing, Ann admitted that she had
never felt so full of well-being. She could work fourteen
hours a day. Contempt now for good repute among the
settlement workers made her more daring and vigorous.
She found a merchant who had gone through the stages
of being poor and Jewish, and well-to-do and anti-Jewish,
into the supreme stage of being wealthy and patronizingly
pro-Jewish, and persuaded him to set up a camp for the
Jewish Boy Scouts on his Long Island estate. (To this day,
did they but know her name, Ann would be cursed by
neighboring Long Islanders, Jewish and Gentile, who woke
up betimes to discover the descendants of Gideon palming
up water from the fountain on the lawn, and singing, without inhibitions, "Dere's a Long, Long Trcll A-windink.")

She taught the girls at the settlement house to clean
their classrooms properly. She ruthlessly discarded the
pure elderly gentlewoman who had been teaching Sex
Hygiene and replaced her with a flippant young woman
who knew something. (All the settlement workers, especially the head, were volubly shocked by this harshness,
and greatly relieved to lose the elderly gentlewoman.)

There were murmurs that the head-resident was going to
retire, to be succeeded by Ann.

She heard it grimly. Before then, she would be an outcast.

She escaped from the prying friendliness of her fellow
workers and dined alone whenever she could.

On an evening some fifteen weeks after she had seen Lafe off on the train, Ann dipped into the basement of the Brevoort, for dinner by herself. The basement, with its French aspect of mirrors along the wall, was humming with literary talk, but Ann did not know authors and editors. She felt secure as she took a small wall-table in the middle room. With pleasantly vulgar anticipation she ordered the larded loin of beef, the snails, the Haut Sauterne. She raised her head, tapping the edge of her menu on the table, thinking of how to wangle free textbooks and a cheap teacher for the class in Elementary Russian, consisting of two cloth-hat-and-cap workers and a venerable Christian atheist. Then her clouded vision cleared sharply. She went cold. Out from the welter of unknown faces leaped that of Captain Resnick.

But he had on his shoulders not the twin bars of a captain but the gold leaves of a major. And he was dining, *tête-à-tête* and far too absorbed to have seen Ann enter, with a girl who was all white silk, young flesh, and hair of black glass.

It was so disastrous that Ann felt nothing at all.

She pronged out her snails like a solemn little girl playing with shells in a garden. She did not eat half of them. She solemnly cut her beef, but she did not taste it.

Then Lafe looked up. She did not remember afterward whether she nodded to him, smiled at him, cut him, or, in her embarrassment, all three. He hesitated. He spoke urgently and intimately to the girl opposite him, and plodded toward Ann, a stuffed smile on his face. He leaned over her, kissing her hand in a wonderful imitation of a Spaniard, and bubbled, "Darling! How marvelous! I just got into town half an hour ago. Was going to call you up right away. I had to escort the daughter of a friend of mine —that's her over there—Leah Birnbaum—nice girl from Scranton, but just a kid, of course—promised her father I'd bring her up to town. But I'll drop her at her hotel, and I'll be free after eight—nine at the latest. You *must* come have coffee with us when you finish your dinner. She'll be awfully thrilled to meet you—of course, she's only a kid, just a *Backfisch*, though quite bright for a flapper, and of course I've told her all about you, what a swell uplifter you are and—uh—oh, she'll be *awfully* thrilled to meet you and—— Look! Will you be free after nine—or say nine-thirty, just to play safe? Got to call up some people. Can't you come up to the Edmond then?"

She let him struggle on, without one generous interruption. She answered gravely, "No. That's impossible. But I really must see you. Come down to the settlement house—as late as ten, if you want to. That will give you time to say good-bye to your Leah. Oh, I'm sorry. But will you come, at ten?"

"Well—all right."

She did not join them for coffee. She went out mutely. She was certain, back at the settlement house, that he would be late; but ten minutes before his time he was announced.

"Of course! How rotten my psychology was. He would be early. That gives him something on me," she reflected, as she marched from her office to the main corridor, where he was waiting.

Strange how the face that from the midst of any crowd had shone dear and peculiar, seemed now, among the students gossiping in the corridor, commonplace and indifferent.

"Let's go downstairs. We can talk undisturbed," she said. She led him to Clubroom D, where Tessie had confessed—where she had confessed to herself.

She sat primly in an armchair. (Afterward, reliving it, she was to hate herself for that superior primness. Why couldn't she have been splendid and violent?)

He closed the door and stood as though supporting himself with the fingers of his right hand outspread against the wall. He was almost weeping. "Ann! Ann! What is it? What have I done? I was going to surprise you!"

"You did! (Forgive me!) Please be honest! I can stand it. Are you engaged to that Birnbaum girl?"

"Engaged? Good heavens, no!"

"Then are you and I to be joyously married?"

"I must say, my good woman, that you don't sound as though you were so devilishly keen about it!"

"Are you?"

"Why—yes, I am."

"When? I assume you're on your way to France now."

"Maybe you assume a lot of things that aren't so! Oh, sorry. I just mean—— There's not as much hurry as you think; time enough for us to be sure what we really want to do. You see, I've been transferred to the personnel corps—given a majority; perhaps you noticed!—and I may not have to go to France at all. Anyway, for some months I'll stay at Lefferts."

"Oh! Then of course there could be nothing that would hurry us." She had tried not to sound bitter; she had not

succeeded. "I congratulate you. Though you didn't trouble
to let me know, to write at all."

"I've been awfully——"

"But I do want this straight. I'm not prying—well, not
unusually. I just must know where I stand. You are pretty
fond of Leah, aren't you? (I watched you two.)"

"Oh, yes, in an uncle sort of way——"

"Huh!"

"—but what of it? Single men in barracks, you know."

"Just this of it. I—that is, you and I—are going to have
a baby."

"Oh, my God!"

"In something less than six months now. Well?"

"Oh, I'll marry you! Hell, I'll marry you! I'll keep my
word!"

"That's all I wanted to know. We'll never be married.
Be kinder to Leah! Good-night!"

She fled out of a side door of the clubroom before he
could stop her, fled to her room, prepared to weep, and
didn't. She was suddenly laughing, sitting on the edge of
the bed, smoking an illicit cigarette, feeling free and
resolute. Weep? Why, it was comic! It was all too complete: the picture of the innocent country girl seduced by
the city slicker who became engaged to the heiress and
was reluctant to marry his victim.

Weep the fair frail, distraught and ragged! Bring out
the irate father with the chin whisker and the shotgun!
On the city directory, lettered "Bible" by the stage
carpenter, let swear an oath of "vengeance, by the
Etarnal!" Come the brave country lover, back from
heroism as corporal in the army; let him return in nick of

time with bags of gold, wed her in happy haste and save her from Shame, what time the false Lafayette Ressington met death beneath the vengeful wheels of the Yorktown Flyer!

"That's how I've been feeling! And it wasn't actually any more his fault than mine, and what's funnier, I don't really want to marry him. No!" She plodded to the bureau, drew out his worn red slippers from beneath the ribbon-flaunting lingerie . . . which she had bought for him. She tried to laugh at herself and at the slippers. That was a failure. She hid them in the closet, and it was a moment before she could go on:

"I don't really feel sinful and disgraced. I'm not really going to quit my social work. It was just the tradition in all the novels and sermons. I'm going to have a baby— entirely normal—nothing more to do with my morals and my work than having typhoid, and lots more interesting. Lafe! You gave me love. I've known love! I'm grateful to you. And tonight you freed me from you. Perhaps I'll begin to be a human being, and not an earnest young woman who's taught Sunday school and read Veblen. And I'm going to have a girl baby. It will be such an exciting time for her, this next generation. But—oh, my God, I am so frightened!"

18

Not till midnight, when the party was over, was Ann able to talk with Dr. Malvina Wormser by herself. The gray little doctor bent over the fire, her legs wide apart, elbow on knee, long cigarette holder in her plump hand. Against her venerable frock of coffee-colored silk she wore an old brooch of seed pearls.

"What have you been up to, Ann? You looked seedy a month ago. Tonight you're quite rosy. What's been the sorrow? All any doctor can do is to find out what the patient thinks she has and then encourage her in it."

"Well, I do feel better. I've stopped worrying about the baby I'm going to have."

"The—— Santa Maria! Honestly?"

"Yes."

"Here's a shoulder. Go on and weep. But honestly, Ann, my poor child——"

"No. All the agonizing is over. What do you advise? Shall I have it? Or an abortion?"

"Good Lord!" Dr. Wormser walked smartly up and

down, stamping her tiny high-heeled shoes, hands clasped
behind her, revolving the cigarette holder in her mouth.
"There's no use being melodramatic. But, my good girl,
don't imagine this isn't a serious business. Weren't you
trying to pump me about an abortionist a few weeks
ago?"

"Yes. But not for me. I found one. But I don't think
I could stand him, for myself. . . . We're all so democratic,
we 'socially minded people,' till it comes to the marriages
of our sisters and daughters, or to an operation. Then,
phut! I *wouldn't* do anything for Tessie that I'd do for
myself! No use lying about it! . . . Think you can help me?
Please understand, I don't insist. I don't want you to take
risks."

"Yes. It is a risk. I might get ten years in Auburn.
Plus everlasting disgrace to me—and what's worse, to all
women medics. Funny! Women are the first, the natural
docs. It's they that bind up the baby's finger and plan his
diet; it's they that have patience and endurance. It's they
that take pain seriously, as something that must be gotten
rid of—most men doctors (except Jewish ones, who have
brains!) say that 'pain is perfectly normal, so why worry
about it'—that is, when the pain is in somebody else's
belly—a man doctor is just as scared as any of his patients
when it's in his own belly—worst patient in the world, a
man doc! Yet in the one profession (besides government
and the third one) that's naturally theirs, women are just
tolerated. But I do owe something to that profession and
its principles."

Ann did not listen. Her ears rang. She felt dizzy and
lost. So she was again to be sacrificed, in the good old re-

ligious way, for "principles." She roused sharply to hear
Dr. Wormser grumble:

"But I owe something to you, too. And I think you're
too useful to let this pack of mad dogs that we call 'society'
chase you like a frightened kitty. Now, listen, my child."

Dr. Wormser whirled her chair about, plumped into it,
and, shaking her finger, spoke with unnatural sternness:

"As an unofficial officer of the State, Ann, I must make
it clear that abortion is a crime. Speaking as a physician,
I advise you against having an abortion. It is abnormal
and dangerous. You may never be able to bear a second
child. And every woman ought to bear a child, if only for
the sake of functioning properly. But, speaking as a
woman, I strongly advise you to have the abortion and
keep your mouth shut about it afterward. As long as men
—and what's worse, the female-women that let themselves
be governed by men's psychology—have made our one
peculiar function, child-bearing, somehow indecent and ex-
ceptional, we have to fight back and be realistic about it,
and lie and conceal as much as they do.

"So! I give you my word, I've done only five abortions.
In each case I thought the patient was more valuable to
the world than what I'm pleased to call my honor as a
physician and a citizen. I won't trust you to anyone else.
You will get a ten-days' leave, starting Friday week.
You will report here at 4 P. M.; we'll go out to my little
cottage on Long Island, do the operation there, and you'll
stay there ten days. I won't even take a cook along. I'll
take my pet nurse, Gertrude Waggett. She's fine. Raw-
boned as an Irish wolfhound, silent as snow in winter
woods. You've made me get poetic! She'll stay with you

when I come back to town. Good-night, my child. Four
o'clock, understand, Friday week. Good-night!"

From the station far out on the South Shore of Long
Island they drove to Dr. Wormser's bungalow. It was
September. The trees had faded to leathery brown and
washed-out golden. Ann looked across lifeless marshes to
a leaden sea; the air was fresh and salty, mixed with the
fishy smell of the marsh, but it was chilly, and she shivered. Dr. Wormser was silent; the tall, pinched-faced,
gold-spectacled Miss Waggett was not negatively but
positively, aggressively silent. Ann shivered again.

By a worn and rutted macadam road through swamps
they came on a long sand spit, littered with summer cottages. Doubtless in July they had been gay enough, with
children whooping and phonographs yammering and
brown young men in scarlet bathing suits. Now, the cottages were forlorn to desolation. The windows were
boarded up; the porches empty of bright chairs; the gray
shingle sidings pitted with blown sea sand.

Barren! And what were these two stern women going to
do to her? She was kidnaped. No one to appeal to, in this
wilderness rimmed with salt oozing swamps and shouting
breakers. Leap out now and flee!

"It's pretty quiet, except the waves," she said.

"Yes." Dr. Wormser came out of her trance and smiled,
like a kind and worldly aunt. "I know. Must seem oppres-
sive. Try to like it. If you can relax for ten days, you'll not
only have the operation over but go back renewed. Wise
old alchemists! Elements—earth and air and fire and
water. We lose 'em, in the city; just turn into nerves, and

arteries made of chalk. Don't try to be intelligent, this week. You're not the bright Miss Vickers. You're an erring sister. Splendid! You may become a real leader of women, not a lady reformer. And I've brought you what you really need for mental fodder—sixteen detective stories!"

"I was going to read through what Freud I've——"

"You are not! You're going to read about nice domestic things, like murders and Scotland Yard. Here we are! We'll get the house warm and operate at nine this evening."

"Oh, no, no! Can't we wait till tomorrow?"

"And let you get more scared than you are now? Huh! Funny about you husky basketball girls. More nervous than social climbers, because you don't take it out in hysterics and new frocks. . . . Ann! Darling! It won't be a bit serious!"

Dr. Wormser's cottage faced on rolling ocean, with grassy dunes and endless beach between. It was as simple as the abandoned summer places they had been passing, except for a collection of books miscellaneous as a crazy quilt, a really capacious fireplace, and, off the kitchen, an operating-room and dispensary with white-enameled wainscoting halfway up the wall. "Only decent surgical equipment, or bacteriological either, for fifteen miles," boasted Dr. Wormser. "I do a good deal of practise here in the summer—city people. In the village, there's just one doctor. Old one. Male, of course. How he laughs at 'hen medics'! I'm his favorite supper joke. And his operating table is an adjustable table that looks like a worn-out barber's chair—maybe not so clean! See, here's my fulguration apparatus; here's my closet for reagents and stains and so on. . . ."

As Dr. Wormser prattled, Ann knew that she was trying to be reassuring; to tell her, with insultingly obvious petting, that she would be competently treated. Ann did not listen. There was nothing in her brain or heart save a cold blankness of pain.

There were two bedrooms, with hospitable possibilities in two couches in the living-room. "You'll take this room on the right—looks right out on the ocean. Miss Waggett and I will bunk in the other."

Ann was too numb to protest.

"Now, while Miss Waggett and I heat up some hot water and get the operating-room warm—got an electric stove; regular little Vesuvius, it is—and get us all a cup of tea, you just trot in and put on a nightgown. Miss Waggett has laid out a nice plain one, on your bed. . . . Ann! You do look scared! Rather wait till tomorrow?"

Only primitive terror spoke in Ann's croaking: "No! No! For God's sake, get it over."

"Right! You bet, darling!"

She undressed slowly, dropped the coarse nightgown over her head, and sat on her bed, rather chilly, twitchily lighting a cigarette. She wondered if, in this death-cell in which she had suddenly been trapped, They would let her smoke.

Miss Waggett was in the doorway, in white overall and cap, gauze over her mouth. "All right, Miss Vickers; all ready."

The slow tramp to the gallows.

Relentlessly led into the operating-room, she found a

new Dr. Wormser, also muffled in white, with a new, huge, hideous, and very efficient-looking pair of spectacles owlishly masking her eyes. She was unrecognizably brisk:

"There we are! Now, Ann Vickers, you damn well stop pitying yourself and working yourself up! *You* an officer in the social army? Rats! Why, every Wop mother that you condescend to knows more about reality! And me—do you realize I sometimes do ten majors in a morning, and most of 'em literally a hundred times worse'n yours? Cheer up, honey! Soon done!"

At just what stage they had stopped giving her ether, she could not remember. In her drugged half-sleep, she felt that it was important to remember. And she seemed to recall a moment in which all humanness, all individuality, all self-respect had been lost in a flame of agony, but she could not be sure whether that had happened to her or to someone else. Over these two tremendous lost problems she pondered wretchedly for hours. Or it may have been seconds. Her brain cleared suddenly of fumes, and she opened her eyes on Dr. Wormser standing placidly by her bed, while Miss Waggett, yet more placid, was setting out a tray with a glass of water.

"There we are! All over! Fine!" chirped the doctor.

All over! Life was free to her again, and if this had been a crime, condemned by all respectable nations—such nations as were this moment, in 1917, showing their respectability and hatred of crime by a display of tanks, poison gas, and liquid fire—then she was confused as to what was crime and what were criminals.

(In Tafford county jail she had taken the first step, now

she took the second, on the path which was to lead her into the darkness of prisons in which sensible people shut away from their eyes the agony and tedium of what they call "criminals." To Gene Debs in prison, Jesus on the gibbet, and Savonarola chained to the flames, she now could add Dr. Malvina Wormser as a scoundrel. Later, she would be able to add Tom Mooney, Sacco and Vanzetti, the I. W. W.'s of Centralia, and the eight negro boys of Scottsboro, Alabama. But she did not know this, now, when she still saw America as the only Galahad among the nations, clad in armor of the best stainless steel, and entirely engaged in questing the Sangrael of international peace and holiness.)

With Dr. Wormser gone, and Miss Waggett silent about the preparation of eggnogs and creamed toast, Ann sat all day, all week, snuggled in most feminine and domestic pink comforters in a deck chair on the porch. From the operation itself, she was recovered in two days, and could have gone home. It was from the wound of futility that she was recovering. She did not see the breakers—to see, they were just a bit monotonous, breaker after excited breaker, as unoriginal and as noisy as a series of politicians. If she did not watch the ocean, she felt it. She had leisure to forget her fussy tasks and be part of the greatness of the earth.

For days she puzzled over her unromantic romance. She did not feel at all "ruined," nor could she get up much pleasant indignation against her "betrayer," against men in general, or against society. She was rather sorry that she probably never would experience the melodrama of being "ruined"; no parent calling upon God to punish her or casting her forth into the tempest with the baby under her threadbare shawl; no deacon of an employer making an example of her; no prospect of illness and starvation while, in an attic through which the winter blast whistled from broken windows, she actively sacrificed herself for the Child of Shame.

That did seem a more stirring life than sitting at her settlement-house desk planning a class in Commercial Arithmetic.

She sat wondering how many other traditionally dramatic situations would, under the bleak light of reality, lose their horrible splendor. . . . Did wartime heroes really hate the fiendish enemy as much as they did salty beef or crabbed officers? And when they were dying in the muck, did they really rejoice such a lot at giving up their lives for their several kings and countries? Were any traditions sound? Did judges always consider their duties as sacred, or did they sometimes, like a schoolteacher slapping an annoying pupil, yield to personal malice? Were Americans always generous and neighborly, Germans always efficient, Englishmen always honorable, and Frenchmen always logical?

Those queries were not to Ann disturbing. From 1890 to 1926, all bright young men and women were expected to engage in a liberal social criticism that was "drastic but sane"—i. e., never carried into action. Through all that generation, the bright verbal violences that had become correct in the early days of Bernard Shaw were favored in middle-class society. It was the period when the sons of senators and the grandsons of bishops spoke with loving anticipation of the rather vaguely dated millennium when "the last king should be hanged with the entrails of the last priest." As the Mid-Victorian age was serene in its assurance that all vicars were pure and many of them intelligent, that all royal princes had good manners, and that Turkey red Brussels carpeting was a handsome floor-covering, so, two generations later, the "intellectuals" were so touchingly free from complexities that they believed all bankers spent their midnights plotting to make the poor poorer; that all members of Congress and Parliament received enormous bribes and invariably died in palaces on the Riviera; that all ministers of the gospel, especially small-town Baptists, kept mistresses in gaudy apartments; and that all socialist agitators devoted themselves exclusively to the cause of mankind and rejoiced in living on bran and cold water.

"Well, but roughly speaking, all those things *are* true!" protested Ann. "Only it's not quite so simple. Is that going to be the next intellectual hurdle; to expect radical propagandists to stop being as simple-minded and obvious as a Missouri evangelist? Wasn't it nice when we all believed that if we just voted the Socialist ticket, then bubonic plague would cease, and husbands would never leer at stenographers, and wheat would always grow forty to the acre, and every child would get his D. Sc. in biophysics at the age of six!"

She began to question the certainties of radicalism as harshly as she had the certainties of respectability. What had she accomplished as a social worker at Corlears Hook? Had she given the youngsters of the neighborhood anything they could not find at the public schools? Would the vote for women really, as she had once prophesied from soap-boxes, lessen crime, assure food and education for all children, and expert medical attention for all child-bearing mothers, and induct hundreds of splendid women states-men into public life, so that by 1930 the country would have scores of women senators and cabinet ministers scarcely distinguishable from Joan of Arc?

Were the statistics-stuffed and liberal-minded social workers whom she met at Corlears House really capable of instituting a vastly better system of government than the greedy and cynical politicians of Tammany Hall and Republican headquarters?

Was she certain only that she could not be so certain of anything as in the good old days; that in the grammar of social science, all the triumphant Therefore's had been replaced by But's?

Then she forgot it in attention to the narcotic detective story which Dr. Wormser had recommended.

In her earlier apprehension of being disgraced, Ann had thought solely of her own dilemma. Neither she nor the realistic Tessie Katz had been so imaginative as to give much heed to the rights of the coming babies. Now, un-reasoningly, her baby became a reality to her, and she longed for it, wistfully, then savagely, accusing herself of its murder. It became an individual; she missed it as though she had actually nursed it and felt its warmth. She began to want it more than she wanted any career, or the triumph of any beautiful principle.

It would have been a girl. "How did she know? Oh, she just *knew*, that was all! Trust a mother to know things like that! Instinct. Something beyond the cookery of science! And how splendid! For this coming generation belonged to women." Let's see (she mused): if the baby had been born early in 1918, it would have been only forty in 1958. By that time, the world might be all one nation; it might all be communized; it might be shattered again into little warring monarchies. Helicopters might be common as motorcars now, or might be forgotten in a waste of dead civilization. Whatever happened her baby would see—no! she sighed, her baby would have seen—as many dizzy changes in forty years as had happened in any other two centuries.

The baby took shape. She would have her Grandfather Vickers's black hair. (Ann refused to credit the hair to Lafe.) She would see that the baby had a healthy body. She should be educated in character, first of all; in integrity. And, in a world where professional castes might vanish along with individual wealth and rank, she should learn to use her hands; not be humbled in comparison with the honest skill of washerwomen and cooks and carpenters and machinists.

The joy she would have in the baby's education——

Then she remembered, aghast, that she had killed the baby. It would never be there to educate.

Her breasts longed for the baby; her imagination longed for extension of her ego through the baby into a vicarious immortality.

It would be named—— Girl babies had of late been named so meaninglessly: Ann, Dorothy, Lois, Gertrude, Betty. A hundred and fifty years ago names had meant something: ingratiating symbols like Charity, Hope, Faith, and Patience. But dumb patience, dull hope, and hang-jawed faith, these were no longer the only merits of fe-males. No, her girl should be named *Pride*, and pride of life, pride of love, pride of work, pride of being a woman should be her virtues. Pride Vickers—the one person whom Ann was always to see and understand!

Ann was not definitely a mystic. Indeed, she believed that she was hard-minded. Yet from now on, without her realizing it, the personality of Pride Vickers was as real to her as that of any Italian child playing in front of the set-tlement house. She was convinced, without knowing she was convinced, that Pride had not been slain but had only postponed her coming; that when another child was born of her, it would be Pride and only Pride.

Not often did she hear Pride's voice, but it was never utterly forgotten as she went back to a world in which she was the efficient Miss Vickers, of whom it was equally inconceivable that she should be vulgarly "ruined," that she should ever be a mystic, or that she should for a second doubt that the instruction of immigrants' children in Shakespeare, basket-weaving, Swedish gymnastics, and the salute to the flag would immediately produce a sweetly reasonable state.

Seven weeks after her return, the Russian Jewish quar-ter about her went mad with the news of the Bolshevik revolution, and she wondered if Pride might not be des-tined to know this November 7, 1917, as perhaps the greatest date in history; as either the beginning of a good new world, or the end of a good old world.

19

As ANN came into Eleanor Crevecoeur's flat, top floor of a loft building, Eleanor and her temporary husband were quarreling. Eleanor was waving her arms, George Ewbank sitting tight.

"Listen, Ann! Of all the bonehead plays! Listen! George is about due to be drafted. If we were married and I chucked my job, so I'd be a dependent wife, I think he'd probably get out of it. And he won't do it. Oh, the fool says he wants to marry me—he better!—and he doesn't mind supporting me. But he won't ask for exemption."

"Feel a fellow ought to do his bit. Once we set our hand to the plow, we got to keep on till we make a safe harbor. Anyway, that's how I figure it," said the mild warrior.

"But you *do* want to marry me?"

"Hell, you know I do. Didn't I get a license once last year?"

"Well, I won't do it! Marry a man that wants to butt into a war that doesn't belong to him? Mamie Battleaxe was right, Ann. Women, cats, and elephants are the only animals with sense."

But George did go to war, and Eleanor, refusing even during the final flag-waving to marry him, turned to Ann in a panic of loneliness.

Ann had never been much given, professional "social worker" though she was, to pious fussing and intrusiveness; to saving people's souls and correcting their diets and censoring their friends. But now she was called on to be as fussy as a mother hen. Eleanor telephoned to her thrice a week: could she go to the theater, could she drop up for a bite of supper and a Tom Collins?

Ann met the intellectual parasites who frequented Eleanor's place as they did any New York flat which supplied free drinks. After two years in New York, she was as innocent of the "Bohemians," the "Greenwich Villagers," as she had been in Waubanakee. She did not know them even from fiction; her notion of refreshing literature was an article on the Assimilation of Latvian Elements in Southeastern Arkansas. Now she encountered all of them: poetic editors of trade journals; nymphomaniac and anarchistic lady managers of tea-rooms; tramp poets whose hoboing had most of it been done in Italian restaurants about Washington Square; reporters who were continually out of jobs because city editors were jealous of their superior diction; daughters of rich up-town bankers who wanted to paint but were willing to take it out in loving. Ann found herself with fifty new acquaintances who called her by her first name and, to her fury, since she hated to be pawed, kissed her lingeringly—male and female. They were all so opposed to the war that she became a patriot; they were so liberal that she turned Presbyterian; they were so besotted that her innocent pleasure in a bottle of wine became a sour teetotalism. She had singularly little happiness out of shrieking parties where untidy youths and maidens lolled in one another's laps and sat before you, on the floor, feeling your ankle and giving you confidences about their glands. Her use of mouth-wash and bath-salts that month increased a hundred per cent. But she continued to frequent their parties because of an authentic worry about Eleanor.

She was fond of Eleanor. She remembered her making cocoa, and slapping a policeman; scrubbing the Fanning Mansion sink, and quoting Krafft-Ebbing; telling scandalous myths about the doubtful purity of Mamie Bogardus, and walking three miles in a snowstorm to address a dreary little suffrage meeting; shocking Maggie O'Mara by her obscenity, and looking all the time like an anæmic Bourbon princess.

She was conscious that, since George's exit, Eleanor had been having a series of lovers. And just now, in mounting resentment of Lafe Resnick and appreciation of Dr. Wormser, Ann was convinced that she hated all men, and that she was enlisted with the angelic females in war against the male oppressors. She particularly hated the complaisant sweethearts who attached themselves to Eleanor's affections and free gin: an old, creeping, fingering playwright who so deftly repeated the latest from the Club that he seemed clever; an explorer who devoted twenty-three months of lecturing to every one of exploring, and who described insinuatingly the strange marital customs of "native tribes"; and a sweet, gentle, helpful Professional Youth who had for twenty-five years been one of the most promising very young authors and most dependable self-invited guests. Ann did not at first quite believe that these marooners were Eleanor's lovers. With George Ewbank, Eleanor had been as domestic as Tib My Wife. Now she could not be true to any lover for a week. She did not much confide in Ann, whom she considered a sound egg but a bit of a prude. Of Lafe and abortions, Eleanor knew nothing, and she condescended to Ann a good deal.

With a certain nausea, Ann thought of lady dogs in the rejoicing spring. Eleanor was always disappearing into the kitchen with one or another softly attentive new male, and taking fifteen minutes to mix the cocktails. She was always leaving dinner with Ann at the Brevoort to make anonymous telephone calls. But Ann could not find that it was any affair of hers as Eleanor grew jerkier, more voluble and meaningless, and as her sunk eyes looked older.

It was Dr. Belle Herringdean who brought it up.

Isabel Herringdean, Ph. D., known to some two or three hundred intimate women friends and to some six or eight men as "Belle," was an executive of Emmanuel & Co., a department store that was one of the wonders of the ages, occupying in modern New York much the same place as the Parthenon in ancient Athens, but altogether bigger and more practical. At Emmanuel's you could buy a diamond-and-emerald bracelet for $17,000, or an excellent imitation of the same for seventeen cents; you could buy nice Gates Ajar funeral wreaths, cotton socks, saints' statues, joke-books for the use of senators, editions of Apuleius on hand-made Japanese paper, floor mops, canary seed, personal manicure outfits costing $178, overalls, tickets to Cairo via Madeira and Algiers, prunes, genuine Chinese back-scratchers, shoes for plowmen, the autographs of Judah P. Benjamin and Zane Grey, chewing tobacco, imported French hats, goldfish, comic valentines *ætat.* 1870, portable country houses, and pins. There were four thousand employees, and the vice president in charge of packing and shipping was an ex-brigadier general, and over the whole army of them was a Personnel Department to decide which, by the inexorable laws of Behaviorism, was gifted in the matter of ladies' cotton pants, and which conditioned to comprehend mouth-organs.

Ann, first meeting Dr. Herringdean at Eleanor's, had been repelled by her and fascinated. There was something of the sleekness and sinuosity and color of the coral snake in this slim woman. She might have been twenty-eight or thirty-eight; her face, enamel-smooth, imperturbable save for quick-glancing eyes, would never show her age. She wore thin suits, with linen collars and men's ties and tricorne hats, and she stood about listening as though she knew everything better than the speaker, while she did graceful things with a cigarette holder.

They were alone at lunch, Ann, Eleanor, Dr. Herringdean.

"Eleanor," said Dr. Herringdean, "isn't that gent you bowed to—coming out as we came in—a new one?"

"Why, I haven't known him very long. He's a great dear. A lawyer."

"That doesn't necessarily make him a great dear. . . . Dr. Vickers, don't you think——"

"Just *Miss* Vickers."

"Well, 'Miss,' then. Though, as a matter of fact, I'm going to call you 'Ann.' I've heard so much about your grand work at Corlears House that I feel as though I knew

you. And you must call me 'Belle.'" Dr. Herringdean
looked at her with such a smile, wrinkling the corners of her
long eyes, that Ann was unwillingly captivated. "And
don't you think, Ann, that Nell does have the damned-
est men hanging around, now that George is gone? Dear
George!"

"You never called him that when he was here!" said
Eleanor.

"I do now, with these human guinea pigs for contrast.
That explorer of yours! I'll bet there isn't a man living
that's braver at taking chances on Pullman diner grub!
And so informing and illustrative! Can you tell when he's
kissing you like a Maori and when like a Kumasi—nice
and slobbery? Ugh! No man living can make love elegantly
and amusingly. Only women!" Dr. Herringdean reached
out her hand, molded like wax, to stroke Eleanor's thin
claw, and uneasily Ann watched Eleanor yielding to that
warm allurement, that cool impertinence.

Suddenly it seemed to Ann that Dr. Herringdean was
all over the place and on all sides of her at once. She never
went to Eleanor's without finding Dr. Herringdean strad-
dling the fireplace and being cynical—a cynicism which reduced optimists like herself to rusticity. No need now to
worry about the male hallroom-boarders in Eleanor's affections. When Eleanor nipped off to the kitchen with one
of them, Dr. Herringdean would stroll after and be heard
delicately mocking the suitor into clumsiness.

When she could get Ann and Eleanor to herself, Dr.
Herringdean talked of great women friends, of auto-
eroticism, of religious symbology. Before she had taken her
Doctor of Philosophy degree in psychology she had had

three years of medical school, and since then she had apparently read every book on sexual abnormalities.

"Isn't it curious," she complained, "that in 1918, in the age of Freud and ragtime and little war-widows, the view about women, even among women themselves, is still that they are angels, lacking all organs except hearts and lungs and rudimentary brains! I tell you, my dears, that until everybody understands that a girl can be a charming morsel, like a rosebud, and still have a healthily functioning colon, there will never be any actual advance in the position of women. After all, the little dewy rosebud is not unacquainted with slugs and manure, and anyone who is too delicate to recognize it had better stay out of the vulgar garden and go back to tatting!" And Dr. Herringdean was off with some absorbing statistics about the periodicity of passion, which reduced the glory of Juliet to dots on Romeo's calendar.

Ann was worried. There was nothing of this so very new to her. She had learned about a rather foreign, impersonal thing called "sex" in physiology class in Point Royal. She had heard Dr. Wormser talk of prostitutes male and female, of the darknesses behind every silver temple veil. But the wise and comfortable Malvina Wormser seemed as different from the lip-licking Dr. Herringdean as Ann's father from Lafe Resnick. Nicer, she fretted, but weren't they less wise? No, she insisted; less exhibitionistic.

"Look!" she demanded of Dr. Herringdean. "Why need one talk of abnormalities? We're none of us precisely so innocent that we think babies always come from under gooseberry bushes!"

"No, my own dear, but you are so innocent that you

think babies always come! And what do you mean by 'abnormalities'? How can anything that happens so often that you can chart it be called an abnormality? There are savage tribes—oh, that's your little explorer again, Nell!— but anyway: there are savage tribes that believe it is indecent to see anyone eating. We don't think so. And sex, any manifestation of it, is just as normal as eating and digesting food and eliminating it."

"Probably. But we don't sneak close together and lower our voices and talk about food all the time!" insisted Ann. "If we did, it would be a bore. There are fat people who tell you by the hour about the wonderful truffles they had in Dijon and the kidneys they gorged in Barcelona. Do you like them? And besides, normal or not, I'd think that a person who considered eating steak was naïve, and who lived only on curry and Camembert, was losing a lot of fun!"

"Ann, my little darling, I always said there was something theological about social work. You're using the typical preacher's trick of mistaking a metaphor for an argument!"

However discomforted Ann was by Dr. Herringdean's conversational peepshow, Eleanor was enthralled, and under that spell she became frank.

"I agree with you about men, Belle," she said. "They are hogs. I can't get along without 'em——"

"Some day you'll see!"

"—but I detest 'em. The worst of it is that all of 'em combine lechery with a maidenly pretense that nothing is happening. They'll chase you all evening with loose mouths, and you're supposed not to notice. But if you, a woman, are crude enough to hint that you'd like to do what they want above everything, they're shocked. You must have no passions! You must sit and wait for their insinuating coughs, and always be so surprised when you find out what they mean! And if any evening they happen to feel noble and virtuous, and you don't, how shocked they are, how high-minded and cruel, even though you've seen 'em looking foolish in pajamas only twenty-four hours before!"

"Haven't I told you that, all of it, about men?" crooned Dr. Herringdean, strolling over to cup Eleanor's chin with her palm, to tilt back her head and smile down on her.

Ann was uneasy. She was the more uneasy a week later when Eleanor announced that Belle was going to move in and share the flat with her. Yet Eleanor was so jolly, so casual about it, that Ann was ashamed. "Be nice living with Belle," said Eleanor. "Of course she's crazy as a bedbug. Loves to shock people by talking about all sorts of crazy inversions. Even pretends to admire cruelty. But I know her. Actually, Belle is one of the hardest-working, most sensible *femmes* I know. I hope she'll like my new beau. He's a peach—you must meet him—first officer on a transport—grand lad—smashes submarines the way you would mosquitoes. Belle'd *better* like him!"

But Belle apparently did not like him.

A month after she had moved into the loft-building flat with Eleanor, adding to it a closet-full of liqueurs, some scores of pictures of young women undisturbed by modesty, and a bookcase of German books on sex, the cumbersome but hearty males who had been wont to look gap-mouthed after Eleanor were vanishing, and the only men who appeared were languid youths with rouged cheeks.

It was dismaying to Ann to see Eleanor, so independent once at the Fanning Mansion, so acidly lofty with impertinent hecklers, in subjection now to Dr. Herringdean. With edged scoffing Belle slashed through Eleanor's chatter; with cold silence she discomforted the old-time friends of George Ewbank, whom Eleanor tried to hold; and when Eleanor was miserable and almost weeping, with warm caresses Dr. Herringdean restored her. Astonished, Ann watched Eleanor turning diffidently to Belle for approval. And for Belle, Eleanor, who had always scorned feminine prettinesses, began to wear an apricot silk lounging-robe embroidered with black peacocks, and silver mules with pompons.

"You don't appreciate Belle," she wailed to Ann. "She's an initiate. I used to laugh at esoteric wisdoms, but I was a fool. She makes one understand."

"Understand *what*, for God's sake?"

"Everything. Life. Real passion of living. And you needn't use profanity. Belle doesn't like it."

"And this from you, Eleanor!"

When Dr. Herringdean had Eleanor thus reduced, she suddenly became acid to her and turned all her spells on Ann. She crinkled the corners of her eyes at Ann. She patted her. She waved her cigarette holder at her. She purred at her. She told her that she—Ann—had treasures of singularly precious but as yet unnoticed powers of love. And always, smiling, almost winking, she acted as though Ann and she were adults who were secretly amused by the silly child, Eleanor.

Eleanor was daily more haggard, twitching like a drug-addict. Indeed Ann wondered if she was not using drugs, and when she mentioned cocaine she noticed that Dr. Herringdean fell uncomfortably silent.

Eleanor had lost what unobvious beauty had lain, for all her boniness, in shrewd friendly eyes and soft brown cheeks. And didn't the good doctor tell her so, playfully and often, while Eleanor sat and tried to look superciliously amused—her thin nails gouging at the thin flesh under her forearms the while. And when Eleanor followed her about the studio, trying to find out what she had done, so that she might beg pardon, Dr. Herringdean snarled, "Of course, my dear Nell, it doesn't matter, doesn't matter, why must we *talk* about it! Of course you *did* offer to have some supper ready for me when I came home——"

"But you said you'd telephone if you wanted some."

"—came home late, assuming you'd understand, all tired out, and needless to say, no supper. Not a thing. Naturally."

"I'm so sorry! Belle! Darling! I'm terribly sorry! Really I am!"

It was then that Ann interrupted sharply, all in one angry word, "Wellimgoinome!"

Dr. Herringdean cooed at her, "Oh, darlingest, we've been boring you. This *idiotic* discussion! Ittle Annie wun away? Don't, dear! Does it look as though I were going to have a very cheerful evening if you leave? With Nell working herself up to a good old Victorian case of vapors, and maybe swooning, to show how aristocratic she is? Wait, Ann, and I'll go with you."

"No, I must——"

Ann never did finish it. She realized that Eleanor was
looking at her with murderous jealousy in her eyes and
twisting fingers.

Ann was in her office late, at nine in the evening. Dr.
Herringdean telephoned to her:

"Ann! I wish you could come down to the studio. Afraid
something's happened to Nell. I know she's in there—key's
on the inside of the door. She won't answer me. Afraid she's
angry with me. You know what an hysteric she is. I got
home late and——*Key on inside the door!* I'm phoning
from the drug-store. Oh, do come!"

Dr. Herringdean sounded really human.

"But she's probably just sore, Belle. A row?"

"Yes. I'm afraid it was serious." But Dr. Herringdean
chuckled. "Of course I was just teasing her—you know
how I am; Nell, the idiot, takes my fooling seriously. I told
her Vivie Lenoir was not only a hundred times as pretty,
which of course she is, but a lot more enfranchised and——
Oh, Nell was so furious! She actually pushed me out of
the door this morning—*me!*"

"I'll come right away—taxi—meet you at the door of
the flat." Ann had no desire to do anything for Dr. Belle
Herringdean, but she might be able to do something
for Eleanor; might even miraculously show her Belle's
cruelty.

When Ann came, Dr. Herringdean was pacing the slate
floor in front of the door to the apartment. She was coldly
lovely in a leaf-green suit that was more a mockery than an
imitation of masculinity. "I've knocked and knocked!
And hollered! Oh, I'll pull your hair out, Nell, my good

woman!" she snapped. "You try, Ann. Nell trusts you. . . . I mean, she did, at least."

Ann pleaded, shrieked. The apartment door was of steel, without transom. On it she bruised her hands. No answer from Eleanor.

"We've got to get in there! Maybe she's fainted. Perhaps she's *enceinte!*" said Dr. Herringdean.

Ann's desire to murder her that moment was not fanciful or vague. Yet she admired the woman as Dr. Herringdean ran downstairs, shouting back, "We'll bust in through the office below. If we wait to get permission from the janitor, take all night."

On the floor below was an unlighted office with a plate-glass door lettered, "The Dandypack Sawdust & Shavings Corp." Dr. Herringdean listened, stripped off a green slipper with an aluminum heel, smashed the glass, reached in to turn the catch, dashed across the dim office, among astonished-looking pale oak desks and chairs, and raised a window.

Ann hesitated a second at a peculiarly open-looking fire-escape. Dr. Herringdean did not hesitate. She clattered up the iron steps, Ann slowly after her. She jerked open a window of the studio and climbed in, bawling cheerfully, "Nell! Little Nellie!"

There was no sound in answer, nor any sight of Eleanor. They looked into the bedroom, the kitchen, the bathroom. At the bathroom door, Dr. Herringdean stood rigid, screaming, "Oh, my God! Don't come in here!" It was too late. Ann saw. Eleanor was lying in a bath of crimson, with a drying crimson film in waves along the white enamel sides of the tub. A smeared safety-razor blade was on the ledge. Eleanor was looking up at them with scared eyes and drooping lips, like a hurt child, astonished by pain, begging for their help. But her gaze was fixed. It did not change.

At midnight, when the doctors were gone, and the police, except for a patrolman who stood on guard outside in the hall, Dr. Herringdean tumbled on a couch. Her arms flopped down beside her as though they were dead things, unattached to her body. She had not been hysterical. Neither had Ann, but Ann could not copy Dr. Herringdean's cold clarity now. She felt flabby; she was sure she had looked guilty.

Dr. Herringdean sat up, lighted her fiftieth cigarette that evening, spoke abruptly: "Ann! I know it's horribly tragic about Nell. But what really gets me isn't her. Poor woman; her worries are over. It's you. I'm afraid you'll be all cut up about her. Listen! I'm being sent to Europe by the store, to look over methods in Paris and Berlin. Come on along—I'll work you in on expense-account. Come on, little darling! We'll have such a grand time! Basking on the sand, in the *thinnest* bathing-suits, my sweet! Oh, forget Nell! After all, she was a weak, sentimental failure!"

Ann liked to believe, afterward, that she had struck Dr. Herringdean. Actually, she did nothing of the kind. She fled—and awkwardly, apologetically.

Safe in her little room at Corlears House, Ann croaked, with great injustice, "Anyway, I won't hate men again. They're better than that!"

Then for years she forgot men and women both, and in a turmoil of work thought only of those inescapable social problems, Man and Woman.

20

For two years Ann Vickers was the head-resident of a settlement house in Rochester. She was apparently successful; she was invited to address women's clubs, church forums, and girls' schools, on such varied and glowingly meaningless topics as "Methods of Americanization," and "The Value of European Folk Songs in the Education of Immigrants." For there was in Rochester a rich old woman, a benefactor of Ann's settlement house, who was so liberal that she allowed Hungarian gypsies to do Hungarian gypsy dances, providing they were willing to learn meanwhile the operation of National Cash Registers and Ford automobiles. The University of Rochester gave Ann, at twenty-nine, an honorary M. A. degree; and she was sixth on the *Times-Register's* annual list of "The Ten Most Useful Women in Rochester." In her settlement house, one hundred and sixty-seven Europeans learned English, so that they were able to read about murder and adultery in the tabloid newspapers; and two hundred and seventy-one girls learned to sew and cook, so that thereafter they could make their dresses at home, at not more than sixty per cent. above the cost of similar dresses at a depart-

ment store, and for fifteen cents prepare a nourishing vegetable soup for four people which would have cost, at the
very least, ten cents at a chain grocery.

Yet daily, these two years, as well as through her last
year as assistant head at Corlears Hook House, Ann questioned the value of settlement work. It was too parochial.
It touched only a tiny neighborhood, and left all the adjoining neighborhoods that did not have their own settlements, which was most of them, without provision for such
recreation, education, emergency relief, and advice as the
settlement could give. It wasn't, Ann decided, much more
valuable than its parent, the good old heart-warming and
tear-bringing system whereby the elder daughter of the
vicar (the one who had never married) amused herself by
taking coals and blankets and jelly to such of the bed-
ridden parishioners as were most slobberingly obsequious
to the vicar and to the squire.

In the modern version, the settlement house, the gayly
mendacious and clutching Jew boy with the big black eyes,
who brought presents to the workers and who most loudly
bawled the Salute to the Flag at Boy Scout rallies, was the
one who got the extra golf pants and the left-over ice cream
and, later, the scholarship in dental school; while the sullen
boy down the street, who had nothing but a genius for
wood-carving and for minding his own business, got nothing at all.

The settlement house (or so Ann Vickers believed) was
nothing but a playground, much less well managed than
the official city playgrounds. It smelled of the sour smell of
charity. It taught, but it did not teach well. The professional teachers of the city schools were better, and con-

siderably more enduring, than the earnest volunteers (so like the Sunday school teachers of Ann's childhood) who, out of a wealth of ignorance and good intentions, for a year or so instructed the poor Jews and Italians and Greeks concerning George Washington and double-entry bookkeeping and the brushing of teeth. The night schools did it better. The ambitious youngsters—the only ones who were worth the trouble—did it better by themselves.

So far as Ann could see, the virtue of the settlement houses was that they had given birth to such impersonal and trained organizations as Lillian Wald's Visiting Nurses Association, and to modern organized charity.

Oh, there were plenty of faults in organized charity— plenty, Ann sighed. It had too much red tape. Often, complete records of families in distress were considered more important than relieving the distress. And charity workers did tend to become hard, from familiarity with misfortune. But so did surgeons, and no one was suggesting that surgery should be handed over to the sympathetic spinsters and grandmothers of the parish. At least, organized charity was impersonal. It based relief not on the smiles and quaint friendliness of the victims, but on their need. It was not restricted to one district; it planned, at least, for the whole community. And it busied itself not with the victims' desires to become better poets or cooks or bootleggers or interpretative dancers—delicate, holy aspirations, much better let alone than pawed over by liberal yes-sayers— but with their need of food, shoes, and money for the rent.

As for her own self, Ann was as sick of living in settlement houses as Joan of Arc would have been of living in one of the more genteel nunneries. She was sick to death of these cultural comfort stations, rearing their brick Gothic among the speakeasies and hand laundries and kosher butcher-shops, and upholding a standard of tight-smiling prissiness among a mob who, tragic or jolly, were veritably living, making sausages, making love, making jokes. It had been annoying to obey (or deftly break) rules as an assistant: to pretend to enjoy coming down to a tough mutton dinner; to pretend that she hadn't been smoking when her bedroom was blue with it; to get enthusiastic year after year over Ikey's scheduled but curiously delayed success in leaving the fried fish shop and getting his degree of Doctor of Naturo-therapy.

But it was worse as head-resident. There was no secret adventure in breaking her own rules; no real and agreeable venom in denouncing a worker for smoking when she had been smoking herself; no avoidance, now, of the Patrons— the rich women, the jovial clergymen, the esthetic stock-brokers, the philosophical-anarchist bankers—who provided the funds for the settlement and thereby, at a price rather less than once was paid for a sturdy black slave, purchased the soul and body of the head-resident.

With the mild horror of a boy recalling a camp where for all one dreadful summer he has been compelled to be athletic, musical, merry, and full of civic righteousness, under the Godlike eye of an anæmic but vigorous schoolmaster in shorts and spectacles, Ann recalled years of dinners in hall, of looking down the cotton tablecloth and the ironclad plates, and listening to the older young ladies among the workers nickering over a story in which the resident male wit had dared to use the word "damn."

"Settlement houses!" Ann groaned. "Teaching short-

story-writing to girls who ought to be learning to overhaul
aëroplanes! Teaching pottery to Lithuanians born to be
excellent farmers! Teaching the grandsons of great Tal-
mudists to imitate the manners of a Yonkers country club!
Teaching basket-weaving as a means of bringing in the
Kingdom of Heaven! Encouraging decent truck-drivers
to become chiropractors!"

She knew that she was tired and unfair. She did recall
great people, sound work: investigation of flies and typhoid,
campaigns for public playgrounds, and contributions to
poor relief. But the fundamental wickedness of settlement
houses, she decided—and suddenly she extended it to all
"charitable work," in all cities, in all ages, whether
churchly or just liberal—was precisely the feature for
which it was most praised in optimistic sermons, enthusiastic magazine articles, and the dim reasoning of well-
meaning benefactors: that, as such sermons and articles
always stated, "it brings together the well-to-do and the
unfortunate, so that the prosperous may broaden and
deepen their sympathies by first-hand contact with the
poor, and come to understand how noble a heart may be
concealed by blue jeans, and the unfortunate may have an
opportunity to learn and to better themselves by this
friendly contact with those who can instruct and help
them."

"Sure!" snarled Ann, in this unfortunate revolutionary
mood.

"Yes! Pad the naked little egos of the charitable! Give
them a chance for exhibitionism! Let them watch themselves being superior to the unfortunate! And encourage
them to do their uplifting in nice, practical ways!

"Soviet Russia doesn't teach bricklayers that it's better
to be soda-clerks or insurance agents or advertising men—
or settlement workers! It teaches them to lay bricks better.
And the Russians don't think that it's a charity to get jobs
and food and education. They belong to them!"

At a convention of social agencies in New York, Ann
met Ardence Benescoten.

New York village gossip said that Miss Benescoten had
inherited fifty million dollars—and she really had inherited
seventeen million—from her father, the miner. (His being
a miner did not mean that he became filthy and risked
death by going underground. Indeed he rarely saw a mine.
He remained in his New York office and thought up ways
of kicking out the leathery-faced prospectors who had
found the mines first and had come to one of Mr. Benescoten's friendly, well-dressed agents for financial aid.) She
was unmarried, at fifty, but it did not seem to annoy her.
She lived with a woman friend, a singing teacher, once
famous as a coloratura soprano. Miss Benescoten was
famous for her charities. She gave discreet donations and
boundless advice to Pentecostal missions in Spain and
Catholic missions in Nebraska, to a home for the widows
of Confederate officers and another for negro graduate
students, a school for faith healers and an institute for
psychiatry, a refuge for dogs and a rather small museum
to which came three and four people a month to study
coins from Crete and Lesbos. At least twice a week her
name was mentioned in the newspapers, as one of a committee for encouraging Mexican art or for raising the "age
of consent"; at least once a month her picture appeared in

the rotogravure sections, either at the laying of a corner stone, or—when she reluctantly forsook her humble works of charity and for a moment resumed her proper place in the best society—on the lawn of her Bavarian *Schloss* at Newport, surrounded by her nephews and nieces, such as Thornton Benescoten, the ranking polo player, Nancy Benescoten, the divorcée, and Hugh Harrison Benescoten, the judge.

Miss Benescoten, on a committee with Ann, growled, "Heard your speech about dental clinics yesterday. You have sense, my dear. Come home to lunch with me today."

Her dining-room was as dim and almost as large as a train shed. The lunch was composed of objects whose names Ann did not even know, though later she recognized them as plover's eggs, cold pheasant in aspic, asparagus vinaigrette, bar-le-duc.

"I've watched you at the convention, Miss Vickers. And I've nosed into your record at Corlears House and Rochester and Clateburn—yes, and in jail at wherever-it-was—amusin'! I run a big charity show of my own. *I* think it's more practical than most of these institutions. (A little more Heidsieck for Miss Vickers, Stone.) Not bound by any of these idiotic rules. Help 'em out whenever they look amusin'. Yes, amusin' way to do charity—not make it painful—diff'rent, eh?"

So, abruptly, Ann chucked her settlement work and became almoner to this modern Grand Duchess.

Ann had a small, smart, black-and-silver office on the third floor of the Benescoten château on Riverside Drive, with a dictaphone, a stenographer, and four telephones—

one public, one outside but private, one to the house switchboard, attended by a footman, and one to Miss Benescoten's own suite.

There were routine duties, the chief of which was the answering or getting rid of begging letters, begging telegrams, and begging callers. After one morning's mail, broken by telephone calls from mysterious persons who "had to see Miss Benescoten personally—won't take but a moment of her time—can't very well explain my business over the phone," Ann had for Miss Benescoten a considerable pity, with a considerable and irritable surprise at the number of fellow-citizens who wanted to get something for nothing. That first morning's mail, of two hundred letters, included a chatty plea from the widow of a small-town carpenter who wrote that she had enough to live on, but would Miss Benescoten kindly send for the carpenter's daughter—including Pullman fare with ticket— and adopt her socially. "In return, am sure she will be glad to help you round the house anyway possible. Has not learned to cook but otherwise would be glad to help you anyway except of course sweeping or scrubbing as is to hard work for girl brought up like her reads French like I do English." A request for a grand piano for a young woman who would be a "musical progeny if only got a chance." Seven requests to pay off the mortgage. Sixteen requests for loans, to be repaid within a month, by blameless persons who would, if Miss Benescoten *insisted*, give as security such objects as "a genuine antique grandf.'s clock don't know how old," an ice-cream parlor in Hohokus, a wedding ring, and a theological library.

A young man whose drawing was admitted by "Prof.

Otto Staub, the best known music teacher in Memphis, also author and lecturer" to equal Frederick Remington and Franz Hals, desired five thousand dollars, to go to Paris and complete his studies. "Kindly answer at once as am now making plans."

An eighteen-year-old girl confided that

. . . though the whole world has fought me and tried to keep me down all these years, I have fought back. *Nothing* can stop me! I am of the stuff of success. It is in my stars, yes, in my stars. I am going to be a SUCCESS. I am going to be most famous author in U. S. Now dear Miss Benescoten, I guess you get a good many letters from *strangers* asking for help, and probably your secretary just throws same in the wastebasket, but I am not asking for help. Or a loan. My proposition is this: If you will just advance me $3,000 (three thousand dollars) I will finish the book (novel) I am now writing have already begun it. I have a splendid plot, never before used, also characterization, etc. If you do this, when novel is finished, I will PAY YOU BACK DOUBLE! So you see I am not asking for a favor, and I guess even with your stocks, bonds, etc. you can't get a better investment than that! Also understand you are a very charitable person, and by doing this, you will be helping the puzzled world by giving them a new Voice, as novel is not mere story but contains splendid moral, also solutions for many problems now puzzling world. I know you are a fine person, not bound by social conventions, so come on, Miss Benescoten, and send check for $3,000 (three thousand dollars) by return mail and of course if you WANT to make it more, it won't hurt my feelings any! don't mind my little joke. P. S. I can't tell you why maybe I'm psychic but I feel as if we knew one another personally and could look into one another's eyes face to face we would call one another Alys and Ardence even if you are so much older than me. Please don't forget and it will be such a dandy surprise if you **do** send it right away return mail.

And pleas from fifty-two organizations devoted to helping mankind in every known manner, from the study of
numerology to the reduction in cost of carpet-tacks.

But the letter from the old lady with the crippled husband did sound authentic. For all her experience of settlement houses—which are regular stops, along with
ministers' studies and newspaper offices, on the pan-
handlers' route—Ann could not harden her heart enough
to keep from agonizing over these trembling scratches
on cheap paper with faint blue lines.

Ann wondered whether a real, orthodox, thirty-third-
degree Bolshevik, "free of all ideological divergences,"
would the more despise Ardence Benescoten for believing
that she was divinely chosen to dispense seventeen million
dollars, or the writers of begging letters for cringing to her.

Out of the two hundred letters, Ann answered twelve,
kept six others to show Miss Benescoten.

She was to see Miss Benescoten each morning, at eleven.
She expected to find the great philogynist's boudoir as
stark as a nunnery cell. It wasn't. Ann passed through an
Adams private drawing-room to a huge bedroom, ivory
and rose: a huge bed with golden nymphs on the corner
posts; chairs of *petit point;* a pink marble fireplace; a
dressing-table like an entire drug-store. Miss Benescoten
was lolling on a chaise-longue, smoking a small cigar, and
being merry with her friend and house-mate, the ex-diva,
Mme Carrozza.

"Oh, Nalja, this is my new pauperizer, Miss Vickers—a
dear girl!"

Madame Carrozza glared.

"May I disturb you for a second, or shall I come back,

Miss Benescoten? I've finished the letters. I think these six cases are worth investigating, especially the old lady with the sick husband."

"Oh!" Miss Benescoten did not sound at all tender or philogynic. "I thought I'd made it clear to you, Ann. We must reject individuals—except, of course, really amusin' worth-while ones, like, for instance, that jolly girl—you remember, Nalja?—that was so much fun, and such jolly ideas about the use of black glass—set her up in a decorator's shop. But these old, poor people—very sorry for 'em, 'm sure; most unfortunate. But they must go to their relatives. We can only take up coördinated causes, that have some direction, do you see, Ann?"

It took the trusting Ann all of three days to discover that she was *not* almoner for the Grand Duchess; that Miss Benescoten did not care in the least about any charity whatsoever; and that Ann's only reason for being there was to get journalistic publicity for Miss Benescoten apropos of her uncharitable charities. A pound of candy for each of ten thousand factory girls—yes, that was an amusin' charity and a real "news-story," with pictures of Miss Benescoten, the celebrated Mme Carrozza, and the Princess Frangipangi handing down the first two hundred boxes from a Glasstop Kandy Ko. delivery wagon. (And it didn't, as the papers said, cost $5,000; Ardence was as shrewd as her father had been; she had, by emphasizing the publicity they would get, bought the lot from the Glasstop Ko. for $780. And there weren't ten thousand boxes; only six thousand.)

What publicity, what feeling of power, was to be had

from paying the interest on the mortgage for old Mrs.
Jones back in the Connecticut hills? But when Ardence
endowed the English Village for Girl Artists—ever so jolly
a red-roofed colony in the Catskills—and opened it to the
strains of a symphony orchestra, which she had made
Ann wangle for her, gratis, there was a whole page in the
New York Sunday papers, and Ardence was voted a medal
by the League of Graphic Arts, and a handsome scroll by
the Association for the Disurbanization of Esthetic Creation.

Ann was expected to write pleasantly diversified ac-
counts of Ardence's latest charity, to take them wheed-
lingly to the Sunday editors in person, to say casually,
"Oh, by the way, I just happen to have some new photo-
graphs," and display a batch taken this week: "Miss
Ardence Benescoten, Heir of Mining Magnate, Inaugu-
rates Night Class for Laundry Workers: Left to right,
Conte Dondesta, First Sec'y Italian Embassy, Miss
Benescoten, Rt. Rev. Dr. Slough, Bishop of Alaska, Bill
Murphy of Laundry Workers' Union."

Sometimes Ann felt like a guest in the Benescoten house;
sometimes like an intellectual chambermaid. For days she
would see Ardence only at brief conferences, and go out
alone for lunch, at the Coffee Pot on upper Broadway;
then, abruptly—causing her to break an engagement with
Pat Bramble—she would be ordered in for state luncheon,
to be shown off to some college president, criminologist,
Swiss psychiatrist, or other social benefactor whom Miss
Benescoten was that day impressing with her wisdom and
her Venetian glass.

Ann was living in a hotel dreary and small as the Hotel Edmond, but large enough to entertain her intimates— Pat Bramble, Dr. Wormser, two or three residents whom she had known at Corlears Hook. It was gratifyingly cheap. She knew that her days with Ardence were numbered, and she was saving. Ardence was generous in money; Ann had eight thousand a year, as against the three thousand, including board and room, she had had at Rochester. She wanted to be extravagant; she pored over python slippers and Talbot hats in the shop windows. But she did not want them so much as she wanted a half year of wandering or of sitting still, away from offices and "case records" filled out with the agony of a human soul reduced to a few figures. She wanted again to find out whether there was still an individual called Ann, with the ability to love and be angry and foolish, or only a human pigeon-hole named Miss Vickers.

She stayed on, spoiling the Egyptians, and all the while wondering whether that much lauded activity of Moses hadn't been a dirty oriental trick. But each week saw another comforting ninety dollars put away in the savings-bank. There was no day on which she did not long to quit; on which she did not feel that she must have the luxury of leaving before she should be discharged. At the Benescoten house there was rich material for irritation. Ardence was alternately snappish and, on days when she admired herself as a benefactor, lush as an overripe banana. There were quarrels. Ardence's butler (real imported Stilton) was never quite sure whether Ann was a servant or a lady. (Neither was Ann, but she cared less than did the butler.) And Miss Benescoten had a private secretary for her own

correspondence, aside from Ann's Department of Righteousness and Publicity, and she was unquestionably a lady.
She was called a "social secretary," and she was the
daughter of an admiral. She told Ann about the admiral,
often. When she came in on a conference and found Ann
insisting that as Ardence had kept the Home for Respectable Postal Employees waiting for a month now, she must
give them some answer, the social secretary would run
forward, kiss Ardence's fat hand, glare at Ann, and whimper, "Oh, Miss Benescoten, they all drive you like a nigger!
Don't let them pester you, dear!"

Two things kept Ann from quitting: the sordid savings-
bank account—comforting and wholesome, like most sordid things—and the occasional presence of Lindsay Atwell.

He was almost bald, and on the bridge of his nose was a
deep gouge from the horn spectacles which he wore when
reading. Yet he looked young enough, this Lindsay Atwell,
with his air of a tennis-player: taut waist, eyes clear of
blur, gray military mustache, and ruddy skin. His bald
head was not pale and glossy; it was tanned and, in a
pleasant way, a little freckled. He smelled of fresh air—
unaccountably, for though he did walk forty blocks now
and then, he disliked the fashion-magazine parade of riding
in the park along with other Yankee and Semitic imitators
of Rotten Row. Nor were his vacations particularly given
to golf or to heroic camping between layers of balsam and
mosquitoes; he said, at least, that he spent them on an
Adirondacks lawn, reading Conan Doyle.

He was, she thought, forty-seven or -eight.

Lindsay Atwell was Ardence Benescoten's lawyer; the most scholarly and least thunderous member of the firm of Hargrave, Kountz, Atwell & Hargrave.

For weeks Ann was certain that he belonged to old things: Harvard, the Racquet Club with the Century Club in sight, boyhood summers in Bar Harbor, and a family known back to Plymouth Colony. She was just thus far right: he was from Harvard Law School. For the rest, he had been born in Kansas, gone to the University of Kansas, and spent his exotic youthful summers fishing for bullheads in prairie sloughs, and reading Walter Scott and Victor Hugo. "But I served rather heroically in the war," he said; "I was in the Advocate General's show, and some-times I didn't get out of my office till after 6 P. M." As for his family, it went back to Cro-Magnon man, but then the genealogy skipped, down to his grandfather, who had been a much esteemed Ohio farmer till the mortgage got him. Lindsay was, in a word, a Typical Well-Bred New Yorker.

He talked rather elaborately, but he did not seem to Ann pompous.

She saw him often. There was much litigation over assembling the parcels of land to make up the thousand-acre tract for the English Village for Girl Artists, and much consultation of Lindsay by Miss Benescoten as to whether she should engage a famous architect or a good one.

Atwell visited Ann in her office, and sighed, "I say, Miss Vickers, there's no use—I've known her longer, and there isn't a bit of use trying to persuade Our Ardence to have Tipple for architect merely because he has ideas and ability. Why, he's unknown, whereas Mr. Tuftwall has led the profession ever since he did the glories of the Falconer Building Tower—all except the general plan and the details—of course he farmed those out! And he has his own press agent, a really enthusiastic one—not reluctant, like you—who would enjoy coöperating with you in getting free advertising for Ardence as well as for Mr. Tuftwall. You must learn that in these modern days even Beauty can be made of practical use!"

Ann dropped her neck, gaped at Lindsay Atwell, and marveled, "Do you mean to say that you're on to Ardence, too?"

"Hush! You'll be criticizing President Wilson, or even Christian Science, next!"

Thereafter, when he came to see Ardence, Atwell wound up in Ann's office, and they talked of James Joyce and other polite but non-compromising topics, and once he took her affably to lunch at Sherry's. That was on the autumn day when, having been scolded by Miss Benescoten for wasting time on the affairs of a newsboys' home which was too well-established now to provide further publicity, Ann curtly resigned, at 3 P. M., six months after taking the job.

She was in a travel agency at four.

Three days later, at Saturday midnight, she sailed for England, with no plans beyond the pier in Plymouth.

What excited her at sailing was not the menagerie saying farewell with kisses, bouquets, and gin, for she was used enough to the voluble crowds of the East Side. It was the feeling of power and resoluteness in the long swift curves of the ship, the glaring white-painted steel walls, and the monstrous commanding roar of the whistle. Power! Not crafty power, like Miss Benescoten's, but the clean power of steel and steam. . . . . And England no longer away than the drowsy drudging from Monday to Saturday in an office!

Down to the surprisingly compact luxury of her rose-and-gray cabin.

Pat Bramble, tired-eyed but demure, in a white lapin coat with high collar, Dr. Wormser, Miss Dantzig of the Rochester settlement, Miss Edes and Dr. Wilson Tighe from Corlears Hook House, were seeing her off, vociferously dropping roses, candy, and copies of *Moon-Calf* and *The Age of Innocence* all over the cabin. Then at the door smiled Lindsay Atwell.

"Oh, I'm glad!" murmured a maidenly Ann. "How did you know about my sailing?"

"Not hard for a really profound legal intellect. I heard you say to Ardence's butler that you were sailing tonight, and this is the only boat out. Ann, I hope it will be glorious. Do this for me! Go down to Cornwall. There's a village there, perfect—St. Mawgan, in the Vale of Lanherne, so old, so quiet, all hidden among the trees, with a Perpendicular tower older than America. Then go through Newquay, and sit on Pentire Head, all gorse and golden samphire, in summer, as I remember it. Sea extraordinarily wide and purple. I sat there hours, leaning against my knapsack. Tell me about it when you return. Good luck—bless you!"

He was gone; and the steamer bellowed, "Onnnnnn! Gangwaaaaay! Onnnnnn!"

21

THERE was a visibility of three miles. The ship was shut off from all the known world, in a gray limbo of rain-spattered swell and horizonless circle of ragged cloud. The dull steadiness of land was gone. There was an even roll which Ann found exhilarating, once her landlubberliness was convinced, from watching the cheerful deck stewards, that this was all normal and proper. Deep in robes in her steamer chair, she felt as though all briskness had flowed out of her, leaving her as detached as the lonely ship.

"From now till I touch foot on the pier in New York again, I'm not for one second going to think about social service or reforms or jobs or forward-lookers or anything else but being adventurous," she vowed.

She was going to dance, here aboard, to flirt, to bet on the ship's run, to have two cocktails every evening. Then she was to see only the Europe of ruined castles, half-timbered villages, cafés, and great galleries; the Europe of the picture postcards.

For guide and inspiration she had taken Andrew Lang's "Romance":

> "*My Love dwelt in a Northern land.*
> *A gray tower in a forest green*
> *Was hers, and far on either hand*
> *The long wash of the waves was seen,*
> *And leagues and leagues of yellow sand,*
> *The woven forest boughs between.*
>
> "*And through the silver Northern night*
> *The sunset slowly died away,*
> *And herds of strange deer, lily-white,*
> *Stole forth among the branches gray;*
> *About the coming of the light,*
> *They fled like ghosts before the day.*"

That was the Europe she quested; a Europe without strikes or statistics or inflated post-war currencies or American tourists trying to find buckwheats with maple syrup. She was so tired that weariness was rubbed into her flesh like ashes in a mourner's hair. But—oh, just a moment or two more of shop-fret. She did have to wind up the inventory of her thoughts about jobs.

Yes, she was glad she'd worked for Ardence Benescoten, for four round reasons: She had discovered that the worst professional "social worker"—the sketchiest investigator of applicants for relief, the snippiest telephone girl at the Organized Charities Institute, the crankiest manager of a free employment agency—was better than the best rich amateur, condescending to committees and treating "charity" as an alternative to bridge. Weren't professionals always better in the long run—whether in charity work, authorship, medicine, automobile-driving, or prostitution?

Second, she had learned so comforting a scorn of the Very Rich that she would never again aspire beyond a cottage with the electric light bill paid. She had met them at Ardence's: the banker who knew senators; the angel of explorations who was sometimes contemptuously allowed to go along as assistant geologist; the manufacturer of toilets who hoped to be minister to Siam; the blanched old woman whose only conversation was the slyness and sloth of her twenty-seven servants. They were not, despite the Socialist journals, a race of supermen conspiring with fiendish foresight to keep down the honest workers. They weren't that good! They were just dull and mostly bored.

Next, she need not worry about what she was to do when she returned. Lindsay Atwell was a trustee of the Organized Charities Institute, and he had spoken to the director. She could have an excellent opening as assistant director whenever she wished.

And the fourth gift which Miss Ardence Benescoten had, without knowing it, given to her was the friendship of Lindsay Atwell. He was there, back in New York; a permanent and reassuring fact, like Dr. Wormser, or smoky sunsets, or Fifth Avenue in the snow at twilight.

There was the diamond buyer. As he crossed from twice to six times a year, he knew all about ships. Certainly, no captain could have been so glidingly eloquent in explaining the automatic steersman, no head steward so emphatic about what to order from the menu and wine-list. But he made all his information apropos of a little affair. He managed to insinuate "Let's sleep together" even when he said, "I saw a porpoise this morning." Ann did not, theoretically, mind being seduced again. Nice time for it, vacation, with no lecture engagements. But she did object to being not an individual woman, but merely a coupon.

There was the boy just graduated from Princeton, going over to study at the Sorbonne. He was refreshing as cold water. But he seemed so young! Herself eight years out of college, Ann felt a hundred, a little scarred and clinging to optimism only by sheer will and obstinacy, when the boy yearned to her, "You're in social work? Oh, I'd like to be! Don't you think that, after all, the most important thing in the world is *justice?*"

Dear child! What did it mean? What was "justice"? She could have answered, a year ago. "He was right, Pontius Pilate," she brooded.

There was the sound, earnest, unamorous, unidealistic group of drinking men in the bar who, by the end of the passage, had almost admitted her as a fellow male. They did not, like the diamond merchant or the theatrical manager, snoop about women's cabins, their hackles rising at the scent of lingerie. They took it out in high-balls and endless guffawing stories. They were the mining engineer, a couple of newspapermen, an Austrian doctor, a cranky and conservative manufacturer from Chicago, an Italian-American antipasto importer, a Scotch bank-manager from Trinidad, and an ex-congressman from Arkansas.

They called themselves the "True Tasmanian Sabbath-Observance and Rabbit-Hunting Association."

They were reality.

Ann scolded herself for that artless conclusion.

How were these hearty, unsubtle scoffers more "real" than poets unveiling the mantled soul, than harried reformers who viewed a human being not as a hundred and sixty pounds of flesh maintained by beefsteak and rest upon horsehair mattresses, but as integers in a social equation that expressed paradise?

"Well, they just *are* more real!" said Ann.

With her drinking set, forgetting a world in which the population was divided between worried "uplifters" and "problems," Ann regained much of the wisdom she had possessed as a child of ten in Waubanakee, and perceived that most men were neither spectacled angels nor tubercular paupers, but solid, stolid, unpicturesque citizens who liked breakfast, went to their offices or shops or factories at seven or eight or nine, admired sports connected with the rapid propulsion of small balls, cherished funny stories and the spectacle of politicians and bishops, quarreled with their wives and nagged their children yet were fond of them and for them chased prosperity, were unexpectedly competent in the small details of their jobs and, despite the apprehensions of prophets, had somehow managed to get through 30,000 years since the last ice-age, to invent coffee and safety-razors and oxy-acetylene welding, and promised to muddle on another 30,000. And they were kind, where they understood. Their most dismaying monkey-capers—wars, gossip, malice, vanity—were due not to inherent fiendishness but to lack of knowledge and lack of imagination.

No! The True Tasmanians again taught her that the mass of ordinary humans were not the hopeless morons and sadists that Mamie Bogardus, Belle Herringdean, and even, when she had to rise before eight-thirty, Dr. Wormser thought them, but sound stock, lacking only some unusualness of the glands, or a chance crisis, to be saints or heroes. And that was good. For if most people were fools, as the highbrows Ann had been meeting seemed to think, then why vote or start hospitals or write articles or support the public schools or do anything whatever but collect a set of Shakespeare and a ton of beans and retire to a cave?

It was not so light or obvious a discovery of Ann's that people actually were people.

For a century the preachers had wailed that most people were not people at all, but subhuman or fiendish, because they drank and fought and wenched and smoked and neglected the church. Now, since war-days, there had arisen in America a sect which preached just as earnestly that most people were not people at all, but subhuman or even Baptist, because they did not sufficiently drink, fight, wench, denounce the church, and smoke before breakfast. In trusting the human race to get along, then, Ann was not merely revolutionary; she was nihilistic.

With mental apologies to the Battleaxe and Eleanor, she guiltily enjoyed the exclusively male companionship of the True Tasmanians, from eleven to one, and five to midnight, delighted at being accepted as a fellow male, who would not be too easily shocked by good clean dirt; the more delighted at being the subject of feverish gossip by all the other women aboard.

The True Tasmanians did not encourage her to go on expecting to see a fairy-tale Europe, entirely of gray towers in a forest green, and herds of strange deer, lily-white. What *they* expected to see, she gathered, was the Savoy Bar, the racetrack at Longchamps, and offices in Cheapside and on the Boulevard Haussmann and Unter den Linden. But she was bound for the Tower of London, the chapter-house at Salisbury, and a cliff of golden samphire above the sea.

Late on her first afternoon in London, Ann left her strait-laced temperance hotel in Bloomsbury. She was so reckless as to walk planlessly, without consulting her Baedeker. She did peer into Lincoln's Inn and the Temple; she was gratified by the half-timber of Prince Henry's Council Chamber, by memories of Lamb and Thackeray, by the tomb of Goldsmith, and the Norman round-church. But after a confusion of bridges and thundering highways, she was in Bermondsey, and she found a London not mentioned in the lush advertisements of the steamship companies.

"You must see the real London," everyone had said to her. Well, she was in the real London, at least *a* real London, in Bermondsey, and she realized that majestic London, like valiant New York, presumably like every city in the world, was nothing but a square mile or two of handsome shops, bedrooms, public buildings, surrounded by square leagues of houses like pens in a slaughter-yard, pinchbeck shops, and dirty factories. The side streets of Bermondsey, drearier even than Brooklyn, stretched out in flat-faced houses in which, it seemed, human beings could no more have a rich and individual existence than ants in a hill. The innumerable children were dirty; the men, returning from work, were tired and threadbare; the women were creeping things.

Intellectually, Ann knew that poverty in England would be no gayer than poverty in Harlem or San Francisco. Yet emotionally she had not believed anything of the kind. By the British authors who, lecturing in America, let it be deduced that they belonged to a civilization mellower and sweeter than American harshness, Ann's imagination had been convinced that all of England was composed of picturesque cottages among meadows constantly, summer and winter, riotous with larks and roses, plus a London made up solely of ancient churches, Buckingham Palace, the smart flats of baronets, the delicate attics of poets, and the speeches of Mr. Winston Churchill.

But here were miles of two-story brick houses grimy with coal smoke. Then the pubs opened. And the London public houses were the most grievous insult to Romance of all that she saw.

She had learned from such itinerant bards as Mr. Gilbert K. Chesterton that all British establishments for the sale of beer were bristling with melody, laughter, jocund signboards, and conversation about sunsets. She wanted to behold these shrines. She noticed shawled women dribbling into a pub on Tooley Street—the Boar and Bull, it was called, but it might more reasonably have been called the Cold Pork and Boiled Beef. Much daring, she followed them in, asked for a glass of beer, and sat on a clean but dreary bench in a clean but drab-hued room. The bar was a pine counter, painted yellow and grained to imitate a wood that never was on land or sea; the barmaid was a tight-lipped, tight-haired lady of sixty, who kept polishing the same glass, as though she had a grudge against it. In front of the bar were two venerable dames in shawls and aprons, and an undersized gentleman with a scarf for a collar.

They coughed as a preface to speech. Ann listened. Now came the lyric worthy of Chesterton's rolling English drunkard in the rolling English lane:

"Good-evening, Mrs. Mitch."

"Ow! Didn't nowtice it was you! Good-evening, Mr. Dewberry."

"Bit chilly today."

"It is, rather."

"Well, good-evening, Mrs. Mitch."

"Evening, Mr. Dewberry."

Silence, then, glum and beer-scented, save for the barmaid assenting to an unseen gay blade in the saloon bar, "Pint of bitter? Right you are! Pint of bitter!"

Ann went home by way of an A. B. C. restaurant and dinner of gravy soup, Brussels sprouts, and mutton. As it was too late to do anything else, she returned to her hotel, the Royal William, and sat in the lounge, with its aspidistra plant and its panels of varnished brown linoleum, and tried to cheer her depressed loneliness by reading the list of peers in Whitaker's Almanack which, with Bradstreet's and the A. B. C. Guide, composed the library of the Royal William.

She, like all Americans, had believed that most titles went back to the Norman Conquest, and she was astonished to find how many peerages had been created since 1890, how few before 1600. Then: "Oh, stop it! Can't I ever forget figures? Dates! Vital statistics! Number of divorces per hundred thousand—nine point seven plus! Wage-scales! Exact distance in kilometers from the Marble Arch to the Metropole, Brighton! What a mind! That's what you get from settlement houses! Can't you ever let your tape-measure of an intelligence go, and live in your imagination? Can't you feel the presence of John Keats and Charles the First?

"No, if you want to know, I can *not!* Charles the First! Just because he had a lace collar and a dentist's beard! I *want* to know wage-scales! Quite a few people with Saturday pay-envelopes seem to think they're as important as aumbries and barbicans!

"But the lovely names! If Father could only have been Leopold E. Godolphin Walmesley Wilfrid Cavendish Tatem Vickers, K. M. G., D. S. O., F. R. F. P. S. G., First Baron Waubanakee, what a chance you might have had, my girl!"

She tried to perform her duty as a tourist. She went humbly to Oxford, but she remembered a gowned and bearded don on a bicycle better than domes and arches. She solemnly went through Kenilworth Castle, and told herself that she could hear the clank of armor; but afterward, over one of those soft white fish which are supposed by the English to be edible, confessed that she hadn't heard one clank, and that so far as she was concerned, Kenilworth was practically ruined.

She did not thereafter see a single castle, a single hiding-place of Bonnie Prince Charlie. She prowled through the factory towns about Manchester (not quite so sordid as Pittsburgh), the modern rayon factories in Surrey, the missions along Commercial Road, the docks at Poplar. She did find Cornwall—a Cornwall not of golden samphire but of harsh stone cottages belonging to tin miners who earned two pounds a week.

And because she saw the workaday England, the boilers and coal-pits and dynamos behind the theater lights, she loved it, and felt vastly more at home in it than in shattered abbeys. The England that she saw now was not dead, like lovely Venice, or slumbering Charleston, or Athens with its marble turned golden and crumbling. Like her own America, it had problems; it fought; it was alive. It was the shrine of Shakespeare's blood, not of his bones!

Inquiring thus, she was not confined to the customary acquaintances of the tourist: vergers, waiters, ticket-sellers, and fellow tourists very weary in the legs and homesick and a little confused between Cistercian priories and cistaceous rock-gardens.

She mailed the letters of introduction she had sworn she would not mail, and she was presently intimate with Labor M. P.'s, women journalists, Hindu nationalists, and pacifist generals, and with at least a decent reverence, she went to Toynbee Hall, father of all the settlement houses. She plaintively admitted that for her there was no use in trying to be cultured about cathedrals, to remember at which address Dr. Johnson used to drink tea (it was tea, wasn't it?) with Mrs. Thrale (if it was Mrs. Thrale), or to learn which Soho restaurant had the wonderful snails and the quaint waiter who had known Anatole France—or maybe it was Voltaire; and she let herself go in talk with her London shop-mates about disarmament (regarding which, she had much enthusiasm and no figures), the plebiscite at Memel, the Œdipus complex, Antioch College, Ramsay MacDonald, and the best method of teaching cricket to Jewish tailors.

Ann had not yet seen the Continent, though her money was low and it was time to go home. But it was spring, English spring. She learned again what automobiles had made all sound Americans forget, the use of legs. She walked in Kew Gardens. With a pair of English girl students she bicycled from Reigate to Tonbridge, from Petworth to Petersfield. Seeing the country thus humbly, pushing the bike uphill, she did not feel herself a foreigner in England; she belonged to it as she belonged to America. Quiet Sussex was nearer to quiet Waubanakee than was Fifth Avenue.

Before she sailed, she had a week-end to herself, without her student friends.

All her life she had never had intimates, except for her father, Oscar Klebs, Lafe Resnick, Pat Bramble, Eleanor, and Dr. Wormser. Yet she had always been in crowds. She discovered now that the purpose of travel is not to seek new people, but to escape from people, and in unfamiliarity to discover one's unfamiliar self.

She went by train to Arundel, and bicycled to Amberley, beneath the Sussex downs. It was the perfect picturesque village, off a Christmas calendar. For several minutes Ann gloated, like any good tourist, and did not think about compulsion-neuroses and the wages of herring-fishermen. She climbed to an oak-sheltered rock high on the downs, and considered the case of Ann Vickers in this complicated world which could include Sussex downs. Liberian slavery,

Belle Herringdean, Prince Kropotkin, who had just died this year, and President Harding, who had just been inaugurated.

She must go back to work. If she returned to "social work," it would probably be for good.

She had to be clear about it. She would never again be thirty, sitting alone in spring sunshine on a Sussex hillside, independent of everyone so far as a human being could be, free to choose jobs and landscapes to suit herself.

It was a definite, powerful realm, this of "social work," of professional dissatisfaction with things as they are. It was unknown to most of the people who sold groceries and weeded potatoes. It was as clearly marked off from ordinary affairs as the navy or the priesthood, and, like them, it was equally passionate whether it was wrong or right. Reform. A whole world—charity distribution, prison improvement, fighting for free speech and free divorce and birth-control and bobbed hair and spring cots in lumber camps—a hectic world composed of saints, grafters, publicity-grabbers, humorists who found senators in Stetson hats funny, senators in Stetson hats who found Wall Street atrocious, earnest vegetarians who warred on beefsteak, cynical doctors who warred on vegetarians, and gay young people who just generally liked to throw dead cats into tabernacles.

That world had its obvious faults. Rather more than the hard-boiled newspaper paragraphers who slurred every manner of "ist," Ann, because she had had to deal personally with them, disliked the lunatic fringe: the undernourished pastors who got into the newspapers by advocating anarchism or even cubism, and the overnourished pastors who drew crowds by denouncing alcohol and prostitution (with attractive illustrations). The people who loved authority and could best get it by dealing with the timid and unresisting poor. The people who wanted to take out on the entire human race the sorrows of their own small childhoods. The demagogues who with equal glee would be elected representatives of Moscow or of Rittenhouse Square.

Yes, said Ann to herself, it is a mad, difficult world. But all worlds, she said, that transcend mattresses and trolley-cars and porridge, are mad and difficult.

"So long," she said, "as there is one hungry and jobless man, one ill-treated child, one swamp in all the world causing malaria—and that will doubtless be forever—I must go on scolding at slackness and cruelty. I must do it even at the cost of hating myself as a prig—a sentimental-ist—a charlatan—an egotist setting up my own itch against the wisdom of the ages (that stupidest of super-stitions!)."

But it was not yet too late to save herself from the frenzy of salvation. She was not a reformer because she had been a failure in practical affairs. She had found noth-ing difficult in conducting an office, being punctual, giving directions to stenographers, imagining what her com-petitors would do—all those occult rites whereby men become presidents, and bathtub manufacturers so princely that their biographies are printed in the magazines. She could "do well" in business. She had been offered the managership of the Women's Department of a Rochester bank.

Why not?

Business—it wasn't just the sordid peddling that the highbrows pretended. It was as normal for a woman or man in the early twentieth century to "go into business" as for a citizen of 1200 to join the crusades. It was the spirit of the age, and how could one affect an age save by being in the spirit of it? Did not business men today control politics, cause ministers of the gospel to preach a message comforting to prosperity, inspire authors to write such tales of detectives as would divert the barons of business? Was it not an inspiring notion to influence the more brilliant youngsters to go into business and thereby render more intellectual the surely not ignoble affair of supplying people with good shoes, tender beefsteaks, latherable soap, and esthetic linoleum?

Wasn't it sense?

"Oh, probably," sighed Ann. She felt weary now. The sun was overclouded and the breeze chilly. "But I've never yet sought sense, in a job or in a lover. I've sought what the soldier calls 'adventure,' what the priest calls 'sanctification.' I *will* go on being a pest and a meddler! For the wisdom of this world, yea, even the wisdom of the Baptists and the Methodists, the laundrymen and garagemen, the Republicans and golf-players, is foolishness with God."

But it seemed to her, as she bicycled back to Arundel, that her daughter Pride was beside her, begging for the security of a home and not for hard paths across windy uplands.

So in the joyous spring—which manifested itself on the Atlantic in two gales and three days of fog—Ann returned to America.

22

S<small>HE</small> had, during her year as assistant director of the Organized Charities Institute of New York, so much to do with discharged and paroled women convicts that she remembered her own fortnight of being elevated and purified in the Tafford County Jail. The ex-convicts whom she now met had not been much reformed; they came out of prisons, even the decentest of prisons, not with repentance but with a desire to get even with Society. So her experience led her into what is known as "penology."

(Penology! The science of torture! The art of locking the stable-door after the horse is stolen! The touching faith that neurotics who hate social regulation can be made to love it by confining them in stinking dens, giving them bad food and dull work, and compelling them to associate with precisely the persons for associating with whom they have first been arrested. The credo, based on the premise that God created human beings for the purpose of burning most of them, that it is sinful for an individual to commit murder, but virtuous in the State to murder murderers. The theory that men chosen for their ability to maul unruly convicts will, if they be shut up in darkness, away from any public knowledge of what they do, be inspired to pray and love these convicts into virtue. The science of penology!)

Ann went for a year to the Green Valley Refuge for Women, in New England, as educational director. She found here not much of which the prisoners could complain, though very much by which they could be bored, for a lady who has these ten years been divertingly shoplifting, getting drunk, being consecutively seduced and arrested, is left unstirred by even the most competent professor of laundering. Green Valley Refuge, a fifty-year-old brick hulk in walled grounds on the edge of a New England city, had been built before the day when prison authorities believed that anything could be done with lawbreakers—aged sixteen or seventy-six, morons or brilliant psychotics, sentenced for torturing children or for breaking Sabbath-day ordinances—except to keep them toiling, keep them frightened, and keep them secure.

Behind the red-brick administration building, with its mansard roof and excessive flagpole, was a cell-block with wooden floors which no scrubbing would quite free from lice and cockroaches, and lacking all toilet facilities save pitchers, bowls, and buckets. There was insufficient room. Succeeding state legislatures, those divinely chosen voices of the people, declined to realize (though the State Board of Control told them often enough) that when a state doubled in population in fifty years, the prison population might increase also. In steel-barred wooden cells, seven feet wide, eight feet long, seven feet high, meant for one person fifty years ago, there were now two persons suffocatingly penned, and many sleeping in cots in the corridors, while the legislature debated what ought to be the fine for a person catching short trout. The scanty grounds of the Refuge had so long been graveled that no manner of digging by the lady convicts would produce flowers and grass.

Yet against all this the chief officers at Green Valley, superintendent and assistant and doctor and steward and now Ann Vickers, struggled, themselves living in bare rooms, abominably paid, fed little better than the convicts. They had got rid of contract labor; they sought to make the prison work a vocational training. A few women convicts who had come in as cocaine-filled, hot-eyed enemies of society actually went out eager to go straight . . . and if they were lucky, thereafter were permitted to cook and wash dishes fourteen hours a day and be treated like virtuous hired girls instead of like fiends.

They were good women, the Green Valley officers, and during such rare debauches as their relaxing over hot cocoa at midnight, Ann loved them as she did Malvina Wormser and Mamie Bogardus.

She was going on in prison work. Yes! She pictured prisons that should be combinations of hospital, technical institute, psychoanalytical laboratory, and old English garden. She would be a power. She would make legislatures understand that the sick in spirit needed more care than the sick in body.

For a year—living largely on faith, beef tea, and tutoring—she took sociology, especially criminology, in the Columbia graduate school, teaching three evenings a week

at a women's reformatory. She shared a flat with Pat
Bramble, a real estate salesman now, still virginal and
shining with wild-rose sweetness, but not at all wild-rosy
in the matter of making clients complete their final payments. And Ann managed to get in one blissful, lazy
Saturday afternoon every week, with Pat, Dr. Wormser,
or Lindsay Atwell.

Lindsay had wirelessed a welcome to her boat when she
returned from Europe. He came often to see her, but he
was as innocuous as the polite young men, the "promising
young men" who would never keep the promise, who hung
around Pat's apartment and helped wash dishes as a way
of singing for their supper. For a time Ann resented it, as
even careerist women do, that Lindsay apparently did not
find her worth making love to. But she saw that he was
tired. He was fighting—always fighting something—a
million-dollar war between a railroad and a coal mine, a
will-case in which one set of wastrels was trying to get
away from another set of wastrels the money a miser had
squeezed out of patent medicines, or sometimes, not often,
opposing an injunction against a labor union. When it was
this last, Ann would get all radical and pleased, and Lindsay would sigh, "Yes, they're a fine bunch, the leaders of
the union. But they made a bad mistake this year. They
didn't hire as good gunmen and gorillas as the Communist
union, so they lost the strike."

He came into the flat beaten with weariness. He seemed
in the presence of Pat, as much as of Ann, to find peace.
Presently he stopped rubbing his flushed eyes, and croaked,
"Can't you two get away tonight?" He took them to
restaurants of which they had never heard—the new,

secret speakeasies now beginning to creep into New York, with authentic wines smuggled in on French freighters. When he said good-night, Lindsay kissed them both, lightly.

Ann lay awake—one minute—to dream of Pride, her daughter. Wasn't Pride very like Lindsay?

Not Columbia nor the convicts she taught nor Lindsay Atwell was Ann's treasure-trove, that year, but Dr. Julius C. Jelke, professor of sociology at Columbia.

Dr. Jelke was a beer-keg of a man, very fond of billiards, port, James Branch Cabell, and white doeskin shoes. He began his seminar in criminology, ardently attended by Miss Ann Vickers, by drawling:

"Ladies and gentlemen, we must consider the state of prisons in America today. We shall find that some of them are decent and human, and some decidedly indecent and inhuman, and this difference will at first seem important. Against such naïveté I must at the beginning warn you. There are no good prisons! There cannot be good prisons! There can no more be a good prison than there can be a good murder or a good rape or a good cancer.

"Even where there seems to be obvious superiority, where Prison A is cleaner, better ventilated, and less given to painful punishments than Prison B, it is not necessarily 'better.' It may be filled with a priggish nagging which infuriates and destroys a good, sane, wholesome yegg more than vermin and lashing. Even those of us who think we are not of Mr. Lombroso's 'criminal types' have been known to prefer slovenly backwoods vacations to the clean houses of self-righteous shrews. *Good* prisons? **Good for** what? For anything save to please the smugness of us, the respectable?

"At its best, any prison is so unnatural a form of segregation from normal life that—like too-loving parents and too-zealous religion and all other well-meant violations of individuality—it helps to prevent the victims from resuming, when they are let out, any natural rôle in human society. At its worst (and it is surprising how many prisons are at the worst, in this age of tender humanity, 1923) the prison is almost scientifically designed to develop by force-ripening every one of the anti-social traits for which we suppose ourselves to put people into prison. (I say 'suppose' because actually we put people into prison only because we don't know what else to do with them, and so, police and judges and laymen alike, we hide them away from us, and show ourselves, adult human beings, the mental equals of the ostrich.) Prison makes the man who hates his bosses come out hating everyone. Prison makes the man who is sexually abnormal, sexually a maniac. Prison makes the man who enjoyed beating fellow-drunks in a barroom come out wanting to kill a policeman—a perhaps not unworthy result of imprisonment, considering that in most cities and villages the mental test for a policeman is that he shall weigh a hundred and ninety pounds and have a skull equally invulnerable to clubs and to civility.

"I will give you a formula whereby you can test the intelligence and thought of all officials, of all persons dealing practically and directly with prisons: Any prison official who is intelligent believes secretly, no matter what he says or writes, that all prisons, of every kind, good or bad, must be abolished.

"And what is to take their place? A hundred and fifty years ago, most even of the authorities who believed that torture (a practice still very fashionable in the United States, under the name of the Third Degree) was shameful and futile, still did not see what could be substituted for it. Doubtless privily they said, 'Theoretically I'm against torture, but after all, I'm a hard-boiled practical criminologist, and until we get something better, we'll have to go on using the rack and the iron maiden—though, being a humanitarian, I believe in putting a nice soft pillow under the scoundrel's neck when you tie him on the rack.'

"Probably we cannot tomorrow turn all the so-called criminals loose and close the jails—though of course that is just what we are doing, on the installment plan, by letting them go at the end of their sentences. No, Society cannot free the victims Society has unfitted for freedom. Doubtless, since the Millennium is still centuries ahead, it is advisable to make prisons as sanitary and well-lighted as possible, that the convicts may live out their living death more comfortably. Only, keep your philosophy straight. Do not imagine that when you have by carelessness in not inoculating them let your victims get smallpox you are going to save them or exonerate yourselves by bathing their brows, however grateful the bathing may be.

"What is to take the place of prisons? Something will. Fundamentally, such institutions as parole and probation for those who merely need a little help and reconstruction. For the ethically diseased, for the incurable, safe-keeping in hospitals. There is no more reason for punishing the ethically sick than the physically sick. And, since the revolutionist in criminology is actually so much more 'hard-boiled' than any Tammany judge, he would not infrequently give a sentence for life to unfortunates who now get only five years. If a man is incurably rotten, if he is an incurable homicide or rapist or torturer of children, then he is not going to be any better after five years in prison. He must be shut away for keeps, not vengefully, but in the same attitude as we shut away incurable carriers of typhoid. *Only* I want his 'incurability' to be passed on, not by a judge whose training in psychiatry has been acquired by playing poker and attending clambakes with the leading politicians of his district, but by trained psychiatrists . . . if such persons exist. If not, let's for a season shut up West Point and Annapolis and see whether it may not be as useful socially to train healers as to train killers.

"The infamy of criminals is a favorite dinner-table topic. But the futility of prisons is a topic as little known among allegedly intelligent people as the teleology of the Tibetans. In certain social problems, a trace of knowledge has now been spread about, so that one expects even a hobo, a Fifth Avenue rector, or a president of the United States to have some elementary notion that war and capitalism—the conduct of business solely for the private gain of the more foxlike human beings—are not sacred and permanent. But that darkness, stench, obedience to inferiors, a mode of life which combines the horror of a bayonet-duel with the petty meanness of village gossip, are not the remedies for complex sicknesses of the soul is a theory as unknown to most judges, lawyers, wardens, legislators, and plain citizens today as it was to the bloody cess-pool of Newgate Prison a hundred years ago.

"The ordinary citizen, when he hears of infamous crimes, always exclaims, 'We must increase prison sentences!' He is right, in his detestation of crime. But what he should say is, 'Since crime increases, obviously the prison system is proven a failure. We must try something else.'

"Before the next meeting, I wish you would read . . ."

Ann came out of it a little dazed. Where, then, were all her plans for coaxing the public to make "good" prisons? Oh, well, she had to work on. . . . There is no good work, she thought, that is not in essence a final destruction of itself that something greater may take its place.

She had passed her New York State civil service examinations. In a few weeks she would have that symbol of cloistered learning, a Master of Arts degree (strange mystic title!). She went to Professor Jelke and spiritedly demanded:

"I've seen a good penal institution—Green Valley. I planned to stay in New York. But now I want to see the worst possible pen, or I shan't know anything about penology as it really is. What do you advise?"

"Well, there are plenty of bad ones. You mean for women? Well, I should think one of the worst was the Women's Division of the Copperhead Gap Penitentiary in the state of Blank. But it would be hard to get you in there. Jobs as prison matrons, especially in backward states, are reserved for the politicians' female relatives who are too mean and ignorant to get jobs keeping pigs. But there's one chance: Mrs. Albert Windelskate, who's on the Blank State Board of Control—wife of a loan-shark, I believe. She's a very charitable and intellectual lady, and pretty terrible. I meet her at prison conventions. She writes me—oh, God, how she writes me! About castrating criminals, only she's too delicate to call it that—she just loves to think about it. I'll write her. By the way: if you should go to Copperhead, my friend Jessie Van Tuyl is doing three years there on a charge of criminal syndicalism. Splendid woman."

Miss Ann Vickers, M. A., was appointed educational director and chief clerk (combined salaries, $1300 and maintenance) of the Women's Division at Copperhead Gap, in a state whose patron saint was William Jennings Bryan.

Dr. Wormser said, "Fine! If you last till the middle of fall, three months from now, what say we spend October out at my cottage?"

Pat Bramble said, "Oh. How much do you get? Lord, is that all? Oh, come on and sell real estate."

Lindsay Atwell said, "Copperhead Gap? I don't know what they do to women there, but I had a man client who went in a forger and came out a murderer. Though of course I mustn't exaggerate; the world has grown better, and so have prisons. We've got rid of torture. . . . Ann! It's so hot this evening—I think I'll run over to Scotland for a month—let's walk up Riverside Drive."

They sat on a bench above the Hudson. The heat had softened New York to a tropic languor. The miles of benches were filled with summer lovers, and past them strolled sailors with arms about noisy girls. The fleet was in; its searchlights clashed in the sky; and the tinpanny bands at Palisades Park across the river were jungle tom-toms.

"Ann!" Lindsay sighed. "I've taken a beastly advantage of you, this past winter. I realize now that I've always assumed you would be willing to play around with me when I was tired. I do get tired, and yet it bores me to rest. You've rather saved my life." He squeezed her hand, but their palms were damp, and he let go. She could feel the pressure afterward, stirring her a little out of the July lassitude.

"You have so much reality, Ann. One doesn't have to fence with you. You're not vain and egocentric, and you don't appraise every man just in ratio as he serves you. For that reason, because I've been so secure with you, probably I haven't realized how desperately fond of you I've become. This horrible plan of yours to go to that pocket edition of hell, Copperhead Gap, has waked me up. Don't! It's mad! Come to Scotland with me—in the proper connubial relationship, I mean, of course. You'd enjoy tramping through the Trossachs, I think."

"If you were passionately in love with me——'

"I would be!"

"When you are, you'll come grab me, and not argue over it, like a will under probate! But I am fond of you. But I wouldn't give up a chance to fight Copperhead Gap for anything—well, almost anything. No."

She wished afterward that she had coaxed him into embracing her, overpowering her. But it was too late, now when she could with such desperate clarity see his kind eyes. What were these "women's wiles" of which she read in novels? Couldn't she master them: be complimentary, be coyly aloof, be wistful, be fluttered by his handclasp, rouse him to a conviction that she was a swooning mystery which he must penetrate?

"In other words, lie and play-act! No, I'm hanged· if I will!" said Ann.

Her solitary bed was hot with July.

"'The world has grown better—we've got rid of torture,'" she cynically quoted him.

23

Mrs. ALBERT WINDELSKATE, that most public-spirited lady who gave her time free to the State Board of Control of Prisons and to the ensuing newspaper publicity, had a summer cottage at Timgad Springs, the principal resort of her state. It was on the way to Olympus City, the station for the Copperhead Gap Penitentiary, and she had invited Ann to spend a day of rest and mutual eleemosynary congratulation.

Mrs. Windelskate met Ann at the station with a handsome sedan, equipped with a pressed-glass vase containing artificial flowers.

"It's so hot! My, you must have just suffered, on the train. I thought we'd go out to the country club for lunch. Your train for Olympus City leaves at three; that will get you to the penitentiary about five. Oh, Miss Vickers, we all think it's just grand you're coming to take part in our prison reform, with your education and training in the East and all. A lot of New York and Boston folks seem to think that in the South and West we aren't up to the latest stunts in scientific criminology, and you'll be able to go back and tell 'em the fine things we've done. Why, they've got a gymnasium now for the female convicts at Copperhead! That was all my idea, my husband and I. We ourselves contributed a hundred dollars. 'I reckon you think we'll go broke, with all our charities,' I said to him, but he just laughed, and he says, 'Oh, I reckon we can stand it.' That's just like him. You wouldn't think to see how smart he is in business—he's in the loan and mortgage business—he does such a lot of good—why, I don't know what a lot of farmers and storekeepers would do in Pearl County if he didn't let them have the money and help them out, and I'm sure he *never* forecloses if there's any earthly way of preventing it, he just does all he can to prevent it, though Heaven knows they're so improvident—buying autos and washing-machines and so on and so forth when they pretend they can't pay the interest. But as I say, seeing him in his office, he's so peppy and efficient and so on, you'd never guess that when it comes to criminology and charity and all, his heart is as soft as—as soft as anything. And then Dr. Slenk—at the prison, I mean—the warden, Dr. Addington Slenk—I was largely responsible for getting him appointed in place of that old crank they had there for warden before—he's such an up-to-date scientific penologist—you'll just adore Dr. Slenk."

(During this delivery of the oracle, Mrs. Windelskate was driving Ann to the Indian Mound Country Club and leading her to the red tile terrace at the edge of the sloping golf course.)

"Of course, as Dr. Slenk says, there is a great deal of nonsense and sentimentality talked about prison reform. Prisons aren't intended to be picnics. If a man deliberately goes and steals, you aren't going to reward him by treating him like a millionaire! As Dr. Slenk says, too many merely theoretical reformers tend to lose sight of the fact that while prisons must primarily regenerate people who have gone wrong, still they must also have a good wholesome *deterrent* effect, so that criminals won't want to come back in any hurry!

"And here in the mountains we get a lot of pretty hard cases, and it doesn't do to treat them too soft. They aren't used to it; they'd just take advantage of you if you gave 'em a lot of luxuries—pie every day, and a lot of bathrooms that I'm sure a lot of decent law-abiding folks like us can't even begin to afford! For a lot of these hill-billies, prison is the *most* regenerating and civilizing force, when it's handled by a fine gentlemanly man like Dr. Slenk. You just can't imagine! Why, at home those folks just live on sorghum and sow-belly, and they're too pleased for words when they get prunes and like that in prison!

"No, as Dr. Slenk says, the great regenerative force is hard, useful labor. In the men's division, we have some perfectly fine industries—a foundry where we make kitchenware, and an overall mill, and in the women's division, a fine shirt and underwear factory. Maybe our machinery isn't quite so up to date as we'd like it, but that'll come in time. It's a shame, though, that the contractors that take our finished goods off us can't be persuaded to pay us what they ought to. No civic feeling! We'd like to pay the inmates a quarter a day for their labor, to encourage them, but we can't afford more than five cents a day, and that really doesn't come to much, even in a long sentence. But still, all this modern industry does teach those poor unfortunate wretches how to take their place in society when they come out. Sobriety! Chastity! Hard, unceasing labor!

Obeying rules, promptly and without chewing the rag! What priceless lessons!

"It's time to order lunch. I hope you like our club. Sweet little clubhouse, isn't it! Do you know, it cost a hundred and fifty thousand dollars. Made of the very finest materials. I often say to Mr. Windelskate, 'There! That's one building that's going to *last*, in this day when there's so much sloppy building.' I do believe in building for the *future*. That's why I work so hard over the poor lost lambs in prison, though Heaven knows I never get any thanks or credit for it, though the Governor, the Governor himself, did say to me, 'Mrs. Windelskate,' he said, 'I doubt if you'll ever know what it means to the institutions and public activities of this state to have a leading woman like you take such a personal interest in them'—though, as I told him, I don't claim to have any special knowledge of all these sociological stunts, but I just do feel you can't afford to neglect the advice and interest of *any* earnest and public-spirited woman! And you'd be surprised how much money Mr. Windelskate and I put into our charities and all, and into our little home—we live in Pearlsburg, in winter, of course. It's ten times as big as Timgad Springs. The last census gave us 27,000 population, and I shouldn't be in the least surprised if when it comes time for the 1930 census, let's see, that will be six years from now, we'll have 30,000 population, if not thirty-five!

"But now about the prison, there's one thing I must warn you about. Heaven knows no one could be closer to the actual running of it than I am. And so when disgruntled people claim the prisoners don't get very good food and sanitation and have to work too hard—it's just too *bad*, now, isn't it! lot of degenerate criminals actually having to work as hard as you and me and other *decent* people!—and when I hear people saying and making criticisms like that—oh, yes, there's blatherskites and soreheads and Heaven knows what all—a so-called liberal preacher, a Universalist, in Pearlsburg, that he'll say *anything* to cause a sensation and get himself talked about! —folks that can only see the destructive side—not one constructive thought in their heads!

"But I happen to know what's the source of all these false rumors, and that's what I wanted to warn you about. There's a prisoner in the women's division at Copperhead that calls herself Mrs. Jessica Van Tuyl. She's a Communist and anarchist and labor agitator and trouble-maker of the very worst sort. I happen to know this Van Tuyl woman was responsible for all sorts of dynamitings and sluggings and shootings from ambush and all *kinds* of outrageous conduct on the part of strikers in the recent coal and tenant-farmer strikes. She was sent up for criminal syndicalism and conspiracy for three years—it should have been life, if our judges weren't so weak-kneed and so afraid of public opinion! And this is the woman who's been managing to sneak out all sorts of lying letters about conditions in the prison, and getting all sorts of false and damaging reports spread about.

"Oh, it's a thankless task, but still I do feel, don't you, that it's the duty of our better families and our better-educated class to go into politics and not leave it to a lot of ignorant, prejudiced, common politicians, don't you think so? I'm so glad you've come to help us. You just watch this Van Tuyl woman, and let her understand how

decent, strict, law-abiding people feel about her. Shall we
have a cocktail before lunch?''

Ann had been given to a certain neatness of hair and
gloves and shoes, but as the heat glared in from the red-
clay hills, as dust danced on the red-plush seats of the day
coach, and the stink of peanuts and baby grew thicker, she
gave up worrying over the fact that her hair was in wisps
over her forehead.

She carelessly noticed a woman three seats ahead who
kept fidgeting, peering out of the window, looking back,
like one to whom travel was unfamiliar and exciting. She
was an ash-gray old negress, in rusty black satin Sunday
dress and a chip hat of 1890. Ann wondered why the
negress was not in the Jim Crow seats at the back of the
car. It was probably because she was with a man who,
though he did not turn his head, seemed from the planes of
his thick neck to be white.

The negress was afraid of something. While she was staring slack-jawed at some alien wonder—the Italian matron
who wore enormous glass earrings and chewed salami out
of a basket; the urbane traveling-man with gray-flannel
suit, silk shirt, and large thumb ring—her neck would
seem to drop down into her body, her lips part and quiver.

"Olllllllllympus Ciiiiity!" chanted the brakeman.

Ann could see the negress's lips, in profile, form, "Oh my
God!" The woman turned about then, and Ann forgot her
in lifting down from the rack her bags, such heavy bags
of books that were all filled with statistics about the tricki-
ness of human nature, about psychology, a thing that the
ash-pale negress up there could never understand.

The station, as Ann staggered out to it—the brakeman gallantly helping her with her bags—was a frame shanty with the red paint peeling, the platform like an open blast-furnace. Against the depot wall leaned half a dozen loafers, barefoot and in tattered straw hats. But in front of them stood out a figure not at all languid; a man tall as a pine, resolute, terrifying; a man with a long yellow horse-face, acute little red eyes, and hands like bloated centipedes. Three front teeth were gone; the rest were black. He wore a gray hickory shirt, red suspenders, a Stetson hat like a circus tent, and a bel. ʾom which hung the holster of a long revolver.

He opened his thin mouth like a snapping-turtle. Toward him a short broad man, with a face like a beefsteak, and as expressionless, was dragging the negress whom Ann had been watching, and Ann saw now—the back of the seat had hidden it on the train—that the old woman was handcuffed to her white companion.

"Hello, Sheriff," bawled the tall pine to the man with the negress. "So this is the old nigger bitch. Croaked her man with an axe, eh? We'll show her something better than an axe!"

The loafers, the sheriff, the tall man himself grated with laughter, like the grinding brakes of a rusty car.

"Yep, Cap'n, here she is—Sister Lil Hezekiah. Sister, want you to meet the gentleman that'll have the pleasure of tying a rope round your skinny neck, you murderin' old hell-cat! God, Cap'n, back yonder I swear she almost bit me!"

"She won't bite me!" The tall man reached out an arm, fingers extended, like the arm of an approaching monster in a nightmare. The fingers crept slowly down on the negress, seemed to thrust into her eyes, clamped on her shoulder, while she dropped to her knees on the blistering planks of the platform, her still handcuffed wrist twisted by the brawny sheriff. She foamed at the mouth, with a panic wailing out of the jungle. The tall man held her while the handcuffs were unlocked, ran her toward a motor truck lettered, "Copperhead Penitentiary," boosted her up into it, and half turned away. Her cobwebbed gray face looked out. He swung and slapped her—it sounded as though her thin skull had cracked—and she vanished into the truck again, while the loafers chuckled.

"They say Sister Hezekiah is a powerful prayer, real Prayin' Pentecostal, even if she did kind of go and git absent-minded and sharpen up the axe on her old man!" giggled the sheriff.

"Well, she better pray! Whyntch you lynch her, like you ought to done, and save the state all this expense?" growled the tall man.

"Why, Cap'n!" stammered the sheriff, surprised and hurt. "You can't lynch a nigger for just killing another nigger! Fact, hadn't ought to hang 'em, for that! But she did almost bite me! By God, I'd like to help bump her off myself! Don't forget I get to see the hanging. Never did see a hanging, Cap'n. Ain't that funny?—not even a nigger. Say, is it true they get their heads yanked right off sometimes when they drop?"

A hand touched Ann's sleeve. She had not been aware, in her trance, that a slouching, heat-drugged, negro driver had been mumbling, "Taxi, lady, taxi?"

"Oh. Taxi? Oh, yes, I want a taxi," she whispered.

"Where to, lady?"

She could not admit that she was going to the prison—that she was a colleague of "Cap'n," the tall man with the long yellow face.

But perhaps the driver would merely think that she was the wife or the friend of a convict.

"To the *prison*," she panted, and indeed the driver did believe, from the terrified hate she put into the word, that she was one of the women who, more than the prisoners, pay for their men's crime.

Main Street, Olympus City, was distinguished by drifted piles of red dust, in which dogs were sleeping or lazily scratching unambitious fleas, one- and two-story frame shops, not recently painted, in front of which, in tilted chairs on the plank sidewalk, the owners were sleeping, and dusty sycamore trees, in which the sparrows were sleeping.

The road from Olympus to the penitentiary was across a clay upland, rimmed with hills. The road was unyieldingly straight, and sped among farms of unpainted small shanties and unpainted large pig-pens, cornfields, and tobacco fields that seemed a little wilted. It was a desert; it was not of sand, but of red soil and yellowy-green leaves, yet it was a desert, and hot, like Death Valley.

"I can't stand it! Hitting that poor old insane woman! I'm going back!" agonized Ann, too paralyzed to do it. She was weak with shame that she had not denounced the sheriff and the Cap'n.

She expected the Copperhead Gap Penitentiary to look

altogether hideous. But she saw, haughty beyond red fields, a shining building of limestone, with tall pillars. The car shook itself up a low hill, through a sycamore grove. At the foot of the hill was a creek, lined with fresh-looking willows. The driveway to the pillared entrance was edged with lawns and rose-beds.

"Why, it's a palace! Perhaps that horrible man, that 'Cap'n' wasn't typical. I'll get rid of him!" Ann comforted herself.

An obsequious negro trusty in well-washed black alpaca opened the bronze gates of the main building and waved her gushingly into a lobby of white marble floor, pink marble columns, and yellow marble stairway, with no hint of prison about it.

"Miss Vickers, ma'am, yassum, Miss Vickers. Been expecting you, Miss Vickers. The warden's office right here on the right, ma'am."

"There's nothing," said Ann to herself, "mean and beastly about all this. If anything, my girl, it's a little too Ritzy for you. Oh, I suppose Dr. Slenk has to put up with what beastly guards the politicians wish on him!"

She hesitated into the warden's office; was ushered by the brisk young woman secretary into Dr. Slenk's private room. It was a handsome, tall apartment, with oak pilasters, a carved oak fireplace, and portraits of Robert E. Lee, John William Golightly, present governor of the state, and the Good Shepherd being merciful to His lambs. The open casement windows let in the brilliance of the lawns and rose-beds.

Dr. Slenk was rising to greet her, his hand out almost affectionately. "Miss Vickers! It's a real privilege to have you with us! I hope you will enjoy your work here. I certainly do. Oh, there's sad tragedies. And we make so many mistakes. But what greater privilege than trying to help the unfortunate, to help the sinner go straight? I hope you'll enjoy your work here with us. Yes, I certainly do! Have a hot journey? And how did you find Mrs. Windelskate? I don't know what we'd do without her help and suggestions. But I'm sure she never did anything more practical than getting you here. Yes, I certainly do!"

He was such a nice little man, Dr. Slenk—as neat as a fox-terrier—the neatest little linen collar and polka-dotted blue tie and white shirt and little black oxfords—the neatest and most literary tortoise-rimmed folding eyeglasses, which he merrily closed and snapped open as he talked.

"Yes, it was pretty hot. Yes . . ." She went on, but she did not know what she was saying; she had no proper notion of making an impression; she was thinking, "I wonder if I dare tell him about that brute at the station?"

"Oh, so you went to the country club with Mrs. Windelskate! Well! I do envy you, on a hot day like this! Wish I'd been there! Lovely place, isn't it, the club—wish we could give our poor Boys and the Women here a place like that, but 'fraid it wouldn't be quite deterrent, hee, hee, hee! Oh! Here comes my right bower—the deputy warden and captain of guards—Captain Waldo Dringoole."

Into the room, like a slouching elephant, was coming the horse-faced high man who had slapped the negress at the station. He wore a blue uniform coat now, but he hadn't removed the umbrella-like Stetson.

"Yes," cooed Warden Slenk, "I reckon you might say

Cap'n Waldo here is the real boss of the prison. I'm just the
gadabout, you might say. I meet the citizens of our good
state, and I talk with the officials and find out what they
want us to do, but it's Cap'n Waldo that really carries it
out. . . . Miss Vickers, Captain Waldo Dringoole! . . .
Cap'n, Miss Vickers is in for the comparatively minor
crime of being a sociologist, so let her off easy—don't give
her the dark cells—not yet! Hee, hee, hee."

He was a jolly little man, Doc Slenk—except during
riots. Always like that, joking and friendly, and snapping
his trick eyeglasses open and shut.

Before Ann could flinch away, Cap'n Waldo had smothered her hand in his vast hoof, and from his rocky elevation
was bellowing down, "Welcome to our city, like the fellow
says, little lady! Saw you at the depot, but I was kind of
tied up. I don't know what the hell a 'sociologist' is, but
if you're it, it's all right by me! But you ain't going to like
it! We got some pretty tough cons here. We try to treat
'em square, but, Lord love you, they just take advantage
of you. Well, you better stick around a month or so—be
good experience for you—and then beat it back to your
colleges and houses of refuge and all that soft-soap bunk.
Say, in your off time, the Old Lady and me would be tickled to death if you'd come to the house and have a bottle
of Coca-Cola with us." Ann perceived that the man was
trying to be cordial. But his gap-toothed smile, as he
loomed over her, was terrifying. "Now you're making a
first beginning, little lady, let me warn you. There's a
lot of cranks and sentimental theorists—*the-orists!*—
especially where you come from, that seems like they got
the idea you can handle a lot of yeggs, that'd shoot you

just 's soon 's eat, by begging 'em to be good boys and girls, and coddling 'em, and giving 'em bathtubs and champagne wine and surprise parties and God knows what all monkeyshines! That's fine for a lot of these theorists that never been nearer a real, honest-to-God prison than a college campus. But me, I'm only fifty-two, but I been right in practical prison work, and sheriff and like that, for thirty-two mortal years, and I tell you the only way you can handle criminals—they simply ain't human, what we call human, and the only way you can handle 'em is to put the fear of God into 'em, so they'll behave themselves while they're in the pen and not want to come back when they get out. Be square with 'em, of course. But just let 'em see you're the by God *boss*, and not scared to punish 'em *proper* if they try to get away with anything! I'm not scared of 'em, and they know it. Long's a man treats *me* right, and does just exactly to the last detail what I by God tell him and no argument about it which way or t' other, why, I treat *him* right, and the damn cons know it!"

(They were seated now: Dr. Slenk beaming and nodding at his desk; Cap'n Waldo flooding an armchair and making the gestures suitable to his oratory; Ann hypnotized, save for her fingers, which nervously galloped on her knee.)

"That's real 'scientific criminology,' ain't it? Cause and effect! Raise hell and you get hell! Anything more scientific than that? And talk about psychology (of course I was just kidding when I said I didn't know about sociology; I'll bet I've read a hell of a lot more real, deep, learned books than most of these guys that claim to be so wise, only I don't shoot off my mouth about 'em)—and when it comes to psychology, here's the real lowdown on it. Why

are criminals criminals? Because they think they're too
good to mind the rules. Then what ought a keeper to do
with 'em? Why, *break 'em!* Show 'em they ain't better
than the run of folks—matter of fact, show 'em they ain't
any good at all, and the only way they can get along, in
prison or out, is by minding *all* the rules, no matter what
they are, and minding 'em quick, and no back-chat! Fact,
it's a good thing to give 'em fool rules that don't mean
nothing, just so they *will* learn to do what they're told,
no matter what it is! And if they don't—*break 'em!* I do!
I'm not afraid to lash 'em (not supposed to, by law, but
we're just talking between ourselves now, not for the fool
legislature). I'm not afraid to keep 'em in the hole for two
months if necessary, with no clothes and no bed and no
light, and mighty little bread, and just enough water so
they're always thirsty, night and day. I'm not afraid to
truss 'em up in the blanket-roll—that's what we call the
straitjacket here—till they feel they're busting. (The
warden isn't supposed to know about these things, so don't
tell him. He passes the buck to me on all that!)"

They laughed knowingly, both men—laughed with shrill
pleasantry, like uncles laughing at the pranks of a baby.

"You see, Miss—Vickers, is it?—here's the point. It's
not only a lot easier for us, but it's a lot kinder to the cons
themselves, to let them know there's no use their trying
to beat the game. My God, it's right in the Bible: 'Spare
the rod and spoil the child'! The quicker they understand
what they're up against, the happier they are. They got to
learn discipline. *Discipline!* That's the greatest word in the
English language! I tell you, if the truth were known, the
worst trick that was ever played on these poor devils was

to do what the fool theorists call 'reforming' the prisons! Chumps like this wind-bag Osborne, and this schoolteacher Kirchwey! Why if I could just have some of the good old punishments, if I could brand the incorrigibles so's people could see just what those skunks are, if I could lash 'em, not on the Q. T. but in public, so's it'd be a warning and a deterrent to everybody, give 'em five hundred strokes with a real cat-o'-nine-tails—stop when they fainted, and go to it again, and put plenty of salt in the scratches afterwards —why, say if I could do that, I'd cure *all* crime in a jiffy! Yes, sir, it's an outrage that a fellow is prevented by the newspapers and these damn so-called reformers from doing what experience teaches us would turn all these wretched offenders into good, straight, God-fearing men! Well, say, sister, I didn't mean to make a Fourth o' July oration! But I just thought you ought to know the real inside facts of the matter at the start, so you can't go out afterwards and complain we were putting anything over on you. I tell you, with my experience I can learn you more real, honest-to-God, practical penology in five minutes than you could learn in these colleges and wishy-washy reformatories in five years. Hey, Warden?"

"Well, Cap'n Waldo, you know I disagree with you about a lot of things. But there is much to what he says, Miss Vickers. We all like to work out new theories of psychology, but as Shakespeare, or whoever it was, says, 'The plow-horse Practice cannot with the trotter Theory keep pace.' Well, Cap'n, will you take Miss Vickers out and introduce her to Mrs. Bitlick and the girls and show her where to hang her hat?"

It may be that Ann's paralysis of rage looked like complaisant stupidity. At least Captain Waldo gazed at her not unapprovingly as he growled, "Well, sister, maybe you'll learn this game, even if you did waste time going to college. . . . Enker! ENKER!" His roar was terrifying. The negro-trusty doorman popped into the office like the humorous servant in a farce.

"Yassah, Cap'n Waldo!"

"Take Miss Vickers's satchels and the rest of her truck to the Matrons' Dormitory, and make it snappy."

"Yassah!"

The doorman yearned at the black-toothed, pigskin-faced giant, Cap'n Waldo, like a worshiper before a sacred statue. It is a question whether Ann was more sick, more frightened, or more homicidal, but all three wholesome emotions were so mixed and confounded in her that she was still silent as she rose to Cap'n Waldo's, "Well, come on, sister."

Outside, Cap'n Waldo sniggered, "Say, you know I don't have to go down to the depot for cons, like I done today. Hell no! I'm the boss! But it's just kind of fun to go, when you got a tough homicide!"

24

Aт the back of the slick and marbled lobby of the entrance hall, with its air of a hotel for promoters and the higher blackmailers, was a low door with no hotel aspect to it whatever: a steel door with steel studs. (What the studs were for, except to look nasty, Ann never did discover.) Cap'n Waldo flourished his ring of keys in the lofty way in which officials *do* flourish keys, and led Ann through the door into a corridor of cement and brick. It was damp, and lighted only by electric lights in small, fly-spotted globes. It was like a large sewer. Up a spiral steel stairway then, in a cement well, as though she were ascending a lighthouse.

"Wait!" puffed Cap'n Waldo. "I'll show you something! Men are most of 'em in the shops or out on the farm, and you can peep in." He sounded as though he were giving her candy. "You ain't supposed to—*men's* division! But I'll let you for once."

He pompously flourished his keys again, opened a steel door, and escorted her out on a floor of dark steel plates cast in a pattern of tiny raised diamonds. She tilted her head in amazement. She was at the focus of a building like a gigantic Y, each arm of the Y three hundred feet long and fifty wide. Here at the focus was a circular lobby, open to the roof, from which she could look up at three stories of barred cells stretching in two double rows the length of each arm. The bright steel bars were like racks of rifles in an unending armory. Toward her these glaring lines swooped like the nightmare of a cubist.

A man, a human being, could no more live in that multiple cage than in a dynamo!

The small prisons she knew—the cottages at the Eastern Girls' Refuge, the steel and wooden cages at Green Valley —were homely as an old-time garret beside this Grand Canyon of steel bars.

The July heat was thickened by stinks of sweat, old food, old toilets, slops, cheap pipe-tobacco, crushed cockroaches, and disinfectant, yet the spreading lines of steel seemed icy. Ann shivered.

"Fine cells, eh?" said Cap'n Waldo. "Sixteen hundred of 'em—enough so's we ain't hardly crowded a bit—only three hundred cells where they're doubled up!" The Cap'n looked at the bars as proudly as King Solomon at his sixteen hundred children. "Yes, sir! Now that's real prison reform! The hardest steel on the market!"

Toward them, on the cell floor where they stood, wavered a half-human figure; an unshaven old man, pale as veal, in a ragged dressing-gown once black and purple, flannelette pajamas of a sickly green, and canvas sneakers.

"How-do, Cap'n! How-do! How-do! Sweet gal you got there! Yessir, sweet! Come here, sweetie!" The old man was advancing in a sneaking sidewise crawl, waving his talons.

"Git out of here, Daddy, or I'll put the bloodhounds on you!" Cap'n Waldo sounded not ill-natured, but the old man crept away, leering at Ann over his shoulder. As Cap'n Waldo motioned her back to the stairway he chuckled, "Funny old cuss, that. We don't hardly make him work at all—still, he's a good block man—sweeps the corridors pretty good. And let me tell you, there's one man that obeys and does what I tell him—yessir, he'll follow me like a licked dog!"

"What is he in for?"

"Oh, he kind of got in trouble with his daughter, and then a lot of neighbors claimed he killed her kid. Don't believe it. Why, say, he's a fine old fellow. Obedient. Though they do say they had to give him a hundred lashes one time, his first sentence."

"Oh. His first one. When was that?"

"Before my time, but—— Let's see. Must have been about fifty-five years ago. But we got him reformed now."

Up two more steel flights, down two, through another sewer-like corridor, and they came into the Women's Division, which occupied three floors at the end of one arm of the giant Y. They entered by the cell-floor. It was not so overpowering as the three-tiered cage seen from the rotunda; there were but eighty cells here, occupied by a hundred women, as against the nineteen hundred men convicts. It was not overpowering, no; it was merely terrifying, to walk past the empty steel-fronted cement cages. Each cell had a double-decker bunk of steel piping, a rickety stool, a staggering little wooden table, a tin bowl and tin pitcher, and a large tin bucket, as sole furniture in a woman's home for two—ten—forty years of her life.

Cockroaches scuttled in front of Ann across the gangway between the cell-rows, and once a rat flashed over. Like the men's division, the corridor stank with disinfectant and the odor of sweat.

"Damn, dirty, lazy wenches—just can't get 'em to kill off the bugs," said Cap'n Waldo cheerfully. "Look now. Got four condemned cells—separate room at the end— special stairs from it goes down to the gallows, in the basement. Makes it handy when we have to execute a woman. You'll see we allow the gals in the condemned cells to have pictures—but limited to pictures of near relations, of course, and only two apiece. We like to do that, to cheer 'em up in their last days. Here they are."

With another flourish he revealed a room of four cells. There was unexpected turmoil. Two beefy men guards, in blue and brass buttons, were thrusting into a cell what seemed to be a crazed dog struggling with claws and teeth to get out of a bag. Ann made it out as Lil Hezekiah, the negro murderess. They had taken her black satin best dress away and her little straw best hat, and put her into a uniform of gingham so washed-out that it looked like a dried old dishrag.

"Shove her in, boys," Cap'n Waldo said casually to the guards. "Got her mugged and fingerprinted? Hey! Don't let her kick like that! What's the matter with you boys? Afraid of a skinny old nigger hag? Grab her legs. That's the way! There!"

As one of the guards closed the barred door, he beamed

on Cap'n Waldo and croaked, "Yeh, got her all mugged. God help the matron that has to make her take a bath, though! She must be crazy, that old devil!"

Then, out of her stunned horror, Ann began to speak, as a hundred times she had almost begun. "She's not crazy, Captain Dringoole! Oh, I'm sure of it! She's simply terrified."

"Sure, I know, honey. She'll be all right now. She'll get used to it, and anyway, we'll yank her downstairs and hang her quick, so it don't matter. They do get scared; ain't got sense enough to see they can't do nothing. But they shut up—see, like this other old coot here. We had a monstrous lot of trouble with her, but now she behaves herself and keeps quiet."

He was pointing at the one other woman in the condemned block, watched by two matrons. She was indeed quiet. She had no face; merely two holes burning in a mask of white cotton. She sat hunched on her stool. She did not move, save that her fingertips crept round and round and round her lax mouth. Her head hung a bit on one side, like the head of a woman who has been hanged.

Cap'n Waldo left Ann at the office of Mrs. Bitlick, headmatron of the women's division, on the floor above the women's cells.

"Afternoon, Sister Bitlick. Behaving yourself? Here's the young lady that's come from Boston-way, I reckon it is, to teach us old codgers how to run a pen. You girls be good now. Think over what I said, Miss—uh—Vickers. In a week, you'll see it just like I do."

"*Well!*" said Mrs. Bitlick, when Cap'n Waldo had gallantly waved his hat and gone. "I declare! First time I ever knew Cap'n Waldo to take the trouble to bring anybody here himself! Most generally sends that fresh nigger, Enker. Reckon you must have made a hit with him. Better be careful of him!" Mrs. Bitlick was laughing, in a vague, pop-eyed, amiable way.

For one half hour then, Mrs. Bitlick (there is no describing her; she looked more or less female, with more or less gray-streaked brown hair; and she more or less wore a blue uniform dress) explained that though Ann apparently *was* a great friend and *favorite* of Mrs. Windelskate, she must put her mind to it and *learn* that here at Copperhead Gap, nobody played no *favors, never,* and Ann must take her *place* and obey the rules for officers just like she'd come from way up yonder on Starvation Ridge.

Mrs. Bitlick said it all rather hopefully, as though no matter what pessimists might think, she herself was certain that Ann would break those rules and be kicked out after a stay just long enough to give them all a good laugh.

"And now I reckon you'd like to go to your room and wash up," said Mrs. Bitlick.

She did not escort Ann. She rang, and into the office trotted a veritable Brownie: round eyes, round nose, round mouth with a round grin; a lively, jiggling, white Topsy, who looked fifteen, who looked as though she had put on only for a masquerade this prison costume of washed-out-dishrag dress and square-toed high black shoes. She grinned at Ann, she grinned at Mrs. Bitlick.

"Birdie! You been smoking again. Yes you have! I can smell it!"

"Oh, no, Mis' Bitlick! Me? I never smoke no more! I

just study all the time on being a good girl when I get out, and smoking is bad—my! smoking leads to all kind of devilments! I just think about everything you and Mis' Kaggs tells me, all the time. You're so good to a po' gal!"

Mrs. Bitlick sighed. "This is Birdie Wallop, Miss Vickers. She's a booster—shoplifter. But she's not like most of the women here. She seems to realize and appreciate what we're trying to do for her, and you can see how happy she looks—she shows what we accomplish. Now, you take Miss Vickers to her room, Birdie, and if I do catch you smoking again, I'll whale the everlasting daylights out of you!"

Birdie wept. Birdie howled. "Oh, 'tain't being scared of being punished, Mis' Bitlick! But it'd break my heart if you didn't think I appreciated all the lovely things you done for me!"

"Huh! I hope so. Run along."

Outside, Birdie Wallop's tears instantly ceased. Her round jaunty eyes looked uncannily through Ann, and she grinned more impishly.

"Birdie! How much do you appreciate the lovely things Mrs. Bitlick has done for you?"

Birdie laid a finger beside her plump nose. "Ask me, lady! Ask me! Say, you're going to have an elegant time in this joint! I'm on. Say, I was a waitress two years, and I know people. When they get to nagging you, you just tell old Aunt Birdie your troubles. Come on."

Along the corridor, Birdie held up a grave forefinger, darted into a room with two chairs, a desk, and perhaps a hundred frayed and faded books, laid a leaflet on the desk, picked up her long black skirts, and did two solemn dance-steps.

"What's all this?"

"Swear you won't tell? I reckon you won't. We know about you—beats hell what a lot of chewing the rag us gals can do in our cells when the theory is we ain't talking! We heard how swell you were. And *educated!* Gee! An educated matron here! Well, see, it's like this. The Reverend Lenny—Doc Gurry—he's the chaplain, and a fine piece of Roquefort *he* is—he'll be in the library this evening and I want him to find that little piece of litteatoor. What a fit Lenny is going to have!"

"What did you put there?"

"Oh, just an ad of 'Old Dr. Thorpley—you can tell him the truth,' that my boy friend soaked off a lavatory and sneaked in to me!"

"Birdie! Do you realize that—do you realize I'm supposed to be an officer here and make you mind the rules?"

Birdie tapped her nose and winked. She had completed the work, begun by Cap'n Waldo, of making Ann perceive that she belonged in no matron's place, but on the other side of the bars, along with Birdie and Mrs. Van Tuyl, with Gene Debs and Galileo and Walter Raleigh.

The room which Ann expected to have as refuge was not a private room at all, but a dormitory with three frowsy beds, three pine bureaus, three chairs, three cracked mirrors, and a bathroom with three skinny towels.

In the farthest bed a woman bleary with sleep raised her head, clearing her throat as she groaned, "Heh? Heh? What is it? Oh. Are you the new matron? Vickers? Oh, God, what time is it? Didn't hardly sleep all day, it was so hot. . . . I'm Mrs. Kaggs, the night-matron. That's your bed, in the middle. Hope you'll try and help keep this room decent. . . . Oh. Mis' Bitlick said you was to put on your uniform that you sent down the measurements for—it's in that middle section in the wardrobe—better put it on now—Cap'n Waldo, the old bastard, raises hell if he ketches us girls out of uniform. Well, I'm going to catch me some more sleep. For God's sake try and be a little quiet, will yuh?"

Mrs. Kaggs instantly burrowed again into her pillow.

Ann stood studying her: an oldish woman, sallow, anæmic, with a mole beside her nose, her face slack in the defenselessness of sleep.

Panting with heat and the odor of carbolic acid and old sheets, Ann dragged off her suit and wriggled into a uniform of blue serge with brass buttons and an absurd Sam Browne belt. In the milky mirror she tried to study herself.

"I look like a tough policeman. I wonder how soon it will get me and I'll enjoy relieving my boredom by using a club?"

She sat straight, in a flimsy chair that creaked to her breathing. She looked out of the window on a cinder courtyard of the men's division, in which three men in blue uniforms with red stripes, and grotesque striped caps, the very jeer and humor of shame, were walking endlessly round and round and round, stooped over wheelbarrows piled with rock.

"I can't stand it! I can't stay here! Not one hour! I'd go mad and kill Cap'n Waldo, and that woman on the bed, and the Bitlick woman! I've got to! Make a protest they can understand!

"No. I've got to stick, just because it is hard. I've been

rather of a failure. Skipped around, job to job; suffrage, settlements, O. C. I., nibbling at reformatories. You're not a promising young woman any longer, Annie. You're thirty-three. But if you can stick this for one year, then maybe you can help blow up every prison in the world!

"But—one year! I've been here one hour, and I'm already a homicidal maniac! I'll end in a cell with Lil Hezekiah. My God, I'd like to! I'd rather be with her than here with Mrs. Kaggs!

"Look, girl, you've got to keep your mouth shut. It's a woman-sized job. You're a spy in enemy country. No matter what you see, till the time comes you *keep your mouth shut!*"

She stood at the window in a cramp of horror. The cinder courtyard burned; the three men staggered round and round and round, wheeling the rocks, a toil pointless and degrading, revealing that as prisoners they hadn't even the free man's first privilege of working for a purpose.

"Yes. 'We mustn't exaggerate. The world has grown better—we've got rid of torture!' Oh, quit agonizing! You, wailing over your little miseries, when you can get away, any time, while those slaves down there—yes, and probably this Kaggs wreck, and the Bitlick—are stuck here for years, for life. And you, with your abortion, your killing of Pride, as much a criminal as any of them. All of us criminals, but some of us don't get caught!"

25

"THERE are no tramps—there are only men tramping," said Josiah Flint. And there are no doctors—only men studying medicine; there are no authors—only men writing; there are no criminals and no prisoners, but only men who have done something that at the moment was regarded as breaking the law, and who at the hit-or-miss guess-verdict of a judge (who was no judge at all, but only a man judging, in accordance as his digestion and his wife's nagging affected him) were carted off to a prison.

So Ann was among women who were not merely prisoners and keepers, but variable human beings, and she did not for twenty-four hours a day go on relishing horrors. Like her Tafford County Jail, the prison was uncomfortable and futile, but it was not magically different from other monuments to stupidity. It was more uncomfortable than the two modern women's reformatories she already knew, but it was no more futile. It was scarcely worse than many institutions to which people are condemned for the crime of being born, such as a Pennsylvania mine and its appertaining shacks, a Carolina cotton-mill town, or a New York speakeasy jammed with clever women who get drunk to forget suicide. Ann came to take most of her disagreeable hours casually. As they say of slothful people, she "got used to things." She slept, breakfasted, worked, quarreled, dined, read the newspaper, slept, in that mechanical acceptance of environment by which mankind endures living in a trench, a North Polar igloo, a tuberculosis sanitarium, or a house with a grasping woman, without going mad.

Had it not been for this healing human complaisance, Ann might well have gone mad, for horrors enough she did see during her fifteen months: Cells with vile air, cockroaches, rats, lice, fleas, mosquitoes. Punishment in the dungeon, lying on cold cement with neither a blanket nor any clothes save a nightgown, with two slices of bread every twenty-four hours. A dining-room filthy with flies, which left their hieroglyphics bountifully on the oilcloth. Food tasting like slop and filled with maggots and beetles. Undergarments coarse as sailcloth, stiff with sweat after work in the shirt-shop. The fact that Mrs. Windelskate's handsome gymnasium was kept locked, was never used, except when Cap'n Waldo found it convenient for conferences with the prostitutes among the women prisoners. The shirt shop with antiquated and dangerous machinery and a dimness that ruined the eyes. Silence for twenty-three hours a day—speech permitted only for an hour after supper, in the exercise yard—though naturally the rule was broken by tapping the walls at night and grunting out of the corner of one's mouth all day long, since it is the duty, pride, and pleasure of all convicts to break all prison rules, exactly as it is the duty, pride, and pleasure of the keepers to enforce them. The only difference is that the keepers celebrate their triumphs, not quietly and decently, like the convicts, but with clubs, straps, and taking away the privileges of letter-writing and walking in the cinders of the courtyard, whereupon the convicts, with natural bitterness at this unfairness, break the rules all the more proudly. The more punishment there is, the more things there are to be punished, and the general philosophy of the whole business is that of an idiot chasing flies.

If Ann got used to the unpleasantnesses, as one does to cancer, she never did get used to the fact that her study of the prison was blocked by the rustic slyness with which Cap'n Waldo pranked up his cruelty. She had expected to talk with the Copperhead convicts, to get their side of things, as freely as at Green Valley. But here there was no rule more strict than that officers might not, except with trusties like Birdie Wallop, talk at any time with any prisoner, save to give orders.

Ann had looked to knowing Mrs. Jessie Van Tuyl, the labor leader imprisoned for the metaphysical atrocity of "criminal syndicalism" as she might have looked to knowing Jane Addams. On her first evening she had gayly started for Mrs. Van Tuyl's cell, but had been halted by Mrs. Bitlick, and told, "No talkin' to the inmates. If you're so well educated and all, you might study your Book of Rules!"

It seemed an excellent notion—she must, like her comrade-at-arms Birdie, know what rules there were to break. She spent her first evening at Copperhead reading such jocularities as:

The only purpose of this institution is to enable transgressors to so correct former bad habits that they may be able to resume a full and happy position in society. For that reason, a prisoner should obey all rules not merely because they are rules, but that he may develop a fuller and richer personality.

"Dr. Slenk or some other Y. M. C. A. man wrote that. Cap'n Waldo never enjoyed good, clean fun that much," murmured Ann.

Do not ever forget that making any commotion in cells at night is not only a serious infraction of prison rules but also a serious disturbance of other inmates. If you do not appreciate this opportunity for quiet meditation so that you may get right with society and your Maker, remember there are others that do, and selfishness is at the bottom of almost all criminality.

No offense is more serious than breaking, marking, or otherwise injuring the furniture in your cell, machinery in the workshop, or any other prison property whatsoever. Remember that the State has gone to great expense to provide you with equipment.

Ann reverted to the diction of Waubanakee, Illinois, and groaned, "Now *hon-estly!*"

With the hypocrisy which is the chief means in all prisons for developing a fuller and richer personality and which Ann was learning as rapidly as any other inmate, she perceived that the way to avoid the rule against talking to prisoners was to flatter Cap'n Waldo and get special permissions. The method had faults. Cap'n Waldo held her hand, suggested evening walks, and looked at her with knowing obscenity. But by managing never to be alone in the gymnasium or her dormitory when he went inspecting —Cap'n Waldo did love to inspect and improve the women's division, especially the bathroom—Ann skated past, wondering when she would be caught and shot, like any other spy.

With his special pass, she was able to call on Jessie Van Tuyl in her cell within a week.

She expected to see a personage, a Joan of Arc, an orator at home. Mrs. Kaggs let her into the stifling cell. The light was so thin that Ann saw only—a typical convict: the dishrag of a uniform, the shoes like blocks. As Mrs. Van Tuyl, who sat reading on her stool, raised her head, her hair was untidy over her hot forehead, and down her face dribbled streaks of sweat. She was the more grotesque that in the midst of this smeary face of an inmate she wore perky eyeglasses. Not for minutes did Ann make out the broad forehead, the steady eyes, the kind mouth, the motherly breast. A Copperhead Gap uniform, a Copperhead cell on a July evening, could make a vagrant out of even Jessie Van Tuyl.

"Why, it's Ann Vickers, isn't it? I wondered if you'd come! Ann, my dear, this is my brightest minute in months! I know Mamie Bogardus a little, and Malvina Wormser——"

"You, Van Tuyl!" It was night-matron Kaggs; she had remained at the barred door, listening. "Miss Vickers is *supposed* to be an officer! You certainly ain't allowed to address an officer by her first name, no matter how well you knew her outside!"

"Mrs. Kaggs!" Jessie Van Tuyl's voice was considerably sharper than the night-matron's. "That poor Inch girl is sick again. I've already told you she's a psychotic— ought to be at Brisbane. I insist on your having the doctor see her right away, tonight."

"Doctor's got no time to fool with that thievin' little nigger! Probably playin' possum."

"You heard what I said! A lovely report I shall have to make to the newspapers when I get out of here!"

"Aw, you and your talk about what you'll do when you get out of here! That's what all you yeggs pull! I'll get the doc, but not because you said so. Was going to anyway! Now, Miss Vickers, remember you ain't allowed but half an hour in there!" Mrs. Kaggs bobbed away like an offended hen.

Jessie Van Tuyl laughed. "If that woman only knew how right she is! I do get a few things done by threatening them with newspaper publicity, but actually, when I get out—— What newspaper would find the fact that slavery exists in the United States, and with torture, important news, like a baseball game, or Coolidge's having a cold? You didn't mind my calling you 'Ann'? I'm one of these dratted sociable radicals. If I were a Methodist, I'd call everybody 'Sister.' Oh, Ann, my dear, my dear! Let me gabble! For seven months, except one visitor a month allowed to see me, half an hour, with a guard listening, I haven't heard or talked about anything except meal bugs in the mush—beat the Inch girl till she fainted—syphilitics use the same bath—tuberculotics can't stitch fast enough—'the conversation damned souls use in hell!' And a beastly fight with Bitlick every time I try to slip some of my food to a starving girl. This is what they did to me for saying that the workers have a right to unite! There! Now tell me the news—the scandal—the low-down! I'm like a trapper in the Arctic, with you landing in an aëroplane. . . . What's Malvina doing? What's the dope on our recognizing Russia? How I want to get out into that beautiful world again, and just stand and breathe fresh air and look at a birch tree for five minutes, then jump right into the first glorious fight that's handy!

"The girl that's sick—the Inch girl? Oh, she's a *very* serious criminal! She's a little colored girl, born in a cabin where her mother lived in sin—lots of sin and frequent. Pure psychotic. She's delightfully named Eglantine Inch. Worked as second girl for a rich tobacco broker in Pearlsburg. Three dollars a week. Her boy friend needed more money—for his automobile payments, naturally. She stole a diamond worth five hundred dollars, sold it for five— and got five years. She won't live out the five years, of course. She has everything a girl could ask for to make her repentant and virtuous. Presumably for her sins the Lord, Who marketh the falling sparrow but seems singularly unaware of convicts, has sent her a touch of asthma, and I suspect syphilis. The doctor just hasn't quite got around to giving her a Wassermann yet. He's not a bad egg, the doctor, but he's a dreadful alcoholic—that's why he's doing time here, like me and you!

"Why they don't send her to the hospital? Why, my dear girl, there's a fairly decent hospital for the men, or so I hear, but there's none at all for the women, because there isn't room—the highly profitable shirt-factory takes up so much space—and because some time in the next ten years they hope to have a nice new separate hell of their own for women, so why make improvements? No, all sick women convicts are treated in their cells, with the same greasy food we get in the dining-hall—only colder and served later, of course.

"What does Cap'n Waldo have on Dr. Slenk, to make him so complaisant? Nothing, really. Slenk is the kind of amiable scoundrel you don't have to have anything on. He just agrees with anybody that has a deeper voice than his. He would agree with me, as he does with the Cap'n (good, old, honest, murderous, lecherous Cap'n!) if I had him here. Incidentally, Dr. Slenk isn't an M. D., as he lets you think, as most people in the state think. He's a veterinarian, and he used to be a horse-trader, and he had one year in a college of osteopathy. How did he get in? By agreeing! By kissing everybody's foot. Didn't he yours? Why, he was almost polite even to me, a criminal! Then, too, he has a brother who's a rich contractor—built part of this prison.

"Graft? Of course there's graft. All the shirts and underclothes we make here, all the overalls and castings and barbed wire the men make in their division, are contracted for by outside firms, who get their labor here for forty-five cents a day, and sell the goods under fake labels, so purchasers won't know they come from convict labor. Good business for them. And for the officers here. I have no proof, but I'm told that Cap'n Waldo, at twenty-three hundred dollars a year and maintenance, drives a Packard, owns two boarding houses at Timgad Springs, and his son is going to Yale. And Mrs. Bitlick and Miss Peebee, who is the shop-matron and forewoman, are partners in a beauty parlor (partners, I said—obviously not customers!) in

Pearlsburg! And certainly the way Peebee drives us to get our tasks done in the shop, to make more money for the contractors, the way she calls in men guards to slap us, drag us to the hole if we don't get them done, would indicate something more than a mere normal love of torture —it must be that even higher inspiration, the dollar! Certainly the contractors, considering that they get power free and labor almost so, have a glorious graft, and either Cap'n Waldo and Slenk and Bitlick and Peebee share the graft, or else they're worse fools even than they seem. Oh, Lord bless me! Sometimes I'm afraid prison will make me a little bitter! Listen, Ann—hear Kaggs coming— *hold on*—keep your mouth shut—stay on here—the world needs you as witness—they won't believe me, a notorious Red—maybe they'll listen to you and believe you!

"*Maybe* they will. Good-night, my dear!"

Ann's days were not entirely given to observing cruelties and talking about them. She had a job. She kept the books for Mrs. Bitlick—she had had fair training at the Rochester settlement, and in any case, she was better than Bitlick, who could not add seven and seven and six and get them to total nineteen twice in succession. She had evening classes in cooking, waiting on table, making up rooms, and fine sewing, along with afternoon classes in reading, writing, arithmetic, and very elementary geography and history for the women, a third of whom had not gone beyond third grade, a fifth of whom were entirely illiterate. Mrs. Bitlick complained that it was "just a doggone fool waste of time for the legislature to make us learn all these hicks and chippies a lot of book-learning—

lot better for 'em to work in the shirt-shop, so's they can get nice jobs when they come out and earn maybe twelve dollars a week and be respectable." But Mrs. Windelskate and a number of pastors and editors had insisted that the inmates be forcibly educated right up through the fourth grade, and to such safe advisers the legislators had been willing to listen.

Ann helped supervise the cooking, which meant that she nagged the kitchen workers into a certain cleanliness. She was not shocked by their cheerful filth; she had learned in settlement work that cleanliness is not an inborn talent but, next to yachting, the most unnatural and expensive form of luxury.

Driven till her brain felt dusty, penned in the office, the classrooms, the kitchens, she failed (and realized that she failed) to see three quarters of what went on in the prison. She felt as though she were living in one of the old, huge, sea-cliff mansions, beloved of English writers of detective stories, in which people are murdered in rooms locked from the inside, shrieks are heard from empty attics, and lurking footsteps rustle at dawn, while the heroine shivers in her bed and wonders if this is really quite nice.

In the corridor, once, she watched two men guards drag a wailing girl, Gladys Stout, a prostitute, from the shirt-shop to the basement stairs. An hour later she saw Gladys staggering up. Her waist was torn, and there was a gashed welt across her shoulders. Ann asked Miss Peebee, the shop-matron, but that lady knew nothing—oh, nothing.

Ann had never yet found a way to see the dungeon—the "hole"—four utterly dark cells, like covered graves, in a crypt beneath the basement, but from it she had heard insane crying.

She got used to seeing girls in the confinement cells, "the solitary." They were like the ordinary cells, that is to say, no nastier than common, but they were segregated. Girls who did not complete their daily tasks in the shop, who talked back to guards, who spoke in the dining-hall or in the procession from shop to cells, were locked up here a day, a week, a month, on bread and water, with no evening hour in which they might talk, no letters, no books —just generally improved and fitted for return to society by being quietly reduced to terrified stupidity.

If Ann herself saw so little, what, she wondered, did the visitors learn who once a week came to be conducted through the prison and enjoy the thrill of beholding *criminals?* On an afternoon off, free of her detestably pert uniform, she joined the weekly sightseeing tour. She hadn't till then known in what a shrine she lived. She walked beside a young woman who resembled Gladys Stout and who giggled, "Oh, gee, look at that guy with the big jaw— I bet he's a murderer." (The guy happened to be a dental mechanic who, when he was out of work and his wife was sick, had stolen some gold.) They were taken by a handsome and jovial guard through the rose gardens to the Ritz-like lobby of the administration building and to the warden's stately office, through the men's cell block, through the men's overall-shop—it was modern and almost clean, and the guard did not show the antiquated foundry —to the men's library, a handsome room containing volumes of sermons and the novels of Zane Grey, Harold Bell Wright, and Temple Bailey—to the magnificent mosaic

chapel, and to the men's exercise grounds, with its impres-
sive parallel bars and rowing-machines, which the prisoners were allowed to use regularly, three hours a week,
providing they had perfectly observed every rule.

"There!" said the guard, as he brought them back to
the gate. "We don't use the cons so bad, do we?"

"You certainly don't. My! There's a lot of *decent* people
outside that'd be glad to have advantages like this!" said
a Baptist.

"But aren't you going to show us the women's part of
the jail?" said a Campbellite.

"That's under repair, just this minute, so we can't show
it," said the guard. "But it's just as nice—women got a
gymnasium, fine library, big classrooms, elegant dining-
hall—say, it's a regular university!"

"If you ask me," said a Presbyterian, "you treat these
crooks too good!"

"Well, maybe we do. But we're firm with 'em. We teach
'em disCIPline. No nonsense. . . . Oh! Thanks!" said the
guard, as an Episcopalian gave him a quarter.

Ann had a look at the shirt-shop, on the floor beneath the
cells, only by occasionally intruding. Miss Peebee, the
shop-forewoman, always glared, and spoke to her about it
prayerfully. (Miss Peebee had a small, earnest Bible class
of girls, including Birdie Wallop, every Sabbath afternoon.) But Ann kept on.

She had never before seen a place in which there was
absolutely no pride in work, no satisfaction in getting a
task done, and no companionship with other workers. The
prison was teaching its pupils that however dangerous

crime might be, anything was better than disciplined labor. The power sewing-machines in the shirt-shop were out of date. The needles were unprotected; often the women had their hands gouged. The long clamorous room was lighted only by small windows high in the wall, and by weary-looking electric globes, and as for ventilation— there was none. The women often fainted at the machines, and were restored by cold water and nagging. No talking of any kind was permitted, except to the forewoman, on business. Miss Peebee sat on a high platform, tapping a light cane. She needed it often, to correct the colored girl, Eglantine Inch, who loved to sing. Eglantine's lips sometimes moved when she was singing to herself, under cover of the roar, and then Miss Peebee was convinced that Eglantine was talking to the girl at the next machine and came down to correct her by lashing her arms. But Eglantine was lucky; she rarely got sent to solitary; she was too fast a worker and turned out too many shirts for the contractors, for all her spells of asthma.

But Josephine Filson, a murderess who had killed her own illegitimate child, was always in trouble. She was slow, she looked vague, she seemed never to arouse herself to pride in sewing hickory shirts; and in her case slackness was inexcusable, Miss Peebee pointed out, for had Filson not been a school teacher and had opportunities?

Ann came into the shop at closing-time—struck in the face by the sudden crashing silence as the machines shut down. Most of the women filed out. Those who had not completed their tasks were held behind, for admonishment. A man guard, with loaded stick, had been summoned. Miss Peebee was waving her cane and shrieking at Jose-

phine Filson, "This is the second day you're short! Aren't
you ashamed of yourself! The solitary for yours!"

"Oh, no, *please*, Miss Peebee!" begged Miss Filson. "I
tried so hard—I've had a headache—tomorrow I'll make
my task, oh, honestly I will! Don't send me to solitary!
You aren't allowed to read there, and I'm right in the middle of such a nice book, about a lord——"

Miss Peebee yelped at the guard, "Solitary for hers!"

The blue beef advanced, yawning. Miss Filson screamed,
clung with wizened fingers and cracked nails to a sewing-
machine. He snatched her loose, marched her out, while
Miss Peebee chattered at Ann, "The idea! Thinks she can
lay down on her task and then get to read! Upon my
word!"

Ann got, that evening, permission from Cap'n Waldo to
visit Miss Filson in her confinement cell.

It was like Miss Filson's own home cell, but she was
deprived of all food save bread and water, and all the
household treasures which were enabling her to get
through a life sentence—a pair of slippers, a postcard view
of Pearlsburg, a yard of crimson ribbon, and a dust-cloth,
stolen from the shirt-shop.

"Excuse me if I was rude," said Josephine Filson. "I
thought you'd be like the other matrons, Miss Vickers;
either they come scold you because you didn't make your
task—and I did do it today, but that poor little Eglantine
Inch stole some off my pile, and I couldn't complain on
her, because she's crazy, poor little thing—or else they
come talk religion to you: how you've been a sinner and
you have to get right with God.

"I used to try and be a good Christian and fear God. But now I've been here and seen Miss Peebee and Mrs. Bitlick and Dr. Slenk—they all claim they're good Christians, and teach in Sunday school, and I'd rather be like the worst woman here, like that Kittie Cognac that sells cocaine, than like them. I wonder if the preachers do know so much? They've never spent nine days lying on wet cement in a dark cell. . . . I prayed for God to come save me, then. He never answered. I reckon God is like your relations—when you need Him, He throws you out, so He won't be shamed by you.

"Yes, I had a baby, and I wasn't married, either. I was teaching in Coon Hollow. I had sixteen pupils, and I got twenty-five dollars a month and board-round. It was high altitude—awful cold. I used to get up at six and walk through the snow sometimes and start the fire and sweep the school. I didn't mind; I had some real bright kids. There was one lovely boy, so bright, and I used to tutor him evenings, and now he's in State University and doing real well! I liked teaching. You can see, I'm not pretty. The boys never paid much attention to me, somehow, when I was a girl. Never listened much. But my pupils would listen to me, and lots of times they'd bring me presents and all—goldenrod and persimmons and everything. I just loved teaching.

"But I never did have a beau—not till then. I was living for two months on the North Road—you know, where you go up from the Hollow—oh, you don't know Coon Hollow, of course; it's real pretty; I used to think before I lost my religion that the hills were like a temple. Well, I stayed first at Ad Titus's, and Ed, he was Ad's oldest boy, he was a big tall boy, only twenty, but he and I used to fool around and dance. I never was one to cut up much, but I did love to dance—you feel so lovely, all your muscles running so slick, why, it's better than horseback. Seems funny, don't it, to talk about dancing and horseback in this cell!

"Well, Ed had a fight with his girl—she was that Lora Dimond's girl, that lived down at Johnson's Forge—and of course, him being that silly romantic age, he just thought he had to have a girl all the time. 'Don't be so foolish,' I used to say to him, evenings, when we was there in Ad's kitchen—it was a big nice room, with a real old fireplace, and so clean and all—my! Mis' Titus would have died if she could see the cockroaches here! I told Ed, 'You do your work and some day you'll be a banker or a lawyer, like as not, and you can have your pick of the girls, so you forget 'em now,' I told him. Well, seems as if the more I talked, the more bound and determined he was that he was going to fall in love with *me*—me, so old and ugly and stupid, twelve years older than he was! I just laughed at him, but one night when his Pa and Ma were away, and we were fooling around, and the dog was barking, Ed he grabs me around the waist and he kissed me so hard—I never have been able to understand—it was just like I'd fainted. I'd never been what you might call kissed before. And I just kind of went crazy. I couldn't think of anything night or day but him—there I'd be standing in the school, drawing a map of Europe for the children—I used to love to draw maps, all the red and green and yellow crayons, and I was really quite good at geography; I could remember things like the rivers of Roumania, and I guess I made the children like it, because I'd always been so crazy to travel and see places and all; and I used to read the *National Geographic* at the doctor's house every month, he took it regularly, and so I could tell the children about Venice and the canals and all, and I reckon they liked it. But, as I say, I'd be drawing a map, but all the while I'd be thinking of Ed—his big hands and his voice, my! it was so deep!— and the way he laughed and you could hit him in the chest all day, hard as you liked, and it never seemed to wind him a mite! And I just couldn't think it was wrong, somehow, to think about him; like I'd found a buried treasure and all the lovely things I could do with it.

"And so one night when he came and crawled into my bed, it didn't seem wrong, it honestly didn't; we were so happy and loved each other so. Oh, I was kind of scared and surprised and all; I didn't know it would be like that. But still, it did make me so happy to think I was making him happy, and by and by I got to like it—I'd been so hungry for love, and—funny!—I hadn't really known I was!

"And then when I moved on to Bart Kelley's and then ol' Mis' Clabber's, I still wasn't but a mile or so from Ad's and Ed used to come every night and hoot like an owl, and I'd slip out, and we'd lie side by side in the woods, holding his hand, and kind of humming old songs like 'My Bonnie Lies Over the Ocean' or 'Joyland, Toyland' or talking about how we'd get some money somehow and get married and go to California.

"He was working for his Dad, but he thought he'd get through and go work in a garage somewhere and we could get married—he was real good at mechanics, but seemed like he never could find a job anywhere. I *told* him, I said,

'Now don't be silly, Ed; I'm just ages too old for you,' but he said, oh, he was so sweet to me, he said, 'Jo, you got more pep than any of these kids.' Oh, I reckon maybe he did mean it, too. I like to fool myself he did.

"We had a game—we'd look up at the stars through the trees (I tried to study a little astronomy, but I reckon I was pretty poor at it)—and we'd think, my! maybe those stars are worlds just like this one, but thousands of times bigger, so maybe the people there are five thousand feet tall, and maybe they have cities with walls of gold, a hundred thousand feet high. 'Think! Ed,' I'd say, 'maybe if our eyes are sharp enough, we can actually see those gold cities. There's the star—nothing between us and it!' I know. I was just a plain, silly, ridiculous old maid, in love with a boy almost young enough to be her son. It must have seemed real comic. Talking about gold cities in stars —and a baby coming.

"When I found out and told him, he was real nice; stood right by me. (If he was here, but thank Heaven he isn't, he'd kill that Cap'n Waldo and that red-headed guard, if he saw 'em coming around running their filthy hands over the girls' bosoms!) But we didn't either of us have any money—I had saved sixty dollars, but I'd gone and bought him a gold watch and chain with it and told him to tell his folks he found it on the road.

"So while we were trying to think up ways, it came summer vacation. Usually I worked in the Notch House, waiting on table, summers, but with the baby coming, I was terribly sick every day, and I stayed with Uncle Charley, he was a Methodist deacon but he was a real good kind man, and he guessed about the baby, and didn't throw me out, but his second wife, she found out and threatened to send me to jail, so Charley had to let me go, and Ed's folks found out about it, and they just went crazy, and they shipped Ed off to Pearlsburg—actually brought in the constable, and made Ed think they'd send him to the reformatory if he didn't get out and stay away.

"He wrote me. Wanted me to come join him. Said we'd make out somehow or 'nother. And I wanted to, so much— I just went crazy thinking about him and me and the baby in a nice little house with pictures, and us three going walking on Sunday. But then—— I was staying with a tough cracker family, across the tracks; Uncle Charley had put up the money. Then Charley's wife and the preacher and some others got hold of me and persuaded me I'd ruin Ed's life if I went and married him, and I don't know, maybe they were right, and I wouldn't want to do that.

"So I ran away, so Ed couldn't find me and have his life spoiled. I went up in the mountains. Stayed with some folks—I reckon they were poor white trash, all right, but they were awful nice to me. Then I tried to walk on. Thought I'd get to some hospital or something—I hear they let in poor folks free, sometimes. But the baby come sooner than I expected. Had it up on the mountain, with just one old nigger lady that lived there helping me—she was ninety, and she couldn't help me much—and then she had so little for herself, I couldn't take any more, and I walked on, with the baby in my arms, and I came to a deserted cabin, and I just set there for—I don't know; I guess my mind was kind of wandering—maybe it was four or five days, and when I came to, the baby was dead, lying in a puddle—honestly, I don't know whether I put it there, or somebody that came past. But then the officers came and said I was a murderess! Me! And the judge— Judge Tightam; he's a famous trap shot, known all over the state, you must have heard of him, I guess—he said I was worse because I had a position of honor and responsibility, and he gave me life. Even yet I can't quite realize it—I'll never go out of here again.

"But Ed's married now and got two little babies. Uncle Charley writes he's doing well.

"But—— You're an officer. Could you fix it so some time I could just walk out in the country just once, one hour?"

As Ann walked away from Josephine Filson's cell, she saw her daughter Pride.

"That's why I'm here. That's why I must stay here. I killed my baby, too," she said.

26

I HATE to say this about any professional crook, but honest I think Kittie Cognac is a stool and a squealer," complained Birdie Wallop. "When you talk to her, Miss Vickers, you make sure you don't say anything you don't want her to repeat to Mis' Bitlick. I know damn well Kittie got Doc Sorella into trouble for telling her about how they starve J. Filson. If you want to belly-ache—and that's a good thing to do sometimes, if you ask me—you go and beef to Jessie Van Tuyl. Saaaay! there's one grand skirt, Van. When I talk to her, I almost feel like going straight. But then I get an earful from Miss Peebee, and it makes me so mad, I know I'll go out and get revenged on the entire damn population of this state for sticking me in here with Peebee and Bitlick and Kaggs. . . . I will say this for Kit Cognac, the old plush-lined hooker, it was her that started us calling Peebee 'Pious Bitch' instead of 'Poor Boob,' like we was simps enough to do before."

Miss Kittie Cognac—she had been christened "Catherine Meek," except that probably she never was christened

—was a blackmailer, badger, dip, snowbird, hotel-prowler, creep-artist, and general thief. She should never have been in this comparatively rustic prison. By what she considered a joke on herself, after escaping the police of Chicago, New York, San Francisco, and Montreal with only two or three years of assorted sentences, Kittie had kidnaped quite a small ordinary child in Pearlsburg and, for all her protests that she was the wife of an English baronet—whom she mentioned in court as "His Grace"— and that her beloved old father lay dying, she had been sent up for sixteen years. Despite the most generous use of money among relatives of members of the State Parole Board, it looked seriously as though Kittie would serve at least five years of her sentence, though now the kidnaped child practically never woke up screaming at night any more.

Kittie Cognac was thirty-five; velvet-voiced, mahogany-haired, with hands like Diana.

At different times she confided that she had been born in Iowa, Texas, Ireland, New York City, and London. London, she told Ann, she knew well; His Grace, her husband, and she had often walked down Savile Row to Buckingham Palace, and while she didn't know the King personally, they had often smiled at each other, at the races at Brighton, in Cornwall, just north of London.

She was the chief trusty of the prison, not merely because, from the money which mysteriously arrived for her each month, she presented all the matrons with candy and silk stockings, and the men officers with cigars and very funny genuwine French magazines, but also because she was the only competent boss among the women prisoners.

Mrs. Kaggs, the night-matron, said admiringly that Kittie could by just looking at Eglantine Inch scare her into an epileptic fit. That was true; she could. And did. Kittie was officially assistant to Mrs. Kaggs; actually she was often the whole night force; let Mrs. Kaggs sleep, kept perfect order, and still had time to receive Cap'n Waldo in the gymnasium. Against all rules, Kittie wore high-heeled shoes and a string of pearls, and her blue gingham uniform was fresh, unlike a dishrag, and hung just below her knees.

"You and me don't belong in a hick jail like this, Miss Vickers," purred Kittie, swinging her legs on a table at one end of the cell corridor, making forbidden coffee in an inconceivably forbidden glass percolator. "You know New York, but these rubes, yes, and I mean the officers just as much as the lags (that's what we call cons in dear old Lunnon), why, they don't know what swell company is, or real excitement.

"Now take one time: I had to beat it out of Chicago on the lam, because they had a warrant out for me for robbing an old preacher. Golly, that was a funny stunt. I was running a creep joint in Chi. I sees an old preacher at a station, regular old white beard, buying a ticket for K. C., and he had a roll would choke a horse. So I makes him and I tells him I'm a stranger in town and I see he's a pulpit-pounder and would he tell me where's the best place to go to church in Chi. He tells me—say, you'd laugh your head off. Coupla years later, I actually did go to hear the old goat he'd recommended, for the fun of it; and just to play hell, I nicked a sawbuck out of the collection basket while I was making a lot of noise putting in one buck. God, that was funny! But I approve of church-going, you understand, and many's the time I've bawled out these sons that make fun of it. Well, I thanks him for being so kind, and wouldn't he come around to the house while he was waiting for the train—I had my old mother with me and Ma, I tells him, is just busting a gut to go to the toniest church in town.

"So one thing leads to another, and I gets him up to my room. Dandy place—swell little bed-sitting-room; nowhere you can hang your clothes except on the top bedpost, and a sliding panel right by it for my trailer to reach in and go through the sucker's pants. So I gets him there and—oh dear, 'Ma must have gone out! We'll wait.' And—this'll give you a laugh, Miss Vickers. You know, I wouldn't be so frank with you like this, but I've decided to reform, and knowing psychology like I do, the first step to really reforming is to be frank with the authorities, don't you think so? I may of been a thief, but I see my way clear now, and they can't none of 'em say I was naturally anything but honest; it was just environment and circumstances made me go wrong! But say, this'll give you a laugh. I got the old sky-pilot sitting there, and damn' 'f I didn't start playing *hymns!* Honest! You see, I was in the choir in Oklahoma, where I was brought up.

"Well, I sort of sat on the old guy's arm of his chair and tried to ginger him up a little so he'd make a pass at me, but nothing doing—the old hound's joy-joy days were over. He took my hand and patted it and what do you think? He started telling me about his Community Church! Can you tie it?

"I gets an idea. It was a pretty hot night. I suggests he take his coat off—he had the oof in bills in his inside pocket, in an envelope. No, he says, it wasn't polite in the presence of a lady. I wanted to lam him one and holler, 'Oh, don't let that stop you, you old son of a hound, I'm not demanding any swell manners—I just want your dough,' but I puts on the Cute Kittie expression and I says, 'But you're *going* to take your coat off, because you're going to help me make some old-fashioned home-made fudge.'

"You see, I had a little electric plate there, and some groceries. I always found it useful—get the sentimental slobs to cooking, when you couldn't get 'em loving. That's my own invention, and I hope to God I get credit for it. Chicago May nor Sophie Lyons nor nobody ever thought of that!

"So I tries to look domestic, and I brings out some brown sugar and butter, and I tells him, 'When I was a littley-bitsy girl in Oregon'—I guess I told him Oregon, or some place in the sticks I never seen. 'When I was a little girl, my four sisters and I used to go to our dear old pastor's and make fudge, and he always took his coat off and helped us. So if you don't, I won't feel at home—and oh, how I miss those happy innocent days back in my childhood home, here in the great wicked city.' You know, something like that, with the old pussy-cat smile.

"Of course he fell. Takes his coat off—but say, the old devil hung it on a chair that ordinarily I had stuck away in the closet so they couldn't do just that. Well, was I sore! But still, I was fair; I always am fair; I didn't blame the old bastard for putting his coat there; I just blamed myself for leaving that chair out; I just told him I was afraid the chair'd tip over, and I stuck his coat on the bedpost, where my trailer reached in through the panel and got the coin, P. D. Q., and filled up the envelope with pieces of newspaper and stuck it back in his pocket, so's if he felt it to see if his wad was still there when he checked out.

"Well, I'd have been kind of sorry for the old coot; he was enjoying our making the fudge so much, and saying he hadn't tasted any for years—it seems his Frau was sick, and he didn't have any real home life, hardly. But—my— Gawd! How bored I got! Me eating fudge! I wanted to slap him! He'd have kept on till the train went! Why, he wanted me to sing some more hymns! (Oh, and say, before I forget it, the big laugh was, the minute we'd cooked the fudge, the old codger—don't you hate these Puritans?— he went and put on his coat again, with the nice sweet pieces of newspaper in the envelope instead of the Redeemable in Gold. Wouldn't that give you the Willies? Like I would try to make him, the old smut-hound, if he was in his vest and shirt-sleeves!) But I got rid of him and saaaaay! I was dead sure he wouldn't look over his wad till he was in his nice little Pullman upper. But he was suspicious—and say, honestly now, don't you think that for all his playing the holy game, that shows he had evil thoughts?—and seems no sooner was he out and waiting for a trolley—no taxis for that bird, the damn tightwad!— when he gives his in-thee-I-do-trust the once-over, and instead of the handsome engravings, there was nothing but clippings.

"Well, I was just getting ready to beat it—and say, this'll give you a laugh: I was singing one of the hymns I'd played for him!—when he busts in on me with a bull. And he has the nerve to try to talk me down! Claims he hasn't tried to make me! And say, here's the real Chrismus-Eve jingle-bells stuff for you. The Dominie claims the jack wasn't his; claims he's collected it from some come-on to build a kitchen and dining-room onto his damn Community Church! And the cop runs me in! Takes me to the station!

"Well, that was all right. I'd fixed it with a guy I knew to put up bail if I ever needed it, with the understanding that I'd beat it out of town but send the bail back to him. And I would of, too, but when I got to New York, I got to thinking, this gentleman friend of mine that put up the bail, he could afford to lose it, while me, I was just a poor girl trying to get along. And who'd done all the work on this case? *I* had, while he'd just put up the money. So I just couldn't see, in justice to myself, why I should pay him back, can you?

"But can you beat that for injustice? Way I figured it, I was giving this old preacher a lesson. Didn't I teach him to not pick up unknown women? Wasn't it worth what he lost? Didn't I deserve the seven hundred bucks I got out of it—for, mind you, I had to give my trailer three hundred for doing nothing but just grab the dough out of the old gent's coat.

"And then he goes home, this preacher, and he commits suicide. Newspapers blamed it on me; said it was because of the notoriety. But was that my fault? Was it? Listen! You know what my hunch is? I think he bumped himself off because he realized he'd gone right against all he pretended to believe in—such a great Christian!—calling a

cop and getting me pinched, and so absolutely denying his
Saviour that said, 'Let him that is without sin cast the first
stone'!

"I don't know for sure just what I'll do when I get out of
here. Maybe I might go in for spiritualism. What a racket
that is! But nothing crooked, you understand, and you do
a lot of good. Of course, you shake the suckers down for all
the traffic will bear, like any other business, but you take
a lot of these old stiffs, say, they get more damn comfort
out of your telling them that Aunt Mariar is ringing 'em
up from Heaven!

"And besides, of course I believe in spiritualism. You
don't? Hell, no, I wouldn't expect you to. That's the trouble with all you earthbound spirits. Mrs. Bitlick and Cap'n
Waldo are the same way. Too dumm, too materialistic to
hear the voices from beyond. Why, many's the time I've
comforted myself in my great troubles—none of you eggs
can understand what I've gone through—by talking with
the spirit of General Grant or some great soul like that.
That's the real reason I'm in stir—because materialists like
you and the judges can't understand me. Yes, I think I
might do the medium dodge.

"And then again I might write a book about how
wicked I've been, and how to get away with it, and how
I've repented. Believe me, I can do it, too! Say, I guess I've
read everything that's worth reading. I bet I know Frank
Harris and Oscar Wilde and Arthur Brisbane better'n
any college professor. Yes, you're damn whistling, I'd like
to get into some nice clean graft like mental healing or
confessions. I dunno. I guess some ways I haven't been a

very good woman. You see, my Dad hated me. Well, all right, all right! I'll show him! He's been dead these twenty years, but I'll show him! To get even with him, I'm going to take it out on every living man I can get my hooks on!"

Ann leaned her head against the wall of the corridor.

"So there *are* convicts who are just as vile as their keepers!"

27

OF THE two women in the condemned cells, the first was hanged at eleven on the night after Ann's coming to Copperhead Gap, and that night Ann knew the restlessness in the prison, the wailing, the pounding on bars, which began at seven in the evening and lasted till dawn.

Lil Hezekiah, the old negress who had come to the Gap with Ann, a sinister classmate in the university of the damned, was in her last week of waiting now, and the death-watch was put on her, night and day; and night and day, two out of the nine matrons watched in front of her cell, two hours at a stretch.

Ann was one of the nine.

The death-watch sat in crazy rocking chairs—the kind that are found in lakeside summer cottages—in the corridor before Lil's cell.

Seven days left. Six days left. Five days left. In five days more the majestic state would take this living human being out and kill her. There she was, probably mad, old and wizened and ashen, yet full of the miracle of life—eyes magically seeing things and thus making them exist, ears delicate to catch the wonder of sound, womb that had brought forth strong copper-shining sons, hands that had woven bright rugs and mixed corn pone—and in five days, four days, three days now, the state in its wisdom and strength would take her and turn her into a heap of senseless and putrid flesh, and be proud of its revenge, and certain that by thus murdering Lil Hezekiah it had prevented all future murder forever and ever.

By the grace of God Amen in our Christian nation wherein we rage not as the Heathen but under the gentle teachings of Jesus do combine in one grand union for the purpose of gently murdering skinny old colored mammies let us now sing the Land of the Free and the Home of the Brave——

Yes, Ann did rave. She disliked murder. She was sorry that this mad old colored woman had committed murder. But, she thought, Lil did not plan it coldly and dispassionately, as we are doing.

Two days now. Twenty-four hours.

Leading penologists of the state, like Mrs. Windelskate and Dr. Addington Slenk, often announced that in this enlightened district, they were rid of the barbaric notion of *revenge* against criminals. That was why they put a deathwatch on Lil Hezekiah, to prevent her committing suicide and thus depriving the community of the pleasure of killing her.

She was not allowed one second of privacy. She had to sleep, think, pray, urinate, ponder on the fact that in a day now she would be dead, all under the bored observation of

Kittie Cognac or Mrs. Kaggs or some other matron. She was an old mountain woman, used to the stillness of high valleys. It prolonged her death agony to see death in the eyes of those peering women night and day, night and day.

But Lil, greatly given always to prayer, had the consolation of daily prayer by the prison chaplain, the Reverend Leonard T. Gurry, though of course Mr. Gurry was a very busy man and could not allow her more than five minutes a day.

He came briskly down the corridor and hailed Ann and Mrs. Kaggs: "*Good*-evening, ladies. I hope you are not too tired with your errand of mercy! But you can rest soon. Only twenty-two hours now!"

"Oh, my dear loving God!" wailed the mad old woman in the cell. "Twenty-two hours!"

Mr. Gurry observed, "Lil! You must never speak the name of the Almighty so lightly!" He let himself into the cell, but he stood with his back against the door, as far from Lil as possible. He was practically certain that colored folk had souls, but he did not like their skins.

"Now, sister, this is one of the last chances I shall have to pray with you—in fact, I can stay only a moment. So, if you will just kneel—just kneel, I said—O Lord our God, have mercy on this poor soul. Forgive her if Thou canst. She has repented of her grievous sin and so forgiveher-amengoodnightlil."

"You do think maybe He'll forgive me? Don't you? Don't you?"

"Oh, yes, yes. His mercy is infinite. But I must hurry."

There was no regulation at Copperhead Gap whereby a trusty could take the place of a matron in a death-watch, but actually Kittie Cognac usually appeared for Mrs. Kaggs, and once Ann and Kittie watched together.

"Be game, old girl," clucked Kittie to Lil. "Keep your chin up. You're just as good as any of these folks."

"Oh no I'm not, miss," wailed Lil. "I was a very bad woman. I reckon I certainly deserves to die. I didn't pray hard enough, that's what was wrong with me. Preacher tole me I ought to pray more, but I didn't. My old man used to get drunk and come home and beat me and my daughter, that's a widow, and I prayed—I prayed—I prayed he'd quit drinking that nigger gin. But it used to just make him mad to see me kneeling—he'd hit me with his shoe heel and so I reckon I weakened in my faith, and I didn't pray where he could see me. That's where I done sinned—that's why God's punishing me—'cause my faith got all weakened that way, and one night when he come home and started kicking one of the grandchildren that was sick, I hit him with the poker, and when he started choking me, I declare to goodness, I just forgot my religion and I busted him with the axe. Oh, I was a bad woman, miss."

"Oh, rats, you weren't so bad." Kittie yawned, and lighted a forbidden cigarette. While Ann was wondering whether she ought to do anything about the cigarette, Lil stood clutching the bars, her eyes angry, mouthing:

"I know what's bad and what's good! I know if I was bad—and who else is, too! I ain't like you women! High heels! Smoking cigarettes! The torches of Hell, that's what they are! I smoked a pipe, but I give that up, too, for the sake of religion, for the sake of my Lord! Cigarettes!"

"Now you look here!" cried Kittie. "A hell of a lot you know about religion, you old axe-hound! What do you know about the great esoteric truths of spiritualism? Can you call up the spirits? I can! Say, listen! Do you want to talk with your son-in-law that's passed over? His name was Josephus, and he used to like your gravy."

"Oh, my God, miss! That's the truth! He always liked it. Oh, is he here? Is he got a message for me? Will he intercede before the Throne of the Mos' High for a poor wicked old woman?"

Ann whispered, "Kittie! Don't! Or do be careful!"

"Sure, I'll give the old gal a five-dollar message!"

Lil was looking on the blackmailer with adoration. She had come alive with the drug of hope which Kittie Cognac had concocted out of a guess about gravy, and Lil's family-record. Her little old monkey face twitched with smiling; her fragile hands, rubbed by long labor to whiteness on the inside, fluttered on the bars; and she made nervous sounds of prayer as the blackmailer chanted:

"Josephus says to tell you that you'll be received in glory. He says the archangels will guide you."

"In glory! In glory! Amen!"

Twenty-one hours, and those bright worshiping eyes would be blank ludicrous things, like boiled onions.

. Dr. Arthur Sorella, the prison physician, looked like Edgar Allan Poe. The matrons gabbled that he was a graduate of Hopkins, that he had been a city surgeon of the rank of two Packard cars, that he had taken to drink when his wife left him. He alone among the officers, as Ann had seen him ghostly in the corridors, had been gentle.

When he came to glance at Lil Hezekiah, Ann begged of him—the other matron on watch, a long red woman whose cousin was a state senator, was safely asleep—"Doctor, you know they execute her this evening. Just ten hours now. Do you ever give them a shot of dope *before?* Can't you, with her? She's so scared! Listen how she's praying!"

"I'd like to. I would if I could. In fact, if there is to be any capital punishment at all, I'd give the poor devils a chance to commit suicide, decently and unobserved; hand 'em some poison they could take when they wanted to. But as it is, I don't dare even give them morphia. In the old days the warden would get a condemned prisoner nice and drunk, so he swung off happily. But the preachers and Good People of this state decided that their God wouldn't get enough relish out of His vengeance if the sinners weren't sober, and aware what He was doing to them."

"But can't you——"

"Hush!" Dr. Sorella glared at her, peeped at the sleeping matron. "Of course, you fool! I always slip them something. If I didn't, I'd have to kill my own self. Kindly don't tell Cap'n Waldo. Listen! Get out of this place! Either it will kill you or, worse, it'll get you, so you'll be as sadistic, in a polite way, as Cap'n Waldo! No human being that ever lived is kind enough or wise enough to stand year after year of having the power to torture people. Me, I don't matter; I'm done. Get out! My God, how I need a drink."

Ann looked in at Lil Hezekiah, holding up her skinny hands in an ecstatic vision of her God.

"So do I!"

They drank fiercely, with no toasting courtesies, from the pint of acrid moonshine he had in his inner coat pocket.

Ann was on duty most of the thirty-six hours before the hanging of Lil Hezekiah. She could most easily be spared. Aside from her accounts, she had no important duties, such as keeping the prisoners from escaping, or driving them to finish their tasks in the shirt-factory—she had, in fact, nothing but teaching, which, as Mrs. Bitlick pointed out, was merely a fad.

She had time off for naps, those thirty-six hours, but she did not sleep. She lay awake in her dormitory, seeing not the reformatory and deterrent spectacle of Mrs. Kaggs, yawning and scratching her armpits, but a Lil Hezekiah, who believed in God.

At half-past ten on an early winter evening, when the air of the corridors was that of a frigid cellar, and the wind harped in leafless trees, Mrs. Bitlick and Ann and Mrs. Kaggs marched to Lil Hezekiah's cell. At Mrs. Bitlick's nod the two matrons on guard tiptoed away.

Lil looked out at the chief matron and sprang up from her knees. She stood slumped, her head almost on her thin chest, her hands weaving. She whimpered wordlessly.

The three strong women in blue uniforms threw open the cell door.

"Now, stand straight there, Lil, and take off them clothes," said Mrs. Bitlick pleasantly.

But they had to hold her to get her stripped to the dark gray skin, to put on the new undergarments of clean coarse cotton, the new dress of black sateen. "Oh, for God's sake,

brace up! You aren't the only one that's gone this road!"
snapped Mrs. Bitlick. To Ann, apologetically, "Hate to
nag even a wench like this at such a time, but folks that
can't take their medicine always make me tired!"

At twenty minutes to eleven the Reverend Mr. Gurry
came into the cell with a brisk and cheery, "*Good*-evening,
ladies!"

He laid a natty handkerchief on the cell floor and knelt
on it, beside Lil, in her new black sateen dress. The dress
was factory-made. The seams were not straight.

The three matrons stood outside the cell. Mr. Gurry
prayed. It did not seem to Ann to mean anything; she
heard only a string of glossy words: Our Merciful Father,
take this soul, for this our great fault.

While the chaplain was praying, Dr. Sorella slipped past
the matrons, into the cell. He was feeling Lil's pulse. Ann
thought he passed something to Lil which, with sly quick-
ness, she popped into her mouth. Her face presently lost
its twitching terror; she began to shout, "Oh yes, Lord!
Amen! Hallelujah! Praise the Lord!"

Dr. Sorella went away.

Ann dropped into a chair, clean-beat.

Mrs. Bitlick grabbed her shoulder, grunting, "Why, the
idea! And you that think you're so superior! Haven't you
got any sense of religion at all—*sitting*, during the last
prayer! I never heard of such a thing!"

So Ann stood again for years while the patter went on,
"And so receive unto Thyself this erring soul," and Lil
shrieked, "Ain't it de truth! Praise God! Amen!"

At five minutes to eleven, tramping heavily, two men
guards came down the corridor, followed by Dr. Sorella

again, and the tappering dance step of Warden Slenk.

Dr. Slenk nodded to the three matrons, but as he entered the cell his face became pious, his voice a very balm of tenderness: "Come, Lil. I hope you have made your peace, my poor woman." He jerked his head sharply toward the two men guards. They lumbered over, seized Lil's arms, snatched her to her feet.

From unknown depths of the prison, from hundreds of cells, a muffled moaning.

Lil was so thin, so frail, and half drugged now. The two guards supported her between them, her feet dragging, her head drooping, but her lips never ceasing to murmur, "Praise the Lord, bless His holy name!" Just behind her came the Reverend Mr. Gurry, praying briskly, and Dr. Slenk, Dr. Sorella, and the three matrons. Ann's knees felt sick.

They stumbled down winding stairs, two horrible dark flights, and out into a room, light-glaring, painted a lively robin's-egg blue, with It in the center—a platform with a stout beam from which hung a noosed rope. Ann scarce saw the gallows; she was embarrassed by the crowd of forty witnesses, standing, staring, goggling, half-grinning in their excitement—rustic reporters trying to look hardboiled, lanky sheriff's officers pleased and professional, shy, eager colored relatives of Lil Hezekiah.

Ann saw the sheriff who had brought Lil to prison. She heard him grunt to a reporter, "Sure, I know the corpse very well."

They rushed Lil through it.

The guards had to lift her from step to step—thirteen steps, painted a lively robin's-egg blue, from the floor to the platform. She looked so little up there, above the mass of red-faced men. While she swayed, supported by the chaplain's arm, they hastily tied her wrists and ankles, most modestly bound her skirt so that it would not fly up, and dropped the noose about her neck, a black hood over her head. Instantly the warden raised his hand, nodding, and two guards, at a table on one corner of the platform, chopped lines of which one—nobody knew which—released a weight. The Reverend Mr. Gurry with neat nimbleness skipped aside, and Lil slumped to her knees. A trapdoor opened downward with a bang, and through it the black-capped form dropped grotesquely, fell, stopped with a jerk, and spun, spun, till Dr. Sorella, green-faced and slouching, caught it.

But it hung there, twitching, as though still alive, still struggling to get free. The veins on the hands swelled till they seemed to crawl. Eight minutes it hung, while Ann fought to keep from going out into the sick blackness that wavered all about her.

Stethoscope at the breast of the twitching thing, Dr. Sorella quavered, "I pronounce her dead."

The spectators crushed out, feeling for cigars, muttering, "Pretty hanging." Ann started to follow. Mrs. Bitlick commanded, "You! You wait! Your work ain't even begun!"

A guard cut the rope, while two others lowered the body to the floor, and loosened the noose.

"Ohhhhhhh!" shrieked the dead Lil Hezekiah, as the air compressed in her lungs rushed out.

Ann rushed to a corner of the room and vomited. She heard Mrs. Bitlick snicker. When Ann came back, the hood had been lifted from Lil's head. Her eyes were forced half out of their sockets. Her mouth was arched with horror, and on her lips was bloody foam.

Mrs. Bitlick, after an interested look at that twisted face, said, "Well, girls, we must wash the poor woman and get her ready for burial. The relations will be waiting for the body."

The men guards carried Lil into a small adjoining basement room, which smelled of decay and formaldehyde. Cap'n Waldo Dringoole appeared at the door and said to the warden, "Go off nice, Doc? Sorry I didn't have time to come see it—had some trouble with that bastard of a registration clerk."

"Went lovely, Cap'n. Never saw a nicer hanging. Bing —and the old gal was gone! Well, let's beat it and leave the corpse to these ladies. Good-day, ladies."

In the little room there was a workbench, with bowls of water and rags, and a coffin.

Ann knew that she was going to be sick again.

Mrs. Bitlick yawned, "Well, come on, gals, let's get back upstairs."

"Don't we have to wash——"

"What? Us wash an old nigger stiff? Hell, no! That was just taffy for the warden. Come on, Mis' Kaggs, give me a hand."

The two women heaved the body into the coffin, slammed on the cover, and cheerfully marched out, leaving Lil Hezekiah to her relatives and to God. But later the relatives failed to return, and she was buried in the jail yard. What God did is not known.

28

FROM her first day at Copperhead Gap, Ann had struggled to clean the women's division of the prison. She discovered that Jessie Van Tuyl had accomplished from her cell as much as she could from her dormitory. Mrs. Van Tuyl had smuggled notes out to the newspapers about moldy oatmeal spiced with moldy worms, about the imprisonment in the same cell of a girl of fourteen and a tertiary syphilitic with running sores, about whipping women who did not finish their "tasks" in the shop. Enough of this had been printed to make the authorities uneasy—for a moment.

"I wish we could get rid of that Van Tuyl woman. Can't we get her pardoned?" Ann heard Mrs. Bitlick sigh to Cap'n Waldo. "Till then, I reckon we'll have to make a noise like reforming. Give 'em some fresh beef, and separate the sick women, more or less."

What, fretted Ann, was the use of tiny reforms, so long as the state permitted this festering old building, these slave-drivers?

But she was a trained and incurable meddler and, so far as was consistent with the vow to keep her mouth shut, she

kept on daily prodding Mrs. Bitlick and Cap'n Waldo.
She argued with the former, coaxed the latter, and to Dr.
Slenk she hinted that "things would get out." She persuaded them to give better food. She was, without proof,
certain that all three of them were grafting on the food;
that they got, and sold, most of the cream from the prison-
farm milk; that they received refunds from the grocers,
the butchers.

The prison food was about equally bad in quality and in
monotony. Week on week they repeated cornmeal mush,
hash, coarse bacon, beef stew, potatoes, baked beans,
bread with corn syrup, willow-leaf tea, sausages from filthy
butcher's-scraps, and stewed prunes; there was never, not
once, fruit or a green vegetable, nor even unskimmed milk
to drink. There were sometimes maggots in the hash,
weevils in the bread, and the stewed fruit was spoiled. It
all tasted rancid. It all tasted nasty. And with a serene
sureness the prisoners starved, till to their other hatreds of
prison, which made them determined to get even with the
state by doing more crime, there was added the murderous
despair of incessant hunger plus incessant indigestion.

Hinting, begging, finally threatening to go out and tell
the world about it, Ann did force Mrs. Bitlick (and it was
curious that there was no addition to the reported expense
for food) to add fresh greens, corn, and string beans; an
orange once a fortnight; cocoa once a week; occasional
lemon juice, apples, and stewed apricots. The milk for
cooking became suddenly and curiously richer.

(From Mrs. Bitlick's remarks, one would have supposed
that the fare now was that of Foyot's.)

Ann tackled ventilation and cleanliness.

Her trouble was with labor. There are, with a few exceptions, only two sorts of prisons: those in which the inhabitants rot away with dulled idleness and those in which, sometimes on behalf of outside contractors, the inhabitants are worked to sick dizziness. In the second sort, the prisons are dirty because the prisoners are too exhausted to do any cleaning; in the first, because they become too lazy.

Ann had to fight for a few women, stolen from the kind contractors, to wash floors, to clean away the accumulated dust and fuzz whereby the screened ventilators had ceased to ventilate. She had to go discouragedly through the whole beg-coax-hint-threaten business all over again for enough hot water, enough soap, scrub-brushes, pails, enough bug-killer, traps for rats. To get two dollars' worth of soap was an entire Dardanelles campaign . . . the next two dollars' worth, naturally, Ann herself paid for.

Then plans toward a hospital for the women.

Ann was to learn, later, that there is no more beloved excuse for bad conditions in any prison, any county jail, than, "Oh, no use monkeying with it; we're going to have a fine new building soon." Now, she was baffled by that excuse at Copperhead Gap. How could she make the officers understand that even for three or four years, it might be well to treat sick women as well as one would treat a sick cow?

But she was wrong in surmising that Copperhead Gap never would build the new and separate annex for women. Since 1925, when Ann left Copperhead, a fine new separate building for women has been erected, with cells light and large and airy, with an adequate hospital room, with ad-

mirable shower baths. The women work in the large kitchen garden or vocational sewing-rooms instead of for a
shirt contractor. It has been erected for some time. In
fact, now, in 1932, it has been erected so long that it is
again satisfactorily overcrowded, with two women in a
cell meant for one; the shower baths are half of them
clogged up and the rest slimy; the handsome tiled floor of
the dining-room (laid by the brother-in-law of Warden
Slenk) is cracked into the hiding places for cockroaches;
and the shining hospital-room lacks a microscope, sufficient
bedding, and in winter, any heat whatever from the radia-
tors (installed by a cousin of Ex-Governor Golightly); and
the really elegant pair of bathrooms adjoining the hospital
just do not work. . . . The chief matron is still Mrs.
Bitlick. . . . As none of the matrons have time for much
teaching, in winter, when there is no gardening to occupy
them, most of the prisoners sit in idleness, and Mrs.
Windelskate is beginning to point out that it would have
been much better if the "so-called reformers" had not in-
terfered, and had left them the good, healthy, character-
building work in the shirt-shop.

What most balked Ann was the belief, sincere in them,
she believed, of Cap'n Waldo and Mrs. Bitlick and the
other matrons that conditions in the prison weren't really
bad. (What Dr. Slenk saw and felt was different and did
not count—he was a politician.)

"I thought at least we might clean the place up," Ann
had tactfully begun to Mrs. Bitlick.

"Clean? What do you mean? It is clean!" marveled
Mrs. Bitlick.

"It is not!"

"Well, I'd just like to see—— I declare to goodness, I don't know where you get your ideas!"

"Well, you come and take a look."

Then Ann pointed out—and it is truly doubtful whether Mrs. Bitlick had ever noticed these little matters before—what seemed to her flaws in the majestic structure of Copperhead Gap, women's division. The night buckets in each cell had a faint sickening reek which filled the cellhouse night and day, year on year. The day toilets leaked, dripping fecal matter on the floor. For all of the women, both for bathing and for washing stockings and underwear —their uniforms only were done by the prison laundry— there were just two tubs, both of iron, rusty, and so ill-set that the mucky water never quite drained out. The bedding was most of it black with filthiness and was usually passed on unwashed from prisoner to new prisoner, so that it sometimes went from a prisoner with infectious syphilis or late tuberculosis to a girl who, however she had offended the local customs, was young, healthy, eager for life. The mattresses were full of bedbugs. Few of the cells had ever had a ray of sunshine since they had been built. And when a sick patient vomited on the floor, which was often—the undying stench of the night buckets alone was enough to cause it—there was no one save the patient to clean it up—when she got well.

Mrs. Bitlick, following Ann, looked surprised when she was forced to see these details, which had been under her eyes not oftener than daily. Back in her office, she was silent, then spoke pontifically:

"Yes, maybe you're right. I reckon we ought to clean

up some. I'll speak to Dr. Slenk again about getting those
toilets repaired. I did speak about it, last year, but I reckon
it slipped both our minds. But, Miss Vickers, you got to
take this into consideration: You and me are used to nice
clean homes. But cattle like these cons, they just don't
know any different—bless you, they don't mind one mite!"

Ann was certain that drugs were plentiful in the prison
—heroin, cocaine, morphine. She suspected Kittie Cognac
of selling them; she was not quite free of suspicion of Dr.
Sorella, whose kind weakness might be as poisonous as
Kittie's vicious strength. But she mentioned no one person
to Mrs. Bitlick when she made her report.

"Well," said Mrs. Bitlick placidly, "if you ketch anyone peddling that stuff, you just turn 'em in, and we'll
give 'em the dark cells. You kind of sneak around and keep
your eyes peeled."

And what did Ann do then? Was she to turn stool
pigeon?

Of adequate physical examination, of competent and
patient treatment for drug addiction, venereal diseases,
tuberculosis, or the welter of psychoses and neuroses, there
was no question whatever. Dr. Sorella had charge of nineteen hundred men and a hundred women, assisted by two
unskilled orderlies, with the part-time services of a couple
of medical hacks from Olympus City who regarded prisoners as a lower species of mammals, to be treated with
quinine, salts, and curses. Dr. Sorella was intelligent, when
he was not drunk, but Dr. Sorella was often drunk.

It is not true that every person who came as a first of-

fender to Copperhead Gap, with only amateurish notions
of crime, learned in that university of vice about new and
slicker crimes, learned the delights of drugs and of prostitution, learned that it was his duty to get even with society
by being more vicious next time. Not every one. A few of
them were too numbed and frightened to learn anything.
But it is true that not one single person failed to go out of
Copperhead Gap more sickly of body and more resentful
for it and more capable of spreading disease among the
Decent Citizens who had been breeding him to their own
ruin.

Mrs. Bitlick was not offended by Ann's statement about
the secret traffic in drugs. She was just bored. But she was
offended, hurt, shocked, horrified, incredulous, and generally Methodist when Ann hesitatingly asked whether they
could not do something about homosexuality in the prison.
Ann knew why Kittie Cognac had arranged to share a cell
with Gladys Stout; she knew why the wicked old baby-
farmer from the dreadful place of graves near Catamount
Falls was so greasily agreeable to the girl pickpockets.
Mrs. Bitlick listened to her, in horror, then screeched,
"I've never in my life heard such a dreadful thing! Miss
Vickers, I hate to say it, but you have a dirty mind! I don't
think you better stay in this prison any longer! I wish
you'd get out! I dread to think of your influence on the
prisoners! Homo——— I've read the word, but I never in
my life before met anyone so dirty-tongued as to use it!"
"Oh, rats!" said Ann, and went away, and from that
day Mrs. Bitlick glared at her.
And the milk began to grow thin again, and when next

she asked for help to clean cells, it was refused. She didn't
quite see what to do about it; the force of public indiffer-
ence and privileged hatred was more than she could deal
with. It took her a while to accept it. She had had a vague
belief, probably from reading novels, that the resolute and
moral hero can always, in the last chapter, conquer the
unconquerable.

It would be agreeable to relate that though the officers
resented her, with a resentment rapidly sliding into hatred,
the prisoners were filled with lively gratitude.

They were not. For an hour they were glad to have
cleaner cells, and for a day they rejoiced in more varied
food . . . though most of them would rather have had the
addition of cream puffs than of greens and lemon juice.
Then they forgot.

Fortunately, Ann was a professionally trained uplifter.
She had learned in settlement two things: that she must
not expect "gratitude," and that people who did expect
gratitude were the eternal amateurs, the eternal egotists.
She was as indifferent—well, almost as indifferent—to the
opinion of the people for whom she carried on "reforms"
as a sound surgeon is to the opinion of a patient on his
technique.

She wasn't even vastly roused by the hatred of the
fellow-officers whom, with so little success, she was trying
to double-cross.

"No," she pondered. "It's not true that women aren't as
selfish, as cruel, and as hard as men. We have all the masculine strength! I'd like to torture Mrs. Bitlick! . . . No!
No! It *is* getting you. That's just the kind of righteous

wrath that *she* has! Women! The times are out of joint, and we not only have to set them right, but we have to take a few million Mrs. Bitlicks along with us. Oh, well, no matter how much I can accomplish here at Copperhead, I'll upset the whole applecart when I get out and tell the world about it! . . . How sick I am of that smell of disinfectant!"

29

BIRDIE WALLOP was in trouble, for all her ability to soothe Mrs. Bitlick, to amuse Mrs. Kaggs.

Birdie had what she called a "boy friend." She was not the only woman prisoner who was so fortunate. Among these hundred women, supposedly shut away by brick walls, steel bars, and frosted windows from even the sight of men, desire for them throbbed more than the longing for food or rest in sweet air. Ann heard the women, during the hour after dinner when they were allowed to converse as they tramped the cinder recreation ground, talking always of men—what He had said, how He had kissed, how generous He had been at the restaurant, the certainty that He would be waiting at the prison entrance. It was a tropism, beyond all human planning.

For a manless retreat, it was surprising how many men contrived to come in. The guards were always snooping about, staring into the shirt-shop where, on the days that now burnt into Ann's second summer, the women toiled with denim dresses open in front. Workmen trusties— carpenters, the plumber, the photographer and finger-printer—appeared, and somehow they never finished their work till the guards drove them out, and from jogs in the corridor you could hear, all day, a whispering, a giggle.

But Birdie Wallop was one of the few who had a "steady." He was an electrician, an excellent electrician, and a beautiful young man with a black mustache. He had also been an excellent telegrapher in the fake wire-tapping racket, and he was doing twelve years. When Ann met him in the corridors, he twitched the greasy uniform cap which he wore as cockily as a soldier's helmet, and smiled as though they shared a secret, and her heart bumped.

He had reported that the wiring along the women's cell corridor was defective, and he labored there all day, while Birdie, supposedly carrying messages, or bringing coffee and aspirin for Mrs. Bitlick's regular and unbeautiful colds, was seen winking at him, leaving notes for him between the braces of his stepladder.

Till Mrs. Bitlick caught her.

Mrs. Bitlick had passed blessedly beyond all desires for sex. It was whispered that she had once been very gay, but if so, she was making up to God for it now.

She came down the corridor and saw the electrician drop a package from his ladder down to Birdie, saw Birdie scoop it into her pocket. She ran, in her rubber sneakers, caught Birdie's arm, snatched the package, opened it. It contained two packages of cigarettes, two books of matches, and chewing gum.

Now Mrs. Bitlick was indignantly and righteously opposed to all smoking among women. And Mrs. Kaggs was equally affected, because Mrs. Kaggs and Kittie

Cognac had a monopoly on the sale of cigarettes to women. Both sprang on her. Birdie was dragged in to a court-martial of Mrs. Bitlick, Mrs. Kaggs, and two or three other matrons—whom Ann joined, without invitation. And the good Kittie Cognac was brought in as witness.

The matrons sat in stiff chairs, in a crescent, in Mrs. Bitlick's office. Birdie stood before them, her smile doubtfully coming and going, as she tried to work its former magic on them. Her eyes were frightened.

"I saw her with my own eyes, smuggling cigarettes!" said Mrs. Bitlick. "Now we know how these nasty coffin-nails get into the prison!"

"Oh!" said the shocked Mrs. Kaggs.

"And I suspect her of smuggling dope."

Birdie wailed, "Honest, I never——"

"Shut up!" said Mrs. Bitlick. "Now, Kittie, you said you had some information."

Kittie advanced, stylishly. "You bet I have. It's Birdie that's been smuggling out all these notes—including those from this Van Tuyl woman, where she belly-aches about conditions! I found one in her cell, like I told you!"

(Ann knew that Birdie had not smuggled out all of Mrs. Van Tuyl's notes, because she had smuggled a good many herself.)

"Well, ladies, I think we've heard enough. You go back to the shirt-shop, Birdie—this afternoon!—and I'll tell Miss Peebee to see you tend to business!"

"Oh, please, Mrs. Bitlick, *please!*" That was as far as Birdie got. Three matrons, hustling her between them, pushed her out, down to the shop.

Ann heard that the friendly electrician was lying in a damp, dark cell.

On the evening after Birdie's wailing demotion, Ann called on Dr. Slenk in his private mansion—a handsome abode, its parlor adorned with a davenport, a radio, a closet of Scotch and Bourbon, and two hand-painted winter scenes by a former convict, in which the snow glittered with powdered mica.

"Did you hear about Birdie Wallop, our messenger, getting sent back to Hard, Dr. Slenk?"

"Yes, I had a report on it."

"I wish—— She's a good child. She really is. I'm sure I have some influence with her, and I think I could get her to promise not to distribute cigarettes or carry notes, and keep her promise."

"I really can't interfere with Mrs. Bitlick's control. I have every confidence in Mrs. Bitlick. And if I may say so, I don't regard it as quite loyal in you to try to go over her head."

"Oh! Loyalty! But I feel some loyalty to these poor women prisoners, too!" Ann was speaking desperately. It was the first time she had ever tried to talk with seriousness to the airy Dr. Slenk. "I've never accused any prisoner. It doesn't seem fair. But when one of them takes advantage of her fellows—— See here, Dr. Slenk; please listen to me. I know! The source of half the trouble we have is this Cognac woman! She's a real bad character! She sells dope and cigarettes, and she arranges sexual perversion——"

The little horse-doctor leaped up, threw his excellent

cigar into the electric imitation of hot coals in the imitation fireplace. "That will do! I've heard enough! Never before have I heard a woman shame herself by mentioning such subjects! And, my dear young woman——" his voice had all the nice nastiness of a spinster Sunday school teacher—"just how is it that you know about these things?"

Ann lost her temper, wholly and wholesomely, for the first time at Copperhead Gap. "That will do! You can't get away with it by making any such accusations! I'd love to have you make them at a public trial! I'm not going to stay here long——"

"No, I shouldn't think you would!"

"—and I might be doing you a favor by preventing a public scandal that would blow you and the Bitlick woman and your 'Captain' Waldo right out of the prison! It's happened before, and you know it! There's graft, cruelty, perversion, everything horrible. I might be able to clean up and save you—for if it all came out you'd never hold another political job, even here, my good man. I suggest that you retire Kittie Cognac to the shop, put Birdie back, and then, for head trusty, put in a woman that's more intelligent and honest than both of us put together—Jessie Van Tuyl. Now, are you going to consider this, or shall I go to the newspapers and start something?"

Dr. Slenk had faded into his chair. His dainty legs, to whose slick trousers and their pressing a prisoner valet gave much of his time, were twitching. The little man was not very brave when he was not protected by some dragoon like Cap'n Waldo or Mrs. Bitlick. He squeaked:

"Oh! But that would be impossible! I'll do what I can

about Birdie—get Mrs. Bitlick to reinstate her after she's
been disciplined a little. And I'll tell her to not give the
Cognac woman so much rope. But Mrs. Van Tuyl! Why,
she's a Com*mu*nist!"

"What of it? Isn't she the most capable woman here?"

"Oh, yes, I suppose she is. But she's a Com*mu*nist!"

Mrs. Bitlick and Ann were in the office at five in the
afternoon. Ann was totting up figures. The lean point of
her pencil made a climbing noise as she ran up the columns
of figures on a sheet laid on the desk. Mrs. Bitlick was
ostensibly reading the kitchen-matron's report, but she
was looking at one blurred spot on it, thinking, and Ann
knew of what she was thinking. Mrs. Bitlick's thoughts
were almost visible—whirling shapes of hatred, lightning
and thunderclouds and quivering masses of dung-colored
fog.

"I'm going to get kicked out," considered Ann contentedly, the while her pencil was tapping. "I'll see
Lindsay, Malvina, Pat! House party at Malvina's!"

She had scarcely been able to write to them, these fourteen months at Copperhead Gap, but they seemed always
to walk with her, shadowy as her daughter Pride.

In the shirt-shop below, the machines shut down, and
the silence crashed. Directly there was a mounting shriek
of mixed voices. Mrs. Bitlick darted out, Ann after her,
Kittie Cognac joining them in the corridor, and they ran
down to the door of the shirt-shop.

While the workers, about to file out, hesitated and
looked embarrassed, Miss Peebee was shaking Josephine
Filson and yelping, "You haven't finished it again! I'll

have the head-matron give you the solitary for ten days,"
and Miss Filson was wailing, "No, no, please not!" Miss
Filson snatched herself free and slapped Miss Peebee,
beautifully, across the eyes and long nose. Miss Peebee
struck her across the face with her long thin cane and
shrieked, "Guards! Ring for guards!"

Mrs. Bitlick pressed the guards' button and, Kittie at
her heels, like an English setter gone warlike, ran toward
Miss Filson.

Birdie Wallop leaped out of the column of women, flew
to the double doors, locked them, threw the key under a
power sewing-machine, and shouted, "Girls! Come on!
Let's kill 'em! Kill Peebee! Kill Bitlick!"

The riot was instantly and confusingly on. No one knew
afterward just what happened. But a mass of women were
dashing at Mrs. Bitlick, Miss Peebee, Kittie, yanking their
hair, tearing their blouses, slapping them, forcing them
back to the end of the room, while the men guards were
already bawling and knocking outside the locked door.

Ann was thinking twenty confused thoughts to the
second. She would joyfully have joined in mauling Bitlick,
Peebee, Kittie. But she didn't want to go to jail—no,
that she couldn't endure. But oughtn't she—wasn't she a
coward? But what of her loyalty to her uniform? And
wasn't this rioting the worst thing the girls could do for
themselves? And didn't Bitlick, Peebee, Kittie beat her
hollow, beat all of them, in physical courage? For the three
women, back to the wall, were fighting ferociously, with
not a whimper, no yowl for mercy—clawing, kicking,
striking back, any one of them equal to three of these rebel
slaves, so long starved of food and air.

Into the mêlée a new figure, voice ringing, fearless as the Bitlick—Jessie Van Tuyl, shouting, "Stop it, girls! Stop it! Do no good! They'll get you afterward! And it's not fair—seventy to three!" With her sturdy body Mrs. Van Tuyl was shielding the exhausted Peebee . . . whom she hated more than anyone dead or alive since time was.

Ann, all her busy little thoughts gone now in the excitement, dashed in, to protect the rioters by protecting the matrons. She tried to get through the mob. She caught the arm of a prisoner who was about to hurl a monkey wrench. And the prisoner, new to her, yammered, "Here's another screw! Let's kill her!"

A more veteran prisoner—a weighty mountain woman, stalwart as Cap'n Waldo, a truly celebrated stealer of pigs, turkeys, and farm wagons—answered, "No! She's Miss Vickers! She's all right!" And, tucking Ann under her arm, the mountain Boadicea removed her as though she were a stealable pig, plastered her against the side wall, away from the riot, and held her there with one hand, while with the other she meditatively tried lobbing spare spindles over the crowd upon the heads of the matrons.

"Make 'em stop! Make 'em stop!" begged Ann. "They'll get terribly punished!"

"Wall, yes, I reckon that's so. But they'll get punished now, anyway, so they might as well have some fun. I reckon they're fixing to kill Mis' Bitlick," ruminated Boadicea.

"There's much," Ann meditated to herself, "to what she says."

The door smashed in, and Cap'n Waldo and half a dozen guards with rifles, blackjacks, and night sticks went to work. It was pretty sickening. They were systematic. Smashed noses. Cut scalps messing hair with blood. Bloody spit. Broken wrists. Eyes blackened. Women twisting on the floor.

Cap'n Waldo himself took care of the huge woman holding Ann, by socking her in the jaw, breaking the jawbone and removing two teeth. "There's two teeth she ain't never going to have no ache in no more!" he shouted merrily, when he recounted it afterward.

It was a difficult verdict, even for a politician like Dr. Slenk. He could, and did, stop for a month the daily hour of recreation and talk of all the seventy women in the shop. (True, only about thirty of them had rioted, and the rest had stood back, cowed.) But in justice, as Dr. Slenk explained to a gathering of all the matrons, with Cap'n Waldo, they ought also to cut their rations down to bread and water for a month and send to the Hole half the rioters (it didn't, he said, with a touch of his old untroubled gaiety, really matter which half!). But they had only four dark cells in the Hole, and as for food, if the hell-cats were dieted as they deserved, they would not be strong enough to get their tasks done in the shirt-shop, and didn't the officials owe this to the good contractors, who were paying the state forty-five cents a day per worker? (How much the good contractors were paying Dr. Addington Slenk, if anything, he did not state then nor at any other time.)

"Well, if I was running it, I'd starve 'em good, and I'd make 'em do their task just the same. Remember what the New York cops say: 'There's a lot of law in the end of a night stick'? Well, there's a lot of encouragement to a loafer in a soaked leather strap!" guffawed Cap'n Waldo.

Ann had then a horrific admiration of Mrs. Bitlick. She was a little frightened; she had asked for a man guard to be stationed always near the shop. But she had courage enough to agree with Cap'n Waldo that it was desirable to starve all the women for a month.

Dr. Slenk apologetically overruled. He knew the contractors better than they did! And it was he who had to minimize the riot for the press. Severe punishment would emphasize it. No. They would just stop the recreation hour for a month, feed only bread and water for two days, whip six of the women, and shut four out of the same six in the dark cells for fifteen days.

The four chosen were Birdie Wallop, Josephine Filson, a Pearlsburg bootlegger, and the pig-stealer who had protected Ann.

Ann was shrieking, "You can't do that to Miss Filson! It will kill her! She isn't strong! And Birdie isn't bad— just a wild kid!"

They turned on her like automata in a waxworks.

Dr. Slenk was ever so plucky now, with Cap'n Waldo and the Bitlick beside him. "Miss Vickers! I've been waiting and expecting you to open your trap! It's a grave question as to whether you ain't largely responsible for this villainous and inexcusable outbreak, you and the Van Tuyl woman! I think we've had enough of your swell Boston culture and sociology! I've been considering whether the time hasn't come to try you on charges of fomenting disorder. Or do you prefer to resign, right here and now?"

"No! You can try me!" Ann was suddenly exhilarated

with hatred. "I'd love to be tried! I'll see there's plenty of reporters present, and not just local men!"

"If you think for one minute," stated the real boss, Cap'n Waldo, "that we're afraid of the newspapers—— But we'll take that up afterwards! But there's one more thing, Doc. Ain't there some way we can put that Van Tuyl bitch—excuse me, ladies, just a slip of the tongue— can't we put her across the jumps instead of the bootlegger gal? The bootlegger ain't so bad—just kind of rough. She don't preach free love and anarchism and revolution, like Van Tuyl."

"No. I'd like to," sighed Dr. Slenk. "But I tell you what we can do. We'll put that insane nigger wench, that's always hollering, in the cell with Van Tuyl, and I reckon that'll keep her too busy to start any more riots!"

Ann realized that she was as completely finished as though she were discharged. Her classes were taken from her; she was permitted to talk with no prisoner; she could go nowhere save to her dormitory—where Mrs. Kaggs and the other matron never spoke to her—and to Mrs. Bitlick's office, for accounts.

She did not see the whipping of the six women. She believed that it took place in a room next to the Hole, in a sub-basement beneath the gallows-room—below even the gallows. She had to get down to the four women penned there. The stairs from the gallows-room to the Hole were watched always by a particularly surly guard. Ann crept about, peering into the gallows-room, as though she were herself a prisoner, trying to escape. You learn sneakiness in a penitentiary, criminal or political prisoner or officer,

high or low. Late one night, while Kittie Cognac nodded
at one end of the cell corridor and Mrs. Kaggs snored at
the other, Ann tiptoed through the corridor, down the
spiral stairs to the gallows-room. No guard in sight. She
could see smoke. He had gone comfortably behind the
gallows for a cigarette. She slipped over to the narrow
stairs to the sub-basement.

The door below was not locked. No need! She came into
a room like the center of a hollowed block of cement; no
doors save the one by which she entered, and a narrower,
lower door across from it; no windows; ventilation through
four holes, six inches square, from the floor above . . . from
the gallows-room. One milky light. In the center of this
cement cube was a wooden upright, with a cross-arm at
each end of which were manacles.

The upright was splashed with dried blood.

The whipping-post.

She fled from it to the door opposite. It was locked, but
with the key in the door. In desperate fear (suppose They
kept her there, once she got in?) she opened on a passageway of rough rocks, dripping, clammy. It was utterly dark.
It was grotesquely melodramatic and improbable.

She made her way, in the light from her electric torch,
along it. She had to stoop, and she could not keep away
from the slimy rocks on either side. After ten feet the passage opened into something like a cave out of pirate fiction
—the Hole. It was a chamber eight feet high, windowless,
utterly dark, of stone and brick, with a damp cement floor.
One side was given over to four cells. In them was neither
bed nor stool. Each was furnished with a night pail, a thin
and dirty blanket, a cup for water—filled once a day, to

accompany two slices of bread—and nothing else whatever, unless one cared to include a human being with the remains of a priceless soul.

Four women were lying hunched each on her blanket in a cell, shivering in sleep.

The first to come out in Ann's torchlight was Josephine Filson. She had rolled half off her blanket; she lay on the chill and slimy cement with her arms thrown out in an attitude of crucifixion. She had a curious breathing, a moan of torture.

"It's pneumonia," quaked Ann.

Hastily, as though looking for help, she lighted up the next cell, and the creature in there sprang up and crouched, clawing at her filthy cheeks, whimpering. Ann at first did not know her. This was a caged animal, a sub-animal, with eyes fierce and stupid, and dirty hanging hair.

Ann saw then that it was Birdie Wallop.

Birdie could not see beyond the blank blaze of the electric torch. She was screaming, "Oh, don't! I'll do anything! Only I won't squeal! I don't know anything about Van Tuyl or Miss Vickers!"

"Hush! Birdie! It's Miss Vickers—Ann!"

"Oh, my God! Have you come to get me out? I'm going crazy! I am crazy!"

"I'm trying! Birdie! What's the matter with Miss Filson?"

"I think she's dying. She couldn't stand the whipping. Fainted, twice. They whipped us. Stripped us to the waist —the men guards. Tied us to the post, with our arms out, and licked us with a strap with holes in it. Look!" Her "look" was a scream. She tore off her waist. Her back was thick not with stripes but with dripping sores. "And every day they've fastened us to the door here, six hours every day, with our arms stretched way up, so we could just touch our toes. Your arms feel like fire. You hang there and God! how you want some water, every minute! Jo kept crying all the time, except times when she fainted, hanging to the door. Know what I'm going to do?" Birdie's quiet was abnormal, like the center of a hurricane. "I'm going to murder somebody when I get out of this. This is what they done to us. I'm not going to go straight! I'm going to kill! But Jo—I guess she won't never get out, never."

Ann turned, staring. Through the door, still open behind her, two torches were shining.

The voice of a guard, invisible behind his glare: "What the hell is she doing down here? How'd she get here?"

The voice of Dr. Sorella: "It's all right. I told her to come. Beat it!" The guard gone, Sorella complained, "Ann! My God, how did you get down here? Don't you know they're laying for you? They'll find some way of framing you—of having *you* jugged down here!"

"I know! I know! Look! Miss Filson is dreadfully ill."

"Yes. Pneumonia. I ordered them to take her out of here. *Ordered!* Me! They wouldn't take my 'order.' Slenk and Bitlick wanted to. Scared. But Dringoole held out. Said it was her own fault if she did die. Said she'd started all the trouble—along with Birdie and you! Let me look at her."

He opened Miss Filson's cell door, listened to her breathing, came out laughing as hysterically as Birdie:

"Order! I gave an order! I'll give another!" In the steady light of Ann's torch, he had brought out his pocket flash, was gulping, "Don't you want a drink? Don't, eh? Wise girl. I've been drinking all night. I'm so far gone now that they won't even take my word for it and save this woman from dying. Come on, get out of here. Want a drink?"

Ann did want a drink. But she did not take it.

As they marched out of the dungeon, Birdie shrieked after them, "Don't leave me here! It's so dark! I'm scared! I'm going crazy!"

Ann ignored every regulation.

She went up to her room, changed from the hatefully pert uniform into Christian clothes, left a note on Mrs. Bitlick's desk, saying that she had been "called away for a few hours," and had the outer guard order out a station wagon for her. She knew that there was a train for Pearlsburg at 8:07 that morning.

At half-past eleven she was taking a taxicab from the Pearlsburg station to the commodious and respectable residence of Mrs. Albert Windelskate, of the State Board of Prison Control.

She had telephoned from the station.

The Windelskate château was of brick and limestone, with mullioned lattice windows featuring heraldic shields.

A maid suspiciously let her into a drawing-room so large and so handsomely furnished that it resembled a hotel lounge, with a hint of furniture warehouse. Mrs. Windelskate was ostentatiously reading *The House of the Dead.*

She looked up casually; she said "Yes?" sweetly; but she was trembling with anticipatory fury.

Ann was warned. She said, as gently as she could, "I do beg your pardon for rushing in like this, without warning. And I do beg of you to listen to me. I feel there's things about Copperhead Gap that only an insider could tell you, and just now there's a terrible emergency, immediately affecting the lives of two, possibly four, women— their very lives!"

Mrs. Windelskate burst, and it has been well said that Hell hath no fury like the wife of a loan-shark seeking respectability:

"My—dear—young—woman! I know all about you! Every particle! I've heard, personally, from Dr. Slenk, whom I happen to know, to trust; whom we entertained in Our Own Home! And from Mrs. Bitlick! How I could have been so deceived in you! I know now that you are a bosom associate of Jessie Van Tuyl—that Communist, that anarchist, that atheist, that trouble-maker! I have little doubt that you are a paid propagandist of Moscow, sneaking into our midst, a spy, like a rattlesnake! I know how you can lie and give false reports! Dr. Slenk has warned me! I already have an appointment to talk to the newspapers and see to it that any lies you try to spread will be nailed on the head before you are able to spread their socialistic poison . . ."

There was more of it, much more.

Ann was not too soft in answer.

All that half hour, the hideousness was for Ann turned almost into comic melodrama by the fact that, waiting in the front hall, obviously peeping in, were the maid, a large negro gardener, and a uniformed policeman . . . to guard Mrs. Windelskate against Ann Vickers.

"Tomorrow, I'll go see the Governor himself," vowed Ann, waiting at the station. "But I'll get back to Copperhead tonight. See what I can do. See what I can do. . . . There's nothing I can do."

She looked at the passengers waiting in the station, the Great Common People, the Safe and Sane, the Men and Women in the Street, the Backbone of Democracy, the Electors of Governors and Presidents, the Heirs of All the Ages, the Successors of King and Priest, the Lords of the Universe, the Creators of the Creator. Traveling salesmen with briefcases, rubicund and jolly, or neat and eyeglassed. Wives of grocers and bank clerks, going to spend a week with Aunt Molly, good clean women who had never consciously lied or hurt. Ample peasant women with lunch boxes, strong and gentle. A priest with his lovely little red-and-black breviary containing words of intimacy with God Almighty, and a brisk young Baptist preacher daring to show his forward-looking liberalism by reading the *Christian Century.* A tall man in black, perhaps a judge, his eyes wrinkled from smiling and from many books.

"Yes, it's you I'm talking to!" Ann shrieked at all of them—though voicelessly. "It's you, the good people, the solid people, the responsible people! It's you, and not the ragtag or the criminals, that are responsible for giving power over thousands in darkness to sadists and sots, so they become torturers, and you don't know, you don't care, you won't listen!"

At the side gate to the prison, nearest to the women's

division, the guard, a not unkindly oaf, growled at Ann, "How are you? Been traveling? Woman croaked today—woman named Filson."

In her dormitory, back in prison uniform, it occurred to her again that she had no notion as to what she could do to help Birdie. See the Governor—— Oh, yes, she would. Would it help at all?

It occurred to her also that she was hungry. She had had no breakfast (save Cracker Jack and Coca-Cola on the train), and no lunch, and she was too late for dinner.

She felt utterly beaten.

Into the room popped Birdie's successor as messenger, another bootlegger, suspected by Jessie Van Tuyl of being a stool pigeon.

"Oh, Miss Vickers! Mrs. Bitlick wanted to know was you back. Did you get some supper? Did you hear about Jo Filson? Wa'n't it too bad! Poor Mis' Bitlick, she cried and carried on like anything—she'd had Jo took out of the Hole and put right in her own room, and then," indignantly, "Jo turned right over and died on her. But I wasn't sent about that. Cap'n Waldo sent me. The jail croaker, Doc Sorella, is took bad. Between you and I, I reckon he's on the edge of D. T.'s, and he keeps calling for you. They've got in another doc, from the town, but he can't seem to do nothing, and he wants you should come and see can you maybe gentle Sorella down a little. Won't you come? Needs you something fierce, the other doc says!"

"Of course I will!"

The messenger-trusty took Ann through short cuts, up

and down and behind and under, to the wing in which
were the men's hospital, the consulting-room, the
operating-room, what was called the "laboratory," and
Dr. Sorella's two-room private apartment. It opened from
the "laboratory," a dirty closet containing a cheap microscope, broken test tubes, reagent bottles, most of them
empty, a bicycle, a pot of geraniums, dead and withered,
and two pairs of rubbers. The messenger gently pushed
Ann into Dr. Sorella's living-room. It had a cot with a
worn imitation Turkish cover; box stove; Morris chair
with one leg broken and bound with twine; table of perky
golden oak; medical books piled on two straight chairs;
and a set of Stevenson on a shelf. It was adequately clean.
Ann fancied that Dr. Sorella himself had cleaned up this
living-room, last night, in his sleepless frenzy of futility.

"This way, right in here!" chirruped the messenger,
laying a hand on Ann's arm with offensive intimacy, pro-
pelling her toward the bedroom door.

Over the floor were scattered the doctor's clothes, and
on a pine bureau was an empty whisky bottle, still reeking.

Dr. Sorella was lying across the bed, his head hanging
over the side. He was wearing a collarless shirt, and covered only by a maculate sheet. He looked dead. But he
was breathing, with a subdued moaning like that of Josephine Filson. His forehead was glistening wet.

"Why! Where's the other doctor—the outside doctor?"
Ann demanded.

"Just stepped into the hospital, I reckon. I'll run fetch
him," the messenger said.

Ann had no sense of disgust. Dr. Sorella seemed not
merely dead-drunk, not "sleeping it off"; he seemed a

little delirious, with a hot fever. Ann bent over him, tried his pulse—it was ticking like a clock. She dipped a towel in his pitcher of water and sat on the edge of his bed to bathe his forehead. (Why didn't that confounded outside doctor come back?) Sorella lurched in his sleep. He would fall out of bed. Straining, Ann tried to lift him back. He struggled. She had to hold him tight to her, in an embrace——

Bang! A flashlight went off, and as she started up, as she gaped at the door, she saw a camera, a smear of faces— Slenk, a little embarrassed, Cap'n Waldo gawping with grins, two guards, the prisoner-photographer, and the stool-pigeon messenger, all snickering.

"So, kidlets, thought you'd sneak off and do a little necking with your boy friend!" Cap'n Waldo guffawed. "Too bad we had to interrupt you! . . . Snarkey! Beat it and bring me rough proof as quick as the Lord will let you. Ought to be a nice pretty picture for anybody's parlor— little Ann and the doc hugging—and him half undressed!"

They had been lucky. The picture, as they saw it in proof—all the matrons, including Ann, with Slenk and the Cap'n—was better than Cap'n Waldo had hoped. Ann was highly distinguishable: her profile, her uniform. Sorella's face was hidden against her breast; her arms were about him, apparently in rapture, beside the bed.

"And we have witnesses!" said Dr. Slenk, gently. "Need we waste any more time? Do you resign now? Shall I send a print of this to the Governor? He's got a great sense of humor. He'd love to show it around to everybody —to all the boys on the press."

"Oh, I—— Will you take Birdie out of the dark cell? Take all three of 'em out?"

"Yes, I'm willing. Well?"

"Oh, I resign. But I'll see Birdie first! And Jessie Van Tuyl! Or I'll stand my trial!"

"Now, by God——" roared Cap'n Waldo.

Dr. Slenk held up his trim little hand trimly. "Yes, we'll even do that. I want Miss Vickers to take home a pleasant impression of us. I'm sure that when she gets a little more experience she won't be such a theoretical little fool. Vindon! Let them three women out of the Hole. Restored to work. Bring the Van Tuyl woman to the gym. Let Miss Vickers talk to her. You see, Vickers, we don't care a damn what you do, now!"

Cap'n Waldo stared in admiration at his chief as he realized that, despite his sweetness of nature, Dr. Slenk was the greatest warrior against crime and radicalism of them all.

30

T<small>HE</small> girl who arrived in New York on the Quaker
Limited, on the late afternoon of September 16, 1925,
looked a little countrified. Her suit was certainly two years
old; it was too long, prudishly so, according to the new
styles, and it hadn't the fashionable flare. She had new
gloves, neat shoes, good ankles, eyes dark and impatient,
a fine skin. She was a restrained person, irritatingly unaware of the inviting looks the traveling-men gave her.
Perhaps a school teacher? Anyway, a woman in trouble.
Often she stopped reading, to brood. Her teeth kept chewing her lower lip.

In the Pennsylvania Station she followed a redcap, with
her bags, as though she did not see him. In the looming
vastness of the station she glanced up, once, rustic and
astonished, and hurried on, looking at the pavement.
When the redcap queried, "Taxi?" she hesitated. "Ye-es,
I reckon—I guess so." In the taxicab she pressed close to
the window, to peep up at the Gibraltar of the Pennsylvania Hotel, muttering, "My!" But she drew back, seeing
nothing outside herself, not even the shoulders of the
driver at whom she was apparently staring.

She had given a West Sixtieth Street address. There, at
one of the innumerable New York apartment houses which
try to cover the smell of cabbage and home laundering
with marble slabs in the lobby and with gilt on an un-
trustworthy elevator, she said agitatedly to the driver,
"Wait! Wait! I'll see!"

She demanded of the negro hall-boy, "Is Miss Bramble
home yet? Miss Patricia Bramble?"

"She ain't here no more. Gone to New Rochelle. Gone
into business in New Rochelle, New York, ma'am.
Yes *sir!*"

"Oh!" It was an "Oh" of indignation, angry helpless-
ness. To the taxi driver she gave another address, on
Fifth Avenue, in the Thirties. She dismounted there at
an old mansion whose ground floor was turned into a
trunk-shop, the upper floors into flats.

She trailed, panting, across the wide sidewalk; she rang
one of a nest of electric buttons and, as the door clicked,
darted in. She crawled up three flights, like a sick woman;
knocked at a dun-colored double-door. It was opened by
a small plump woman with shrewd eyes, and unfashionable
lace at her wrists, who cried, "Why!"

Ann swayed in and dropped on a couch, too gone, too
beaten, to speak.

"My dear, what is it? How did you get here? Never
mind. Just sit there," said Dr. Malvina Wormser.

"Send—send—" Ann was gasping like a fish—"send
Gertrude Waggett down—pay off taxi—running up fare—
bags."

Dr. Wormser whooped. "Death and despair ne'er shall
keep your good old New England economy from working!"

"Well, I'm a poor prison matron, and I resigned from Copperhead Gap three evenings ago. I resigned, I did. Some people call it that. I'm all right now. I won't be tragic any more."

She wasn't. But she was boiling over with a crusading wrath. She was going to end the whole prison-system by telling the world what it was like. She talked half the night, inconsequent but sharp as a news reel. . . . Tea at Warden Slenk's; Mrs. Bitlick in mufti, with short skirts above piano legs; Cap'n Waldo in white duck, his coat like a circus tent; Cap'n Waldo telling the comic anecdote of the convict who had spent weeks in tunnelling under the walls —idiot thought he'd get home to his wife for their wedding anniversary—all the while the guards knew about it, and watched him, snickering, and let him dig—caught him on the last night, as he emerged outside the wall and, laughing so they could hardly lay on the lash, whipped him and stuck him in the Hole. . . . Birdie Wallop solemnly practising on the mouth organ. . . . How fried maggots look in prison hash. . . . Jessie Van Tuyl's imprisonment in solitary for a week, for having slipped one slice of bread to a woman in solitary. . . . The brief epic, full of American democracy, of a girl of sixteen, a virgin, wild and gay, but ignorant of everything save village flirtations, who entered Copperhead two days after Ann, for having stolen bananas from a storekeeper and having slapped the man for accusing her. She was in prison for one year, and she received the education which is a purpose of prison along with revenge and deterrence, for did she not share a cell with a woman of forty, wise in such matters as blackmail, carrying the gun for a gang leader, prostitution, cocaine? The education took. Two months after her release, she was back, to do life, for murder. . . . The refusal of good Dr. Slenk to let the prisoners have any Christmas celebration whatever, because there had been a "bread riot"—the prisoners had thrown their bread on the floor, one day, when it was weevily. . . . Tadpoles in the stale water that would not drain from a bathtub. . . . Miss Peebee yelping at the timid Dr. Sorella for ordering out of the shirt-shop a woman with a swollen and infected hand. . . . Cap'n Waldo striking a woman full in the mouth when she refused to share a cell with a syphilitic. . . . Three matches for ten cents, obligingly sold by the firm of Kaggs & Cognac, and thereafter the pleasant scent of cigarettes all night, in cells where smoking was Strictly Forbidden. . . . A woman evangelist telling the prisoners, in chapel, that their kind officers yearned over them and longed to make them better women. . . . The time when a broken pipe dribbled an inch of water over the floors of the dark cells in the Hole, and the four women confined in them were not removed for a whole night, but slept sitting up, in the water. . . . The state legislature which, after defeating a bill to spend $200,000 on a new women's annex for Copperhead Gap, voted $250,000 for a Soldiers' Memorial—a series of statues around a cenotaph. . . . The eminent state senator (an ambitious father, a kind grandfather, a college graduate, a trustee of the State University, a practically honest wholesale grocer) who made oration: "These vile women prisoners already live like a lot of queens—three fine meals a day, without having to stir one finger to prepare them like my old mammy did, by thunder! A handsome recreation ground just for them to walk in. Modern bathtubs, while most decent Christian women in this state still have to use the family washtub. A doctor and a preacher at their beck and call; free classes in languages, sewing, and, I have no doubt, bridge-whist and how to make pink tea! And now the gentleman from Carter County proposes to build 'em a still lordlier mansion! Just what is his idea? Does he want to make prison life so lovely that every woman in the state will be committing crime just for a chance to break into prison?"

Dr. Wormser let her talk—encouraged her, indeed, and did not look tired, as Ann raved on till three in the morning. (Sometime during the hours, a light supper had miraculously appeared, and Ann been coaxed to taste an egg.) By three, the bitterness had been drawn from Ann, and an optimistic belief restored that the Great Common People would do something about it, if they only *knew*. And Dr. Wormser had already planned what editors Ann was to see.

Charley Erman, managing editor of the morning *Chronicle*—he was the best man to see; a friend of Dr. Wormser; a liberal newspaperman on a paper which, though conservative as an Episcopalian banker, yet loved nothing so much as printing a Socialist speech attacking the *Chronicle*. And then, of course, an article or two in the *Statesman*, the liberal weekly which had been the first publication in America to assert that not Germany only, but also France, Britain, and Russia had heard the news about the Great War before 1916.

In two days, Ann was again a New Yorker, not an awed and desperate rustic. Dr. Wormser had prescribed some new clothes and expensive lunches. Ann was rich. Out of the $1,500 salary she had received in fourteen months, she had saved $997.93. (The rest had gone for cigarettes, books, railroad fare, and loans to released prisoners, of which 100 per cent were still unpaid.) She bought a suit, more silk stockings than she needed—which is the definition of luxury—an evening frock, and a jade-colored cigarette holder, and she went to a revue, which she left abruptly in the middle, because of a very funny sketch in which was shown a Modern Prison, with valets bringing champagne in ice-buckets for the happy burglars. . . .

Lindsay Atwell was away, still on vacation in Vermont. Two days after Ann had telephoned Lindsay's office, he telephoned her from Dorset, "My dear, I *am* glad you're back! New York has been intolerably dull without you. Would you like to be associated with the New York prisons? Right you are! Judge Bernard Dow Dolphin—New York State Supreme Court—is staying here. He has a great deal of influence. I'll speak to him immediately. See you soon."

Well, she would rather have heard that her lips were rubies, but warmer, and that he longed for them but—— It was nice that he was so practical and keen.

Charley Erman, managing editor of the New York *Chronicle*, had been spoiled by service as a foreign correspondent: he sometimes drank tea at tea, instead of hinting for a cocktail. He was drinking tea now, in Dr. Wormser's dowdy living-room, while Ann talked of Copperhead Gap as coolly as she could. . . . Birdie Wallop,

who was Topsy and Ariel and Skippy, hanging by her
wrists for hours, against a rusty barred cell door, in darkness, her back bleeding, her throat like flannel with thirst;
all this for defending Jo Filson.

And prisons or county jails like this (did the newspaper
want to send her out to make sure?) in Missouri and Mary-
land, Oregon and Ohio, Kansas and Illinois—a little
better, a little worse.

Erman cleared his throat a lot. "Well, what do you want
us to do?"

"For myself, nothing."

"I know! I know! A newspaper's worst trouble is with
people that don't want something for themselves but for
the world. I haven't any doubt that everything in your
prison is as bad as you say, and probably worse in other
jails. But it's all been said—in Mrs. O'Hare's *In Prison*,
for instance, and Frank Tannenbaum's *Wall Shadows*,
and Fishman's *Crucibles of Crime*, and—oh, dozens of
books. But people mostly don't pay attention to things
that aren't under their eyes. No one ever made a revolution for people more than a hundred miles from himself.
But the real point is, you have no *news*, since this condition
goes on all the time, and a newspaper exists to publish
news—new things. If there's a prison riot or scandal, we'll
publish it all right, and every detail about lack of sanitation, bad grub, cruelty, or anything else. We did just that
with the scandal about tying up women just a couple of
years ago. If you want to go back to Copperhead and get
up a petition that will make the Governor act, or if you'll
just assault the warden, or do something that will get you
tried and bring out the facts, we'll publish it, plenty—

and you'll probably go to prison for five years. Want to do that?"

"I do not!" Ann sounded shaky. "Once, I thought I would never be afraid of anything. But I'm afraid of going to prison, dead afraid!"

All the other newspaper editors said, "Yes, we don't doubt it, but there's no news. It's horrible, but it's old stuff, and people wouldn't read it."

The editor of that distinguished liberal weekly, the *Statesman*, was sighing, "Yes, I'm sure you're not exaggerating, Miss Vickers. And there are even worse prisons. Have you read the articles we've run in the last two years about the French Guiana penal colony, and the Florida chain-gangs?"

"No, I haven't. I'm afraid I didn't get to them."

"Do you see? Nobody much does 'get to them.' You say you feel a ghastly futility because you can't get the world to listen to you. Well, for thirty years I've been trying to get the world to listen to honest accounts of all sorts of preventable abuses, and the result is that even people like you mostly don't 'get to them'! What do you suppose I feel? I've more or less, after a good deal of cussing, learned to be patient. I'm afraid you'll have to. And—— So many abuses! Sometimes I want to chuck the whole Cassandra business and just go fishing. I like fishing. And when I fish, at least I do catch fish!

"Let me show you the tips on assorted outrages that have come to me just this morning alone, in letters or propagandist publications or telephone calls, begging me to tell the facts and get something done, right away."

He fumbled at the pile of papers on the Gargantuan desk in his minuscule office. "And mind you, all these people want me to help them communicate to the world, as you do. Um. Let's see. Well, here, for instance: Political prisoners are starving in Roumanian prisons. Miners are starving in West Virginia, and their representatives are shot down, and a perfectly respectable school teacher who protested about it was deported in the middle of the night, and his family left terrified and penniless. The natives of the island of Pafugi, British possession in the South Seas, are exploited by the white sugar-planters—paid twenty cents a day. The descendants of the liberated Southern slaves who settled in Liberia have now made the descendants of original inhabitants slaves. Emma Goldman says the Bolsheviks treat anarchists worse than a New York State Republican. Chinese workers in textile factories, owned by fellow Chinese, get six cents a day. The residents in a Western Y. M. C. A. hotel say the secretary is a degenerate, and got a fine decent young workman who protested pinched as a criminal syndicalist. In an Eastern university, a professor with twenty years honorable service was dismissed because he praised the Mormons.

"A thousand others! And I've run so much about prisons. I ought to hush up for a while. But I'm going to let you, if you'd like, tell the stories of Josephine—Filson, was it?—and Birdie Wallop, and the old lady, I forget her name, who was hanged, in three short articles, say about two thousand words."

She wrote her three short articles in a fever; they appeared handsomely in the *Statesman*.

They made as much noise as a bladder hurled into the ocean. They had as much effect as a tract left in a speak-easy.

There was a complimentary editorial about them in a liberal church paper. Three newspapers quoted a paragraph apiece. A new magazine called *Woman Triumphant* (born but to die, alas) sent an ambitious young lady interviewer who reported Ann as asserting that she had been head-matron of a penitentiary at Rattlesnake Gap, and that with the warden, Dr. Dringoole, she had instituted classes in sewing which had reformed all the prisoners.

She had a long letter from a gentleman who observed:

It is sentimentalists like you, who want to turn prisons into picnics, who are largely responsible for the present crime wave.

(For there was a crime wave in 1925, as in 1932, 1931, 1930, 1898, 1878, 1665, 1066, 11 B. C., and most years in between.)

The best informed and most experienced authorities on crime now state that lashing, with a provision that the lash must draw blood, should be universally restored, as the only deterrent against crime which a crook really fears.

But the chief response to Ann was in the *Proletarian Pep*, the chief Communist journal of America:

With characteristic impertinence, the *Statesman*, the wishy-washiest of all milk and water liberal sheets, has been publishing some pieces by a woman named Vickers about conditions in a Southern jail at Copperhead Gulch. This writer is a Social Fascist, like all contributors to the *Statesman*, also Socialists, and agent provocateur, under a disguise of so-called Liberalism secretly helping the Capitalists to bring about war with the U. S. S. R. How true this is can be seen from the fact that she does not even mention Comrade Jessie Van Tuyl, who is imprisoned in this jail at Copperhead Gulch, and it is a fact known to all comrades who are free from ideological deviations that Comrade Van Tuyl, and her alone, is responsible for whatever reforms are making at Copperhead Gulch. That this tool of the Capitalists, Mrs. Vickers, could have been there and apparently not even aware of the presence and leadership in jail of Comrade Van Tuyl shows where she stands and the necessity of all comrades being alert to the smug hypocrisy of Social Fascists, and supporting *Proletarian Pep* which because of its struggle to unmask the conspiracy of the Liberals to overthrow the U. S. S. R. is at this moment in serious financial straits. All comrades are urged to set aside five per cent. of their wages for *Proletarian Pep*.

Two years later Ann learned that Dr. Sorella had committed suicide by drinking poison in his bedroom at the prison.

31

ANN VICKERS had been superintendent of the Stuyvesant Industrial Home for Women, the most modern prison in New York City, for only a year, assistant superintendent for two, yet through her book *Vocational Training in Women's Reformatories* she had become known to all sociological and juridical groups in America, and she was receiving today, in January, 1928, the degree of Doctor of Laws from Erasmus University, Connecticut.

A Day in the Life of a Great Woman. . . .

Her train left the Grand Central at seven-thirty, and she had time only for a cup of coffee and a doughnut, sitting on a high stool at a counter in the station, in that amazing underground city of cigar stores, magazine shops, haberdasheries, on streets whose sun and stars were electric lights. She shook her head at the redcaps and carried her own bag, containing her academic robes, a private box of candy, and the latest prison handbook of the National Society of Penal Information. At five thousand a year salary, without quarters or maintenance, you don't carelessly give tips to porters, if you are the superintendent of a women's penitentiary, because every woman prisoner has the same idea of borrowing from the superintendent when she is about to leave and enter upon a life of holiness and sobriety.

The Great Woman did not read long, during her two-hour journey. She sat quiet, not jiggling, looking out of the window, apparently unseeing. Her dark eyes seemed resolute yet contented. She glanced at people quickly, as though she were used to sizing them up and giving them orders, yet she had none of the roving, hungry look of an egotist who expects to be noticed. She could be very alone in a crowd, one thought.

At the Erasmus station she was met with grave hand-shaking by the president of the university, two professors of sociology, and an officer of the State Federation of Women's Clubs.

"We shall feel deeply the honor of having you as an honorary alumna of old Erasmus," said the president, be-ing a small man.

"Did you have a comfortable journey?" boomed one of the professors. As though she had come from China.

"My home club is just aching for the privilege of getting you to lecture for us, whenever it's convenient, though we do appreciate how terribly busy you are, with that great Institution in your charge," breathed the clubwoman. She was quite pretty, too.

"If you'd care to come up to my house, my good lady would be enchanted to help you don the academic vestments," said the president, smiling to indicate that he was being slightly humorous.

At the presidential mansion, when Ann had put on the dolorous robe and funny hat that are somehow associated with the labeling of learning, the president's wife said brightly, "Is there anything I can do for you?"

Ann longed to remark, "You bet there is! I'd like a human cup of coffee and an egg." But you don't, when you are becoming a Doctor of Laws, ask for coffee and fried eggs, do you? She remained classic and calm. That was ever so important a part of being a Great Woman, she was learning: being silent when she didn't know what to say.

The convocation was held in a hall like an armory, very modern, all steel girders and curving walls of cement and loud-speakers. There were a good many undergraduates—Ann suspected that the sociology professors had dragged out their unwilling students—more clubwomen, and most of the faculty. The hall was a quarter filled.

Before the ceremony, behind the stage in a neat room adorned with autograph letters from William James, Henry Adams, and Robert Underwood Johnson, Ann was introduced to the other celebrities who were to receive honorary degrees: the president of a Schenectady bank, who had given a hundred thousand dollars to the Erasmus School of Higher Business; the governor of a Mid-Western state; and the world-authority on the botany of Beluchistan. She would not have noticed any of them, had she merely met him on a train, but since she knew they were celebrities, she was thrilled by them.

The Governor said, "You must come out and look over our prisons some day, Dr. Vickers. You'll find 'em right up to date. Dark cells and whipping forbidden. By law! We got a real modern penological system."

She chanced to know that no state in the union had more prisoners strung up by the wrists, spread-eagled against cell doors, than the good Governor's, and none had more weary, degenerating idleness among prisoners but— how do you reply to a Governor in such a case?

The bank president said to her, and he said it merrily, for he was a renowned after-dinner speaker as well as so renowned an amateur of education that he was already an A. M., a D. C. L., a Litt. D., and an LL. D. four times over—he said: "Well, Dr. Vickers, here's something I bet no one ever called to your attention: I've got a lot of respect for the sympathy you show for the Unfortunate, but personally I think it's misguided. Way I look at it, prison ought to be made just as disagreeable as possible, so's it'll have a deterrent effect and make folks not want to go there!"

The botanist-explorer shook hands and winked at her. She loved him.

It was a handsome procession.

The president, sixteen faculty members, two members of the Board of Trustees, and the four candidates for honors, all in their academic robes, with hoods of black and scarlet and purple, preceded by a gaunt, white-mustached man carrying a silver mace, marched out of the back of the hall, around to the front, through a mass of students and photographers, and up to the platform, while Ann, trying to move majestically behind a pair of heavy but enthusiastically polished black shoes, said to herself, "I ought to feel impressed—this is a fine thing—it certainly is—a great moment—I wonder what the dickens Mrs. Keast is doing about the butter for the prison?"

She got more applause than the other three when she stumbled over to the president, at the reading-stand, to wait with watery knees and receive her diploma. And it irritated her. "Getting rolls of parchment! Applause! What am I doing here? If I were any good, I'd be in a cell with Jessie Van Tuyl." Meantime the president was baying, " . . . difficult to know whether we should the more honor Ann Vickers for her learning in the complex co-ordination of sociology and psychiatry which constitutes contemporary criminology, or for the greatness of heart which has enabled her to take to herself the sorrows and suffering of the misguided . . ."

And then she was Dr. Vickers, with a diploma under her arm; and then, somewhere, minus her robes and with a fresh rosebud in the lapel of her suit, she was addressing a large luncheon at the Faculty Club, with perfectly enormous applause whenever she came to a halt—no matter what she had said before the halt—and presently she was on the train again, very tired and, for all her efforts at cynicism about honors, very proud of herself; and just before six she was bustling into the Stuyvesant Industrial Home for Women, of which she was superintendent. Immediately all purple honors and degrees were submerged in details of butter for the prison dining-room, the unfortunate conduct of Prisoner No. 3712, who had been caught distilling alcohol in the kitchen at night, and the feeble pedagogy of the teacher of dressmaking.

The Industrial Home for Women, in the Borough of Stuyvesant, in Greater New York, was an entirely modern prison, but adapted to a jammed city. There was no room for gardens, but there was a central court, with a fountain, a not very extensive bed of flowers, handball courts, and standards for basketball; and on the roof, nine stories up, there was room for all two hundred of the prisoners to walk in the sun at once, with no sense of jail about it save a high wire screen necessitated by notions of suicide.

The assembly-hall had none of the damp garish stoniness of chapel at Copperhead Gap. There were theater seats, subdued decorations in crimson and dull gold, a stage with curtain and scenery.

There were no cells. Each prisoner had, at least when the prison opened and was not overcrowded, a room to herself, with wire-glass windows but without bars. The rooms were ten feet by eight—not large, yet luxurious by comparison with other jails; each with a bed, a chair, a table, a wardrobe, bookshelves, such pictures as the prisoner cared to bring, running water, and, on the linoleum floor, a rug. Each dwelling-story had a sitting-room with books and magazines, open from after-supper till bedtime to all inmates not undergoing punishment, and on each floor were shower baths and toilets. . . . They were clean. . . . The plumbers regarded Ann as a holy terror.

A rug on each floor! No one could quite believe it!

It was extraordinary, a matter for discussion at penological conventions, that a woman should have a $1.98 rug on the floor of this, her only home!

The entire building was of steel, cement, brick, and glass. It could be kept spotless; under Ann, it was. Whatever else she might leave to Mrs. Keast, the assistant superintendent, Ann herself, with the doctor, inspected every corner three times a week; and the sight of a cockroach caused the entire staff to be mobilized, to the martial sound of wire swatters and Flit-guns.

The inmates wore blue Indianhead uniforms all week. They were suggestive of uniforms only in being uniform. On Sunday—when they were not, as in respectable prisons, locked in cells from Saturday noon to Monday morning, but allowed to go to chapel, read in the sitting-rooms, loaf on the roof, as they wished—they could wear their own clothes.

At no time was any rule of silence enforced.

There was, in the Industrial Home, a small, very modern knitting-works, which made sweaters, mufflers, caps of colored wool. It paid back to the state a part of the expenses of the prison, and the workers received from thirty to seventy cents a day—no vast sum, yet several times as great as was paid for labor in the other prisons of the world. But the heart of the prison was what Ann sentimentally called the "Salvage Corps."

There were vocational classes, as good as she could make them: classes in cooking, housekeeping, stenography, sewing, dressmaking, millinery, fur-repairing, which turned an almost satisfactory percentage of the petty criminals into self-dependent wage-earners. Ann was as unscrupulous as most reformers in getting teachers for nothing in these classes. There was the most complete parole department in America, and it regarded itself (with a certain encouragement from Ann) as existing only to help discharged prisoners, not as a set of cats trying to trap the mice. And most important of all in the Salvage Corps was the office of the psychiatrist. He was a good psychiatrist—or so Ann thought. His business was to study not the crime that had been committed, but the individual who had committed it, and to find out why. He could not, or so Ann insisted, be greatly shocked by a woman who had killed a blackmailer; he could be perturbed by a woman clerk who had stolen stamps.

With the psychiatrist was a full-time general practitioner. Their salaries were, on the books, eighteen hundred dollars each a year. They received seven thousand each. The extra money came from Lindsay Atwell, Ardence Benescoten, the Carnegie Foundation, and the Dr. Ann Vickers who did not use redcaps. It was doubtful whether it was not in some way a form of graft and pull. Certainly Ann had used pull enough when she had been assistant superintendent, three years ago, and the Stuyvesant Industrial Home had been built. She had pestered Lindsay to influence the state authorities to keep bars off the windows of the women's rooms—the number who were willing to escape by jumping out of a sixth-story window was negligible—to install the basketball equipment, to keep all wood out of the construction, and to employ the two full-time doctors.

There were no executions. Ann was a little ashamed to have that supreme task done for her at Sing Sing.

Her greatest trouble was the wits. The wits in the newspaper columns and cartoons. The wits in the magazines. The wits of the dinner-table. Whenever a cartoonist had nothing whatever to draw, he could make sure of commendation by depicting the Industrial Home as a funny university, as a funny speakeasy, as a harem. It did hurt, that the wits should make their living out of being humor-

ous about women in agony, and other women who tried to
save them from that breaking agony by making them feel
decent and clean and trusted again.

The staff rushed up to the Great Woman when she arrived at her desk at the Stuyvesant Industrial Home after
the ceremony at Erasmus University.

The telephone girl had a message from Mr. Lindsay
Atwell to the effect that he had to address the banquet of
the New York County Home Florists Association, and
would not be able to telephone Dr. Vickers that evening,
but he certainly did congratulate her on—— "Gee, Miss
Vickers, there's one word I didn't get. It sounded like
'doctorate.' Is there such a woid? Say, lissen, gee, I'm glad
they made you a doc, Miss Vickers! Ain't that *funny?* My
boy friend said, he said, 'She's never studied medicine.'
'Say, lissen, fathead,' I says to him, 'if Miss Vickers wants
to be a doc, lissen,' I said, 'the State Medical Board would
be tickled to death to *make* her a doc and——' Gee, I was
tickled pink! Say, Doctor, what do you do for a headache?"

The kitchen and dining-room matron, a quiet woman,
said, "May I congratulate you, Dr. Vickers? We are all so
pleased! About the butter, now. I know it's bad. It's the
politics. Honest, Doctor, I can't do better. If we don't get
it from the Aegis Dairy Company, we're in Dutch with the
district leader. And I'm not getting any graft out of it
either. I swear I'm not! I wouldn't do that to you, Miss
Vickers!"

"I know. . . . I know. . . . I'll do what I can."

The psychiatrist ambled in to say, "Ann, I've never
been so pleased! Shall I call you 'Doctor'? Was it fierce?"

"Well, if you want to know the truth, Sam, I was proud as Punch!"

Then a minor New York paper was calling, asking for an interview. And the Sevigné Club of Lima, Ohio, was calling, long distance, asking her to lecture for them—"I'm afraid we can't pay you a very large fee, Doctor, but we'd be very happy to pay your expenses and to entertain you, of course." And her old Settlement, in Rochester, was calling, long distance, to invite her to Settlement Old Home Week. And the chief janitor of the Industrial Home was at her desk, cap in hand, muttering, "Doc, I got to have a couple more ash-cans, right away—I stole one, but that's all I could get." And there were telegrams, like yellow snow. Twenty telegrams were still in front of the Great Woman when Mrs. Keast, the assistant superintendent, came in.

Ann had once said that Mrs. Keast was "Mrs. Kaggs plus New Hampshire inhibitions." Mrs. Keast had been Ann's rival for the position of superintendent of the Industrial Home. She believed in purity. She was reasonably honest. She was unreasonably terrifying. She had, possibly as a result of fifty-five years complete abstinence from tobacco, alcohol, laughter, sexual excitement, and novels, a dark bagginess under her eyes, and twitching fingers. . . . She hated Ann rather more than she hated the rest of the world.

"Oh, good-afternoon, Miss Vickers. I don't know whether you would care for my humble congratulations, but I venture to give them to you, anyway. I *suppose* that I ought to call you 'Doctor' now!" She neighed exactly like an indignant horse.

"Well, I don't think it matters very much."

"Well, I'm *sure*, Dr. Vickers, I'm sure I hate to interrupt you on your great day, I'm sure it *must* have been a great day—for you! I hate to interrupt you with the practical problems that have entered today—while you were away!"

"Well, that's just too bad. That's the way life is. What're the problems?"

Mrs. Keast sniffed.

"Well, the first is the woman that was caught making moonshine while she was in charge of the kitchen and dining-room at night."

"Yes. I don't like that. I'll talk to her, later. But what's the other?"

"Well, there's a woman brought in this afternoon—while you were away!—for blackmail, and she just won't listen to reason. Regular recalcitrant. Cursed me! I've got her in the Jug."

There were only two forms of punishment at the Industrial Home: docking of sitting-room privilege, and solitary confinement in rooms as clean as the others, and as light, but solitary and apart; and these two punishments Ann used as little as possible. But Mrs. Keast and the other veteran matrons preserved some savory memory of the older days of licensed sadism by referring to these confinement cells as the "Jug."

"All right, all right, Mrs. Keast. I'll see her before I go home."

Mrs. Keast sniffed herself away.

The Great Woman rang for her secretary, Miss Feldermaus, who giggled, "Gee, isn't it *dandy*, Doctor," saw a few more subordinates, read a few more telegrams of congratulation, went quite cheerfully down the corridor to the "Jug," alone, unlocked the cell, and heard from the Recalcitrant therein: "Well, Annie, and how the hell are you? Hear from your boy friend, the Copperhead prison doc, often? God, that was a swell picture of you and him!"

The lady in the cell was Miss Kittie Cognac.

Ann laughed.

Kittie did not look so elegant as she had three years ago, nor quite so vicious.

"Why, Kittie, my dear! In again?"

"Hell, no! I'm skating across the Atlantic!"

"Hard luck. Oh, just a moment."

Ann bustled out of the cell, leaving the door open. Kittie dashed after her.

"Want to escape, Kit? I don't mind!"

The woman stood glaring.

On a wall-telephone, Ann called the prison psychiatrist: "Dr. Alstein? Miss Vickers speaking. Will you please come to D2, right away?" She looked around. Kittie's hands were clenched, her eyes darting like lizards. Ann called again on the telephone: "Mrs. Keast? Miss Vickers. Will you have a room prepared for Miss Cognac? I'm taking her out of solitary. What? *Yes, that's what I said, Keast, understand!*"

But as she spoke, Ann was thinking, "Dr. Sorella was right. It's getting me, beginning to make me a tyrant, this prison life. No human being is good enough to be a jailer!"

Dr. Alstein was racing down the corridor—a small, compact man with kind, neurotic eyes. Then Kittie spoke:

"How are you, Doc? Aren't you the guy that tried to make me in a speak last week?"

"I am not!" The doctor spoke with quite unprofessional rage.

"Oh, ain't you? Well, it was some Jew boy that looked like you. Well, Annie, so you and the doc think you're going to soft-soap me into being a hypocrite like you two! You! Miss Vickers! Dr. Vickers! You round-heel!"

Dr. Alstein blazed, "Doctor, shall I——"

"No!" cried Ann.

"All right. But she's going back to solitary."

"No. She's not. It would flatter her too much. Doctor, here's your case. My friend Kittie is essentially an ego-maniac. I knew her at Copperhead. But she's rather com-petent, and I'm planning to see that when she leaves this health resort of ours, she'll be set up in a smart gown or hat shop. She'll be a success. But meantime it will be a little difficult to convince her we're friends of hers. And we'll have to get her off the snow, cold-turkey. Do you mind, Kit? I hate to have to do it this way but——"

Kittie Cognac was crying. "Oh damn you, damn you! Won't you even get insulted?"

As she went down in the elevator, Ann remarked to her-self, "Annie, I have never known you to be so hateful as when you took that sweet and forgiving and superior atti-tude toward Kittie Cognac. Poor Kit! The Alstein was much more human—losing his temper. Miss Vickers! Dr. Vickers! The Woman Leader! You poor semi-literate brat! Giving you a degree! If they only knew!"

And so the Great Woman came home, by subway—not

many Great Women can afford taxicabs—and in her apartment she sat by the telephone, thinking, "I wish I had a date for this evening. I wish some nice person would call me up and invite me to dinner and the movies, the way they would Tessie Katz or Birdie Wallop."

For dinner, she made for herself, as women do when they live alone, a cup of tea and a slice of toast, and as she consumed them, standing before the drain-board of the sink in her kitchenette, she brooded:

"Funny how I hate the phone when it rings in my office, all day long. But now—— I wish Lindsay would chuck his cursed Florists' Dinner and come. Florists! I wish I had a husband, who came home nights—no, no, not every night, but sometimes, for a surprise. I wish I had Pride. My daughter! I would be proud of her. I'm afraid I'd send her to a terribly conservative school, and be proud of her horrible smart friends, like any other Waubanakee mother. And I killed you, I murdered you, Pride, and so I am Dr. Vickers, superintendent of a prison! And with a great sum obtained I this freedom. But Paul said, 'But I was free born.' He was not! No one is!"

Ann Vickers brewed herself another cup of tea. It was bitter.

32

HER apartment was as modern as the Stuyvesant Industrial Home and, though she didn't like it, almost as hard. It had been pleasant enough to take the trouble of housekeeping when she had shared with Pat Bramble. But now, when once or twice a week she had to go out and address Dinners with a capital D—Dinners of the League for the Urbanization of Agricultural Communities, or the League for the Rustification of Industrial Centers, or the Committee on the Employment of Non-Recidivist Penal Offenders, or the Alumnæ of the Phi Tau Delta Sorority of Point Royal College, or the Illinois Society, or the St. Stephen's Women's Sociological Study Circle (Brooklyn), or the Citizens' Independent Mutual Union of the Borough of Stuyvesant—when sometimes she had to stay at the prison till midnight—when gentleman reporters telephoned to her daily for her opinions on bobbed hair as an accessory to crime and the effect of novel-reading on crimes of lust—when brightly tender lady reporters called to get her opinions on divorce—when lady ex-convicts waited at her door for advice and a slight temporary assistance—when insurance agents called up in the evening to explain that hers was a peculiarly hazardous occupation (they had statistics about the number of prison officials who had been killed in riots)—when 750,331 young women wrote to her monthly, asking for her autograph or for suggestions on how to get to New York and enter the romantic realm called "Social Work"—when you could never tell whether Lindsay would appear at six or seven or eleven, and want a snack here or take her to the Casino— when there was no Pride whose fresh air and quiet must be considered—when, in fact, she had become a Great Woman, and generally lonely, it was too much to fuss over housekeeping and innumerable bills, and she had taken a little flat in the new Hotel Portofino, in the East Nineties, halfway between the prison and the place of theaters and restaurants.

It was not a very large hotel. But to make up for that it had untold marble, telephones, radios, bellboys with monkey-jackets and grins and crisped Sicilian hair, mysterious and unhappy-looking old men with blue denim jackets and long gray mustaches who were always going somewhere with kits of tools to repair something that never quite got repaired, proud Persian carpets and rather less proud Japanese prints, supplies of White Rock, and telephone girls saying, "Yeah? Well I givum the message, I don't know where he is."

Ann had a living-room with the clean, hard, efficient brightness of steel and cement and prickly plaster. Tall windows with metal mullions. From them you could see the East River, and hear the beckoning hoarseness of steamers which she imagined were outbound for Seville and Götteborg and Mangalore. Unyielding floors of linoleum laid in cement. High walls—straight walls that went bleakly up and up to a ceiling of rigidly squared beams enclosed in plaster.

She had made it as human as she could with her small store of kind, human, old things. The lounge on which Professor Vickers had slept on Sunday afternoons. His set of Dickens. The *David Copperfield* that she had read every year since she had been ten. The *Water Babies* that he had given her, and *Idylls of the King* with Glenn Hargis's signature. Four soft chairs, and little tables, and lights by the chairs so that you could read. Shelves of brown dim books about criminology and penology and psychology and all the dim desperate sciences in which she sought wisdom.

Beyond this tall living-room was a bedroom rather smaller than she had had in Waubanakee, Ill., and a bathroom so small that she had only a shower bath. And the kitchenette—New York was the greatest city in the world, so she had no room for a spacious stove or a line of copper pots, but there was ever such a nice electric coffee percolator, and she had a large tomcat named Jones.

A good many people came in: Malvina Wormser, Lindsay Atwell, Pat Bramble, whenever she was in town, and a clique of social workers, such as Russell Spaulding. He had been christened James Russell Lowell Spaulding, and he signed it "J. Russell Spaulding," but, for reasons Ann never did discover, he was known throughout the whole world of radical-dinner-attenders as "Ignatz." She had met him at the Organized Charities Institute, of which he

was a department head. He was unmarried, at forty—
three years older than Ann—and zealous at being a Man
about Town as well as a Progressive Humanitarian. Mr.
Spaulding was large, round-faced, and given to little jokes.
As a small boy, Ann guessed, he had been the wistful fat
one on whom the gang in his Boytown in Iowa had played
all their jokes, and he had never quite got over trying to
impress the gang—trying, in New York, to impress a
shadowy, unescapable Iowa. Ann liked him because he
was kind, because he never minded being invited to dinner
at the last moment, and because he remembered to telephone you, when you were kept home by 'flu, as depend-
ably as did Lindsay Atwell.

33

He was so thin and fine and gray and gracious, Lindsay Atwell. His ruddiness had faded. Pat Bramble insisted that he was an old cat, but Ann saw him as a greyhound. He remembered flowers and candy and birthdays. He kissed her, tenderly and not too briefly, but nothing more. Sometimes she reflected, "If that man doesn't propose to me pretty soon, I'm going to propose to him," but she always forgot it. He was as familiar to her as her right hand, and as unregarded.

He came in for what New York politely called "tea," when she was particularly tried, and particularly glad of his restfulness. A bad day. Kittie Cognac was turning so sweet and pious that Ann knew she was up to some deviltry. And Ann's pet prisoner, No. 3701, an ex-school teacher in prison for stealing rare books from libraries, had been caught selling false teeth out of the dental infirmary. "A swell reformer I turned out to be!" sighed Ann, in the jargon of the day. She felt clinging. When Lindsay came, she kissed him, to his placid surprise, till she almost strangled him. But she did not tell him she was tired: being tired was his privilege. She drew the bridge lamp nearer to the deepest chair, gave him the evening papers, and went out to the kitchen to mix the cocktails.

As she dumped the magic ice-cubes out of the electric refrigerator, as she measured and shook, she hummed excitedly, and planned. "What a blessed security we'll have when Lindsay and I are married and he comes home every evening like this! He'll be a Justice of the Supreme Court of the United States, and I think I'll be Governor of New York. Together, we'll have royal power. Like a medieval king and queen. I'll give him some of my belief in the coöperative commonwealth. He'll give me something of his common sense. But how can I be in Albany and he in Washington?" She laughed, as she carried in the cocktail shaker, on a silver tray with glasses and a prim, unfeminist doily. "I'm a little premature, to worry about that!" she jeered to herself.

Lindsay sipped judiciously. He folded the newspaper before he laid it down, with its edges exactly parallel to the edges of the little table beside him, and judiciously he spoke:

"I think you ought to know, Ann: I am going to be married. To Margaret Salmon—you remember, the banker's daughter."

Ann sat quietly. She, who usually did things jerkily, put down her cocktail carefully. "Yes? Miss Salmon? A nice girl. I remember her. At your flat."

(But inside her, the Ann who had defied Cap'n Waldo was raging profanely, "You are not! You're going to marry me! That Salmon flapper, that limp, skinny bone-head that can only dance—drives a car so badly she's

always getting wrecked and—— Oh, my dear, this is the
end, Lindsay, my dear!")

"You are the first to whom I have told this, Ann, because I dare to think of you as my best friend. Yes. My
best friend." He stopped. He scratched his upper lip with
his left forefinger. He was standing now, still holding his
undrained cocktail, but his hand was trembling, and he set
down the glass. A few drops on the little table. He absently
wiped them off with his pure handkerchief before he faced
her again. "Ann, I had hoped once I might venture to ask
you to marry me. You are the most worth-while woman I
know, and the dearest. But I'm afraid you're a little too
big for me. I have a career of my own. And if I married
you, I'd simply become your valet, I'm afraid, my dear."

"Yes. Yes, perhaps. Yes, it might be so."

("It would not be so, you fool! I'd protect you and help
you——")

"You see, it's just because I do think you and your
career are so important—— You know. I wouldn't even
want to interfere, Ann. Encourage."

"Yes, well, I think perhaps I do appreciate——"

"But, on the other hand, it seems certain I'll have the
Democratic nomination for Justice of the State Supreme
Court and—— But I'm afraid that you—— Oh, in all
helpfulness and sweetness. You'd want to advise me, and a
judge has to stand alone—or sit, ha, ha!—and—— And in
daily life you'd be fretting about me—— You see, sort of
smother me with kindness. You see, because you *have*
resolution and a point of view of your own, and conceivably I'd let you control me and—— You see?"

"Yes, well, I suppose perhaps that's so."

"And, dear, you must come to appreciate my Margaret! You probably think she's unformed but—— Such a fine, delicate nature—simply too shy to express herself publicly, but so dear and—— Oh, Ann, oh, my God!"

He was kissing her in the awkwardness of passion, almost sobbing as he kissed her ears, her hair, her throat, her shoulders. Then, crying, "I can't stand it!" he was fleeing out of the room, out of the flat.

She did not move; just stood, with her arms out toward the door.

For an hour she sat far forward in a deep chair, stooped over, biting a knuckle. A hundred times she thought, "I'll telephone him. I will! No. I won't!" She rose, mechanically, her head filled with the vision of him and of his kisses; she drained his cocktail, washed the shaker and glasses, put them away, and unseeingly caressed Jones the cat when, to make her notice him, he vainly played at cat-and-mouse with a ball of paper. "I'll telephone him. I must! I can't let him go, not to that beastly little flapper!"

She turned on the radio, but after a moment of Terry Tintavo crooning "That Atlantic City Mooooon" she snapped it off viciously.

Mostly, through her hour of agony, she sat like a softer "Thinker." She "went to pieces." That is the accepted phrase. The fact is the opposite. The scattered pieces of her at last flew together; the pieces of Ann Vickers that had been dropped in so many corners: in Humanitarianism, which, being interpreted, means putting diapers upon old evil judges and old evil tramps; in sketchy dabblings at psychology, in affection for friends, backdrifts to the con-

ditioning of a village childhood, fear of being afraid, desire
for an impossible perfectionism with some good saline
humor about that spectacle of herself trying to be perfect,
in a muted pride at having become a species of Great
Woman, in the romantic guidance of the shreds of Keats
and Tennyson that she still remembered, in the drag of
such daily and inescapable ordinarinesses as unpaid bills,
and the taste of fresh peas, and the smell of pinks on a
street barrow, and the corn on her toe that made a little
ridiculous some interview with a state official, and how
much to tip the hotel janitor who, after all, had only fixed
her bathroom light this past month, and the ever-imagined
sound of Pride's crying, and her neighbors' radios when
she wanted to sleep, and the regret that she had forgotten
to send flowers to Dr. Wormser on her birthday—all these
dissevered pieces of Ann Vickers flew together and she
became one integrated passionate whole, a woman as
furious for love as Sappho.

To the eye she was a modestly dressed and comely
woman sitting on the edge of an overstuffed chair in one
cell of a skyscraper hotel scientifically provided with electric lighting and electric refrigeration, in the cinematic
city of thousand-foot towers and steel and glass and concrete. But all the layers of niceness and informed reasoning
and adaptation to the respectability of concrete had been
stripped off, till she was naked, nude as a goddess—a
woman tribal leader in the jungle.

Rarely did she think in words, but chiefly in emotions,
explosive and scarlet. Yet now and then her inner words
were clear:

"I do want to add a millionth of a degree to civilization.

Like Florence Nightingale. (Not so cranky, I hope!) I do
like a job of some dignity and respect. I like power. I do! I
do not want to spend my life paying grocery bills! And I
can put it over. I have! Power and initiative and the
chance to give Kittie Cognac a chance.

"And I don't care one hang for all of it! I want love; I
want Pride, my daughter. I want to bear her. I have a
right to her. I want to teach her. I would be glad if some
ranchman out of an idiotic 'Western novel' came along and
carried me off. I'd bear his children and cook his beans.
And I wouldn't become a drab farm-wife. I'd learn grains,.
soils, tractors. I'd fight for the coöperatives. I'd go into
politics. And all the time I'd have Pride and my man——

"But maybe I couldn't have Pride and my ranchman
and still have ambition, any more than I can have Pride
and Lindsay and ambition. How simple we were when we
used to talk about something called 'Feminism'! We were
going to be just like men, in every field. We can't. Either
we're stronger (say, as rulers, like Queen Elizabeth) or
we're weaker, in our subservience to children. For all we
said in 1916, we're still women, not embryonic men—
thank God! I'm glad of it, because while Lindsay has his
judge's robes and his leech of a Margaret, some day I'm
going to have my daughter Pride!"

Russell Spaulding on the telephone.
"Don't suppose there's a ghost of a chance you're free
for dinner 's evening, Ann. You're probably dining with
the president of Columbia or the Pasha of Pezuzza."
"Oh! No! Russell! I'd be enchanted—— I take it this
is an invitation?"

"By my halidom, yea! I'll be right around."

Her only side-thought was, "I do hope he won't be *too* joky."

Mr. J. Russell Spaulding of the Organized Charities Institute, variously known to reform circles of New York as "Ignatz" and as "Russell," was a competent social worker who had read the books, who could chivvy underpaid stenographers at the O. C. I. as efficiently as any manager of an insurance office—one of the first qualities of any executive in a humanitarian movement—and who could in ten seconds tell whether an applicant for charity really wanted to work. (Which, charity subjects being like carpenters, authors, fishermen, aviators, and doctors, most of them earnestly did not.) Yet with all his qualities as a leader of men, Russell reminded Ann, in private life, of a good old farm dog, hearty and simple, frisking and crouching and shaking his broad behind with the longing to go for a run.

By the time he came Ann had changed from a suit to the first frock at hand, had washed her eyes and gargled, and was convinced that she had concealed her sorrow as only a Great Woman, used to facing and denying the public, ever could. He bounced in, crying, "How about some grand Chinese eats—chicken pineapple, eggs fou yung—— Why, Ann, darling, what is it?"

"What is what?"

"Something's worried you. Tell old Uncle Russell."

He loomed. He was so taller and wider than Lindsay; his chest so more keg-like than Lindsay's fastidious bosom; his wavy black hair had a natural pompadour. She wanted to lay her head on his shoulder and howl. But she said briskly, "Not a thing. Oh, just the usual fusses at the Industrial Home. I want to forget 'em. And if I do look a little palely loitering, it's probably because I'm famished. Let's go eat."

His big hands, a little flabby, pinioned her arms. He kissed her forehead, brotherly, and grunted, "Well, I shan't butt in, my good Doctor, but if I can do anything, proud to met you. Yes, let's forget it. But no Chinese chow for you this evening, my good woman. What you need is—— I know a Wop speakie where nobody will recognize even good and great leaders of public opinion like us, and the Chianti is practically drinkable. Come on!"

And he wasn't *too* joky. He wasn't apparently sympathetic. He talked shop—that only really satisfactory talk aside from dirty stories and love, which latter is itself a form of shop-talk. He had her furiously debating with him about eugenics, Commonwealth College for Workers, minimum hours for women's labor, reorganization of the textile industry. Lindsay would have been charming and witty about the theater and Trouville, and Ann have been delicately happy. But with Russell, she was aggressive and emphatic and already half-healed.

Back home, Russell said cheerily, "Lookit. If you aren't going off with your boy friend Atwell next Sunday, why don't you and I try to get hold of Malvina Wormser and Bill Coughlin and have a picnic in Westchester?"

"I'll phone Dr. Wormser and phone you tomorrow. Thanks a lot, Russell."

He stooped for a kiss, then didn't, and went off leaving her to weep—only the weeping did not come now. It seemed a grief dead these hundred years, and Lindsay was someone of whom she had only read.

But the mention of Dr. Wormser made her long for that fount of life. With Malvina, she could weep. And if she did not weep, she would die.

It wasn't so late—quarter after eleven. She telephoned, and in half an hour was across the fireplace from the dumpy little woman, smoking, and saying with careful gravity, "Malvina, I think the jig is up—my pretending, or at least wanting, to be a woman as well as a glorified school-ma'am. Lindsay chucked me tonight. I haven't come for encouragement, but more, sort of, to make a public and official registration of the fact that something, God knows what, makes it impossible for any real man to love me."

"That's not true, Ann. You have something, I have something, all superior women have something (I s'pose we *are* superior, aren't we? I dunno) that makes the *pretty* real men afraid of our overshadowing 'em—the men who are ambitious, not commonplace, yet won't stand comparison with better stuff. We have to depend either on men so small that they get their pride and egotism out of being known as our associates, or on men so big they're not afraid of comparison with anyone.

"It has nothing to do with sex attractiveness. You and I have passion, some charm. In fact, Ann, you must get it right out of your head that it's only ambitious women that suffer so. It's men, too. A first-class man marries a mean woman, and after she gets over her first awe of him as a celeb, she puts in the rest of her life, till he chucks her, in trying to convince the world that she's as good as he is. She suffers, almost to insanity, over the fact that most people see her only as the great man's wife. She tries to make him feel guilty for it.

"Even among friends of the same sex—A and B start out as youngsters, apparently equal. A makes good. B doesn't. It's a terribly rare and fine B that will endure it, and won't try, by recalling A's early breaks and throwing them at him, to make him feel humble.

"Good heavens, Ann, it's world-old. It's the story of Aristides the Just. Three fourths of the mass hate superior people. Verily I say unto you, there shall be more rejoicing over one good man pulled down to the mob than over nine and ninety that are elevated for an example to mankind.

"It's only an improbable accident when a woman and a man who are both of them big enough not to be jealous of each other's bigness do meet—and then, probably, when they do meet, one of 'em will already be married to some little pretentious squirt and they can't marry—but thank Heaven, there hasn't yet been passed a constitutional amendment preventing the sacred old custom of illicit love. In a long life devoted to meddling with other people's intimate affairs, I don't know of half a dozen successfully married couples who are both important people. But it has nothing to do with your feminine attractions, my love.

"But—— Curious. If a woman were handsome as Diana, a better physicist than Lord Rutherford, President of the United States, world tennis-champion, mistress of seventeen languages, a divine dancer, and possessed of a perfectly functioning adrenal gland, still she would be miserable and humble in the presence of any bouncing chorus-girl, if no male had ever looked at her moist-eyed. And I'm afraid it will be the same world without end, amen. Hell!"

Somehow, when Ann went home, she could not feel tragic—just dreary and futile and not at all a Great Woman, but a Little Woman.

Their picnic was agreeable. For three weeks Russell Spaulding was chubbily attentive and blessedly unquestioning. Ann did not telephone to Lindsay. He called her, tentatively, suggesting a party with his Margaret, but she begged off, with hoarse politeness.

Ann was alone in her apartment, at mid-evening, engaged, as a weighty part of prison work, in studying a pamphlet, "122 Economical Ways of Preparing Rice." She was humming. A knock, and her careless, "Come in."

No apparent response. She looked up. Lindsay Atwell was in the doorway, staring. His hat was in trembling hands. There was something indefinably aged and degenerated about him. His collar was proper enough, but his fastidious tie was a little crooked, his hair not quite sleek. He looked like a sick man, and hopeless. He stumbled as he came toward her desk. She did not rise. This was a man she could barely remember.

"Ann, I'm going crazy! I can't stand Margaret! She's a little peacock! Oh, I need your richness and realness—— Forgive me! Marry me!"

"Why, I'm sorry, Lindsay, but Russell Spaulding and I were married yesterday afternoon. Announcing it tomorrow."

"Why? Oh, God, why?"

"Why? Oh, I suppose because he asked me to. And I do like him, you know. Yes. Of course I do."

34

It HAPPENED to be convenient for these two people, busy about all good works, to be married Thursday afternoon, but for that night Russell had a dinner of the Single Tax Advancement Program and, the next night, a committee meeting of the Friends of Russia, and he delicately stated that it might be very nice if they didn't do anything nuptial till Saturday, when they would start their three-day honeymoon at Malvina Wormser's cottage.

"Sure. All right," said Ann.

They arrived at the cottage at six of an early-spring evening, with moon. Russell had been very funny on the train, telling how the editor of the *Statesman* had spent an hour at the committee meeting trying to combine entire loyalty to Soviet Russia with entire pacifism and loving-kindness toward counter-revolutionaries.

There was no porter at the station. She admired—she was always forgetting how strong Russell must be—the way in which he tossed their bags on his shoulder and wafted them into the station; the executive way in which, by telephone, he ordered a taxicab.

In Dr. Wormser's pine-ceiled long living-room, with its

scent of wood and salt breeze and books, she was morbid about Pride, who had been murdered in this house. But she forgot, as Russell lifted her from the floor, held her to his breast.

"Hm! Some feat! I'm not a lightweight," she said.

"To me——" Peering, she decided that he actually was not joking. "To me you're just a fragile little thing, to shield and baby and protect, for all your giant brain!"

"Well, that's a new way of looking at it. But if you should ever meet a friend of mine called Katherine Cognac, don't tell her that. How about some supper? Did you really remember to bring the grub?"

"Honey, your old man may be a frost as a sociologist, but as a picnic provider, he's IQ 100. He's the king of boy scouts!"

"Russell, my dear, say anything else you want to about yourself, but never that."

She did not sound particularly merry.

But she was touched by the thoroughness of his shopping. Out of a wooden case, which he had carried in as easily as though it were—well, as easily as though it were a pretty heavy wooden case—came half a Smithfield ham, Irish bacon, a chicken, two squabs, veal chops which they immediately popped into the electric refrigerator, cans and boxes of corn, tomatoes, instant oatmeal, flapjack flour, Roquefort—— She loved a grocery store, as do all healthy dreamers, and here was one of their own.

Apron about his waist, singing "Smile, Smile, Smile," Russell helped her prepare the first honeymoon meal, deftly setting the table. In fact, he was almost too helpful and merry. Ann wished, presently, that he would be quiet.

She was tired with a nameless tiredness. She wanted to dine well, to sit silently looking at the moon-webbed sea, to be kissed thoroughly, till she reeled, and go off to sleep with a man's arm around her.

"'There's a long, long trail a-wiiiiinding——'"

"Damn it, let it wind!"

"Why, darling!"

"Oh, I'm sorry, Russell. You know. I sort of got tired of that song during the war."

"Then I'll sing that funny one, 'She was poor but she was honest.' Or—— Maybe I'm too noisy. Getting married is a little nerve-racking, isn't it! But delightfully. I'll be a li'l' mouse, then, as much as a hundred-ninety-pounder can be a mouse—mouse crossed with elephant—cockroach crossed with hippopotamus—Lord might have invented much more amusing animiles——"

He did run on. But seemingly he did not expect her to listen, and she was almost happy. They sat and regarded the guaranteed spectacle of moon on ocean, and he held her competently—neither with a stale and fishlike timidity, nor with too avaricious a passion.

Abruptly, at eleven, he said, "Let's go to bed."

"Well——" She felt virginal and frightened.

In the living-room he seized her hand, led her to the window seat, drew her down. She was nervous till she saw his face; then she wanted to laugh. He looked so lugubriously sentimental, and his voice was so Y. M. C. A., at its manliest and most ponderous:

"Ann, the moment has come—— We are both of us people of the world, and I think we're rather unusually endowed with senses of humor, but let us for once forego

humor and treat this hour as sacred. Perhaps I should
have told you before, but anyway, I must now. While I
have certainly never been a roué, I am not quite altogether
a virgin."

"What?"

"No, I grieve to say, not altogether a——"

"Well, neither am I."

"You're not?"

"No—not quite."

"Oh. Well, of course, that makes it—— Still. Of course.
You're a modern."

"I am not! I'm a woman! I hope that's not merely a
modern creation!"

He struggled. His face worked like that of a puzzled
little boy who seemed large only because he was glimpsed
in a magnifying mirror. Then his face cleared; he laughed:

"And by golly, I'm glad you're not! Oh, Ann, I'm a
sentimentalist, a make-believer, a wind-bag, an exhibitionist! I'm a reformer only because I'm an exhibitionist! (I'll
kill you, my good girl, if you ever remind me of my confession!) I guess I was planning a fine juicy scene—nobly admitting how very bad I've been! Oh, I'm a typical sentimental liberal! And you so big, so honest, so—— No, by
God, you're not! Not tonight! You're my girl! Come here!
How do you unfasten this?"

She had liked Russell. At least she had liked his liking
her. This night, from the moment when he had admitted
his tendency to childish play-acting till the moment when
she woke in his arms, they two curled close together as
piled plates, she believed that she loved him.

Once convinced that he need not be delicate and reverent, Russell enjoyed being bawdy. Next day he made a good deal of swimming naked, of setting the table clad only in straw sandals and an apron, and he told her stories that were not only slightly filthy but, much worse, very old.

For a day, she enjoyed abandonment to lively coarseness, nor did she later mind it. But after many Kittie Cognacs, she did not think that coarseness was in itself particularly interesting. She began to find Russell a little too noisy, too proud of his athletic powers, in their greater intimacies. He was as lacking in restraint as Lindsay Atwell was lacking in boldness.

She meanly sneaked away from him when he was peeling potatoes on the porch and, leaving him babbling on in his belief that she was in the kitchen, she ran down the beach and sat in the bowl of sun between two dunes. She looked happy and young as she ran, and her hair fluttered at the edges of the red handkerchief tied round her head. But she grew serious as the sun lulled all of her save the little machine that ticked unceasingly in her skull.

"He's a child. He does mean well. He is not a fool. (I do wish he wouldn't be so joky, and I wish to Heaven he wouldn't tickle my sides!) But he's a child. He's vain. He's pretentious. I don't want him as the father of my children —of Pride.

"No. It's not true. He'd probably be an excellent father —understanding and jolly. But I don't want Pride to reproduce him. That's what a woman wants in her child: to perpetuate the man she loves.

"Oh, my God! How could I have done this? Just to get

back at Lindsay, just to *show* him! Russell! This bumble-puppy! This joker! This teaser that thinks it's funny to call me 'Doctor'! This fat rustic that hankers after bouncing love, under hedges! I that was proud and free and powerful! To get myself into a position where I have to share the bed of this clown—and what's worse, have to listen to his jokes!"

She hissed with fury.

But the sun was coaxing, the waves were gay, and she was a healthy woman who had been starved. She crept back, and was gratifyingly received on the window seat. But after that she took precautions that she should not have the children of Russell Spaulding, of Ignatz, of the playboy of liberalism.

35

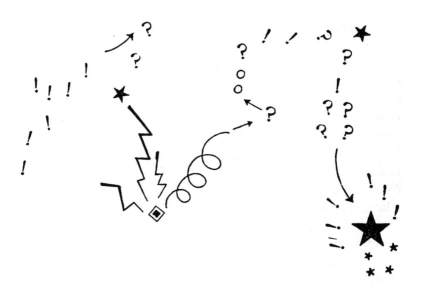

Spirals, stars, rays, beams, zigzags——
TALK
as, radical talk, progressive talk, liberal talk, forward-
looking talk, earnest talk, inspirational talk,
as, of Roget, of Thesaurus, to,
cry, roar, shout, bawl, brawl, halloo, whoop, yell, bellow,
howl, scream, screech, screak, shriek, shrill, squeak, squeal,
squall, pule, pipe, yawp, vociferate, raise the voice, lift up

the voice, call out, sing out, cry out, exclaim, rend the air,
shout at the top of one's voice,
as, in a radical party in a radical party a radical party,
as,
of,
Tom Mooney
prison paroles
Stalin
sterilization of the unfit, unfit for what
kulaks
Gastonia
homosexuality
commission form of govt
syndicalism
Haiti, conditions in
Nicaragua, conditions in
China, conditions in
Upper Silesia, conditions in
Liberia, land of the noble free, conditions in
homosexuality
capital punishment
birth-control
gold standard
glands
Sacco and Vanzetti
Ramsay MacDonald
Senators, conditions in
A. F. of L.
A. F. of Matty Woll
social equality
race equality

what is equality
homosexuality
Majority Communist Party not a chance without Bill
Foster
but if Bill Haywood had lived
homosexuality, conditions in, prejudices against, why not
Tom Mooney
tariff, down with tariff
steel industry, conditions in
no conditions in it
homosexuality
Rand School
social diseases—why social
Macedonia irredenta where is Macedonia
Mexico irredento
the J. A. B. of the A. I. C. P. & the C. O. S.
the I. L. D.
the L. I. D.
the A. A. A. A.
not the A. A. A. never
the T. U. U. L.
the L. I. P. A.
the N. A. A. C. P.
the American Civil Liberties Union
the Theatre Guild
Clarence Darrow
Freud
Adler
Jung
Bertrand Russell
John Dewey

Al Smith
Sam Gompers
the United Front
the Llano Colony
Mooney and Billings
why never Billings and Mooney
conditions
TALK
as,
to,
cry, roar, bellow, blare, bark, bay, yelp, yap, yarr, yawl,
grunt, gruntle, growl, neigh, bray, mew, mewl, purr,
caterwaul, bleat, moo, croak, caw, gobble, cackle, gaggle,
guggle, buzz, hiss, blatter,
as,
TALK,
with,
all the several sorts, manners, and classes of persons interested in Reforming the World whether from lively
morality, astringent fanaticism, the most excellent pleasure of hell-raising, the on-holding of weekly salaries, the
to-wealthy-women-common desire of seeing learned reb-
els obsequious at their dinner-tables,
indeed, all these votaries of Justice,
as,
editors of journals of revolt
Communist agitators out on bail
statisticians
presidents of garment workers' unions
Columbia instructors

members of the Lucy Stone League
Socialist reporters from Republican newspapers
wives of bankers who get back at their husbands by bailing
out Communists and feeding them champagne when they
need porridge they both need porridge both the banker
husbands and the Communists but the bankers' wives,
the bankers' wives, the jolly bankers' wives they'll be
damned if they'll cook porridge for the faith—'tis prettier
far, tra la, tra la, to have the butlers pour out the champagne for the starving Bolos again and again
lobbyists for Roumania, for North Dakota, folk song,
Navajos, vegetarianism, song birds, and the instruction of
bright little Jew-boys in sculpture to be of use to same later,
tra la, in modeling gents' suitings
foreigners (1) with beards (2) with beards
all these coin-bright uplifting souls and all full, not as in a
Greenwich Village literary party, of gin but full of
TALK

The talk of that evening, at a party densely populated
with radicals and progressives, came quivering back to Ann
as she lay in a twin bed, beside Russell's. (She liked a room
of her own but he thought this was "ever so much jol-
lier.") She recaptured it not as sounds but as figures of
flame inside her shut eyelids.

Despite her years of "social work," she had been intimate with only a few friends. But Russell was a Beau
Brummel of liberalism. He had to hear many voices. He
was unhappy if he was not invited to every public occasion.
He was miserable if he was not recognized by every celebrity—of his world.

For there are as many sorts of celebrities as there are
occupations. Only a few men are universal celebrities; in
1932, for example, in all the world there were only Colonel
Lindbergh, George Bernard Shaw, the Prince of Wales,
the Kaiser, Freud, Einstein, Hitler, Mussolini, Gandhi,
Hindenburg, Greta Garbo, Stalin, Henry Ford, and, most
of all, Al Capone; and of these fourteen, five will be forgotten by 1935. But there are engineers famous among
engineers; there are doctors whose record time in snatch-
ing out appendices is known to medicos in Kamchatka and
Paris; there are dry-cleaners whose appearance on the
platform at National Conventions of Laundrymen causes
the zealots to rise in hysterical cheering; there are authors
whose names remain familiar to book-reviewers a year
after their deaths. So, in reform circles, the man who put
through the short ballot in Nebraska and the woman who
was for a year juvenile court judge in Miami are known
literally to dozens, and with such maestri Russell itched to
be seen. He attended banquets. He introduced speakers.
He signed petitions to Congress to abolish poverty and sin.
He rejoiced in being one of seventy Honorary Vice Presidents of associations to rescind blue laws or to release
from jail all right-minded rioters who had been imprisoned
for beating policemen. And in between these more stellar
activities, he just liked to Go Out.

Ann had been given to going out—to theaters, to concerts, to sedate hours by Dr. Wormser's fire. But Russell
longed for places where there were talk and liveliness and
vocal solution of the insoluble. Not drunkenness—no
loose Bohemianism. At his parties there was no need of
gin. They could get enough kick out of the wickedness of

prosperous Russian kulaks, and the virtue of prosperous Dakota farmers.

At such an evening of spiritual diversion Ann again met Pearl McKaig, that meager and earnest young woman, with a brow like a hard-boiled egg, who once in Point Royal College had rebuked her for being too affable a politician. (It seemed strange to Ann now that the awkward, naïve Ann Vickers of those days could ever, even by Pearl, have been viewed as too suave and amenable!) Pearl had come to New York as a social worker; had been a propagandist for coöperative stores; after the war, a propagandist for Macedonia; then plumped into the deep river and become a Communist complete. She was an organizer for the Trade Union Unity League, Communist rival of the American Federation of Labor; she preached Communism on anything from a soap-box to the rostrum of a Kansas City church forum; she wrote for the *Daily Worker*, explaining that all Socialists and liberals were secret agents of J. Pierpont Morgan; and she wore, changelessly, a brown wool suit, cotton stockings, Ground Gripper shoes, and a zipper jacket of imitation chamois. Pearl regarded evening clothes, churches, James Branch Cabell, meat, having servants, Walter Pater, Herbert Hoover, Clarence Darrow, patent-leather shoes, cigars, wine, going fishing, Joseph Hergesheimer, the Ritz Hotel, first-class quarters on steamers, Oswald Garrison Villard, investments in steel stock, Trotzky, the Prince of Wales, the Pope, the New York *Times, Evening Post, Sun,* and *Herald Tribune,* Heywood Broun, silk underwear, cigarette holders made of anything other than paper, Japan, charity societies, smutty stories, diamonds, Aucassin and Nicolette, Harvard, polo, William Randolph Hearst, single tax, Ramsay MacDonald, golf, Christmas, Velasquez, rouge, Tolstoy, bath-salts, Peter Kropotkin, avocados, the *Saturday Evening Post*, bankers, lawyers, doctors, lying in the sun except as it was done purposefully and in the presence of other nudists of all three sexes, Evelyn Waugh, Poland, H. G. Wells, Norman Thomas, Roy Howard, linen handkerchiefs, rising later than 6 A. M., Pullman cars, the *New Republic*, Anglo-Catholics, Three Seeds in the Spirit Baptists, Christian Scientists, the *Redbook*, the *Cosmopolitan*, the *New Yorker*, H. L. Mencken, John D. Rockefeller first second and third series, Will Rogers, all motor cars except Fords and second-hand Chevrolets, Dean Kirchwey, *Vogue*, the Chicago *Tribune*, Cardinal Hayes, Jane Addams, the National Association for the Advancement of Colored People, Palm Beach, roulette, gin, truffles, dressing-gowns other than those of a blanket aspect, taxicabs, and Dr. Ann Vickers, as being equally bourjui, vicious, individualistic, old-fashioned, and generally treacherous to the Workers and the U. S. S. R.

She said to Ann, with the cold steadiness of a deaconess, "Are you still trying to patch up the capitalistic system by reforming it? I suppose you reserve your darkest punishment-cells for political prisoners."

"I certainly do!" said Ann, with the boisterous idiocy which chemically pure souls like Pearl produce in human beings.

During their honeymoon Ann had suggested to Russell that they take, as with their joined incomes they could afford to, a cottage in a suburb and have a home instead of a roost along with the other crows of Manhattan.

"Oh, no, I think you're *wrong*, dear!" protested Russell. "We'd lose the intellectual contacts you get in the city. It's so important for us. Think, in one evening at Maurice Steinblatt's you can meet the people and get the lowdown on negro share-croppers and the Lipari Isles and the foreign bond scandal. Oh, no! In the suburbs, they're nothing but a bunch of bridge-players!"

Ann had never played bridge.

She wondered for a disloyal second if bridge might not be restful after a day of trying to persuade wild young women that the nunnery grayness of a Model Prison was pleasanter than speakeasies.

They had a flat, because it was large and cheap, in an ancient, almost prehistoric apartment house built in 1895, with an exterior of minarets and Moorish arches. It was above an extension of the Sixth Avenue Elevated, which, along with trolley-cars, motor cars, trucks, and milk wagons kept startling Ann all night long, making her jump from sleep as though leopards were yawping by the reed walls of her jungle camp. It had cockroaches. It had a smell of damp walls and cocoanut matting.

But the living-room was thirty feet long, eighteen feet high, a superb place for radical parties, or even liberal parties, which are larger though not so vociferous per unit. Between them, Russell and Ann had some eleven hundred books, divided into sociology, poetry, and detective stories, and they made a learned display. In this intellectual solitude one could pretend that there were no elevated trains coming—until an elevated train did come.

Here she heard oceans and surges and surfs of talk, and it was quite as undifferentiated as one surf from another.

The walls of their living-room were covered with a paper imitating brown stamped leather, divided into panels by strips of pine optimistically stained to resemble mahogany. But they could not afford to change it, not just yet, and Ann discovered that Russell rather admired that Sixth Avenue baronial air.

At one corner was an alcove which was almost a separate room. When they were taking the place, Ann saw him looking at it wistfully, then urging, "You take this, dear, for your study."

"No. You take it, Ignatz. I'd really rather work in the open. And I don't do much at home except just read."

Tenderly, a little amused, she watched him conduct visitors into—sometimes he called it his "Den," sometimes "Study," sometimes "Office," and she was sure he would have called it his "Studio" if it hadn't been so small. On the few evenings when he had no excuse to go out and could coax no one to come in, he would retire there in a secret, excited, youthful way, and she would watch him pasting stamps in his album. He was a devoted collector. He had piles of, to her, utterly mysterious catalogues and notices about Charkhari Pictorials, Triangles, Surcharged Stamps, Imperforate Sheets, Airmails. He looked through a magnifying glass and bounded in his chair and scratched behind his ear and clicked his tongue against his teeth as he found treasures in approval sheets. He showed visitors his stamp book as his brother Henry, in Syracuse,

showed the kodak album of Junior from the age of one to
the age of eleven.

In August, five months after her marriage and a week
after their summer vacation, which Russell had insisted
on spending at a Progressive Political Conference at a
radical camp in the Adirondacks, Ann heard from Pat
Bramble, in New Rochelle:

DEAR ANNIE:
How do you like being married? Why don't you come out and
see me, week-end? Things gehen nicht too well bei business.
There's a real estate agent in this town, Lester Pomeroy by
name, a regular Babbitt, the tall, thin, jolly, kind, dumb sort
of Babbitt who's been getting all my customers away from me.
He may be dumb but he does know how to handle people who
want a $75,000 palace with a sunken goldfish pool for $35,000—
six hundred dollars and a cigar down. He's snatched all my trade.
So I have married him. Come see us. Bring Russell if you must.
Love,
PAT.

She went. She did not bring Russell.

Pat and the cheery Mr. Pomeroy had set up in a con-
ventional and highly comfortable imitation-Colonial cottage: chintzes, wing-chairs, davenport, the Five Foot
Shelf of Books, gramophone, kitchen with colored tiles and
electric refrigerator, a small lawn with a round bed of
dahlias, a two-car garage. Pat wore a flimsy, flowered
house-dress and a beam of almost idiotic content.

"Oh, Ann," she caroled, "I'm happy as two larks! My
old man adores me. He thinks I'm a combination of Mrs.
Browning and Mary Pickford. We're going to have kids, if

I'm not too old. But, oh, Annie, it isn't the mild romance, such as it is. It's just the sordid, commonplace vulgarity of being protected—I mean as far as money is concerned; not having to get up early in the morning, every morning, and hustle to an office to battle with a lot of hard-boiled males all day. I can actually lie abed, if I want to, and have the maid bring me breakfast! And I discover that, all these years, what I've been putting into suburban real estate was my longing for houses and shiny new dish-pans and gardens and mop-closets for *myself!* I wonder a little if you don't put a lot of submerged longing for children into your care of prisoners. Let me show you the house. As a salesman, I would rate it about E2. As its mistress, I rate it about Windsor Castle plus. But listen: I'm not lying down. I can tip even Mr. Lester Pomeroy off on a few things about the mulish race of women and how to sell 'em. I sold a house myself, last Tuesday, and I get the commission! But not to *have* to do it—grand! Come see the shack!"

If Ann could not be quite so sentimental as Pat over the Russian linen luncheon set, the gas dryer, the candlewick bedspreads, she longed for them.

They sat on the sliver of lawn, in basket chairs, rather quiet. It was, Ann bitterly thought, healing not to hear Russell's busy and intellectual boisterousness.

That evening, neighbors came in, solid, agreeable people, and they had bridge, sandwiches, beer.

She lay in a fresh, gay bedroom and listened to the silver-colored river of silence. There was a jew's-harp orchestra of insect sounds, but it was only the background to the stillness.

She had been righteously irritated once by arty people who talked about hearing colors and smelling hexagons and the smooth, cool feeling of flute notes, but for the past two months she had definitely seen the city's noise, the unceasing, grinding roar at night, as a brown and evil harbor with burning ships.

She woke to robins and brightness, with no grease of the elevated in the air.

"Pride and I will have a place like this," she said.

36

AFTER months of marriage, Russell alternated between boyish exhibitionism, a delight in his singular possessions, and a lofty prudery when Ann slipped into any of the words which made him giggle in anecdotes by men. In neither case was he natural; in nothing was he ever quite natural; and his self-consciousness kept Ann from rising into the security of naturalness. But the little surface, social irritations were what occupied her, when they had been married for six months.

He most irritated her by treating her as a Little Woman. (He called her that.)

He decidedly wanted her to be Big enough to hold an office which would make them both socially important; he did not mind her paying the rent and grocery bills; he was irritated when she did not show off properly at public dinners and when she fell into clichés like "The first problem of penology is the safe-keeping of prisoners." Only, privately, she had to be a Little Woman—otherwise how, standing beside her, could he be Big Mans? (He had told her of a girl who used to call him "Big Mans." But even in her tenderest moments, when he had brought her Viennese chocolates and been funny, she'd be hanged if she would ever be as littlewomanish as that.)

She asked him, once, to stop in at a bookshop and get Blözen's *Gestalt Psychologie*. It was important. She would base her talk to the Mt. Vernon Current Problems Club upon it. She was home before him, and had her German lexicon all out and dusted. He came springing in, like a vernal ram, and gloatingly held out to her a bunch of chrysanthemums of approximately the size and appearance of a wheat-sheaf.

"They're glorious! You're a darling. Did you get the book?"

"What book?"

"Oh. Honestly! You promised! The German book about psychology!"

"My gracious! What an important little student we are! Just going to get right into the depths of things and be one of our best little serious thinkers! Now what would we do with great big seewious books if we did have him?"

He tried to pat her cheek. She jerked away, raging, "Oh, damn it! All right! I won't bother you again! I'll get my own books!"

"Why—why—did I make you sore?" he gasped.

A girl discharged on parole from the Stuyvesant Industrial Home had come in this evening to see Ann—as they did, dozens a month. The girl had served a year for stealing silk from a dressmaking loft in which she had been a seamstress. She "wanted to go straight," she said, but she could find no work, and she could get no help, only

curt moral lectures, from her parole officer, a high-church
but high-powered lady who was agent for the Lighthouse
League for the Redemption of First Offenders. Ann gave
the girl a note to a pleasant, intellectual, and quite amoral
lady who ran a dress shop in Greenwich Village and, when
the disapproving Russell wasn't looking, slipped a ten-
dollar bill (which she couldn't afford) into her hand. The
girl gone, she paced the floor oratorically, while Russell
looked cynical in the deep chair which Ann had once called
her own:

"Parole! It's the key to punishment, and nothing's so
neglected. Can't blame the parole officers. Most of 'em are
much too busy, and a lot of 'em are too ignorant. If I had
any decency, any energy, even any sense, I'd chuck my
prison job, I'd go into politics, I'd force through a bill
providing as many millions for parole as for prisons, if not
a lot more, and make it obligatory to give as much attention to paroled, scared, sick-minded ex-cons as to sick-
bodied tuberculars, I would. And I believe I could!"

Russell crowed, "What a great thinker—what a great
popular leader we are! My yes! Oh yes, dearie, sure! If you
went into politics, Tammany Hall would just do anything
you wanted. Annie d'Arc—and how!"

She was holding forth at dinner at their pet millionaire's
—the one who surely would, though he apparently never
did, endow all the little theaters and all the little magazines
and all the Russian films and all the young poets and all
the industrial schools for discharged convicts. Ann was,
with plain tale and flourish of figures, maintaining that
not one in ten of the prisoners, men or women, who are

supposed to have a trade has really mastered it. The company seemed interested. Probably she was pontificating a little; probably she was forgetting that she was a wife, and taking herself as seriously as a male golf player. But it did hurt—not merely infuriate but hurt, deep in her heart where dwelt her loyalty, when Russell publicly drawled:

"Well, now you've settled that for us, dearie, just explain Russia, and tell 'em about bio-physics!"

With a paradox that was only seeming, he bored Ann by praising her in her presence; telling strangers at a dinner what a penologist, an executive, a psychologist, she was; how bravely she had downed dozens of riots in a rather vague Southern prison; and how sweet and forgiving she had been to the mutineers afterward. Then, in the taxi home, when he had thus glorified her and shared that glory, when she had enjoyed the show more than she admitted, and was a bit insistent and opinionated, he would prick her with, "Well, dearie, I'm glad you had a good time, but I think if you'd made a little effort, you might have gotten Dr. Vincent to talk *some* of the time, too!"

He was particularly explanatory in the taxi if someone had ignorantly called him "Mr. Vickers."

"I corrected the idiot! I admit that of course I am merely the husband of the celebrated Frau Dr. Prof. Supt. Vickers, but still, I do have a certain small, meek, wifely place of my own in social work!"

Yet it is true that even this never vexed him quite so much as the diminishment which threatened the house of Spaulding-Vickers when some very young or very old

professor tried to contradict Ann about the psychology of
prisoners. Then that old grizzly, brave old Russell, rose
and waved his paws and growled, "My dear fellow, Miss
Vickers has had a good deal of practical experience along
with the theory, you know!"

After such evenings, he was a lover.

There weren't many such evenings. Mostly, he enjoyed
pushing down the marble Diana he had helped to erect.

She wasn't always meek to him.

When he went beyond amusing himself by hurting her
stout affection and her longing to love, when he was really
cross and natural and told her that she was a rotten
penologist and a worse executive, then the Dr. Ann Vickers
who handled murderers came into the room. He crawled,
slavering apologies, and then she despised him—then, and
when he boasted of himself not as a competent, journey-
man giver-away of other people's money, but as a sociologist.

He did boast that way. He talked of himself as a "social
scientist." He often said, "In my research, I may seem
perfectly passionless, but I do have one uncontrollable
passion—a passion for accuracy."

If that was true, thought Ann, it was one of the great
Thwarted Passions of history.

With all his proud attention to mastering her, Ignatz
did do a good deal of quiet, earnest flirting—or "necking,"
as in this era it was technically called. He was always a
Toucher and a Feeler and a Stroker. Even with men, he
liked to link arms, to pat shoulders; and with women he
could only by violence be kept from kissing the cheek,

hand-cupping the shoulder, encircling the waist and, in more promising cases, stroking the ankle. At the larger parties, Ann became, after eight or ten months of marriage, accustomed to seeing him slip off to pantries or balconies with, invariably, the slinksiest, short-skirtedest, most mouse-haired of the intellectual young ladies present, and they would come back looking brightly ashamed.

Ann felt definite urges to murder him.

It wasn't so much his offenses toward her sex loyalty. That was growing thin in her, month by month, as she realized that she was to him not a shrine but merely another station on the railway. It was the insult to her dignity that he should prefer the rattiest young females to her. She could have endured it if he had peeped only at wise and lordly women. . . . So she told herself.

Yes, she could have murdered him with only the slightest readjustment of her life. She thought again how curious it was that she happened to be on this side of the bars, when she might—Malvina might, Pat Bramble might, Eleanor Crevecoeur might—so easily have been on the other side, for murder, adultery, or any crime that was not ignoble or mean.

She suspected that he in his flirtations never went farther than geographical stroking. She suspected that she would have despised him much less had he been courageous enough to go farther. Nor was he ever overt enough so that she had excuse for a good, strong, wholesome domestic eruption and kicking him out. She wished she had such an excuse, as they slid greasily into a swamp of irritable dullness.

Anyway, she would not have him for the father of Pride.

He was too weak, too coy, too glib; a creek over pebbles.

But—here was the heart and hell of woman's tragedy: if she did not have Pride in the next two or three years, she could never have her. At forty-five Ann would be young, just mastering ambition, yet too old for children. Russell, any cursed careless man, not really wanting children except as they might mirror him and butter his vanity and by their adoration comfort him when older people were too bored to listen, could none the less have children at sixty.

The cards were stacked—and no amount of spirited Feminism would ever unstack them.

A race now, a desperate one, between her unwillingness to let Russell Spaulding father her child, and the time when no one could father it. But all the same, she could not let him get his flabby hands on her and on Pride. No!

She was to attend a Women's Reformatory Conference, in Atlantic City, and for a week now she had plunged into material about the effect of diet upon prison discipline. She was reading sixty medical authorities all at once—and absently, really thinking aloud, she quoted them to Russell at home.

He flared, "Being married to you is like sleeping with the Taxation Problem!"

She was instantly remorseful, "Oh, am I neglecting you? Oh, my dear, I'm afraid I have a single-track mind! Let me get this dratted Atlantic City conference over, and I'll see if I haven't it in me to be a good wife. Perhaps I might make you fall in love with me, instead of just being curious about me!"

Marvellous kiss.

It was said at Atlantic City that Dr. Vickers's address on prison diet was brilliant, almost revolutionary. The hardest-boiled of the Midatlantic matrons was so moved that when she returned to her reformatory, she gave her customers nine prunes a week instead of five, and added stewed apricots, and once every summer, fresh sugar corn. But while Ann was sweeping her audience away, she was thinking pitifully of Russell.

She had the curst blessing of being able to see the other person's side even when she was fighting him. Disciplining Kittie Cognac, she could never get over a sneaking notion that Kittie had not had a fair training. Now she saw that Russell had some reason for being irritated by her greater notoriety, by her distressing independence; some reason for leading out upon balconies flimpsy little fools who would lean upon his noble chest and breathe up at him. Russell was kittenish, Russell was shallow, but Russell was a competent artisan, and kind.

She came home from Atlantic City and worked at being a devoted wife—the worst way, naturally, of being one.

But it seemed for a few days to succeed.

Russell was delighted when she produced no ideas after office-hours, when she seemed willing to sit still for quite a few minutes while he played "This little pig goes to market" with her strong fingers, when instead of leaving the dinner menu to the cook, she sought out the artistic and poignant dishes which his adventurous soul and stomach loved: Nuremburg Bratwurst, chicken chow mein, fat fried mushrooms like the hats of kobolds, corn pudding, ravioli, Stilton cheese soaked in port, corn waffles with maple syrup . . . he would delightedly have eaten them all at the same meal.

He promptly became authoritative, and never asked her before inviting to the flat the friends whom she least liked —even when the maid was out, and she had to trot to the delicatessen for food, and after supper wash the dishes.

It was an odd scene; the final fruits of Feminism. There had been a supper of four. After it, Dr. Ann Vickers, superintendent of the Stuyvesant Industrial Home, and Mrs. Werner Balham, who in public life was Miss Jane Emery, highly paid director of the Craftsmen's Furniture Shops, washed the dishes, while in the living-room Russell and Mr. Balham, a literary man whose visible production these two years had been one eight-line sonnet and one five-line sestette in *transition*, sat placid and discussed the rise in real-estate values, and looked down on the two females when they came in and began to talk privily about cooks.

Russell had marched in the first Suffrage parade up Fifth Avenue, and all such demonstrations afterward; Werner Balham risked rotten eggs by campaigning for Feminism among the Boston Irish; both their wives had more tiring and more lucrative jobs than their own; but it never occurred to either of them that these working wives should not order their husbands' meals, hire and—especially—fire servants, see that their husbands' socks were darned, that the studs were removed from their dress-shirts before sending them to the laundry, that telephone messages regarding such crises as engagements to play golf were taken down complete, with the caller's name, address, telephone number, place of meeting, also time of the train to the golf course, all accurate. To neither hus-

band did it occur that if their wives had been out late at
an evening business "conference," that was no reason
why, when they came home, they should not comfort their
husbands by making fudge or Welsh rabbits or shaking
up a scrambled egg.

The cards were stacked against you, Ann. No doubt they
will be against your great-great-granddaughter. But since
birth and life have thrust you into the game, at least be
warned that the cards have been stacked.

37

I N NOTHING, not even in the recurrent habits of a drunkard or a man of evil temper or a suspicious woman, is the
pattern of life more surely repeated than in marriage. If
Ann had never been an obsequious wife to Russell, no will
to be one could make her so for more than a fortnight. She
was off again, on the scent, vociferously hunting the foxy
opponents of wider probation for first offenders, forgetting
that Russell was (to Russell) so important a person that
she ought to devote to him all her romantic dreams instead
of squandering them on the two-point-six failure announced
in a Rhode Island report on recidivism.

Their break came surprisingly.

Russell romped home, glowing. They had a free evening,
also a splendid steak for dinner, and everything looked
rosy. She could tell by his tremendous lightness that he had
a secret, and when she said, "What have you got up your
sleeve? Something nice?" he leaped up and chanted:

"Listen, baby, I've got the chance of my life! You know
old Shillady, the big hotel-chain man—contributed a lot
to the O. C. I.? Well, he's got an idea that the future money

isn't in the big expensive hotels like his—they're being overdone now—but in the cheap places, for workmen and so on. He has an idea for a chain of big cheap city hotels, superior lodging houses, really. Well, of course, with all the lodging houses and lunch-rooms and so on that I've run for the O. C. I., I know a lot about that stuff, and he's offered me the assistant managership of the whole chain, at twelve thousand a year—think of it! twice my salary now!—and a good chance ahead for the managership and maybe thirty thousand dollars a year *per annum per omnia saecula saeculorum*. God, isn't it *mar*-velous!"

"Why—— Oh, Russell, do you really want to go into business?"

"Why not?"

"Oh, it's so awfully stupid!"

"Well, I'll be damned! From you, of all people! You that are always questioning the value of charity, always taking dirty little digs at people that think they can 'save the world' by the single tax or abolishing cigarettes!"

"I know. I know. So does Dr. Wormser question the value of everything in medicine beyond setting broken legs and giving salts and insulin and quinine. But that doesn't mean she'd take a job in a grocery, not at a million dollars a year. Why, Russell, however little we do accomplish, if anything, a social worker has a profession, like a lawyer or a doctor or an artist or a priest or a schoolmaster or a soldier, and he has obligations to it, he has loyalties, almost, you might say, mystic, and if he has to give it up, it's tragic for him. You don't need this money. We make enough between us——"

"And now I suppose you'll throw it up to me that

without your salary we wouldn't have enough to——"

"My dear Ignatz! That's so obviously what you would say that I'm surprised to hear you say it!"

"Well, if you think I'm going to go on tagging after you—— I'll be a millionaire, one of these days, and——"

"And you'll get a dreat big shoot-gun and shoot all the Injuns and be an engineer and drive the choo-choo cars! Do you intend to wait for the million before you grow past the mental age of seven? A million dollars! Now, won't that be elegant! And what will you do with all this nice lovely money? I'll tell you: you'll be a philanthropist, and you'll be able to explain to an adoring tableful of young uplifters that in taking up business, you haven't given up any of your ideals! I'm going for a walk!"

Repentances there were, and apologies, and smoothings out, but for once Russell held to his purpose. He did resign, to help start the hotel-chain and, seeing his joy in having for the first time in his life enough money to take taxis without calculations, Ann was certain that she had been unjust to him. But as to herself, she was not going on as an appendage to lodging houses organized for the purpose of making millions from the dimes of working men.

The lease on their Byzantine apartment was up on January 1, 1930, a year and three quarters after their marriage. Russell had to go to the Pacific Coast, on affairs of the hotel syndicate, and he left it to Ann to find them a new apartment, one more modern, worthy of a rising young lord of hotel keeping—in America a rank almost equal to a peerage in steel or soap or motor cars.

She found an excellent apartment for him. Her own books and chairs and linens she moved back to her old hotel apartment.

He stormed in on her, when he came back, but his he-man storminess blew over before her cold eyes. "What's the idea, leaving me flat like this? Just what have I done?" he begged.

"Nothing, my dear." She was kindly enough now, no longer cold. "But it's such a good chance for the break, and the break is inevitable. Let's not drag on, trying and failing and trying and failing again till everyone is sick of it, as most married couples do when they crash."

"D-do you want a divorce?"

"Not particularly."

"Then let's—— Oh, if you must, we'll live separately. For a while. Try to see where we stand. Honestly, it isn't just that I don't want people to laugh at me because I couldn't hold you. I have loved you, better than I ever did anybody. I do love you! I don't understand! I don't know what I've done! And I don't know what I'll do without you!"

He stood humbly, a large man, fumbling at his lips, and out of his plump middle-aged face looked the eyes of a terrified child.

Then she was lonelier than ever she had been in her life; much lonelier than when she had dwelt in this barren hotel before, for there was no Lindsay Atwell nor Russell Spaulding to call, and Pat Bramble Pomeroy rarely came into town.

Russell did creep pleadingly around, every week and

once she let him stay the night. But it was strained, too eager to be eager.

Yet such was her loneliness, such the purposelessness of her undesired freedom, that late in March, when Russell quivered in to say that people were beginning to laugh at him, she consented to come back. Only, she said, she must have another couple of months to herself—to discover, to explore herself again, as she had after Point Royal and the questions of Pearl McKaig, after suffrage and Clateburn, after settlement houses and Lafe and Ardence Benescoten.

For that exploration there were no charts.

38

Dr. MALVINA WORMSER was giving a party.

The word "party" indicated, in that ultimate climax of civilization, 1930 in New York, many things. To the artistic, it meant gin and necking. To the raucously inartistic, it meant gin and necking. To persons so rich and respectable that they had not yet begun to whimper about the "Depression" that was just begun, it meant contract bridge and gin. But to the forward-looking group, it meant just Talk.

Dr. Wormser had no great strength with which to dominate the idea-merchants, but she had something better: a deep placidity, so that she could sit amiably indifferent by the fireplace, smiling on her party, neither bored nor so inspired that she would not sleep that night. She would be operating at ten tomorrow morning, fresh and serene. Surgeons and sea-captains and aviators—they are solid people in an insane world.

Ann watched her, across the room, enviously. Ann herself was bored. She was sitting on a couch, listening to a young person who assured her, on the basis of magazines he had read, that in Soviet Russia all problems of sex had been solved. He went on to sketch his more important ideas about industrialization of farming (he had been born in New York, the nephew of a rabbi, and he knew all about farming except just what it was that they grew on farms).

Ann yawned internally, "I think I'll go home and turn on the radio!"

She roused then to a human curiosity. Shouldering into the room came a sturdy, red-bearded man, not very tall, but of a bulldog build, a red bulldog. His beard was short, coarse, aggressive; his eyes were lively, and his forehead, under rusty and bristling hair that was turning gray, was fine, veined, distinctly paler than his apple cheeks. His hands were those of a prize-fighter, but they were manicured. He wore excellent dinner clothes, the tie atrociously knotted.

Ann had never been introduced to him, but she had seen him, at a public dinner. He was Judge Bernard Dow Dolphin, of the Supreme Court bench of New York State. He was an acquaintance of Lindsay Atwell; he had been of value in lifting Ann to her position of superintendent. He was a competent scholar, a giver of sane and honest verdicts—and he was a notorious devotee of wine and wenching; he delivered authoritative lectures in the law-schools —and he was an associate of all the most extravagantly dressed, cynically dissipated higher politicians of the state. Lindsay had told her that among all the temporary royalty of the great kingdom of New York State, with its twelve and a half million people, there was no oligarch more virile, more competent, more contradictory, more honorable as a judge or more crooked privately, than Judge Dolphin.

In political circles he was known as Barney Dolphin.

He was a B. A. of Fordham University, with honors and with his letter in baseball; he was a graduate of the Columbia Law School, with a year at the Sorbonne; he was an honorary LL. D. of three universities; and he was said to speak French, Italian, Polish, Yiddish, English, and East Side with correctness and fluency. He also belonged to the Elks' Club of Brooklyn and played a classic game of billiards. He was the first authority in New York City on railroad bonds, and he had once played poker for thirty-two hours straight. He could quote Balzac, Zola, and Victor Huge (*sic*) by the page, and he had never heard of Michelson, Millikan, or Compton. He was supposed to be a millionaire, and it was also supposed that the speculation which had led to this state of bliss had been honest. He was reported to own still the brick shanty on Morton Street where he had been born, and to retire there to cook corned-beef and cabbage for himself when he was tired; and merely in fact was this story untrue. He was a favorite at Bradley's Casino at Palm Beach, and at the Queens County Orphanage. He was fifty-three years of age, and he could run the hundred yards in thirteen seconds. He was a practising Catholic, but his name had been uncomfortably in the air as a possible co-respondent in three divorce suits. He was a merry man on the bench, but he could flash into horrifying cold rage at lawyers who sought to advantage themselves of that merriment.

Ann watched Judge Dolphin stalk through the chatterers up to Dr. Wormser. His quick eyes seemed to snatch

the soul out of everyone he passed. He kissed Dr. Wormser's hand and held it. The young men came to speak to
him, and he answered them with the swift, heart-warming,
and entirely meaningless smile of the politician.

It was half an hour before Judge Dolphin drifted Ann's
way and, glancing at her noncommittally, murmuring,
"May I?" dropped on the couch beside her. The earnest
youth who had been tutoring her was gone, and she was
exhausted. She had to rib herself up to say warmly, "I
have something to thank you for. I believe you were in
good measure responsible for my getting my job. I did
write to you, but I've never had the chance to thank you
in person."

"Oh. Oh yes."

"I'm Ann Vickers, of the Stuyvesant Industrial Home."

His glance at her was swifter than ever, and more blade-
like. Then he shook his head. Every hair of his bristly small
red beard seemed a wire, throwing off sparks.

"Nonsense, my dear girl! You a reformatory superintendent? Where's the glasses? Where's the thin lips? Where's
the look of detecting a bad smell? Where's the patient-
martyr expression?"

"Oh, I'm worse yet, Judge. I'm the matron kind. I
mother the poor souls, and they have to stand for it."

"Yes, that may be true, but you don't look to me like
the black lace mitts and little gray home in the West.
You look reasonably disillusioned."

"I'm not. I feel melancholy."

"This talk?"

"Yes."

"You a Communist?"

"How do I know? I don't know anything about it. I'm certainly not against it. But I'm bored by listening to these people."

"Yes? I've been here——" he glanced at the watch on his broad, hairy wrist—"thirty-two minutes now, and forty seconds, and I've heard these kibitzers settle everything except their rent. Let's go off and get a drink somewhere and kill a policeman, and then I'll sentence both of us to go live in your pretty jail."

His eyes—they fastened on hers, without evasion, with a mocking boldness that she had never known in any male since Adolph Klebs; they said that he considered her an extremely warm and tempting woman, and rather handsome, and that he would be pleased to live with her a good deal this side of her "pretty jail."

"Let's be serious," she begged. "I'm singularly poor at persiflage tonight."

"You're missing your Russell, then? Or just plain lonely?"

"You——"

"Certainly. I know everything. My business, as a politician. I knew you when I came in tonight. We were at the same dinner, two years ago—the Vestal Association—you sat at the last table on the right from the speakers' table, and you sat between—— Wait! Wait! Don't tell me!" He snapped his stubby fingers; a dry, clicking sound. "You sat between Dr. Charlie Sargon and that dean from N. Y. U. And while I was discoursing learnedly—I *was* by God—on aëroplane ordinances, I was looking at you— you were smoking Turkish cigarettes, from a leather case, Wop or Viennese, I should think—and I was looking at

you, and thinking what a sweet mouth you had to kiss—
life in your lips, not wet parchment, in this town of parchment women! But of course I gave up such evil thoughts,
as a good Judge should!"

She was goggling. It was dismayingly accurate. She felt
helpless—the more helpless when he laughed at her and
tucked her hand over his arm.

"Honestly! You know yourself, Miss Vickers, that
women in the uplift racket—and may the saints bless 'em,
for it's a fine, self-sacrificing, lovely gang of noble souls
they are, to be sure—but mostly, they get cold-blooded or
cautious or dictatorial; they want to boss a gang of meek
yes-women or they want to be received socially, like prin-
cesses; but you, says I to meself, Miss Vickers is still, for
all her learning, the darling, I says, she's still the lovely
tomboy of a swift-legged darling of a girl that she was when
she was a kid, and, yes, I *did* kiss the Blarney Stone, as you
are about to remark, Ann!"

He laughed at her again, tenderly, and squeezed her
hand between his prize-fighter forearm and his side.

She smiled at him, a little hazily, and complained in a
small voice, "I suppose I would have said something about
the Blarney Stone. One does. Actually, are you Irish?"

"One quarter. And one quarter each, Cockney fish-
monger, Swedish, and Austrian. But like all the Tammany
bhoys, like Al Schmitt, I'm *ex officio* Irish, just as Herbert
Huber is *ex officio* Iowa-California-Yankee. Write us a
thesis on the new solution of racial minorities—transform
your great-grandparents to fit your geography. But you
said, let's be serious. I do want to be serious about one
thing, darling; I want to thank you for giving such a swell

chance to—do you remember?—girl, twenty-two, Carma
Krutwich, stenographer? I had to send her up for forging
a small check, when I was in the Court of General Sessions.
Couldn't help myself. Told her to come back to me when
she was paroled. She did. She said that after you took
charge at Stuyvesant, you treated her better than anybody
since she was born; put her in your office, lent her books,
used to drink tea with her. How that girl Carma does love
you! I suppose you know she's going straight now, engaged
to a grand kid?"

"Yes. I had them up for beer and a rarebit, last week."

"You would! . . . She told me, if she were a man, she'd
marry you, if she had to commit couple of murders to do it.
I say, Ann, do you know in whatever blessed spot or
bourne, in what strange corner of the ice box, keeps
the gin? Malvina won't bring it out for another hour
yet."

She noticed, in the kitchen, that he took a particularly
small nip of it, but that he seemed to relish it, throwing
back his head, his beard like a cropped Assyrian's.

"Let's get out of this, Ann. We don't want to listen to
any more talk. If we want to know anything, the printing
presses are still running, I believe. Let's drive somewhere.
Elegant night, for March. Come on!"

"All right."

Dr. Wormser cocked her head a little when Ann came
up with Barney Dolphin to say good-night. It made Ann
feel young and agreeably guilty.

Judge Barney's car was a cream-colored roadster with
low-set red leather seats. It seemed long as a locomotive.
He fished a fur robe from the rumble, tucked her in neatly,

with no insinuating fondling. He was quick, and impersonal as a coachman.

"Are we going anywhere in particular?" she asked.

"I don't know. On Long Island. We'll stop and get warm whenever you want. By the way: Barney Dolphin is the name."

He said nothing more, for miles. They slid over the Fifty-ninth Street Bridge, with its prospect of business buildings down the river. Though it was midnight, the spots of lighted windows marked the incredible heights; fiftieth story, sixtieth. Who was up there, in those mountain plateaus, so late—what desperate bankrupt, what triumphant *condottiere* of business ambushing his victims, what little office lovers trysting in airy towers? They lurched through streets of banal shops and barren apartment houses, passed a craggy desert made from a million tons of waste ashes, sprang forward into open road, and smelled the salty Sound. Nothing existed save the monstrous portliness of the great cream-colored hood before them, and a tunnel of light with sandy road-banks and scrubby trees for sides. The motor was smooth; it merely hummed triumphantly as the needle went up to sixty miles.

Creeping cold came insinuating under her fur robe. As her breast began to creep with chilliness, he slid to a stop and silently gave her a flask, from which she drank excellent Scotch. He tucked in the robe again and whisked on. He talked now, not glibly and a little foolishly, as at Malvina's, but slowly, as though he were bothered:

"Like it, Ann?"

"Love it!"

"I do. It's my one best escape from reality. Can you stand it if we drive late?"

"Why——"

"Anything really crucial at the Industrial Home tomorrow?"

"Of course! Always! Number 3701 has been stealing doorknobs, just to keep her hand in, nothing else being detachable. Number 3921 is suspected of getting heroin. Number 3966 has suddenly turned religious and sends a message to the Superintendent that the Archangel Gabriel says I'm all wrong. Mrs. Keast, my assistant, has had her feelings hurt again because I was so curt, and the end of her nose is redder than ever. The new formula for hash is rotten. The Pentecostal Brethren want to hold services in the chapel at the hour set for Mass, and *is* this a democratic country, and what am I doing—selling out to the Pope? Crucial? Heavens, yes!"

"Then I think we'll keep on going. I'm not due in court tomorrow at all, and naturally, if it doesn't matter whether I get tired or not, that will be sufficient rest for you."

His hands lay on the wheel, seemingly without pressure. He drove as a man eats. His eyes were on the road every second, but never with strained intensity. She wondered— how came she to think of him, when she hadn't for years?— she wondered if Adolph Klebs didn't drive like this, if he was still alive.

Save that they were somewhere on Long Island, she had no notion where they were. She did not believe that she had ever seen this road; it was a road out of the movies, with no geography, no reality. She could make nothing of it save the sandy banks, untidy with jack-pine needles, the filling-stations, lunch-stands, lone houses, all meaning-lessly running backward. Sometimes there were red tail-lights ahead; instantly they had slid back out of sight, without Barney's seeming to have moved the wheel. Once, for three seconds, the headlights brought out a parked car and, in the front seat, a girl's head on a man's shoulder. Then Barney hugged her, but he did not look at her, did not seek to kiss her.

He was talking, abruptly:

"I'm glad you came, tonight especially. I've been wor-ried. I'm going to be investigated. New committee of the legislature. You see, I've made a lot of money, *I* think honestly. I won't pretend I haven't had good tips on the market, but I don't think I ever paid for 'em by any in-fraction of justice. My judicial record seems to me sound as a bell. But the publicity hounds may prove that any error I've ever made was pure racketeering. And all the babies I send up, won't they be happy to see the press sniffing and snouting into my private affairs! I'm worried. It's been a devil of a comfort to have you here—as though you understood everything, without my having to tell you, Ann."

"Have they anything on you?"

"Yes: this. I've always been as careless as the devil about my private acquaintances. I know gamblers, big bootleggers, grafting contractors, bucket-shop proprietors, all sorts of doubtful characters, and I play cards with 'em, I drink with 'em. I'd send any one of 'em up like a shot— or I hope I would—if necessary, but until they're indicted, they're my friends. I find them considerably more amusing than lawyers who play chess and go to the opera. But my little buddies do give the investigators a beautiful lot of clues that ain't there! Do my pals shock you—considering how violently I have added you to them this evening?"

"No." She studied. "Really no. My secret as a prison keeper—and it would probably ruin me if anyone but you and Malvina Wormser knew it—is that I find myself liking, and even admiring, the prisoners more than most keepers and guards. Some of the prisoners are really bad. Slimy. But so many have just been more adventurous—not willing to sink into dressmaking and cashiering all their lives. There was a darling I knew in the South, one Birdie Wallop —I hear she is running a successful restaurant in Spokane now. She used to come to me——"

For a quarter of an hour she talked of Birdie. She broke off to suggest, "Isn't it rather unusually late—Barney? I can't get at my watch. Where are we going?"

"Yes. I'm afraid it's time to turn back. But we're almost out at my country place. Two miles more. Let's stop in there and have some cold turkey and a bottle of beer out of the ice box. Place is practically closed—my wife and girls (two daughters—young ladies now)—they're in Europe, and I just go out occasional week-ends. But there'll be something to eat, and we can get warm before we turn back."

She knew, she said to herself, that he had been craftily heading for his den all the while. She felt that she ought to be indignant. She couldn't be. She liked him, through to the marrow.

She wondered what sort of a place he had—painty little new bungalow, shabby Colonial cottage, or prim mansion with mansard roof and plaster walls. She did not care.

The two miles, at their speed, took two and a half minutes, and while she was still speculating they turned in between concrete pillars, rattled through the gravel of a quarter mile of curving driveway, and came up all-standing before what seemed to be an immense house in brick and limestone Georgian. She had a feeling that Barney would ring and be admitted by a butler and footmen. But he led her to a small side door and through a white passage to a kitchen out of a house-wife's dream of Paradise—linoleum floor, tiled walls in canary yellow, long gas range, coal stove with a hood, sink of Monel metal, and on the walls a family of copper pots, from grandfather pot to baby, surely imported from France.

An ice box seven feet wide, electric.

In it beer, a cold chicken, a cold duck, caviar; and in the pantry a vast box of English biscuits.

"Too cold for beer, don't you think?" said Barney. "I'll make you a cup of tea. Like it?"

"Love some! I'm cold to the bone."

"Wish it weren't so late; I'd cook you a whole dinner. I may be an illiterate jurist, and even a Harvard man can beat me at hand-ball, but I'm the best damn cook outside the Colony restaurant." His way of turning on the gas, lighting it, reaching for the teakettle, the professional sureness of it, proved his words. "My Mulligan stews are reverently spoken of even by the best bartenders, and my pineapple sauerkraut has caused exiled German princes to weep tears of pure Löwenbräu."

He refused Ann's help. Russell would certainly have taken it. She noted again that it is a myth that the soft men are "handiest about the house." She could see Barney

Dolphin as a camp cook, an army cook, a ship's cook, enjoying it, while Russell puttered in kitchens and gawped and got in the way. Barney stripped to his shirt-sleeves, and she noticed his solid shoulders. She sat on a high stool, warm now, happily watching him. He deftly made chicken sandwiches, made toast for caviar. He had their supper ready in ten minutes, and they ate it at the kitchen table, not very talkative, exchanging grateful scandal about judges and court officials and prison experts.

Elbows on table, chin on hands, he looked through her eyes into her brain.

"It's cold out, my dear. It's late. Why not spend the night here? We'll start as early as you'd like in the morning —or as late."

She ought to protest, at least to fence. But she did want to stay. She was, after years of loneliness, curiously at home in Barney Dolphin's presence. She avoided his eyes, she played tattoo with her fork. She impersonally heard herself saying, "All right."

He came around the table to kiss her, with a professional sureness which captivated her while she felt that it ought to shock her. They went down the white passageway to an entrance hall, with portraits which seemed to her old and handsome, and up the staircase. But she halted, nervously. On the landing, illuminated by a strip light, was the portrait of a woman as cool and clear and slender and proud as though she were made of rock-crystal, and beside her were two girls, fragile and disdainful.

"It is your wife?" said Ann. She sounded stricken.

"Yes. Mona. And the girls. Good-looking, I believe." His hand was urging her upstairs. He led her to a bedroom

like a corner in the Petit Trianon, with a too-gaudy bathroom off it. The toilet table was of glass and lace and—
she suddenly detested it—huge bows of pink ribbon.

"This isn't *her* room, Barney?"

"No. No. Honestly. It's a guest room. And I don't mind
saying I think it looks like a kept woman's boudoir. I'm
not responsible for all the frills. But the bed does have a
swell mattress, anyway. I'll bring you some night things."

When he came in with a pile of dressing-gown, pajamas,
cold cream, an enormous bath-sponge, she had donned
again the evening cape she had taken off in the kitchen.
She was sitting cross-legged on the bench before the
dressing-table, her back to the table, staring out into the
room, elbow on knee.

"Worried, dear?" His voice flowed over her, caressing
her like a warm bath.

"No, but—— Oh, Barney, it is a little sudden, but I'm
afraid I like you immensely. Defenselessly, almost! I think
you like me."

His kiss explained that he jolly well did, and something
was going to be done about it.

"But we can't make love here," Ann insisted. "It's
Mona's house, so utterly hers. If we were strays, meeting
by chance off in some inn, I wouldn't care. But I can't hurt
her, Barney, and it seems to me (perhaps I'm idiotic) that
the essence of her is here everywhere. I can't betray her,
not quite that much."

"Look here. Will you go off for a week-end with me,
next week-end?"

"Ye-es—yes, I will!"

"Then sleep sweetly, and tomorrow I'll have you up at

eight—that gives you five hours—and you can change
your clothes and be at your office at ten-thirty, and on
the way we'll make plans, my dear!" To his good-night
kiss she murmured, not really knowing that she said it,
"My very dear!"

She dreamed that she was standing, a prisoner, before
Adolph Klebs, in judge's robes. He looked down at her
ironically. She loved him, and was a little afraid of him,
and utterly attendant on his whim.

She woke to Barney Dolphin sitting on the edge of her
bed, in the morning light. His arm, in pajama sleeve, was
warm about her neck, but his morning kiss was almost dis-
appointingly innocent, and he said only, "Up, my darling,
and away, to the little criminals."

There was a sort of bath crystals, apparently geranium,
new to her and luxurious.

A frost-bitten unplaced servant had breakfast for them,
and as Barney smiled at her across the toast and honey
and coffee, she felt that she had been his mate for years.

39

AT MIDNIGHT on Saturday, March 29th, they started
out in his cream-colored torpedo for the Valley of Virginia,
meaning by the magic of speed to push the calendar ahead
into full spring. They had dined lazily and late and well,
assured lovers—they who had known but four kisses yet,
and supper at a kitchen table.

Ordinarily Ann was capable of a judicious nervousness
about fast cars, but tonight, with a confidence in Barney
Dolphin that seemed based on years of his swift resoluteness, she drowsed happily on their flight. Towns, railroad
crossings, thunderous underpasses, they were only visions
in her dream. She woke once at angry voices. Barney was
arguing with two enormous state policemen with Sam
Browne belts. He seemed, she thought foggily, to be laughing, to be handing the policemen a bill and a drink from a
flask. Then the encounter was sunk in her sleep. She never
did know whether it had happened in New Jersey, Pennsylvania, Delaware, or Ultima Thule. She was so warm
and snug in her double robe, and he seemed never to be
tired when she leaned against his shoulder, which con-

tinuously, smoothly, flowed in motion as his hand moved with the wheel.

She was conscious, once in the night, of a very little voice, probably that of Annie Vickers of Waubanakee trustingly driving with her father: "'S nice. 'S all very nice and proper. I like it here"; and conscious of an arm that was around her for a moment.

She was awakened, scarily, by a sense that the comforting sway and drumming had ceased. She sat up, startled. She was alone in the seat, and the car was stopped, in a city. By some completely mysterious means she had come to a narrow street that curved as New York streets rarely do; a narrow foreign byway with high buildings of smoky brick. She blinked, and her whole body felt hungry for Barney's secure presence. Rubbing her eyes, feeling exploratory and observant, she decided that she was before a lunch-room. And Barney was coming out, carrying a tray, smiling, a little ironic. With immense gratitude she took a thick china cup filled with the most superb coffee, and the hottest, in history.

"Where are we?" she muttered, half asleep again.

"Baltimore, my beloved. The home town of Mencken and the crab—not necessarily related, however."

"Um. That's nice. Kiss me."

Then, immediately, they were in front of the Mayflower Hotel in Washington—how the devil the hotel had suddenly got there beside their car she could not understand— and Barney was calling, "Now for some real breakfast and a wash, my beloved, my kit, my sleepiest of cats!"

(But when *he* talked the Little Language, it was so lightly that he wasn't cloying, like Russell.)

He lifted her out. He laughed. "I'm not sure but we ought to stop here, sleepy. By the time I get you to Staunton, you'll be an infant in arms. Just now you look about ten. I'll be pinched for kidnaping—and have a Republican judge sit on the case, at that! Wake up, darling! Waffles! Toast and honey!"

They came at noon to the hamlet of Captain's Forge and a little inn of brick with a white portico, on a bright hillside over a valley of streams and quiet fields. It had been a plantation manor house; the lawns were springing with daffodils and jonquils; and on the parlor wall, over the white fireplace, was the sword of a Confederate general. They had a suite of lofty bedroom, sitting-room with horsehair furniture and portraits in oval frames, and a balcony over a lawn edged with rhododendron, and this place seemed to Ann the first of all places since her father's house in Waubanakee that was, immediately and enduringly, Home.

They dined vastly, on fried chicken with corn fritters and fresh peas, and slept all afternoon, close-clasped, absolute in their unquestioning closeness to each other; slept on that vast black walnut bed, whose headboard was prickly with carven walnut pears and wreaths and roses, with the jalousie making a twilight striped with gold.

Their days at Captain's Forge were on the surface bland and idle. First of all they saw immediately that it was a great nonsense to suppose that they would go back on Monday; and they telephoned very long and lying telegrams about the vague affairs which would keep each of them here for a week.

They walked, they swam, they picnicked. They played, though both were rusty, a fast, vicious, unlaughing tennis. Once, in a fast drive, they whisked all the way to Richmond for an evening at a secret and gilded club, but for the rest they were content to be absorbed by each other, by country airs and the smell of April earth. Ann re-read John Howard, Elizabeth Fry, Beccaria—the Wesleys, the Erasmuses, of prison reform—and Barney growled, "I don't know why the hell it ever seemed to me like a slick idea to give up my classical Italian—the only Italian I know now is 'due bananas' and 'quanto costa the fine?'—in order to pursue the playing of rummy with Tammany district leaders. Still, the Lord may know His business. If I'd stuck to my books, I might be dean of a law-school by now, or a Justice of the United States Supreme Court, and then I'd never have met you, and I must say I prefer kissing you to toying with the justices' whiskers in the shade. Gurrumph!" He dived into *La Figlia di Jorio*—on the balcony, in a willow chair, with a siphon and a bottle of superior moonshine and a box of cigars on a little iron table, and Ann, in brocaded dressing-gown and mules, reading *The Magic Mountain* for the third time, but dropping it on her lap to glance contentedly at Barney, to stare, in a trance of happy formless thoughts, down the green funnel of the valley.

Russell Spaulding (a man who was, Ann amazedly recalled, related to her by marriage) talked always in his lighter amorous moments of "playing" at things, of "making believe," and he engaged in these diversions so hysterically that he was as embarrassing to Ann as the spec-

tacle of a fat man dancing at a nudist colony. Barney
Dolphin had probably not used the expression "make believe" since he was thirteen, forty years ago, and the verb
"play" was in his rhetoric applied only to cards, golf, and
baseball. Yet it was Barney who excelled in the fond,
secret games of lovers: the pretense that she was the shy
nymph flying; the pretense that she would not go to bed
when he did, but would sit up reading unless he carried
her off. He was grave about it, and did not hustle the
game by gabbling, but let it glide on in slow sweet idiocy.
He could afford to be grave. He had enough energy in him
not to have to be noisy.

She noticed most, and most liked, the fact that they
could understand each other instantly, wordlessly, with a
coup d'œil. They went to a revival of that attractive church,
the Episcopal Evangelical Pentecostal Union of the New
Saints in the Living Word. The pastor (by day an excellent
carpenter), perhaps weary of the same old sins of the same
old members of that congregation of twenty-two excitable
souls, was delighted to see in Ann and Barney new customers. He shouted, "And I want to tell you that fine clothes
and living in *cities* ain't going to save folks from going to
damnation for their sins no more than wearing *overhalls*."
Barney's glance slid past hers and they glowed in shared
laughter without having to laugh, without having to whis-
per the wisecracks of a Russell——

"Oh, why can't I stop this comparing the two men!"
she admonished herself. "It's childish! Making compari-
sons! And it isn't fair to anyone."

But the truth is, she was unbelievably happy, and it
is a part of human happiness to make comparison with

wretcheder days; it is the softest joy of relaxing in a warm bed to recall the chill walk homeward.

Unbelievably, unholily happy—and in especial because she knew that Barney was equally happy.

There was a third who was with them always—Pride, her daughter. Certainly Ann was doing nothing to prevent Pride's finally coming out of the everywhere into the here, as the school reader in Waubanakee had expressed it. She saw Pride now as inevitably his daughter, Barney's. How, she sniffed, could a girl like Pride be fathered by Lindsay Atwell or Russell Spaulding or Lafe Resnick or Glenn Hargis or even Adolph Klebs?

"I will have my child, as I have my man!" she vowed. "A working woman has a right to her child and her lover. Oh, I don't suppose she has any specific *right*. Probably there are no 'rights'—only the chance of having good glands and good luck. But whatever the philosophy of it may be, I'm going to have, Barney and I are going to have, our daughter!"

They were driving to the nearest town for the magazines. Not once looking at her, speaking steadily, Barney said, "I suppose you'd better know more about this legislative investigation of me. It will probably break just after we get back to town. I exaggerated a little when I said I was completely innocent. Mind you, I do think that in criminal cases I have been a little unusually scrupulous, and unusually careful. I've never let myself get bored and mechanical. But there have been civil cases that—oh, there was no real question of justice on either side; they were simply battles between two equally crooked gangs of guerillas and gorillas masquerading as high-minded business corporations; and in those cases, sometimes I have been guilty—or it would be fairer to say, I've been *realistic* enough to side with the bunch I liked best. I've never taken a bribe. I have taken tips on the market, and such things as the location of new trolley lines, and I've had directorships. But never bribes. . . . Though I don't know that makes me any the less guilty. Perhaps just more cowardly. But it does happen that they can't *get* me. But they'll have a lovely time bothering me. And—I've flattered myself you might worry, my darling, and I wanted you to know that I shan't be the abused goat of the piece, but something much more like the city slicker, the crafty villain, the crafty smiling villain. Do you mind?"

Drearily she told herself that this one man whom she loved beyond all human beings represented, then, precisely the cynical, vulgar dishonesty in public officials that she had been most passionately fighting.

She told herself that, quite clearly, but she did not hear herself.

She saw Barney hammered by the press, betrayed by fellow politicians crookeder than himself, losing his debonair sureness, becoming more gray, wondering whether he ought to resign and, if he did resign, how he could get through sapless day after day after day.

"No! No!" she wailed, and clutched his arm desperately. "They shan't get you! Reform if you want to, but don't resign! Don't you resign! We'll tell them to go to the devil!"

He turned his head toward her, and he smiled gratefully.

He was talking, for the first time, of Mona, his wife.

This was in darkness, when they sat on the balcony, smoking, with the smell of lilac bushes and wet grass slipping through the smell of Turkish tobacco.

"I wonder if you've wondered if I've had many love-affairs? Well, I have. I suppose that's notorious. I've never tried to conceal it—to conceal much of anything, for that matter. And I'm not sorry. I've never been sorry for anything I've done, I guess. Only sorry this way—it may make you doubt me when I tell you the flat, hard, honest truth: that you're the first woman I've ever definitely loved, spiritually, and decidedly physically; and if you were willing, I'd just see if I had my check book along, and you and I would start off tomorrow and never come back, never— go on till we landed in a coconut plantation in Tahiti.

"I've known a lot of cuties that amused me when I couldn't stand Mona's perfection. She's like a gilt Louis Seize chair, and a husky lout like me expected to sit up straight in it, all evening, every evening! So you go out and get a nice little pillow-cushion to squat on——"

"But, darling, what kind of furniture do I become in your metaphor? A Simmons mattress?"

"No! A throne—but with modern upholstery! But I mean: No sane person could ever find fault with Mona. She's righteous, she's beautiful, she's quiet. She would have made the best abbess in Christendom. And in seven minutes by the clock she can turn me from a normally decent and competent person into a foul-mouthed, awkward

bum! She forgives you for what you might do before you do
it, and then the least you can do is to satisfy her by going
ahead and doing it. She's so lovely. And oh, God, I am so
happy to be here with you! . . . Mona comes back to
America in June. It paralyzes me a little. I'm going to see
you every day—and most nights—till then? Shall I?
Shall I?"

Dimly, "Yes, every day—every night."

In its sleep a night bird drowsed three notes.

They had only one quarrel, that very sharp; when he
made fun of her for "coddling" prisoners. She won. Before
it was finished, he had rather meekly admitted that he had
seen little of the prisons to which he had sent so many convicts, so casually, for so many years; he had uncomfortably
promised that he would go prison-inspecting.

"Yeah, and I might have had more sense than to have
brought *that* up!" he said afterward.

They drove back to New York slowly, savoring every
mile of spring; they got in at dinner time and, as he had an
evening engagement that could not by any possibility be
broken, he did not leave her flat till ten next morning.

She was so proudly happy next day that she had to be
kind, even if there was no one around who would tolerate
being bekinded. She telephoned to Russell that she was
back. She was, yes, willing to have dinner with him.

Russell arrived with gusty boasts about his success as a
hotel-keeper, and he took her to dinner at Pierre's. But
when they returned to her flat after dinner, his boisterous

spirits drooped, and he began shamefacedly to fumble at love-making. He was so childishly lonely, so transparently lustful, that, from the heights of her own happiness, she looked down at him in pity and let him stay. He believed, he almost said, that it was his own magic and wisdom as a lover which exalted them that night. He believed that he was her husband!

When he was gone, in the morning—she pushed him out with the excuse that she must hasten to her office—she sat in wretchedness. "I feel like a prostitute! I must never do that again! So soon unfaithful to Barney—and with that human puppy, that man Spaulding, on the cheap ground of 'not hurting his feelings.' Ugh! How did I ever stand it? I never shall again. I'm glad I took extra care. But it only makes me feel more sordid. . . . Why hasn't *he* telephoned?"

She slipped into the courtroom where Barney was to try a case, into the back row of seats, near the door. Among the counsel ruffling through papers or chatting at their long table she apprehensively recognized Reuben Solomon, the most famous trial lawyer in New York. Could her Barney manage so ferocious a fighter?

The court attendant beckoned the room to rise. Ann sprang up, proud at this tribute to her man, when all of them, even Reuben Solomon, stood at attention, upon His Honor's entrance; prouder yet of the black silk robe which Barney wore carelessly over his smart blue suit.

She studied the courtroom. It was rather stuffy and ugly, with spotty brown plaster walls, on which one stain resembled a map of Africa. The only decoration was the twin golden fasces behind the judge's high desk. Yet to Ann it seemed a beautiful room and cheerful.

She awoke to a tilt between His Honor Judge Bernard Dow Dolphin and the great Mr. Solomon.

"None knows better than the Court that the questions of my learned opponent are entirely improper."

"Mr. Solomon, need I again remind you that this is not your office, but a court of the State of New York? If you again forget it, I shall take pleasure in fining you for contempt. You will proceed, Mr. Jackson."

Her Barney!

As she left the courthouse, she realized that she knew intimately two judges. Lindsay Atwell also had recently been elected a Justice of the Supreme Court of New York. She had scarcely noticed the news at the time; she only half remembered it now. Lindsay was something out of a dream, blurred and unimportant.

She saw Barney every day, even the day on which Mona came home from Europe.

He was to meet her boat at eleven and drive with her to Long Island. At three in the afternoon, Ann's secretary, the bustling Miss Feldermaus, skipped in excitedly: "Gee, Doctor, see who's calling: Judge Dolphin of the Supreme Court!"

Barney had never called on her at the Industrial Home; had telephoned as rarely as possible; and when he did telephone, had given the code name of "Mr. Bannister." For women's prisons are precisely like Y. W. C. A.'s, smart finishing-schools, and Lesbian restaurants, in their heated friendships, their furious loathings, their gasping curiosity, and their incessant gossip.

"Oh, yes, Judge Dolphin. Is Dr. Malvina Wormser with him?" said Ann affably, looking at a sewing-room report with more interest than the document deserved. "Uh—shoot him in. Say what he wanted?"

"How d'you do, Dr. Vickers," he said, as he came in.

Barney looked gray and stern. He wore a double-breasted blue coat, a wing collar, a peculiarly moral and lofty black four-in-hand, and ridiculous great horn-rimmed eyeglasses. And he carried a stick.

She adored him—her man, dressed just as politely as anybody; wearing his blue serge almost as well as he had worn a sweater and grease-specked bags in Virginia.

She jerked her head at Miss Feldermaus, to get rid of that slowly moving, curiosity-devoured maiden.

Barney kissed her hastily, while she murmured, "No—no," and kissed him back.

"I couldn't do it," he said. "Mona. I was determined I'd be cordial, maybe lover-like. But when she came off the gangplank she looked at me forgivingly, and she said—God, she was polite—she said, 'I hope it doesn't bore you too much, my coming home so soon.' I told her I was due in court and—I came here. I'm going, now. I just wanted to see you a minute—you know—just one quick drink of you, and how I needed that drink! We'll dine at six? Eh? Chuck it! Six, at the Brevoort, and then, God help me, I'll go out and eat chipped ice on Long Island!"

He was opening the door, calling back for the benefit of no one knows how many pricking nymph-ears, "Yes, I really hated to send her up. I think you can reform her.

Sorry I haven't time to see some of the prison. G'd-afternoon, Dr. Vickers."

And gone.

She laughed—at his eyeglasses, at the way in which he remained and now would always remain immanent in her office. Then she wanted to cry, at the tragedy of the Good Woman who was accursed by having a red-bearded husband, and the tragedy of the red-bearded husband who suffered from having a pure, high-minded, frugal, and imbecile wife, and the tragedy of Ann Vickers, who had an excellent chance of being crushed between them, with the squeaking of Little Russell Spaulding just as an added torture at the death.

Three and a half weeks later she had reason to believe that she would have a baby.

40

Sʜᴇ would most certainly have her baby. It did not occur to her to murder Pride again. Whether it was because this was Barney's definitive edition of Pride, and not the limp-bound version that might have been issued with Lafe Resnick as father; or whether, with a certain cowardice, she was willing to let the world think poor Russell was the father, while previously she had had no husband to throw to the wolves; or whether she really and edifyingly had repented of her former murder of Pride and learned humble wisdom thereby; or whether it was because this was, at forty, probably her last chance to have a child—all this no one knows, she did not know herself. Probably it was for all four reasons, with a dozen other complicated desires thrown in. But she did not mark them, nor puzzle over them, nor try to think herself into an attitude of virtuousness and credit. She merely went about singing, "I'm going to have Pride! I'm going to have my daughter! I'm going to have Barney's child!"

She did not tell Barney for another month, not till she was altogether certain.

He cried, "I'm delighted! I'm delighted! Unless you
mind?"

"Of course not! I wanted your child. Terribly."

"Scared?"

"Not a bit. I'm strong as a horse."

"Then I'm simply tickled beyond words. I was born to
be a patriarch. And you the mother of a tribe. If we'd met
twenty years ago, we'd have ten kids, all hellions, and a
thousand-acre farm and seven thousand books now, and
I'd be almost a decent human being, instead of an office-
holder. Ann! Our kid!"

They were in her little flat. As so often now, they had
preferred a chop and salad brought from the hotel restaurant to the danger of meeting friends of Mona and having
to be bland to their hostile curiosity.

He kicked back the absurd card-table at which they had
dined. He lighted a cigar. She watched him. He seemed,
after his ruddy enthusiasm, suddenly weary and serious.

"Ann. Listen carefully. I'm not speculating. I'm suggesting this seriously. Is there any reason why, with our
child coming, you and I should not get up and git, the
three of us, right now? Think of where we could go—Paris,
the Tyrol, Algiers, Bali, Devonshire, Cuba—anywhere!
I've got enough money to take care of the two families. My
girls are grown-up. Don't need me. They have the Long
Island society bug, anyway. They think I'm vulgar—no
doubt correctly. I'd try to get Mona to divorce me, but
if she didn't—what of it? Think of a villa in the hills behind the Riviera, and breakfast on the terrace, instead of a
prison corridor and fighting with Sister Keast for you, instead of a stuffy courtroom for me, and a lot of fat-jawed

politicians asking favors! And we wouldn't be just exiles—escapists. I might have been a scholar once; I want to pick up things again. Six months, and I'd be back in Dante and Ariosto. And there's a devil of a lot you don't know, that you could grind on over there, my girl—painting, music, sculpture, architecture—you're ignorant as a rabbit! And our kid brought up to something besides radios and basketball. I mean it. *Why not?* I don't think I've ever accomplished one damn thing worth while—never heard of a judge that did—they're just actors spouting the lines written by the legislatures, who are infamous playwrights. I suppose you have done something. Per-haps! But haven't you done your share? Must you give up your whole life to the Kittie Cognacs? I could be ready to start in two weeks, if you wanted to. Come! Yes?"

"Barney, I can't think of one single reason why we can't, but I know we can't. I think it's that we're both terribly active people. We have to carry out a job, even when it seems a little futile. We *say* we'd be content studying Ariosto, taking music lessons, exploring Crete. We wouldn't. We'd become restless and homesick and take it out on each other, and then I might lose you. I think probably my only chance to keep you is to have a job, be somebody besides just 'that damn woman that's here in the room all the time.' And I like my work—and you will again, once you get this cursed investigation over and stop feeling shaky. Kittie Cognac is like a novel I've read three quarters of. I want to read the rest. And I've actually got Number 3921, Sallie Swenson, alias Cohen, to swear off heroin, I think. And—— I can't! Let's plan to meet a year from now, by accident on purpose, and have a month in

Italy. But not stay and become shadows. We're too pink and meaty—we wouldn't make good shadows. Oh, my dear, I want so much to go with you! I can't. And you couldn't. You, with the funny face and the absurd red beard and the atrocious reputation as a Casanova, that I adore!"

Not till midnight, tossing in her bed (regretfully alone), seeing the two of them in a lemon-colored villa above silver-colored sands, did she remember that neither of them had thought of a man named Russell Spaulding.

"Whom God had put asunder, from the first, let no man, not even a preacher, try to join together," she piously observed.

Not for a week did she, the perfect Protestant, see that for Barney, who was proud of knowing bishops and of having met cardinals, it must have been devastating to talk about being divorced and remarried. She probably could never comprehend how much he had given her in that . . . the very cloak and garment of his soul.

She told Dr. Wormser about the baby.

They sat in the same position, on either side the fireplace, in the same flat, as thirteen years ago, when she had confessed to Malvina about Lafayette Resnick. But it was a different Ann Vickers from the embarrassed pregnant virgin of the settlement house. She was radiant, resolute, and almost flippant in her joy, so that Malvina needed not to be so pattingly tender.

"What? Again? My God, Ann, it's getting to be a habit! Who's the father this time? Russell or Judge Dolphin? Or have you been getting into bad company?"

"I've never said one word to you about Judge Dolphin!"

"You haven't, eh? Well, I've seen you look at the man. It was an indecent look. You might just as well have sung *Tristan and Isolde* in John D. Rockefeller's church."

"Well. Anyway. No use lying to the family doctor."

"Heavens, no, nor any use in telling her the truth. A family doctor is, by definition, a person with such a reputation for congenital idiocy that she, or he, is expected to believe that the aftermath of a five-day bout with the speakeasies is 'a little attack of gastric 'flu, Doc'! Are you going ahead and have this new child? I would, if——"

"Have her! Yes! I'm mad to! I'm walking all over God's Heaven about it, right now! But you must get this straight. This isn't a 'new child.' This is still Pride, that we wouldn't let come before, and she's given us another chance, the blessed soul!"

"So? Interesting discovery. You might just let me send a note of it to the *Journal of the American Medical Association*—and the *Christian Science Monitor*! Oh, my darling, don't look hurt! You look like a child that's been jumped on just when she thought she was being so good—your lower lip's all quivering! I'm just as glad as you are about it, and I bet Barney is. Is he?"

"'Tickled to death,' he says."

"He better be! Oh, well, I won't be feminist. Wish I could have pinched him off myself, though there have been a fair share of nice men around, in my own day—so long ago. But you seem to have a problem or something, when I stop gabbling. (I feel like a grandma to the baby—is she still named Pride?)"

"(She certainly is!) Yes, there is kind of a problem. Shall I tell Russell that the baby isn't his?"

"Won't he know? Could he conceivably have been the father?"

"Well, it's *just* possible. With his delightful vanity, he'll be sure it's his."

"Then don't tell him."

"Why not?"

"Why? My God, why? Who's to be the gainer by it— except your own egotism, which you mistake as a high sense of honor? How will it help you? How will it help baby? How will it help Barney, to make a homicidal enemy for him? How will it help Russell, to tell him he's been a complaisant cuckold? And most especially, how will it help Pride, to have this known, so that she may hear it some day? Not why not, my good wench, but *why?*"

"Because Russell'd find it out, and then be all the angrier—or the more hurt. I'm not a good liar. Wish I were! And then, too, it doesn't seem fair, with him; like taking candy from a child. I might try to lie to Barney or you; try to get away with it. But you may be right. I'll think about it."

And so, when she left Dr. Wormser's, from the drug-store on the corner she telephoned to Russell at his apartment. It was only ten. "Oh, yes, do come up, please do!" he begged.

He came out into the hall to meet her, urging, "Look, dear, I've got some friends here—Townsend Beck and Dr. Martin and Julia Casey and a couple of awful big hotel-men. Townsend—darn him, he thinks he's such a tease!—he's been trying to kid me about your not being here. I told 'em you were coming back, now I'm settled down to the hotel management here in New York, and I was so glad when you called up! You are coming back? For keeps?"

"Perhaps. We'll see."

("Russell *would* make a good father for Pride. He loves kids. He'd play with them—pickaback—bear—little horsie. They wouldn't find his coyness trying, or even his little moralities. He'd read aloud to 'em. He'd even change diapers. He wouldn't be stern like Barney, or ever drunk. . . . How lonely I am for Barney! And I saw him this noon!")

This, swiftly, as she followed Russell in and dropped her wrap.

"Laaadies an' gennelmen, it gives me great pleasure this *even*-ing to present to you that rare and celebrated animal my *wife*, and to an-*nounce* to you that Dr. A. Vickers Spaulding——"

("Good God! I suppose that I am 'Mrs. Spaulding,' legally!")

"—has come to agree with your humble servant, the chairman of this meeting, that there is posolutely and absotively nothing to this experiment of two marrieds having separate apartments, no matter how busy each— and—ev-ery—one of them may be with different jobs, and that the said Doc Spaulding and her old man will from now on join forces again!"

Much cheering from the group draped over chairs, couches, piano bench.

Russell was full of cheerfulness and mastery. His raid on commerce had made him more certain that he was a man of the world, and with even greater firmness than he had once shown in regard to charity woodyards and tickets to the Municipal Lodging House, he held forth on the mysteries of the cheap hotel business: cost of cotton sheeting per ten thousand yards, great value of gelatine in hotel desserts, problem of keeping bums from loafing in lobby, also same in reference to lavatories, value of bill-board advertising (1) near R. R. terminus; (2) on roads frequented by tourists in flivvers. He was as learned as an archeologist or an osteopath, and when the guests departed, one of the "awful big hotel men" took Ann aside to inform her, "Russell is bringing a whole lot of new ideas into our profession, let me tell you. Even with a swell job like yours, it must give you a great kick to have a husband that's got a creative imagination like his."

He breezed on being masterful, even when they were alone, unconscious that he was ambushed and defenseless. . . .

"Sit ye doon, now, and we'll have a good chin-chin, Anniekins. Well! I'm talking poetry! But listen: I've been thinking. I see where I made my mistake. I never applied the principles of executiveship, in which I think I may with all modesty say I have been rather successful both in charity-work and in business, to my private life. I used to coax you instead of insisting, even in cases where I knew I was right; and of course a high-spirited woman despises a man who doesn't take the lead. I tell you I've learned a lot out of being in business—learned reality, instead of all this theorizing. (And you jumped me for going into it! Wisest thing I ever did!) So now—— Let's cut out all the palaver

and the If, And, and But's, and make it a business-like
proposition, and just decide, bing! to do the only normal
and possible thing for a married couple: to live together, of
course! And if you can't run the household *and* your job,
why, chuck your darn job! I can afford it now, even with
the Depression. It would make a new woman of you. You
wouldn't take yourself so doggone seriously if you could
stay home and have a good rest and get things in their
proper prospectus—perspective, I mean. There! Shall we
call it a deal and say no more about it?"

"But I'm afraid, Russell, there are one or two things we
must say about it." She tossed her hat on the couch, got
herself into a deep chair, lighted a cigarette. She might as
well be comfortable during the Inquisition. He stood beaming on her, a man about to conquer his Little Love who
seemed so wayward but who, in her skittish secret way,
really adored him.

"For certain reasons, Russell, it may be well that I
should come back to your bed and board——"

"Oh! Horrid phrase! Be more romantic——"

"—but it must be on a basis of that reality you talk
about. Russell, I am going to have a baby!"

"Eh?" Apparently he remembered their accidental
night of love, these two months and more gone, and he
shone. "But it's splendid! I'm simply enchanted, dearie!
I've always wanted a child, oh, God, so much!" He ran to
sprawl on the floor by her chair, to kiss her hand with
great vehemence and wetness. "A child! To play with and
watch grow and be able to teach—maybe he'll avoid some
of the mistakes we made! To give me some excuse and
reason for all the work I do! I'll send him to Princeton!

Our boy! And I didn't think you'd ever be willing to have one!"

"Russell! This isn't easy. Maybe I'm a fool to tell you, but it isn't your baby."

"What d'you mean? Whose is it?"

"Well, primarily it's mine."

"Who is this man? How far along is the baby?"

"Little over two months."

"Then—— Let's see. Then it could be mine!"

"Oh, yes, conceivably. But probably not. And listen to me, Russell; I'm not going to be questioned, I'm not going to be bullied, I'm not going to be audience at a self-dramatization. The child is mine and always will be. I haven't the slightest right to ask the slightest thing. You can turn me forth into the snow, but that would be slightly ridiculous, as it's June and I can afford taxis and I have a nice flat of my own. I'm incorrigible. I'm going to have a baby, and I'm glad of it. And by the way, she's going to be a girl, not a boy. But she must have a home. You would, I believe, make a good father. And a girl-child ought to have a male parent. Though she's *mine*, and will be! I'm a matriarch! There isn't the slightest obligation or claim on you. But you assert you want me and want a child. Do you want me with this child, my child—which is possibly all you'll ever learn about its parentage?"

"Good God, woman, don't, at least under the circumstances, talk like a prudish spinster putting a hallroom-boy in his place!"

"I guess I did sound prim. It's just—it isn't easy to talk about this casually. I suppose it's not exactly a daily situation!"

They laughed. That was better. He was instantly serious again.

"I won't pretend I'm not hurt, Annie. I had hoped you would want a child of mine, some day, somehow. And at first you were passionate. And then—I don't know what I did; oh, my dear, I never understood; you turned so cold with me, or so bored, or irritated! Oh, my dear, I was miserable! Part because of you. Part because I've always been crazy to have a kid. . . . I've cut out pictures of babies from women's magazines and hid them in my desk. Always pictured myself coming home at night and cute little tot toddling down the cement walk to me, and lifting it 'way, 'way up in the air, and it squealed and said, 'Dada'——"

The man was pouring sweat in his revealed agony.

She came to live with him, to have a father for Pride, after a fortnight spent mostly with a Barney grieving and unusually silent.

41

It was no easy thing for Ann to bear a baby, at forty. But it was easier than her kind friends would give her credit for. They had such a good time, such a splendid vicarious pleasure, in cautioning her, fussing over her, finding out what she wanted to do and coaxing her not to do it.

Russell wanted her to go to bed at nine every evening—with the results that she always woke at the grisly hour of four and lay turning till eight, and that she was always handy there for him to try to make love to. Pat Bramble Pomeroy wanted her to come and stay in New Rochelle, so that, by daily commuting, she would be rather more wearied than by staying in the city roar. Julia Casey (of the O. C. I.) wanted her to try vegetarianism and sun baths. And Mrs. Keast, assistant superintendent at the Industrial Home, urged, "My, we're all so proud that we're going to have a baby! The whole staff of the S. I. H. are just going to claim it as ours! Now, if you'll permit me the suggestion, why don't you take a four or five months' leave and devote yourself to this sacred duty?"

While Ann was mouthing sweetly, "Oh, that's awfully thoughtful of you, but I simply couldn't let you take all the extra responsibility, Mrs. Keast," she was secretly raging, "Yes, and give you a chance to worm yourself in and carry out the great sacred duty of getting my job away from me!"

Two people did not fuss: Dr. Wormser and Barney Dolphin.

She had insisted on Malvina Wormser as obstetrician. "All these accursed male obstetricians," said Ann, remembering her days as a settlement worker, "say that pregnancy is 'just a normal process' and make the astonishing conclusion that therefore morning sickness isn't nauseating and labor pains aren't painful! I don't want any sentimental sympathy now. I don't want to be dearied. I want to be treated like Superintendent Vickers. But when my time comes, I want all the sympathy I can get, I do!"

Barney did not talk overmuch; did not irritate her by asking for the sixteenth time that day, "And how do you feel now?" He just gathered her in and tucked her against his shoulder, where she belonged.

Before she had lived with Russell for two weeks, she knew that she had been an inconceivable idiot, and that she was not unlikely to be killed by her folly. She had erected her own trap and, with such good sensible reasons, such laudable planning for Pride's welfare, had bustled into it and heard the door bang. She was as much a prisoner as any woman in the Industrial Home—she was more a prisoner, because the privacy of their cell-bedrooms was sacred.

By the end of that two weeks Russell was to her a pillow pressed over her head, a diet composed entirely of cream puffs and strawberry ice-cream soda, a perpetual course of bedtime stories, a cornet that never for a minute stopped playing "My Wild Irish Rose," a hot bath scented with black narcissus in which she was bound with silken cords.

He was so damned kind, all the while, and so insistent on making her admit how damned kind he was, and so damned forgiving—no, she snarled, she simply couldn't express it without the "damned's."

He treated her like a child who has been caught stealing or making nasty, and whose anxious parents are determined to love it into niceness.

Russell was feeling his oats. In this first year of the Great Depression, when tens of thousands of employees were being discharged or cut in salary, Russell had soared from twelve thousand a year to fifteen thousand. He had, it seemed, a hitherto unlaureled genius for beef stew, communal shower baths, prevention of towel-stealing, economy in the candlepower of incandescent bulbs, and all the other bright metaphors and adjectives of the art of keeping cheap hotels. And this year men who had formerly paid three dollars for a room were seeking rooms at a dollar, and was it not nice that who should profit by this save old Russell Spaulding, who was not a commercialized business man but an industrial engineer, fully equipped with ideals! He was a Success; already a Success to a degree of fifteen thousand dollars; and he was no longer much impressed by his wife's being a Doctor and a Superintendent and a Speaker. No day now but he was begged to Speak—at Kiwanis Clubs, at Conventions of the Shoe and

Leather Industry, at the Annual Banquet of the Caterers'
and Restaurateurs' Association. And when he became a
millionaire he would endow colleges, and not have to be
content with one mangy LL. D. but be handsomely a
Litt. D., a D. C. L., and probably a D. D.

He could afford to laugh at the Little Woman's pre-
tensions, to ignore her irritating vanity and be kind to her;
and how inexorably kind he was! He not only sent her to
bed at nine, but came in at nine-thirty and took her detective story away from her and turned off the light and
tucked in again the well-tucked comforter. He brought tea
in the morning, and if she did happen to have slept clear
through, he woke her, so that he might enjoy the spectacle
of her satisfaction at being bekinded.

And while he did not know who was the Guilty Hound
that had ruined her—his friends said something about
Judge Bernard Dow Dolphin, but he knew that could not
be true, because he had never seen Dolphin, and certainly
Ann never had a letter from him nor a telephone call—
while he had not identified him, Russell beneficently made
sure that Ann, the poor kiddie, should not be pestered by
the rat any longer.

She knew that her letters were being steamed open.
Dear Russell, he was so all-thumbs about sticking them together again! She knew that whenever she telephoned the
door of her bedroom was eased open, oh, so delicately and
slowly, that Russell might listen.

She had not exaggerated, she sighed, in thinking that no
prisoner in the Industrial Home, no, nor any in Copperhead Gap, was held quite so tightly as Ann Vickers, on her
voluntary commitment. But she tolerated it without one

word of anger, without more than a few quick breaths of
rage, because she knew that if she said one word she would
say a thousand; that she would leave Russell the same
night; and that Pride would be without a father.

"Besides," she fretted, "Russell has really been most
awfully kind and forgiving, and I've got to play the
game."

And of course she did not play the game, and every day
she did see and desperately kiss the improbable Judge
Dolphin who never wrote to her, never telephoned to her
flat.

The Governor had appointed a commission of members
of the legislature, with retired judges and a couple of
deans of law-schools, to investigate the courts and jurists
of the state. It was the investigation the prospect of which
had worried Barney, but apparently he was no more the
subject of its searching than any other judge. The investigation went on mildly. They questioned every sort of
magistrate, clerk of court. The press, at first excited with
the hope of a good horrible scandal, became bored.

Barney was relieved. "Nothing will happen. They're
dumb. If I were on that commission, I'd get something on
the boys," he grumbled to Ann.

He had borrowed from a friend a flat in which Ann and
he could meet for lunch, or tea when engagements prevented lunch. They cooked their own meals, or indolently
got along with shredded wheat and cream. The flat was in
an enormous apartment house on the East River, and it
was not likely that she would ever be traced in it; but to
make sure, she always took a taxicab (insane extrava-

gance!) to a corner two or three blocks away. She fancied
that she was being followed. Followed by Russell, by the
Mrs. Keast who so jealously wanted her job, or by enemies of Barney? It would have been a relief to be discovered
by Russell or Keast and have it out; but rather than let
Barney be compromised she would have given him up . . .
almost.

Whatever they talked about at lunch, they came back
to the same anxieties.

"I'm getting up a hatred for our Russell boy that's
pretty homicidal, Ann."

"I don't hate him. I just—— Oh, he just merely makes
me get sick on the hearth-rug. I'm a prisoner."

"You're no more of a prisoner than I am, my lamb—
I'm caught by you. Me, that used to think I could always love 'em and leave 'em. Me, that once thought
myself such a man of the world, such a man's man—His
Honor, Judge Bernard Dow Dolphin—Barney, that has
fallen as completely in love with a wench as any young
Romeo, come here and sit on the floor and put your chin
on my knee and try to look intelligent. And—— We can't
keep this up! We've got to elope. Pride may as well begin
to get used to belonging to irregular parents, right now, at
her early age. Let's go!"

They might have gone. They were near breaking. Then
the investigation came, and he could not, or thought he
could not, "resign under fire," still less run away under
fire. If it was a banal and merely traditional reason, it still
seemed to them real beyond question.

But daily they met—romantic lovers, not very young;
crunching shredded wheat in a terrible little dining-room

with imitation exposed beams and latticed windows that opened on a brick airshaft three feet wide, instead of sipping Lachrymæ Christi in a moony loggia.

They seemed to drift circling in a backwater. Nothing would happen again; forever Pride would be slowly coming, but never come; forever Russell would be prattling at her, and Keast would, with vinegar-dripping long nose, be watching in hope that Ann would have to give up her work; and at his home Mona be coolly disgusted by his commonness.

Then he exploded.

When she came into this dingy borrowed place that was their only home, he shouted, "I've done it! I ditched it! Last night, apropos of nothing at all—in fact, she was unusually polite and had put out whisky and a siphon for me—I said to Mona, 'I don't think you're enjoying this. Would you like to get a divorce? I'll give you grounds. Don't worry about hurting my position. That's in the fire-sale already.'"

"And——"

"Oh, it wasn't too good. She said, 'I shall never divorce you—much though I should like to be free of you and your vulgar political friends—because of the family, and because of our religion, and because I am still waiting, as I have all these years, loyally and single-mindedly, for the day when you are tired of your mistresses and get ready to appreciate the purity of my affection.' God! She was like a crystal chandelier talking. So!"

"Have you many girl friends?"

"Since I met you? None. Not one. Believe me?"

"Yes."

"I'm glad you do. It happens to be the truth, in this case. Still, I don't recommend it as a precedent in general. Darling!"

"You know, don't you, Barney, if we three ever do go off together, it doesn't make the slightest difference to me whether we are married or not? Mona is welcome to the lines, as long as I have the man. . . . I've never spoken of it: I do know that you're a good Catholic, or would be if you could, and I do know what anxiety you went through before you were willing to divorce and remarry."

"Oh! You noticed that!"

"And as for Pride, she can jolly well take what her father and mother have. Oh, she'll probably either turn out a lady, like Mona, or a religious political fanatic, like Pearl McKaig, and in either case, she'll disapprove of her old man and old lady. We'll probably wind up sitting on the steps of the poorhouse, smoking our pipes together, while our Pride slides past in a Rolls-Royce!"

"Well, that might not be so bad. I swear there's better talk and better pinochle in a poorhouse than in a Rolls-Royce, and less trouble dressing for dinner—— Oh, Lord, I can't even be joky, like dear Russell! It's all so damn absurd. You and I that were born to go tramping together —with Pride following us, carrying a little rucksack! . . . Russell, Mona! How in hell did we manage to get ourselves shackled to those complete strangers? My dear, whatever grafting I may have done has been ethical compared with my sin (to her and to myself and now to you and tomorrow to Pride) in thinking I was in love with Mona, and bullying her into marrying me. I had the lowest of motives— cowardice. You see, I was ambitious. I expected to be Governor, Senator, and I knew that I had a certain energy, unfortunately combined with affection for vulgarity and dissipation. I thought that with anyone so passionless and correct and reserved as Mona, I'd have to become a cautious and exemplary lad. Tried to escape from my innate recklessness by marrying into a nunnery. Of course it failed. I deserved it. But the other victims didn't deserve it. Oh, Lord, I'm getting moral! Love often takes one that way, I'm told."

It did not add to Barney's cheerfulness that the securities in which for years he had cannily invested were fast losing value. He had never been a gambler in his investments, however much he had enjoyed those friendly poker games by which the privy councilors of Tammany rest themselves and settle the political fates of a few million people. He had never bought on margin, but had invested in stocks safe as Gibraltar—rails, steel, motors—and then Gibraltar had quietly slid into the ocean. "I'd have had a lot more fun and made just as sound an investment if I'd had sense enough to change all my money into silver dollars and sit on a pier and throw 'em one by one into the East River," he said.

The Great Depression had been on for a year. It had the one blessing that, since dinner parties talked of nothing else, at least they no longer talked about Prohibition, which topic had occupied the great intellects of the United States now for ten years. A few people, even presidents and bankers, were beginning to stop saying "We have turned the corner and are on the up-grade; the Depression will be over in three months." A few were begin-

ning to wonder whether such prosperity as America had
known from 1890 to 1929 would ever return; and a rather
smaller number to consider whether it might not profit our
great land to lose the theory that a family which does not
have a radio, at least two automobiles, a bedroom and a
bathroom for every member of the family, and a membership in a country club, is a spiritual failure and a moral
menace and in general an offense to the Lord God.

The Great Depression did not depress Ann. It strangely
exhilarated her. She saw poverty again accepted as natural
and non-mortal. She felt that if ever Barney and she should
somehow, somewhere, be poor together, they would be
part of a new, taut, lean spirit creeping into the swollen
land.

Pearl McKaig, the Communist prophetess, called on Ann
at the Industrial Home.

"I want to talk privately to you, Ann," she said, in the
tone of a school-principal.

"All right, Feldermaus, outside!" said Ann to her little
secretary.

The door had not closed before Pearl demanded, "Do
you let her call you 'Vickers'?"

"I do not!"

"Then why should you call her 'Feldermaus'?"

"Because she adores me."

"So you take advantage of her?"

"Certainly—just as you are taking advantage of my
notorious good-nature to bring me your message of bad
cheer, whatever it may be. Shoot!"

"It isn't exactly a message but—— Ann, I had great

hopes of you, once. I thought you were one of us, the
Workers, the uncompromising Reds. And just for a hand-
ful of silver you left us, just for a ribbon to stick in your
coat. You have never denounced the Mayor or the Governor. You seem to serve under them quite contentedly. And
now I hear that you are carrying on with a rich political
grafter."

"Oh, leave my personal sins out of it!"

"You can't, these days. We're in the crisis of history.
A revolutionist must have character, and he has no time
for the pleasant little sins. There's such terrific things
happening. The whole coal-mining situation, especially
West Virginia and Kentucky, is simply a war——"

"My dear girl, I know something about Southern industry myself. When I was in Copperhead Gap——"

"Yes. All the rest of your life you'll talk about having
been there, *once;* about having fought, *once;* and you'll be
so smugly pleased. You think that you're still a proletarian
and a revolutionary penologist. That's how Liberals always fool themselves. Pretty soon you'll be perfectly satisfied with the prisons, and all the rest of the Capitalist
system, and you won't even know it—you'll make
speeches, and refer to yourself as a Radical, and you'll be
more useful to the Big Beast than any open and avowed
reactionary!"

"Um. I'll tell you, Pearl. I'll run my grafting lover right
out of town, tonight. And I'll open the prison doors and
let all the girls leave—presenting each of 'em with a tract
by Lenin as she goes out. Will that satisfy you? Well, I'm
grateful to you for saving my soul again. And now—I'm
busy. *Fel-der-maus!* Come in and take dictation."

But it did bother her, just the same, and she said to herself, "There's more than a little in what Pearl says—there's a *terrific* lot in it." But in the immanence of Pride and Barney, she forgot it.

January came in, and time for her to take leave from the office and await the baby. She felt radiantly well and normal, but she was bulky; her step, which had always been eager, was slow and graceless; and at little pangs of pain she was frightened. If it would only begin! If she could only get it over!

It was infuriating to be a human mollusk, scarcely able to waddle through the flat.

42

Everyone had told her that the labor pains, when they came to warn her, would be just an hour apart—that is, everyone save the doctor, who had said, "Good Lord, I don't know how far apart they'll be! But don't worry. You'll recognize 'em when they come, all right! Your room is ready at the hospital. You can be there in twenty minutes, and I'll be there in half an hour."

Ann was asleep, at three in the morning, when she was shocked awake by a pain like a dynamite explosion in her belly. She had never known there could be such pain. Beside it, toothache, earache, the torture of a leg she had broken in girlhood, were only mild twinges. She was drowned and choking in pain, powerless in its flood.

And she was glad. "It's come! Pride is coming! And I'll be a human being again, not a feather bolster!"

Now, inconceivably more than ever, she needed Barney and could not endure it that Russell should be with her, should have the apparent right to touch her. (Even in her pain, she took out a second to marvel, "Husband—lover! How insanely we use words! If ever a woman had a husband, Barney is mine; and Russell is a lover that I took in a moment of indecent weakness and have been too weak to throw out.") But for Pride she must endure even this sacrilege of Russell's bustling presence in her holy hour. She must call him—must get up—must get to hospital—quick—— No. The pain was gone; she was in fresh breeze after fog; she had an hour yet of surcease before she need call him. And as she feebly pawed for her watch and looked at it, just seven minutes after the first pain exploded the second.

She sat up and yelped, "Russell!" with no more fantasy about it.

He galloped in, a large ball of putty in the faded pea-green flannelette pajamas which he loved on winter nights; and he was so swift, so kind, so unplayful, that she liked him. ("Curse the man, if he would only be more consistently objectionable, how much simpler life would be!") He had the hospital, Dr. Wormser, and the night watchman of the apartment house, who was to fetch a taxicab, on the telephone apparently all at once, while she lay back, feeling secure enough to give herself up to the agony of the pains, which were coming regularly now, seven minutes apart. All sense of dignity passed from her in the compulsion of suffering. She writhed, she tore at the sheets, she shook the side-board of her bed in her feverish grasping, and she heard her own voice in a frightened keening.

She was too blind with the paroxysms, and too damply feeble and relaxed between them, to know much of what was going on. She had a notion afterwards that Russell and the maid had raised her, got her into dressing-gown and top coat and slippers, with a shawl round her shoulders, supported her down the corridor to the elevator, into the taxicab, up the hospital steps. She was a little puzzled at seeing Malvina Wormser magically there.

Then the pains were coming three minutes apart, and she was holding the hand of a stalwart nurse, wringing it till it must have ached, and presently she was so anesthetized by the pain itself that she realized it only as a ceaseless hurricane in which she was lost with no sense of separate pangs.

And all the while it was something different from suffering. She hadn't the feeling of waste and futility that other anguish had given her. It seemed to have sense, because she was producing life. If her body hurt dreadfully, so that she howled like a child, her spirit was triumphant. This was martyrdom not for a cranky Cause but for Life; to create the miracle of miracles. She heard Malvina gently repeating, "Bear down—try—keep awake—I'll give you a little anesthetic when the time comes—bear down—try!" and obediently, worshipping Malvina, she strove, till the glorious moment when Malvina said affably, "We can take her in now."

She believed that she was singing aloud. She believed that Barney was there, and that she was lifting her heavy hand to wave to him. But all the attendants saw in the corridor, all that a weeping and yearning Russell saw, was a pale, draggle-haired, blanket-covered woman, motionless and silent on a wheeled stretcher.

She came out of fog and the gray thickets and the floating shadows of faces, Oscar Klebs and Glenn Hargis and Lil Hezekiah and Eleanor Crevecoeur and Barney Dolphin.

She seemed to be on a bed in a blank white room, with a woman in white apron and stiff blue gingham dress sitting by her. She was puzzled. She had to think this all over. She would, right away, but she must rest first. She came out of the fog again and instantly, a little proud of herself for being so astute, knew that she was in a hospital room. Her mouth felt parched. She tried to raise one of her hands, folded on her belly, to rub her lips, and realized, startled into full wakefulness, that she was no longer a full hot-water bottle, but miraculously slim again and solid—and then, then only, that she must have given birth to Pride.

"Oh! Oh, tell me, nurse! How——"

"Splendid! Everything perfect."

"My daughter——"

"You have just the loveliest little baby boy!"

"Nonsense!"

They brought in her baby.

They told her he was a fine big boy, eight and a quarter pounds, but she was afraid to touch him, so absurdly fragile were his minikin arms and hands and kobold blob of a nose. He wasn't unduly red and wrinkled, though he certainly was no cream and roseleaf fairy child. Over his ruddy skull was a flush of pale fine hair which, she was certain, would be a red thatch. "Oh, you young Fenian! You shanty Irish! You darling!" was her greeting.

There was nothing fragile about the way in which the son of Barney Dolphin seized upon her breast and demanded his rights.

Within two days she would have called anyone who hinted that she had been expecting a daughter a fool.

Within four days she was planning his course in Columbia, Berlin, and the Sorbonne.

But as she had never thought of any name save Pride, she was in naming him a little less cocksure and loftily maternal.

When Russell came in, beaming, late that first afternoon—the baby had arrived at eleven, and ever since then he had been receiving congratulations by telephone, and buying speakeasy champagne for very important men in the hotel and charity businesses—he caroled, "Well, it went just fine! You had surprisingly little pain."

"Oh, I did, did I!"

"Well, anyway—you know what I mean. I've been in and seen him. I think he looks a lot like me." (And Russell was as dark as the baby was red.) "Now the great question comes, now that we have this grand boy, what shall we call him? I'll let you have first say, though. What had you thought of?"

"Oh, I, uh, I hadn't really decided."

"Now, listen—I just suggest it, and you don't need to take it seriously if you don't want to—but how about naming him after his Daddy—Russell Spaulding, Jr.?"

She was too furious to speak. She lay looking pensive—she hoped. She realized that Russell was beginning to believe the baby was his own; that in a few months he would believe it completely; that legally the baby actually was spawn of the Spaulding; and that no one could be more stubborn than a weak-gutted man like this, once he was challenged. So quite civilly, where she wanted to curse, she said:

"I never cared so much for Junior names. So confusing. And the child is always in danger, unless he's simply miraculous, of being overshadowed by his father."

"Yes, perhaps that's true. Well what do you think of this: Henry Ward Beecher Spaulding. I think that name has a lot of class, and he could call himself either 'Ward' or 'Beecher,' both nice high-grade names, if he didn't care for the 'Henry,' and it would be a nice thoughtful thing to do to commemorate a great man like that. He's in danger of being forgotten in this day of cheap sensationalism and publicity-seeking in so many pulpits. Of course, I'm an agnostic, as you know, but still, I do respect the fine old stalwart spirituality of our forefathers."

"But, Russell," feebly, "I thought from Captain Hibben's life of Beecher—— He made Beecher a good deal of a charlatan; not the kind of leader that—" she gulped, but she got it out bravely, pale in her hard little bed— "that, uh, Liberals like us would want to honor."

"That's all a bunch of hooey! Hibben didn't know what he was talking about! The fact is, I'm distantly related to Beecher—kind of a fourth cousin of my mother's—and so I know he was one of the really great, fearless, forward-looking thinkers of his day. Yes. Henry Ward Beecher Spaulding. That would be a dandy name."

"I'll think it over. I'm terribly all in, dear. Perhaps you'd better let me rest now."

"You bet. Well, I'll come in again just before ten this evening. Mustn't neglect the Little Girl now she has given us a handsome son! . . . Ward Beecher. . . . I think he ought to go to a Middle-Western State University and get the sense of democracy that's so lacking in these damn snobbish Eastern colleges! I'm glad I was an Iowa man myself, let me tell you!"

She made secret Jesuitical arrangements with her night nurse that when Russell came in before ten the nurse was to look agitated and throw him out with speed.

She did.

When he had fled before that sternness which is common to American traffic policemen, secretaries to British cabinet ministers, and nurses universally, Ann gave her son—her son!—his late supper (her breasts trembled as though they were stroked by a lover's hands), then wriggled into a position for exhausted sleep, and did not sleep. She missed something. She tried to keep from admitting that it was Barney, but she caught herself speculating whether, before Nature's last sardonic trick on women, she would have time to bear Barney another child.

She was looking at the door, saw it hitch slowly open, as if by itself, and Barney was there, smiling. He came swiftly to her, sat on the edge of her bed, raised her—while she held her arms out to him and struggled to sit up—and kissed her, with no word. When he had laid her head on the pillow again and stroked her cheek, she felt utterly healed.

"It's the Saints themselves have watched you!" he said. "I've been on the phone to Malvina Wormser all day. I knew about the boy ten minutes after he came. And I've been standing in a doorway across the street till Spaulding (that louse!) was gone and I was sure he wouldn't come back. But I'm not going to do any more sneaking like this!"

"How did you get in, after hours?"

"Bribed two people, bullied two more, and made love to

two others—exactly the right mixture. And I have a letter from Malvina in my pocket, in reserve, if I need it."

"Have you seen our boy?"

"I certainly have!"

"Approve of him?"

"Enormously."

"You agreed with me you wanted a girl. D'you mind?"

"I lied. I wanted a boy, like the devil. My only son! And listen to me. I'm not going to give him up to any damned Russell-laddie——"

("But he's so touching!")

"—and I'm not going to give you up to Russell any longer. I don't know how but—— We'll go into that later, when you're stronger. . . . I love you!"

"Darling, what shall we name him?"

"Matthew. After my father. (No, he wasn't the saloon-keeper; that was *his* father; my old man was worse—he was a contractor, with a heavy fist, a great sense of humor, and no ethics—a West Street Lincoln.) Besides, Mat is an honest, decent nickname for a kid to have."

"Yes! Mat Dolphin, my son—I'm already scared of him! Mat! What a come-down! When I was a girl, I thought that if I ever had a son I'd call him something nice and romantic—a Lady Novelist's name—Peter or Raoul or Noël (especially if born in summer!) or Geoffrey or Denis. Then Mat! And I love it—and you! What a gorgeous brown suit! I've never seen it before. English?"

"Made here. Heather, from Isle of Mull. Smell nice? Sniff."

"Lovely. A man invited me to tramp through the Scotch highlands once."

"Yes, Lindsay is very fond of them, or says he is. But I warn you that he never actually tramps more than five miles a day."

"Beast! You always know too much. If I were married to you, I wouldn't get away with seeing lovers in my bedroom after ten o'clock."

"You would not! I saw your friend Lindsay the other day."

"That's nice. Keep him. I'm in love with a wild Fenian, and I want no respectable men about me. '——that sleep o' nights!' Lindsay? I don't remember the name. I remember no names——" She yawned, immensely. "Remember no names in the world except Barney and Mat."

"You're to go to sleep now."

"Sit by my bed a minute. Pull that chair over and sit by my bed. Just a minute. And hold my hand."

Safe now, guarded and warmed by his hand, she was instantly asleep. It may have been an hour later, it may have been two hours, when she was awakened by the nurse's coming in and clucking with professional horror and personal sentimentality. Her hand was still in his, unmoving, and in the subdued light she could see him sitting stiffly, chewing an unlighted cigar. His arm, she wailed, must ache abominably. "You poor darling, you go and rest now!"

His good-night was to kiss her drowsily closing eyes, unspeaking.

"And I used to think, in Feminist days," she brooded, as she floated into sleep, "that the whole physical side of love—kisses, caresses, little pattings—was vulgar, and suited only to high-school boys, milkmaids, soppy spin-

sters, people who sing about Moon and June and Spoon.
Holding hands? Banal! I was going to have a high spiritual
romance. Sit across from the well-beloved and discuss the
funding of municipal gas works, I suppose! I *have* a high
spiritual romance! And Barney's hand seems to me, this
particular day, like the sheltering hand of God!"

43

THE nurse-governess was excellent—Miss Gretzerel, a lively young woman from Switzerland, with a Swiss passion for languages, cleanliness, and children. The nursery was excellent—it was arranged for Mat himself, and not for the amusement of Mat's parent; it was free of all furniture save the crib and a bureau of small garments and two straight chairs; the walls were innocent of yellow ducks and tender mottoes and could be scrubbed ruthlessly. To them Ann had given rather more excitement and planning than the average jobless young mother with duties in the way of bridge and dancing.

Ten times a day she wanted to telephone from the Industrial Home to Miss Gretzerel, and didn't. No matter how seamed her mind was with the details and worries of work when she left the office, they were smoothed away as she realized, taking the subway, that she would see Mat now. As she reached the apartment, she invariably began to fear that something might have happened, and throwing her hat down in the hall anywhere, she tiptoed into the nursery as desperately as though it were the crisis of an illness.

She saw, immediately, that Mat was certainly the most beautiful, the strongest-backed, and the most precociously intelligent infant in the world. She tried not to tell people about it at dinner-parties, but she hugged to her heart the knowledge that this extraordinary child could fold its feet together like a kitten folding its paws, that at the age of three months he certainly recognized her, that his miniature nails were of a perfect almond shape, and that he never cried except for a reason.

Her one grief was that she could not nurse him after two months. With this she had to pay for being what the world quaintly considered a "free woman."

Russell was, apparently, as devoted to Mat as she was, and frequently she wished to Heaven he would be less devoted—as from time to time she had wished that he would be a little less everything. He brought in preposterous toys which the baby couldn't even see: lovely woolly lambs and puppies and pussies with their fluff filled with streptococci; funny little wooden bears, with which the baby banged his own forehead, to his belligerent and noisy astonishment. And Russell talked baby-talk—he gushed, "Izzums the littely, ittely, bittely?" and tickled the baby's feet. The fact that frequently the brat enjoyed this cuteness thoroughly and screamed with pleasure made it all the worse, and gave Ann her only moments of questioning whether Mat really was a Voltaire, and whether he really was Barney's child.

Finally, Russell, when not checked by public violence, tried to show the baby to visitors, after it had gone to sleep.

It was Miss Gretzerel who put a stop to this sacrilege.

But it was Ann who had devised the plot against the fond
ex-officio father.

The fascination of the baby's tininess, the adventure of
watching him grow, the old avowal that he should make
none of her mistakes and be cramped by none of her igno-
rances, the sweet, simple belief that he was much hand-
somer than any of the kodak pictures of other babies
which her friends showed her, these emotions, plus her
work, plus the increasing danger in seeing Barney, so
absorbed her that she was only a little annoyed and worried by Russell's growing determination that he would be
her lover again.

It had been part of Russell's general evasion of life not
to admit, except by fumbling hands in the darkness, that
there was such a thing as love's embraces. But now, in his
irritation, he grew verbal and specific enough. He reminded
Ann that he had been very generous in taking her back
and giving his name to a child who might not be his own.
He hinted that she was thinking about her lover and
possibly even sleeping with him. As all of this was absolutely true, it was hard for Ann, who did have a certain
equity of mind, to work up indignation in answering him.

She wanted to jam a suitcase full, take Mat under her
arm, and go off forever.

She couldn't, not with Mat.

And just now of all times, she could not go to Barney.
Aside from his position, his danger from investigators, he
was busy marrying off his older daughter. She was "doing
well for herself": marrying a boy who was going into the
diplomatic service, the son of a corporation counsel with
an estate on Long Island.

In the "society sections" of the New York Sunday
newspapers there were portraits of "Miss Sylvia Dolphin
—a lovely March bride."

Ann showed these to the highly interested Matthew
(when Russell and Miss Gretzerel were safely out of hearing) and pointed out, "That is your half-sister, Mat. Do
you recognize her in her new Lelong?"

Mat belched.

A horrible, perhaps childish fascination drew Ann to the
wedding. Anything related to Barney was so important.
She stood as far back as she could in the crowd alongside
the awning at St. Patrick's Cathedral, behind an old
Irishwoman shaped like the back of a taxicab, and saw
the procession come out.

Sylvia looked——

"Well, she looks like a bride. I don't think I ever did,"
thought Ann.

Her new husband——

"And he looks like a college man; let's see; just how am I
related to *him?*"

Then Barney came, to sub-Tammany cheers. She hadn't
realized that he was reasonably tall. Or was it just the
burnished top-hat, the morning-coat, sleek as a snakeskin,
the pale gloves, the spats as worn by the peerage, the gold-
headed stick? Ann gazed on him with fond, foolish adoration. "That's my man, there!" She longed to tell the bus-
bottomed Irishwoman about it.

But her lodestar was Mona, Mrs. Dolphin, the blameless innocent who to Ann had become "that damned
woman, that leech."

Yes—twisting a little, risking a little, Ann could, for

the first time, see Mona now, on the other side of Barney.

Well, and she was as cool and proud as she had been in the portrait on the turn of the stairs, and she wore superbly a long sable coat with a flaring high collar. Crystal—yes. But there was no inner light there, as the portrait-painter had feigned. She looked bleak. And her nose was sharper, her mouth thinner, than in the picture, and she was beginning to have altogether more of a mummy aspect.

"Graceful and dead, and Barney, the wild Fenian, has to live with her!" thought Ann.

On her way up in the subway—before she was restored to importance and Great Womanness by the adoration of Miss Feldermaus, the jealousy of Mrs. Keast, the demands of prisoners to see her and have their lives straightened up —in the stale subway air, crowded among people who flopped against her as the train took curves, a strap pulling her arm out of its socket, Ann saw the picture of the matter as it might have been described: The rich and powerful Judge Dolphin, with his beautiful wife, well-to-do in her own right, both of them fairly acceptable in that sound and beautiful society which could buy viscounts for daughters; these important people attending the marriage of their daughter to one who would presently be permitted to mix cocktails for third secretaries of Portuguese legations; and in the crowd, watching the proud procession, a working woman who was Barney's despised mistress. . . .

"But it isn't like that, Barney, is it? What would I do if it were, if Barney didn't love me? I think I would die. I think not even Mat would keep me living."

She worried it. Miss Feldermaus was surprised (though

philosophical) at her crossness in the matter of the canned string beans.

At four, Barney telephoned in one of his rôles, the Hebrew Protective Home for Delinquent Girls, hoping that Dr. Vickers would be able to look in at five and talk with one of their more difficult girls. "We have something interesting to show you," said the message.

The Hebrew Protective Home proved to be a speakeasy on Eighty-fourth Street, and though there were plenty of delinquent girls around, they were being treated only with cocktails.

Barney solemnly rose as Ann came in, assumed his top-hat with a stagy pat on its top, and turned round and round.

"Am I beautiful?" he demanded. "Do I look like the Duke of Westminster? You may never see me like this again."

"But why the splendor?"

"Don't you remember? I told you. Sylvia married to-day."

"Of course. I remember now. I'd like to have been there."

"Really? (Mike! Two side-cars!) I'd have seen you got an invitation if I'd ever supposed—— I thought perhaps you'd rather not meet Mona. You wouldn't like her! At least, I don't! But I am so sorry——"

"It doesn't matter. Probably I'd have leapt up, once I saw you as beautiful as this, and have tried to drag you from her."

"Come and do it, the next wedding! My other girl's engaged. Looking at you, my dear!"

That was the only time, even by inference, she had ever lied to Barney Dolphin.

Two aching people trying, in a sleazy illegal café, to be light and very humorous.

With Barney more nearly free, his daughter safely auctioned off, Ann began to be obsessed by the thought of fleeing to him from Russell's increasingly damp pawing. Russell became—oh, she was sorry, not angry at him; she knew that it was her own exasperating refusal that maddened him—but he became a lecherous hobbledehoy. He bolted into her bathroom when she was in the tub. He made feeble, embarrassing, smutty jokes. He (she was sure) deliberately punctured a hot-water bottle so that it flooded his bed, and made it an excuse for wanting to share her couch that night, and was not unreasonably tart when she suggested the davenport in the living-room "because she was so sleepy—just tonight—if you don't mind."

She did not defend herself.

"I sadly perceive," she thought, "that this much lauded business of preserving one's chastity can be much nastier and meaner than prostitution. I'm horrible to that poor man, and he's been as decent as ever he could be, and maybe just a little decenter. I must get out. How can I, with Mat? I must. Cottage in the suburbs; Gretzerel and Mat and I, with a five-dollar-a-week girl in to help get dinner and wash the dishes. I can afford that."

It was a rather jarring coincidence that the next evening, after a number of other pointed moral remarks, Russell wound up a spirited sermon with:

"And another thing. You think you're such a damned

good mother. Says you! I've listened to you. Confiding to the other old hens that you just *love* taking care of Mat (and I *still* don't like that name; 'Ward' would have been ever so much smarter and more original)—how you prefer taking care of him to bossing prisoners and addressing the Universal Meddlers' and Uplifters' Association! Sure! Your self-sacrificing devotion consists in paying Miss Gretzerel to do all the dirty work! For one thing, of course, if you had the *slightest* consideration for the good of our child, and not just for your own convenience and self-glory, we'd be planning to get a house in the suburbs, where he could have fresh air and quiet and build up decent nerves, instead of this stinking, noisy city!"

"But, Russell, when we were first married I wanted to get a house outside the city, and you insisted we needed the stimulus of the intellectuals——"

"Heh! 'Intellectuals!' You know one difference between you and me? I can grow. I discard worn-out ideas. There was a time when I thought business men were the bunk, a lot of nit-wits, and these 'intellectuals' had a corner on ideas. Well, I've learned different, and I tell you, I want Mat to be surrounded, as he grows up, with a lot of keen, practical, efficient people that do things, stock-brokers and dentists and advertising men and so on, like you'll get say in Mount Vernon or Cos Cob, and not by a lot of bums and radicals and mere theorists. Now I want you to listen to me—if you can for one moment forget how important you are! Next Sunday we're going to hire a car and drive up Westchester way and see what we might be able to do in the way of renting a suburban house."

"It will make it harder to see Barney, to live there,"

she was thinking, the while she said meekly, "I should be glad to."

Russell made a good deal of the fact that, purely on behalf of her and of his son Mat, he was paying twenty-five cents a mile for the limousine in which they had driven out to find among the higher-class suburbs of New York their Isle of Innisfree.

It was one year and two weeks since she had driven all the hours of darkness beside Barney Dolphin to the Valley of Virginia.

Russell talked about the Depression, train service from Mount Vernon, the amount of cod-liver oil Mat ought to have, the future of the Depression, and Pelham real estate as an investment. Ann sat bolt upright on the dove-gray upholstery and smoked too many cigarettes too rapidly.

They looked at a dozen respectable houses with two-car garages and the quietude that is afforded by nearness to a through highway. The houses cost from twenty thousand to thirty-five. None of them had more than twelve hundred square feet of lawn and a handsome pair of trees.

Now Russell, Ann knew, had saved ten thousand dollars; she (daughter of Waubanakee), for all her small salary and the enthusiasm with which reformed ex-prisoners borrowed, had by cheerful meannesses managed to pile up three thousand. That was all they had between them, she pointed out.

"But, good Lord, we don't have to pay the whole price down. Pay maybe five thousand, and take ten years to pay the rest."

She fell into such a panic as squeezes a first offender

when he hears the judge say, "Ten years hard labor." Was she going to be caught? Could Russell by some magic, by that sticky strength of the weak, trick her into this, so that for ten years she would have to stay with him, and help him pay, lest she be "letting him down after he had gone to work and taken the house just for her and her child"?

She could not see the trap. She could smell its wintry steel.

They did come, through a mistake in the card-listing of an otherwise reputable dealer, to one house she liked, near Scarsdale. Forlorn and shabby among the mansions, stucco and brick and hollow tile, Tudor Georgian and California Spanish and Evanston Colonial and Connecticut Swiss, there stood abashedly a farmer's cottage built in 1860, in an irregular, ragged, weedy lot, a quarter mile from any thoroughfare. The asking price was $5,000. The timbers were sound. It had a large living-room, a kitchen, no dining-room, running water but no bathroom, two large bedrooms, one small bedroom, and a Main Street porch looking down a valley filled with dogwood.

It was called Pirate's Head Cottage. When Ann asked for the story behind the name, the agent explained, "Oh. Well, that's what they've always *called* it, see?"

Ann calculated rapidly: a bedroom for Mat and the Gretzerel, one for herself, and a tiny coop for Barney— whether or not he used it all night was no one's business.

"This is such a sweet funny old place," she said.

"Why, you're crazy; aside from its being a wreck, not half enough room," said Russell.

The whole way home he talked approvingly of the most

machine-made house they had seen. It cost twenty-five
thousand, but they could pay for it in eight years. Ann
listened with the cold sweat of a man being taken to Sing
Sing, to the death-house.

She was, she told herself, "up against it." She must no
longer muddle along.

She could flee to Europe and the golden exile with Barney. He still had money enough, despite the Depression,
and almost daily he proposed flight. But they were too old
ever to become part of any European community. "We
should have met and thought of this when I was ten and
Barney twenty-four. Careless!" They would be permanent
tourists, pointless as eagles in a zoo. And Mat would never
strike roots anywhere; he would become a dilettante, a
shadow among feeble shadows, moving among American
countesses, and women whose one purpose in life was to
suck as much money as possible from the ex-husbands
whom they had divorced for the sake of alimony and the
ease of an existence without duty or pride or honor,
among imitation writers of imitation free verse, mysterious
colonels and doctors and marquises who had never quite
soldiered or practised medicine or been recognized by the
peerage, among waiters and riding-masters and gigolos,
quiet dipsomania and more than suspected cocaine—a
world that was in Europe yet never for a second European,
a world of loafers without grace, of gangsters without courage, of orchids faded brown. No! Better for Matthew even
Russell's bouncing moralities than this life of red-velvet
curtains gone threadbare and greasy.

Or she could definitely settle down to being Russell's

wife and lover by cultivating deafness and frigidity. But would it be good for Mat to have such a mother, bitter with sacrifice?

Or on her own, with Mat, she could face the loneliness of independence, with Barney as lover if he would stick it. But would he not weary of this hole-and-corner business? It was curious that, for all his political bargaining, his doubtful favors to acquaintances, his one-time fingering love-affairs, Barney was no intriguer, no amateur of bland secrecy. He had never hidden what he was. He was friend or foe outright. And how would this irregular alliance seem to Mat when he came to an age where he was conscious of his schoolmates' snickering gossip?

"In other words," said Ann, "whatever I do will be wrong, so why worry? And isn't it a bit naïve of you to assume that you can decide what you'll do? Of course you'll just drift on, and nothing will happen—nothing will ever happen."

On Friday, April 3, 1931, everything began to happen, all at once.

44

At 3 p. m. on Friday, April 3, Prisoner 3921, who was in the Industrial Home on charges of blackmail and selling drugs, and whom Ann sweetly believed to be cured now of heroin-using, was released with a reception in the office, during which Number 3921 (Sallie Swenson, Sarah Cohen, and Sue Smith were among her other names) drank tea and wept and gratefully received ten dollars, and said that Dr. Vickers was her benefactress, her inspiration, and, to all intents and purposes, her private saint.

At midnight, the same Friday, Sallie was arrested for assaulting the bouncer of a respectable, law-abiding speakeasy while in a great state of liquor, and on her way to the station-house in the patrol-wagon she smote a policeman with a rock mysteriously concealed in her bosom, and sang "Mademoiselle from Armentières" in the original version.

As there was no particular news in New York just then, a police-court reporter thought Number 3921 might make a good story, and talked to her. Sallie, Number 3921, had the jitters and a terrible case of remorse. She said that the whole trouble was that instead of being disciplined into goodness at the Industrial Home, whence she had just been released, she had been treated with such cowardly laxity that she had become rather of a naughty girl. Finding the reporter strangely interested and being fond of the male attention she had recently lacked, Sallie added that when she had been sent up, just for a little blackmail, she had been an innocent country girl who knew not the taste of alcohol or nicotine, to say nothing of drugs, and that she had learned to drink and smoke from the pampered women in prison.

The newspaper made a second-page spread of the story on Saturday morning, just in time to furnish meat for two worried though celebrated Manhattan preachers, neither of whom had, before reading the paper, any notion of what Message he was going to give the hungry congregation next day. But they had already announced the titles of their sermons, so that on Sunday morning, under the separate labels of "Gangsters and the Gospel" and "When Will the Judgment Day Be?" the two prophets delivered almost the same sermon, to the effect that the reason for the crime wave, as shown by the testimony of Miss Sallie Swenson, was that prisons had become such dens of luxury and indolence that criminals were no longer deterred from their nasty tricks by fear. One of the reverend experts on mercy advocated the resumption of lashing; the other brought out, as a new device, silent and solitary imprisonment for years, with nothing for the prisoners to do but read the Bible and think of their wickedness.

Ann laughed, reading these thunders on Monday morn-

ing. No one could take seriously these doctrines which had
been so fetching in the year 1800.

That afternoon she received an anonymous telegram:

See sermons revs ingold and snow today papers at last folks
getting on you wolf in sheeps clothes.

That morning there were nineteen abusive letters on her
desk at the Industrial Home, three of them anonymous.
The newspapers were trying to telephone to her even before
she had reached the office. She was touchy, ready for a
fight, but she decided—unwisely, no doubt—that the tact-
ful thing would be to avoid the reporters, to avoid publicity. She took the day off, spent it with Pat Bramble in
Connecticut, and did not return till midnight.

When she got the papers Tuesday morning she went insane right in the midst of the corn-flakes and cream. One
somewhat sensational paper, the *Banner*, had given an
entire page to the case of poor Sallie vs. the Industrial
Home, and headed it, "Do Palace Prisons Tempt to Vice
and Crime?" Several other preachers had rushed in to
save the nation. One said in an interview that he had authoritative information that in a "certain reformatory
for women criminals" the head of the institution smoked
cigarettes with the prisoners and was afraid to discipline
them. A Flatbush organization of women which had for
months been unable to get into the publicity, no matter
how many resolutions against Russia, whisky, atheism,
and mixed bathing it might pass, tried again, with a resolution condemning Ann and asking for an inquiry into the
Industrial Home by a committee to be appointed by the
Governor. This time they pulled it off. Their resolution

was printed in a box, surrounded with female portraits so blurred that the ladies might as well have been women ambulance drivers, the inner circle of Sappho, or members of the No. 3 Company of "They Do It in France." But they were asserted to be "prominent society women of Flatbush who protest against degeneracy of penal system."

Investigation by committee appointed by the Governor! Now, raged Ann, she really knew how Barney felt.

The kernel of the whole page was an interview with Ann's assistant, the good Sister Keast.

In the absence of Dr. Vickers, mysteriously summoned out of town, Mrs. Keast had admitted, said the reporter, that possibly they had been too easy on Miss Sallie Swenson. They were trying the experiment of loving the girls into goodness. Mrs. Keast herself did not agree with this method, having had an experience perhaps more diversified than most penologists. But her chief, Dr. Vickers, and the other members of the staff were such lovely people that she was willing to submerge her own practical experience and help them test their theories.

The dullest reader could see from the interview that if Mrs. Keast had her rights and were superintendent, she would put an end to all this nonsense, stop coddling these fiends, and make angels of them by such novel means as the dark cell, the cat, bread and water.

Ann went up the front steps of the Industrial Home like a cyclone. She was pushing Miss Feldermaus's button, and holding it down, before she took off her hat. "Send Keast in—quick!" Then, to the fish-mouthed assistant superintendent, "Keast, did you give out that interview in the *Banner?*"

"Oh, wasn't it dreadful! Of course I didn't give it! They sent a reporter here, and I told him I didn't care to talk to him, and all I said was that we were glad to experiment with new methods, and then he went and made all that out of it!"

"Keast, I was to go to Philadelphia today and speak at a women's club luncheon. I'll have you go for me, and you better start right now, this minute. You won't be able to get back till late this evening, so you needn't report till tomorrow morning. Here's the memo—the chairman's name and place of luncheon, and here's your ticket. You better skip, quick, and make the ten o'clock train. I'll phone 'em you're coming. *Feldermaus!* Get me this Philadelphia number here, quick! 'Bye, Keast."

Mrs. Keast out of the way, Ann was telephoning to a *Banner* reporter whom she knew as a devotee of Malvina. He asked someone who asked someone who asked someone else, and in fifteen minutes he telephoned Ann the information that Mrs. Keast herself had written the interview in the *Banner*. The reporter had added only a lead and two paragraphs of description.

Ann was in the prison, that day, for fourteen hours, from nine in the morning till eleven at night, and most of the time she spent at her desk.

When Miss Feldermaus dragged exhaustedly home at midnight, she informed the family, "Gee, what a day we got! But fun? Listen! I ain't see the Big Chief enjoying anything so much for months! She's been looking kind of down in the mouth, but today, baby, she was ole Mis' Dynamo herself, and did she eat up the fight—say, she was throwing somebody out of the twelfth story one per minute, and laughing all the time. Some day—and some boss! Gosh, I'd like to see that kid of hers! I'll bet he could take on Gene Tunney and Max Schmeling together, right now!"

And indeed all that day Ann was saying to herself, "Trying to *decide!* What idiocy! Of course it's been decided for me, as I knew it would be. Lone Ann and lone Mat together. And the Job, always. No husbands. . . . But I hope Barney will come sometimes and not hate me too much for being Ann Vickers again!"

She took out the dossier that she had been making on Mrs. Keast, pasted the *Banner* interview and annotations in it, and telephoned to the Governor, who had always been friendly to her, disposed to back her in any reform.

"I hear you are getting a little pounding today," said the Governor. "That's splendid! That puts you right in line for being Governor yourself some day."

"Heaven forbid! The prisoners have to stay and hear my speeches, Governor, but audiences might walk out on me. I want to read you a few facts about my assistant—and enemy—Mrs. Keast, who wants my job, and whose interview, which she wrote herself (I have the proof), will be used as the base of all attacks on me. . . . This Mrs. Keast is a cousin of Mick Denver, the Democratic ward leader; she is a sister-in-law of Walton Pybeck, the upstate Republican leader; they pooled and got her in here before I came. She was dropped at the end of her second year in a Chenango County high school for gross failure in examinations, and she's had no scholarly training of any kind since. She was in that horrible Fairlea Cottage Reformatory for Women, in the Northwest, when they had the awful

riot, and was accused of grafting on food and of hanging
up recalcitrants to a beam, with just their toes touching
the floor, so that one died; but they hushed it up and didn't
try her—just let her out, and she came back East." There
were a dozen more items in the dossier, then: "I've let her
stay here, watching her every second, so she could do no
harm, because it kept the politicians' hands off my sheep-
fold and let me go ahead. Now I'm going to fire her. If she
balks, I'll make these charges. She doesn't know how much
I know, I'm sure. What I want is, will you back me up?"

"You're sure of all your items? You can prove them?"

"Yes, documents, and I have the names and addresses
of witnesses."

"Then I'll back you. Good luck, Doctor."

"Thanks, Governor."

"I wish," reflected Ann, "that I could call him 'Your
Excellency' and make it sound right. But I'm afraid I'm
not a good Excellency-caller. . . . Feldermaus! Get me the
Hudson and Inland Realty Company, Yonkers. Hustle!"

To the real estate agent who had accompanied Russell
and herself through Westchester, she murmured, "Dr.
Vickers speaking—Stuyvesant Industrial Home. You
showed me some houses. Eh? Yes, if you insist, I am also
Mrs. Russell Spaulding. You remember that small old
house on the edge of Scarsdale—Pirate's Head Cottage?
No, I don't *want* a larger house. But I don't care a damn—
pardon me, I mean—well, that's what I really do mean,
I don't care a *damn* about tiled baths, and gas garbage-
incinerators. You asked five thousand for Pirate's Head.
What's the very lowest price the owner would take? Eh?
Oh, nonsense!" (And she had been so meek, that Sunday;

such a Mrs. Russell Spaulding!) "I'll consider paying thirty-six hundred—twenty-five hundred down, and the other eleven hundred in two years. Yes, you take it up with the owners and tell them to make up their minds quick or I'll withdraw the offer. Eh? Oh, nonsense; nothing is selling now, with this Depression; they're lucky to get any offer."

She wanted to sing.

"I have a home for Mat and me! And maybe Barney will come sometimes on a Sunday. . . . Let's see; when Malvina comes, I'll take the little room and give her my big one. When Barney comes—— Precisely!"

The Hebrew Protective Home for Delinquent Girls called up and said, surprisingly, "This press stuff bother you—anything I can do? Fine!"

The next telephone call, in a tired dragging voice, was, "Ann? This is Pearl—Pearl McKaig. I take back what I said—some of it! I'm glad you're getting pounded by the reactionaries. Maybe it'll bring you back to us, dear. Good luck, you darn old Liberal!"

While she was calling up the newspapers, all of them, speaking now brusquely, now with a quite false jollity, she was already planning the restoration of Pirate's Head; the lawn with daffodils scattered through it for spring, and a small garden of zinnias and dahlias and hyacinths edged with violas, and one bed devoted to the unfashionable flower she best loved—the cat-faced loyal pansy. While she snapped at city editors or cajoled them, she was adding to the cottage a bathroom (but only one, with white pine wainscoting and no vain tiles), and deciding on old-fashioned wallpaper for the living-room, and a white mantelpiece. . . . "Let's see—that little shop in New

Canaan—pick up an old mantel quite cheap—— Hello, yes, yes. This is Dr. Vickers of the Stuyvesant Industrial Home speaking, and I want to talk to the managing editor, at once—Dr. *Vickers*."

She was inviting every newspaper in town to send a reporter (preferably female, but she did not insist) to prowl through the Industrial Home, to talk with any inmate or guard, unsupervised, and to get the truth, in answer to the sermons and the patriotic ladies of Flatbush.

They came. She received them not too effusively. She asked them only, "Do you prefer to go through by yourself or with a guard?"

When they had finished they assured her that they were her partisans, and when could she have lunch with them?

She breathed easy then, and had a moment to give to the question of old rag-carpeting on the stairs of Pirate's Head.

The Hudson and Inland Realty Company telephoned back that she could have the cottage on her own terms.

She telephoned to Flatbush and invited the executive committee of the "club of prominent society women" to tea.

She made notes on the not very promising possibility of getting Jessie Van Tuyl, once felon and saint at Copperhead Gap, now conducting a college for working women in Detroit, as her assistant superintendent.

The last of the reporters left the Industrial Home at eleven at night, and Ann kissed Miss Feldermaus, apologized, "I've driven you to death today, you poor darling!" and went home herself, so happily that (after she had crept in for a glimpse of Mat, asleep with his fists belligerently clenched) she was very kind and jolly with Russell, with the result that she had to lock her door and listen from behind it to furies which, she admitted, were completely justified. She got up early, Wednesday morning, to enjoy the corrections about the Industrial Home in the press, and the first headlines she saw were in the *Recorder*, first page, first column, top of column:

TWO JUDGES ARE INDICTED
BY NEW YORK GRAND JURY
FOR RECEIVING BIG BRIBES

JUSTICES BERNARD DOLPHIN AND HENRY SIEFFELT
ACCUSED OF CROOKED VERDICT IN
QUEENS SEWER CASE

SECRET SESSION OF GRAND JURY STUDIES DATA
OF INVESTIGATION AND MAKES
SURPRISE REPORT

Ann had a notion that there were favorable accounts of the Industrial Home in all the papers. She did not read them. She never did read them.

45

Wᴵᴛʜ Malvina Wormser beside her, holding her hand and purring with sharp little indignations, Ann sat through all four days of the People vs. B. D. Dolphin. She neglected her own fight. She rather wished that Mrs. Keast would attack her now. It would be a relief to have someone like the Keast to slaughter.

The two women were supposed to be, they supposed themselves to be, good feminists, righteous citizens, honest members of the working class, and they were choking with loyalty to a man who, as the trial went on in that dreary and unaired courtroom, appeared to have been a complaisant crook.

Not at first, not till she had noticed on one wall the stain shaped like a map of Africa, did Ann perceive that it was in this same courtroom that she had seen Judge Bernard Dow Dolphin in silken robe nodding to the people who rose in reverence at his entrance. Another judge, in another silken robe, sat at the same high desk below the twin golden fasces which symbolized the sanctity of the Law, and they all rose to *his* entrance, they were all satisfied now with *his* inviolable wisdom.

For a second, when she had first entered, Ann had thought that the new judge was Lindsay Atwell. He was not. But, "That's all it lacks of being the perfect irony," she raged.

She looked little at the judge. She saw the back of Barney's head as he sat, apparently indifferent, near the counsels' table; she saw the rigid profile of Mona Dolphin, to one side in the front row, and the gum-chewing jaws of the jurymen, lords yesterday of groceries and garages, lords today over a man's honor.

The case was dismayingly simple. The contractors for certain extensive sewers had let out a part of the work to sub-contractors, who had later sued for more payment. Barney, presiding in the case, had persistently ruled for the prime contractors, and after it had been made a director of the firm. At this time also he had deposited one hundred thousand dollars which he could not or would not explain.

It was a weary recital of figures, dull to listen to—altogether as dull and as fatal as cancer.

But Ann was neither dull nor weary on the second afternoon, when she glanced back and found Russell Spaulding sitting in court, glaring. She whispered to Malvina, "Oh, God, there's Ignatz! Don't come out with me." She tried to look at once casual and wifely as she joined Russell at the closing of court, sweetly murmuring, "Curious case. But I didn't know you were interested, Ignatz."

Russell merely grunted, and they moved into the marble corridor. He had said only, "See here!" when Barney and Mona were suddenly on them, and Barney halted, checking his wife by seizing her arm. Mona stared, unsmiling;

Russell stared, frowning; Ann guessed that she herself
looked like a schoolgirl caught with her sweetheart; only
Barney seemed cheerful and unembarrassed.

"Oh, Mona, this is Dr. Vickers, head of the Stuyvesant
Industrial Home, women's reformatory. She's a good cus-
tomer for the ladies I send up . . . did send up. Dr. Vickers,
my wife."

"And this is my husband, Russell Spaulding, Judge."

"I think we met once at Dr. Wormser's," said Barney.

"Did we? I don't recall it," said Russell, as offensively
as possible.

Mona Dolphin stated condescendingly, in an imitation-
Mayfair accent, "But I thought the Judge said your name
was Dr. Vickers, Mrs. Spaulding."

"It is. I keep my maiden name in my work."

"Oh? Rully? Very interesting. How did you happen to
leave medical work?"

"I'm not that kind of doctor."

"Oh. Are there other kinds? Very interesting. I really
think we must hurry now, Bernard. Good-day. Charmed-
metyou,msure."

And Russell and Ann were alone in the corridor. Ann had
seen Malvina scuttling off, fleeing the typhoon.

Ann started toward the stairs.

"You *wait!*" snarled Russell. "There's a couple of
things we're going to get straight, and right now, this
minute, before you have the chance to think up any new
lies! This crook Dolphin been your lover?"

"Why 'been'? Is!"

"Oh. so you're not going to lie, this time! Well, it's

been, not *is*, now! I absolutely and finally forbid you to see him again, any time, anywhere, and that includes coming to any more of this disgusting trial, to yearn over your pet grafter and bribe-taker! Understand?"

"Oh, yes." Now Ann did sound weary. "Very well. I'll be out of your flat before midnight, I and Mat and the Gretzerel, and this time, of course, it's for keeps."

"But, Ann, Ann! I don't want you to, don't want you to go, and especially I don't want Mat to go! I love Mat! No matter if possibly he might not be my son—but he is!"

Russell was frankly weeping, regardless of a gaping police sergeant who lumbered past.

With Mat and the nurse, she was in a hotel before midnight.

Mona's daughters were with her on the last day of the trial. They were as still and cold and hawk-nosed as their mother. "How they'll hate me when they know!" thought Ann. She shivered. But she made little of them; she was too intently studying the faces of the jury during the concluding speeches of defense and prosecution, clutching Malvina's hand in despair as she saw dull eyes, bored yawning, aching shoulders rubbing against the backs of the jurymen's chairs.

"They'll never see it—that Barney isn't *like* that—that at worst he just played the game as his organization did—that he needed money for his accursed crystal virgins, not for himself—that if he did anything wrong, he never will again—oh, I could choke them—they'll never understand him," agonized Ann . . . the feminist, the professional social worker, the expert criminologist.

Feverishly she watched the foreman, a fat, contemptuous man who chewed segments of a cigar.

When Barney's chief counsel, summing up Barney's own testimony, repeated that his client "could not reveal the source of the hundred thousand which he banked at the time of the suit between the contractors, because it would disclose an important and perfectly ethical real estate deal, and not only embarrass his partners in the deal but actually ruin them, so that this bold and determined silence on the part of Judge Dolphin reveals him not, as the prosecution has so causelessly hinted, as a plotter and taker of bribes, but as a man of such high honor that he would suffer any obloquy, any unjust punishment, rather than betray his associates in negotiations of which the very essence was a perfectly proper secrecy"—when the learned advocate had thus appealed to his friends the jurymen, with a brow of alabaster innocence and eyes of hurt tenderness, Ann saw the foreman shake his head a little and, champing the juicy cud of cigar, grunt cynically. When the prosecutor roared "the more competently Mister Dolphin's vast array of the highest legal talent demonstrate the man's former learning, subtlety, and seemingly unimpeachable position, the more inescapable do they make the conclusion that there can be no temporizing with his present obvious guilt"—then the foreman nodded and spat.

The judge was brief, mild, generous, and generally damning. The case was given to the jury at noon.

Ann tried to get herself to go away till they should return. This, Malvina assured her, would be very wise for both of them. So they stayed in the corridor, wearily, ambling up and down with sore feet, slipping out for a malted-milk-egg at a drug-store and, in panic, dashing back before the drink was finished.

Barney had come out with Mona and his daughters, still-faced and waiting as they; he had brightened at sight of Ann and Malvina and come resolutely to them. "Don't worry. I know what the verdict is—being, you know, a highly trained jurist. It will be 'guilty'!"

Mona and the daughters, twenty feet away, were staring at Ann through imaginary lorgnons.

Ignoring Malvina, recklessly, Barney growled, "Oh, God, Ann, if I could just go off with you for one more week-end, I wouldn't mind the five years they'll give me in Manawassett Penitentiary! I suppose I must get back to my family. . . . Ann!"

She watched Barney and his women drift off to some haunt downstairs.

Malvina said suddenly, "I suppose Barney *is* guilty?"

"Yes, I suppose so—technically."

"Well——"

That was the entire conversation on the ethics of the matter between Dr. Wormser and Dr. Vickers.

Ann looked at a clock. She was certain that an hour and a half had passed since the jury had gone out.

It had been exactly twenty-five minutes.

She might call on Lindsay—on Judge Atwell. Yes, she might do that. Be a good idea. Kill time. And be courteous. Yes, might do that. . . . Oh, by and by; not quite yet.

"We might walk around the park," said Malvina.

"Yes. Might."

They did not move toward the stairs.

They sat on a wide window ledge.

"I really ought to dash uptown and see a patient and come back," said Malvina.

"Oh."

Malvina did not go.

Thirty-one minutes had passed.

When an hour had got itself by, and they had made a raid on the drug-store and returned, Ann mumbled, "I'm just going to explore this building a few minutes. You wait here." She had to be alone. If she were alone, she would be able to think of something bright and helpful to do.

She didn't. She continued to feel as helpless in the express-train of the Law as Lil Hezekiah in the hands of Cap'n Waldo.

Then she saw Barney and his women. They were seated in an otherwise empty courtroom, their backs to the half-open door. As Ann stared in—not quite realizing that she was eavesdropping, so much a part of this family did she feel herself—she heard Mona's high, even voice saying, "The girls and I will do the *real* suffering—have to face the disgrace you've brought on us, while you'll be safely hidden away. But we'll be waiting to take up our cross when you come out, and try to be as forgiving——"

"Yeah?" said Barney coarsely.

Ann fled.

The jury came in at seven minutes after four. The courtroom filled so quickly, so confusingly, that Ann was separated from the comfort of Malvina and jammed in beside Mona, with Barney on Mona's other side.

"How say you, guilty or not guilty?" buzzed the clerk.

The foreman grunted, "Guilty."

Ann looked at Mona. Her lips were moving. She was praying. Ann looked at Barney. He was praying. But she little noticed it, for she herself was praying.

As two deputies came from behind the rail, Barney rose, nodded to them, and walked forward to sit between them, a convicted felon.

The judge did not delay pronouncing sentence. He had apparently long been ready. He wound up his lofty sermon:

". . . that you may repent and if possible obtain forgiveness, that thinking on it day after day you may realize that never was a crime committed with so little justification, I sentence you to six years at hard labor."

They were leading Barney through a back door. Ann *had* to run to him, to say good-bye. And she couldn't. In desperation, in agony, unconscious of what she was doing, of everything save that this woman beside her was also a part of Barney and he of her, she grasped Mona's hand.

Mona snatched her hand free, sprang up, and stared down at Ann, moaning "Oh!" as though she had stepped on a rattlesnake. She pushed her way out of the courtroom, while Ann sat hunched, all pride, all dignity, all courage gone from her.

46

D<small>R. ANN VICKERS</small> was discharging (but she said "firing") her assistant, the good Mrs. Keast.

"I'm giving you a chance to resign—to put it as cowardly bosses always do, Keast. If you don't, I'll break you. You have plotted against me ever since I came here. I don't think you have done any actual financial grafting. You have merely tried to cut my throat. So if you'll just sign this—it's your resignation, and very well and modestly put, as I know, because I wrote it."

"You think you can get away with this, Miss Vickers! I have friends——"

"Yes, I know; you met State Senator O'Toolohan at eleven o'clock last night at his house. No, I haven't employed a private dick, but I have some good friends among the city cops. I have, I guess, every detail of your plotting written down—and I don't keep the original dossier here in my office, either, so there's no use your going on trying to find the combination to my private safe, evenings after I'm gone!"

"You—— Now, you look here, Miss Vickers——"

"Dr. Vickers, please!"

"—I don't care a hang what you may think you've got on me. But what I've got on you! Wouldn't you look just dandy, *Doctor* Vickers, *Superintendent* Vickers, Mrs. Spaulding, or whatever your name may be, if it were to come out that you were the mistress of a crooked judge that's doing time in Manawassett? Go ahead! Have me up on charges, and see what charges come out against you! Resign I won't!"

"Keast, that shows you never did understand. I don't care one damn what you charge me with. I don't care whether I lose my job here, so long as I get rid of a cancer germ like you. I wouldn't a bit mind going into business and making money—as I can. . . . By the way, why was it they didn't indict you for murder when the girl you hung up by the thumbs at Fairlea Cottage Reformatory died? Do you happen to have been informed that the attorney general that protected you died two months ago? Well, let's stop this squabbling. Sign here, and we'll be good friends and no backbiting."

Mrs. Keast signed.

Ann was at her desk, drawing labyrinths on the blotter, and meditating, "Beastly! You, the melodramatic! Is that how you have to control your staff? Cheap melodrama!

"No! I won't apologize to myself! Melodrama does happen, these days. Hijackers murdering bootleggers. Premiers assassinated. Aviators crashing on cottages and burning up the old ladies in them. Babies kidnaped and murdered. Kings kicked out of their country and starving in cheap hotels. Methodist bishops accused of stock-gambling and rigging elections. Billionaires committing suicide and proving to have been forgers. Five-year-old boys in nice suburbs playing gangster and killing three-year-old boys—and gangsters, fresh from taking people for a ride and shooting them, dashing home to take pansies to their dear old mammies on their birthdays. A skinny little Hindu that drinks only goat's milk baffling the whole British Empire. Fourteen-year-old negro boys condemned to death for rape they didn't commit, and supreme court justices solemnly affirming the sentence. Submarines that won't come up and aëroplanes that won't stay up. Hundred-story buildings and fifteen-year-old boys driving gasoline locomotives on public highways at seventy miles an hour and some days actually not killing anybody. A nation of one hundred and twenty million people letting a few fanatics turn it from beer to poison gin. Known murderers walking the streets, dining with judges. British peers going to prison for fraudulent company reports. And I don't think I could quite last through this incredible melodrama of Barney's being in prison if I weren't a little melodramatic with Keast.

"I wish she did dare attack me. I'd be proud to have the world know he is my lover!"

She visited Manawassett State Prison.

To her, the prison expert, there was nothing horrifying in the somber walls that, like a tomb for the living dead, towered up to cut the rack of July thunderclouds; nothing intimidating in the guards outlined atop the walls with rifles crooked in their arms; but little terror in the thought that Barney was penned there, a criminal, a convict. She had known too many convicts to consider most of them as in any way different from her other friends. But the old perception of the utterly fat-headed futility of the whole business came to her anew; the childish belief of that super-cry-baby, the state, that stone walls, steel-barred gates, bad food, and the supervision of guards too stupid to become trolley conductors, were magically going to teach loyal gangsters like Barney Dow Dolphin to become sing-leaders in the Y. M. C. A.

She sent in her official card and was welcomed by the warden in his office. On the way there, she did have one qualm of terror for Barney as she looked down a cell corridor and caught the old stink of disinfectant, cockroaches, cheap food, and vomit, which in the decency of the Industrial Home she had almost forgotten.

The warden was an acquaintance, and better than his prison. They had stood together at prison conferences, fighting against capital punishment, fighting for more parole and better paid parole-officers and more prison education. "This is a grand surprise, Dr. Vickers! Would you like to see our shop?"

"Later I would, but—— It's probably a little irregular, but I want to talk with Judge Dolphin, privately."

"Um. Yes. Against the rules. He's supposed to see visitors in the visitors' room, but as you and I are fellow scrappers, I think I can fix it. . . . See him here. . . . I have to be away for half an hour, anyway. You won't be disturbed."

She wondered how much the warden knew, but she wondered it carelessly, without apprehension. Of only one

thing in her life could she never be ashamed—of her devotion to Barney.

The warden summoned Barney (and that was a gloomy
enough moment for Ann, when he said to a guard, "Send
in Number 37,896") and left her there, the door open on
the outer office, where worked half a dozen prisoner clerks
in dolorous baggy gray uniforms. Ann heard the outer door
open, saw the clerks look up, heard them call out, "Why,
it's the dear old judge, the bastard that sent me up, and
now look at him!" and "Good-morning, Your Dishonor!"
and "Oh, baby, you certainly don't look like a jedge
now; you look like a hijacker!" and, simply and sweetly,
"You sanctimonious crook!" Barney hurried into the
private office, his head down, not seeing her. He too was in
drab and shapeless gray; he was unshaven; his hands were
calloused and dirty. When he looked up, he grunted with
surprise. "Oh! They didn't tell me!" He closed the door,
stood hesitating. Then her arms were round him, his head
was heavy on her shoulder, and they were babbling in the
terror of ecstasy.

"I'm going to wait for you, Barney, and teach Mat
that you're coming back. I'm going to make all the money
I can. I'm going to have Pirate's Head ready—if you
should want to come!"

"God knows I'll want to come, fast enough, but look
here, Ann; you don't want Mat to have a scoundrel for a
father."

"But he already has that scoundrel for a father! And he
isn't a scoundrel!"

"Oh, yes I am—I was good and plenty guilty, at least

technically, and a man who is egotistical enough to be willing to take any high position, whether it's judge or senator or surgeon or bishop, has no right to make even technical errors. I deserve it. Look here!"

Barney sat opposite her. It hurt more than his ragged face, more than the smut on the plump suave hands of which he had once been proud, to see how timidly he sat far forward in the chair. And he did not as of old speak coolly, but too eagerly, like one who has thought it out in solitude and who longs to get in all the explanation he can before his auditor becomes bored:

"I think I would have given the same decision in that sewer case even if they hadn't 'expressed their appreciation,' as they called it—I *think* I would. And I considered myself superior to a good many other judges. No one ever succeeded in bribing me to give a decision I thought was wrong—and you can't ever have any idea how often they tried, in this blessed era of racketeering. No bootlegging combination ever got me to let off a crook or a murderer, or to prevent the parole board from sending a man that had broken parole and was going on racketeering back to stir.

"But I know now that I was that worst of weaklings, a middle of the roader, a compromiser. I haven't turned moral; I've just turned realistic. I should either have been an out-and-out perfectionist, who wouldn't take as much as a five-cent cigar from anyone connected with any case, or else an out-and-out grafter, frankly saying that most occupations today, from selling toothpaste to preaching radio sermons, are just grafts, and a man is a fool that doesn't take all he can get. I wasn't either. I was respectable . . . and played billiards with the known mouthpieces for big shots and, like so many Pure Citizens, I had for bootlegger a known murderer. I wasn't either wolf or wolfhound. That's what makes me sick: the weakness and cautiousness of it. That's what I want to repair, when I get out. I want to be either a racketeer or a saint—so far as Old Man Mat Dolphin's son can be a saint. And if you really can wait for me (oh, God, I hope you will—but you mustn't, for your own sake—but I hope you will!) and if you do wait, I'll have to take a shot at the sainthood. You have leanings that way yourself, except for your slight tendency to illegitimate children—you darling!"

"I'll wait! I'll be at the prison door! Try and lose me!"

"You know, I won't have much money left—this Depression and everything. I did make a trust fund that will take care of Mona and the girls. Needn't ever think of them again. But for us and Mat—not so good. I may have ten thousand saved out of the wreck. We could go West and get a farm or something, but the isles of Greece, the isles of Greece, where burning Sappho loved and sung, I'm afraid we'll never see them."

"A lot I care! I want to see just one thing—you playing with Mat, even if I am a Professional Woman—a prison-keeper! Oh, it gets me every day now; it wrenches me, like labor pains, to think of myself as a keeper of prisons and you as a prisoner!"

"There is one curious thing—going back to what I was saying about being such a good judge. Now that I'm one of them and like 'em (even the dear little teases that ride me about having been a judge, and God knows I don't blame 'em for it)—I see what decent fellows a good share of the convicts are, and I realize that when I felt most severe and righteous and gave the stiffest sentences, then I was most vicious, perhaps, and when I was unethically sentimental and easy, perhaps I was nearest to dealing out justice. I never thought I'd be a jailbird. I never thought I'd be desperately in love with an intelligent woman. I never thought I'd question the supreme power of judges to decide whether certain circumstances demanded that a man should spend eight or ten or fifteen years in a moldy hell. Apparently, I just never thought. . . . Oh, I babble on! I've been silent, in cells, these two months! Tell me more about Mat, more about you, more—more!"

"Your poor hands—they look so ragged. You ought to be in one of the offices or in the library."

"No. I was offered both. I felt it was kind of a graft. I want to do penance. I'm sewing gunny sacks. It doesn't help much! Penance! I used to talk to people about that. Self-conscious, unnatural, priest-made self-righteousness! Still, I don't want any favors. I can take whatever they give me. In fact, the only graft I want now is to see you as often as I can. Quick! Somebody coming!"

One terrible kiss before the warden came in.

She saw him once a month, then, and each month was longer, and six years seemed hysterically intolerable, and in her hair the gray was thick.

47

Aɴɴ was astonished to discover how much money she could make when, for the first time in her life, she gave attention to this dull art. She concluded that the chief quality of millionaires was not their orderly planning, their gift of selecting assistants, nor their imaginative forecasting of the world's future needs in such fascinating matters as gasoline and pocket-flasks and oatmeal in red packages, but just their being stupid enough to want to sacrifice living to money-making.

She was going to have a place for Barney, for Mat.

She lived now in an apartment larger than her old hotel suite, but less fashionable and cheaper. Her sole luxuries were the nurse for Mat, and his milk, his white woolly suits. She had bought Pirate's Head but (naturally) she had found that to furnish it and put in a bathroom and comb the disorderly yard cost enormously more than she had expected.

She had been easy meat for club secretaries who wrote, "We do so long to have you address us but just this year I am afraid our exchequer is rather low and we shall not be able to pay you anything but expenses." Now she had a lecture agent with no illusions about the preferability of credit to cash, and two or three nights a week she was in forums or clubs or churches from Hartford to Baltimore, lecturing at from fifty to a hundred and fifty dollars a time, on practically all known subjects connected with criminals, feminism, education, and a vague mystical topic called "psychology."

Through Malvina Wormser she was offered the chance to write a syndicated newspaper department called "Keeping Girls from Going Wrong." It made her fairly sick. She was never quite able to determine whether Barney's decision in the sewer case or her syndicated gush was the more criminal, but on hot evenings late that summer, when Barney had been in prison for three months, then on effervescent September Sunday mornings when she longed to pick up Mat and flee to the hills of Westchester, then on winter nights when the flat grew frigid after midnight and she sat working with a coat over her bathrobe and a flannel nightgown, she toiled on answers (and sometimes, when the genuine crop was scanty, on both questions and answers) to working girls, small-town girls, or frightened women, who wanted to know how to love and be safe, whether a sober lover was preferable to a drunken husband, how to become human again after having been dehumanized by a "reformatory," and whether silk stockings always led to the gallows.

There were in Ann's manner of writing no *fines herbes*, neither tarragon nor chervil. It was the honest corned-beef hash of literature. But she was so much in earnest, she labored so ceaselessly, that she impressed some scores of thousands from Bangor to San José, and certainly she did win that sure proof of achievement, the disapproval of her acquaintances.

Russell, calling up (in vain) to invite himself to her apartment, ended a rather tart colloquy with, "You know what gives me a laugh? The way you jumped me for being mercenary when I went into business, and then you turning out this wishy-washy rot for the newspapers!" Pearl McKaig telephoned to say that Ann was by her articles in no way contributing to the Five-Year Plan of the U. S. S. R. But Malvina, whose taste in literature was that of a rabbit, said, "Grand stuff, darling, and often I think it probably means something." And Barney, whose taste was excellent (his favorite authors being Herman Melville, Samuel Butler, Saki, and P. G. Wodehouse)—Barney never saw the articles, never knew.

She developed a sneaking habit of going into tourist agencies, railroad offices, land bureaus, to filch pamphlets advertising Western orchards and ranches. They resembled a Pentecostal preacher's descriptions of Heaven. Every day Ann saw herself with Barney and Mat in a cherry orchard in the Santa Clara Valley or an apple orchard on the Columbia River. She reveled in violently colored pictures of mountains and bridle trails, or bungalows deep in orange groves. But she was no great amateur of scenery for its own sake, and she saw it always as a background, brilliant and quiet and secure, for her man, her child.

With these tasks she had one other. She shopped constantly and unscrupulously for pardon for Barney. She pushed herself into membership on a State Federation of Women's Clubs committee of prison inspection, which necessitated her seeing the Governor's advisers often, and cunningly (or so she hoped) she brought in the name and virtues of Barney and what seemed to her the fact that just to be convicted was sufficient punishment for such a man.

On the committee she was aware that the Great Woman, Dr. Ann Vickers, was not quite so reputable a character as formerly. They respected her knowledge, but they watched her. She was aware that though she had silenced Mrs. Keast, there must be wandering rumors about her "moral character." She, the Sunday school girl of Waubanakee, the Y. W. C. A. virgin of Point Royal, did not care a hang, providing she could keep some semblance of virtue till Barney should be freed.

Hardest of all, hard almost as seeing Barney led out a prisoner, was interviewing Judge Lindsay Atwell for him.

She had encountered Lindsay three times in the four years since they had broken off, and always casually, at receptions or committee meetings; they had politely asked after each other's spouses and lied suitably in answer and in general been damnably cordial.

She telephoned, and called at his office, a few feet from the place of horror where they had broken Barney . . . where Barney had broken so many others.

Lindsay was thinner and grayer and most worn, like an old greyhound.

"This is a great pleasure, Ann—if I may still call you that?"

"Of course, Lindsay. Always, I hope."

"You look extremely fit. And your husband is well?"

"You mean Russell?"

"Why—why——"

"Of course. Silly of me—absent-minded of me. Well, to be frank, I have broken with Russell. Haven't even seen him for a good many weeks."

"Oh, I *am* sorry!"

"Don't be! I'm not at all sorry. We parted in quite a friendly way, you know; just found we couldn't get along."

"Oh, yes. Yes. But your baby—I hear you have a baby —I was highly pleased, Ann, and, need I say, envious? I'm sorry to say I don't quite remember whether it is a boy or a girl. . . ."

But they had talked polite imbecilities for only ten minutes when she blurted, "Lindsay, I want your influence for something that is very important to me; very close to my heart, if you won't think I'm too sentimental. I want to get a pardon for Judge Bernard Dolphin."

Lindsay was rigid. "Dolphin? But why are you interested in him?"

"He's a great friend of—uh, of Malvina Wormser, and so, of course, of mine."

"I should have thought his only friends, if he has any left—you must pardon my cynicism, but you see I *know* him!—I should think they'd be only ward politicians and bootleggers."

"But you can't know him! He had—or has—one great vice that was also a great virtue: his loyalty to whatever group he happened to be in. He played the game, as they say."

"And as they say, my dear Ann, it was a very bad game! I wonder if you can understand how very much the honor of the Bench means to me? You mustn't consider me too narrow or severe if I say that I regard Dolphin much as you used to regard that despicable warden, or whatever he was—you used to call him 'Cap'n' something—at Copperhead Gap. I think you know the depth of my esteem, and I will even say affection for you. In all humility I acknowledge that when we used to see each other—and it has been my timidity rather than my lack of desire that has prevented my endeavoring to see more of you—but as I say, in those days it was always you who upheld a higher and more passionate standard of social ethics than I was capable of. But now—— Absolutely no. I shall never do anything, in word or deed, to shorten the highly merited punishment of this man who sinned against the temple he was, by his very office, serving."

"Damn his purity! Damn his virtue! That man hasn't enough blood in his veins to be tempted! And most specially and particularly damn his rounded periods!" thought Ann in the subway.

But she was feeble and incompetent in her cursing, and she was taking refuge in it only to conceal her dreary certainty that Barney would go on shut off from life, shutting her off from life, for all his sentence.

And the next month, which was April, two years since she had been with him in the Valley of Virginia, eleven months since his conviction, she thought so often of suicide that only the presence of Mat, his funny grins, his funny swift crawling, his chuckle of "Mama," kept her from that escape.

It was hot, for May, and that evening Ann's newspaper work seemed intolerable, her flat seemed intolerable. The flat was on 108th Street, not too far from Central Park for Mat to enjoy the luxury of grass and trees and air; yet it was over toward the East River, in a district of fire-escapes with crusted black paint, breweries, coal-and-ice dealers in swarthy basements, kosher butchers, Hungarian coffee-rooms and, among the gaunt gray tenements, an occasional frame cottage left from a hundred years ago. It had not quite become a slum, but it was distinguished from slumhood mostly by the fact that it was less cheerful. No shawled Jewish mothers sat on doorsteps chattering; the children who littered the streets, playing ball, falling under grumbling trucks, were less gay than the starveling gipsies of the slums. But they were loud enough, and on this hot evening, when all the windows were open, the children's shrieking was to Ann like an ache pounding inside the top of her head. She stood on the flimsy fire-escape balcony, smelling the fried fish, the cabbage, the dampness from laundries.

In the long four years yet that Barney must stay in prison, even with time off for good behavior, would her relationship to him become known, so that she would lose face, lose her job, have to take what work she could, in this time of unemployment? For suddenly the precariousness of jobs was terrifying hundreds of thousands of independent feminists who had been able to say airily, "Oh, to thunder with my husband and my father, yes, and the boss, too.

After all, you know, I can always wait on table!" They could not wait on table, now. They could not be airy. It was a beautiful time for male bosses—except that they were likely to lose their own jobs.

Would Mat, fresh now and pink and undefiled, have to play down there with the others, among the dust-heaps and torn papers and garbage cans?

She was conscious of a knocking at the outer door of her living-room. Her apartment house still kept up some claim to selectness by having a hall-man, but he wasn't much of a hall-man; neither rage nor tipping had ever persuaded him that he must telephone about visitors; and every manner of peddler, beggar, solicitor for dubious charity, came knocking. She sighed, went in to her desk, and picked out on her typewriter, ". . . so girls who feel they must revolt against their parents might try reading that famous old play *King Lear* before they decide——"

The knock again, and her careless "Oh, come *in*." No apparent response. She looked up. Barney Dolphin was in her doorway.

She gaped. She sat panting, loose-lipped. Then life exploded, and she knew that it was Barney, and she had run to him, wailing, had pulled him into the apartment. She locked the door. He might be an escaped prisoner! She pushed him down into a chair and knelt by him, her arms twitching as she grasped his poor hands and kissed them.

"Yes. It's all right. Governor pardoned me today. I'm free. Not even parole. Cheer up! Ann, my dear, my dear!" And laid his cheek against her hair and sobbed as she never could.

She tried to take care of him. She bustled to the kitchen

to get a whisky soda for him, but thrice before she even chopped the ice she had to rush back to make sure he was there. He had hold of himself now and was trying to look at ease, to sit erect in his chair, but he slumped after a moment.

His face was of that gray known only to prisons and hospitals. His lips were tight—no longer easily humorous. His hair seemed to have been hacked off with dull gardening scissors. His clothes were wrinkled. But it was his eyes that hurt. They followed her, begging her to care for him—no, begging her to let him stay here till he should catch his breath.

But she sang, "I'll make him well again—lips and eyes and hands!"

He gulped the highball wonderingly, muttering, "My God, the first I've had in a year! Listen——"

"Wait! Before you talk!" She ran to her bedroom, brought back a pair of slippers, unlaced his shoes, put on the slippers.

"Why, they fit! How come——"

"I bought them a year ago, Barney. They've been waiting for you."

"Um. Service here better than in the pen!" He almost smiled.

She remembered in an instant of bright shame her one-time devotion also to the red slippers of Captain Lafayette Resnick. Life was all bound together—even by slippers. She forgot it as she cried, "What happened, Barney, what happened?"

"Well, I think your friend Judge Lindsay Atwell helped."

"Honestly? Oh, that's wonderful! I did misjudge him so."

"Yes. Quite. He headed a committee of lawyers that went to the Governor and got so righteous on him and tried so hard to bully him into keeping me in the pen for life, at least, that the Governor got irritated, I guess. He pardoned me suddenly, without notice. The warden came into the tailor-shop this afternoon (I'm a pretty good coat-cutter now!). He was grinning, and I wanted to stab him with my scissors. But he said, 'Judge, come into my office,' and there he told me, and had me change clothes in his own house, and I was so dazed I was on the train before I understood that I was—my God—free! I can walk down streets! I can speak to strangers! I can go into a public library! I can buy cigarettes! I can come to you! And I'm still dazed. I must look terrible. But it didn't get me, not quite. I'll come around, if you'll help me . . . if you want me!"

She said what was to say.

He rubbed his eyes, put down his glass only a quarter empty. "I better go slow on that, I guess. Not used to it. No, I forgot, that wasn't all. The papers had gotten onto the news somehow—too late for the evening papers, though—and the reporters were waiting at both the back and front gates of the pen. The warden smuggled me out in a jumper over my clothes, driving a laundry wagon —only useful thing I've ever done, I guess, besides meeting you! So the reporters will be after me hotter than ever, now. I suppose I'll have to go out to Long Island this evening. But, Ann, my Ann, I did have to have a few minutes of paradise with you before I faced them—and her."

"You are not going! You're going to stay here tonight. No! You're——"

She raced to the telephone, ten years younger, an era gayer. "O'Sullivan Hire Company? I want a limousine, at once, to go up to Scarsdale. Dr. Ann Vickers, superintendent Stuyvesant Industrial Home. At my flat, 108th Street. Right away."

She knelt by him again, but she was not taut now, nor he.

"I've bought Pirate's Head, you remember? There's only three rooms actually furnished, but we're going up there tonight, on our real honeymoon. I'll have to come down every day, but I'll hustle back, and you stay till you want to see the reporters . . . and Mona and the girls. Can do?"

"Yes!"

"Meantime have your lawyers arrange whatever is necessary and have them see the reporters—tell them you've slipped away on a yacht to recuperate from your unjust imprisonment—any good honest hooey, dear."

"I know. I start my new moral life by lying?"

"Exactly. There's been enough martyrdom in this particular family lately, my love! And I haven't kissed you yet! And I've dreamed of it for a year!" She sounded incredulous.

"Perhaps we've gone beyond the need of kissing."

"I trust not!"

"Well, I shouldn't wonder if we discover our animal natures haven't been too etherealized by penance. Oh, my God, Ann, I can't believe it—it's impossible—I'm with you, free. I'm even allowed to talk too much!"

Before the car came for them, he tiptoed into the nursery and stood a long time brooding on his son, sleeping so serenely, so unearthly fair and unspotted by life, in that low light. An absurd gray flannel monkey with a red cap lay at the foot of the crib. Barney kissed Mat, and crept away, and now he was smiling. It was Ann who had to strive against tears, for that smile was saddest of all.

The whole way to Scarsdale he held her hand tight, even when he leaned over to kiss her. But they talked dispassionately. They were realistic enough to go into finances. He would have eight or ten thousand left and, she proudly told him, she had saved two, besides partly paying for Pirate's Head.

"We can go West, where they don't know," she said, "and buy a farm and live there till you're readmitted to the bar, or whatever it is."

"I can probably sell real estate meanwhile," he said. "I'm good at it."

"But first, let's have the fight out. Russell will divorce me fast enough. I think Mona may you, now—or do you want her to?"

"Of course!"

"Meantime, let's just go on placidly living together. Let the scandal start! I'll be fired, but I'll have such a happy time showing up all the politicians, including a state senator that offered me ten thousand dollars to let a girl escape! It will be a grand last fight. And then I'll be ready for another job. (I'll always have jobs—you may as well get used to it—it makes me only the more stubborn a feminist, to be in love!) And by the way, there may not be any scandal, if we welcome it. They'll think we have something up our sleeves. Sound good?"

"Glorious. I'd rest a month. But—— Ann dear, I can't sit at home, poking around a garden, doing nothing else, while you face the fight and earn the living. If I could have a month, and then we went West, began working, right away, it would be fun. But to be a pensioner for month on month—— I almost wish you hadn't bought Pirate's Head!"

"Oh. Well. I thought perhaps you'd feel that way. So I have a provisional purchaser who'll take it off my hands at a small profit. But I thought I wouldn't tell you till I found out just how you felt. What about Oregon and apples and mountains and Mat and you and me?"

"Well, I never cared much for apples. They always seemed to me a chilly fruit. But I'd like a year of the mountains and then——" He dropped her hand a second, he scratched his chin, and said seriously, "Ann, I think I'll get busy and make a million dollars in real estate."

She did not believe it. The day of that sort of reasonless fortune was possibly gone. But it delighted her that already, in two hours, the pleading beaten man had again turned into the ambitious and boasting boy that all sound males are at heart.

He fretted, presently, "You say you're not afraid of a scandal, but don't you think it may be easier on you if you resign from your prison?"

"No. *You* wouldn't! I'm not conscious of doing anything for which I should resign. It's so *right*, to be with you! And it wouldn't help, to resign. They'd just think I was running away."

"What about the future effect of the scandal on Mat?"

"Listen! This is a new age. By the time Mat is sixteen he'll have to look in a dictionary to find out what the word 'scandal' means. No! My motto comes from that good old pirate, the Duke of Wellington: 'Publish and be damned!'"

They came to Pirate's Head, and she loved him so very much that she even spared him, for this evening, the duty of admiring her built-in bookcases, her linens, the painted furniture. Till the late moon rose they sat outside, close clasped, and they were so sure of life that they could be silent.

When she awoke, to daylight, he was gone from their upper room. She was utterly terrified. Suppose he really had broken prison; come to her just for a night? She ran to the window and stopped, laughing softly.

Barney was pacing the raw new garden below, in shirt-sleeves, smoking a pipe. He stopped once and waved the pipe. She guessed that he was planning how the rose plot might be better laid out.

When she came down he had breakfast ready for her.

"But that was wonderful of you, Barney!"

"Is the coffee good? Is it really good? Is it?"

"Marvelous!" (And by coincidence it was.)

"Well, that's good. Ann!"

"Yes, milord."

"I think that soil where the rose-bushes are planted is wretched. You ought to put in enormous quantities of fertilizer."

"Yes——"

"And I wouldn't be in too much of a hurry to sell this place, even if we do go West. We have—I should say *you* have, an excellent investment."

"Of course, I'll do what you think."

"And while I was in the pen, I read your paper on the relationship of crime and tuberculosis, in the *Journal of Economics*. I'd question your figures. Shall I check up on them?"

"Oh, would you? That would be terribly kind. Oh, Barney!" said in meek ecstasy the Captive Woman, the Free Woman, the Great Woman, the Feminist Woman, the Domestic Woman, the Passionate Woman, the Cosmopolitan Woman, the Village Woman—the Woman.

He paced the floor. In horror she saw that he was unconsciously following a fixed pattern: nine feet up, two feet over, nine feet back, two feet over, nine feet up, unchanging, while he grumbled, "Though it's the most unholy nerve in me to criticize you in anything, my dear!"

She said, and she made it casual as she could, "Did you ever think, Barney, that we're both out of prison now, and that we ought to have sense enough to be glad?"

"But how are you——"

"You, you and Mat, have brought me out of the prison of Russell Spaulding, the prison of ambition, the prison of desire for praise, the prison of myself. We're out of prison!"

"Why! We are!" Again he paced the floor, but his path now was not nine feet by two.

THE END